The MAGICIANS' Guild

The Black Magician Trilogy

The Magicians' Guild
The Novice
The High Lord

The MAGICIANS' Guild

TRUDI CANAVAN

atom

ATOM

First published in Great Britain by Orbit 2004
This hardback edition published in September 2005 by Atom
Reprinted 2005

A CIP catalogue record for this book is available from the British Library.

ISBN-13: 978-1-90423-366-1
ISBN-10: 1-90423-366-1

Typeset by Palimpsest Book Production Limited,
Polmont, Stirlingshire
Printed and bound in Great Britain
by Mackays of Chatham plc, Chatham, Kent

Atom
An imprint of
Time Warner Book Group UK
Brettenham House
Lancaster Place
London WC2E 7EN

www.atombooks.co.uk

This book is dedicated to my father, Denis Canavan.
He provided the spark that lit the twin fires of curiosity and creativity.

ACKNOWLEDGEMENTS

Many people have given me valuable encouragement, support and constructive criticism during the writing of this trilogy. Thank you to:

Mum and Dad, for believing I could be whatever I wanted to be; Yvonne Hardingham, the big sister I never had; Paul Marshall, for his inexhaustible ability to reread; Steven Pemberton, for gallons of tea and some very silly suggestions; Anthony Mauriks, for the discussions on weaponry and demonstrations of fighting; Mike Hughes, who foolishly wants to be a character; Shelley Muir, for friendship and honesty; Julia Taylor, for her generosity, and Dirk Strasser, for giving it a go.

Also to Jack Dann, for giving me confidence in my writing when I needed it most; Jane Williams, Victoria Hammond, and especially Gail Bell for making me feel welcome among non-sf writers at the Varuna Writers' Centre and Carol Boothman, for her wisdom.

And I couldn't forget to thank Ann Jeffree, Paul Potiki, Donna Johansen, Sarah Endacott, Anthony Oakman, David and Michelle Le Blanc, and Les Petersen.

A warm thank you to Peter Bishop and the Varuna team. You helped me in ways too numerous to mention.

Last, but not least, a special thanks to Fran Bryson, my agent and hero, for taking the books that step further; and Linda Funnell, who said 'yes, please!'.

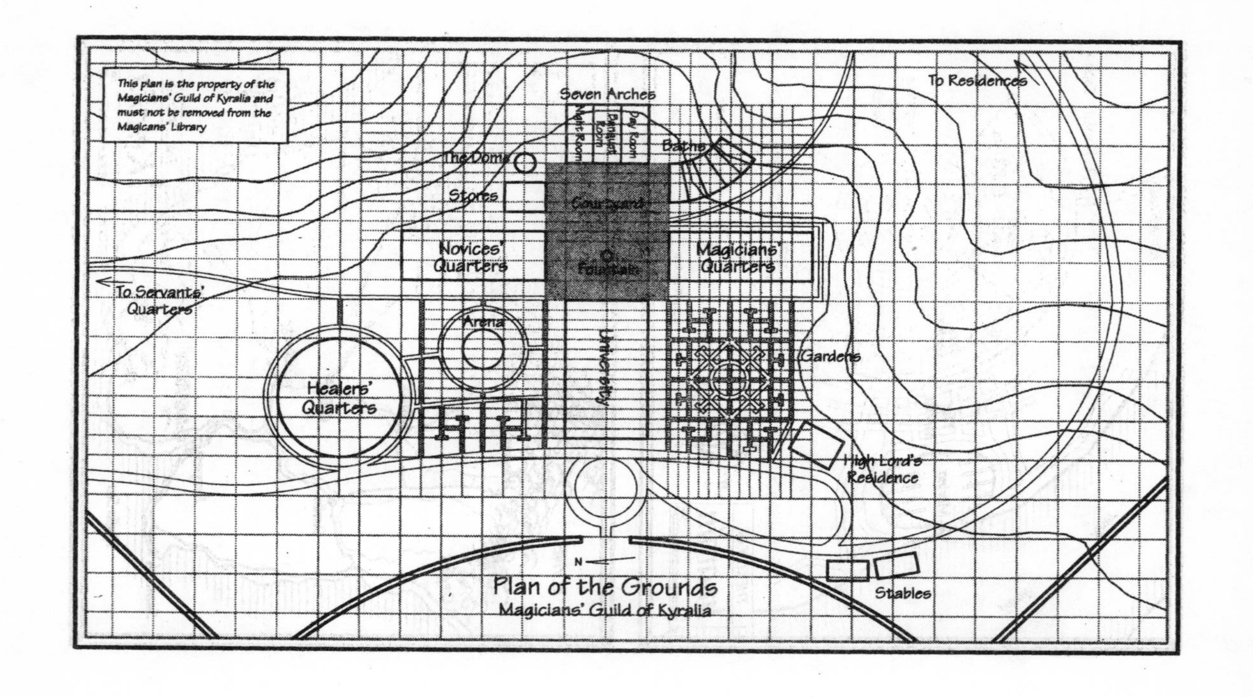
This plan is the property of the Magicians' Guild of Kyralia and must not be removed from the Magicans' Library
Seven Arches
Night Room
Banquet Room
Day Room
Baths
The Dome
Stores
Courtyard
Fountain
Novices' Quarters
Magicians' Quarters
To Residences
To Servants' Quarters
Arena
University
Gardens
Healers' Quarters
High Lord's Residence
N
Stables
Plan of the Grounds
Magicians' Guild of Kyralia

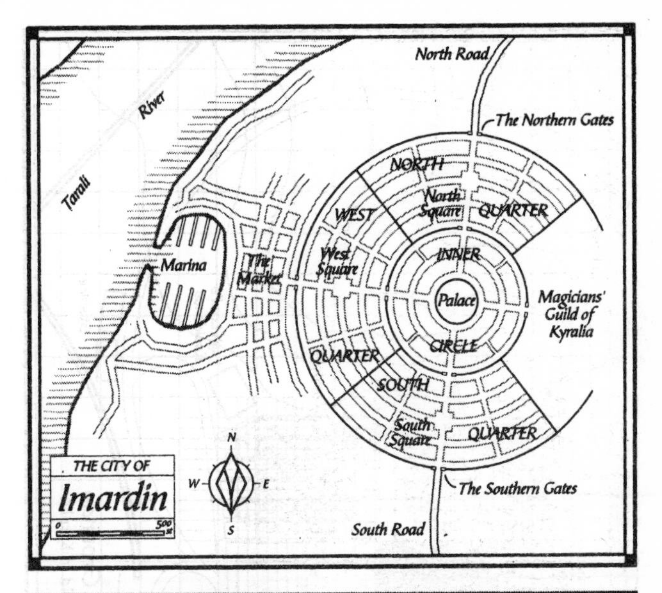
North Road
The Northern Gates
Tarali
River
NORTH
North Square
QUARTER
WEST
West Square
Marina
The Market
INNER
Palace
Magicians' Guild of Kyralia
CIRCLE
QUARTER
SOUTH
South Square
QUARTER
THE CITY OF
Imardin
N
W
E
S
The Southern Gates
South Road

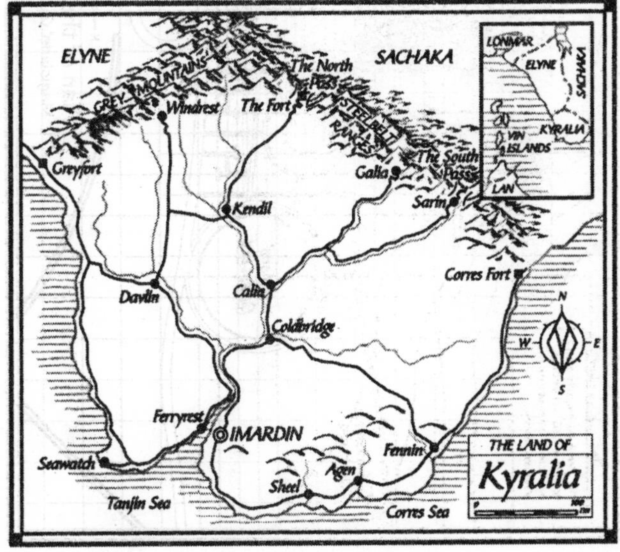
ELYNE
SACHAKA
GREY MOUNTAINS
The North Pass
Windrest
The Fort
STEELBELT RANGES
LONMAR
ELYNE
SACHAKA
KYRALIA
VIN ISLANDS
LAN
Greyfort
The South Pass
Galia
Sarin
Kendil
Corres Fort
Davlin
Calia
Coldbridge
N
W
E
S
Ferryrest
IMARDIN
Fennin
Seawatch
Agen
Sheel
Tanjin Sea
Corres Sea
THE LAND OF
Kyralia

PART ONE

CHAPTER 1

THE PURGE

It is said, in Imardin, that the wind has a soul, and that it wails through the narrow city streets because it is grieved by what it finds there. On the day of the Purge it whistled amongst the swaying masts in the Marina, rushed through the Western Gates and screamed between the buildings. Then, as if appalled by the ragged souls it met there, it quietened to a whimper.

Or so it seemed to Sonea. As another gust of cold wind battered her, she wrapped her arms around her chest and hugged her worn coat closer to her body. Looking down, she scowled at the dirty sludge that splashed over her shoes with each step she took. The cloth she had stuffed into her oversized boots was already saturated and her toes stung with the chill.

A sudden movement to her right caught her attention, and she side-stepped as a man with straggly grey hair staggered towards her from an alley entrance and fell to his knees. Stopping, Sonea offered him her hand, but the old man did not seem to notice. He clambered to his feet and joined the hunched figures making their way down the street.

Sighing, Sonea peered around the edge of her hood. A guard slouched in the entrance of the alley. His mouth was curled into a sneer of disdain; his gaze flitted from figure to figure. She narrowed her eyes at him, but when his head turned in her direction, she quickly looked away.

Curse the guards, she thought. *May they all find poisonous faren crawling in their boots*. The names of a few good-natured guards pricked her conscience, but she was in no mood to make exceptions.

Falling into step with the shuffling figures around her, Sonea followed them out of the street into a wider thoroughfare. Two- and three-storey houses rose on either side of them. The windows of the higher floors were crowded with faces. In one, a well-dressed man was holding up a small boy so he could watch the people below. The man's nose wrinkled with disdain and, as he pointed his finger down, the boy grimaced as if he had tasted something foul.

Sonea glared at them. *Wouldn't be so smug if I threw a rock through their window*. She looked about half-heartedly, but if any rocks were lying about, they were well hidden beneath the sludge.

A few steps further on, she caught sight of a pair of guards ahead of her, standing in the entrance to an alley. Dressed in stiff boiled-leather coats and iron helmets, they looked to be twice the weight of the beggars they watched. They carried wooden shields, and at their waists hung kebin – iron bars which were used as cudgels, but with a hook attached just above the handle, designed to catch an attacker's knife. Dropping her eyes to the ground, Sonea walked by the two men.

'—cut 'em off before they reach the square,' one of the guards was saying. 'About twenty of 'em. Gang leader's big. Got a scar on his neck and—'

Sonea's heart skipped a beat. *Could it be . . .?*

A few steps past the guards was a recessed doorway.

Slipping into the shallow alcove, she turned her head to sneak a look at the two men, then jumped as she saw two dark eyes staring back at her from the doorway.

A woman gazed at her, eyes wide with surprise. Sonea took a step back. The stranger retreated too, then smiled as Sonea let out a quick laugh.

Just a reflection! Sonea reached out and her fingers met a square of polished metal attached to the wall. Words had been etched into its surface, but she knew too little about letters to make out what they said.

She examined her image. A thin, hollow-cheeked face. Short, dark hair. No-one had ever called her pretty. She could still manage to pass herself off as a boy when she wanted to. Her aunt said that she looked more like her long-dead mother than her father, but Sonea suspected Jonna simply did not want to see any resemblance to her absent marriage-brother.

Sonea leaned closer to the reflection. Her mother had been beautiful. *Perhaps, if I grew my hair long*, she mused, *and I wore something feminine . . .*

. . . oh, don't bother. With a self-mocking snort, she turned away, annoyed at herself for being distracted by such fantasies.

'—'bout twenty minutes ago,' said a nearby voice. She stiffened as she remembered why she had stepped into the alcove.

'And where are they expectin' to trap 'em?'

'D'know, Mol.'

'Ah, I'd like to be there. Saw what they did to Porlen last year, little bastards. Took several weeks for the rash to go away, and he couldn't see properly for days. Wonder if I can get out of – Hai! Wrong way, boy!'

Sonea ignored the soldier's shout, knowing that he and his companion would not leave their position at the entrance of the alley, in case the people in the street took advantage of their distraction to slip away. She broke into a jog, weaving through the steadily thickening crowd. From time to time, she paused to search for familiar faces.

She had no doubt which gang the guards had been talking about. Stories of what Harrin's youths had done during the last Purge had been retold over and over through the harsh winter of the previous year. It had amused her to hear that her old friends were still making mischief, though she had to agree with her aunt that she was better off keeping away from their troublemaking. Now it seemed the guards were planning to have their revenge.

Which only proves Jonna right. Sonea smiled grimly. *She'd flay me if she knew what I was doing, but I have to warn Harrin.* She scanned the crowd again. *It's not like I'm going to rejoin the gang. I only have to find a watcher – there!*

In the shadows of a doorway, a youth slouched, glowering at his surroundings with sullen hostility. Despite his apparent disinterest, his gaze shifted from one alley entrance to another. As his gaze met hers, Sonea reached up to adjust her hood and made what would be taken to be a crude sign by most. His eyes narrowed, and he quickly signed back.

Sure now that he was a watcher, she made her way through the crowd and stopped a few steps away from the door, pretending to adjust the binding of her boot.

'Who're you with?' he asked, looking away.

'No-one.'

'You used an old sign.'

'Haven't been about for a while.'

He paused. 'What you want?'

'Heard the guards talking,' she told him. 'Plan to catch someone.'

The watcher made a rude noise. 'And why should I believe you?'

'I used to know Harrin,' she replied, straightening.

The boy considered her for a moment, then stepped out of the alcove and grabbed her arm. 'Let's see if he remembers you, then.'

Sonea's heart skipped as he began to pull her into the crowd. The mud was slippery, and she knew she would end up sprawling in it if she tried to brace her feet. She muttered a curse.

'You don't have to take me to him,' she said. 'Just tell him my name. He'll know I wouldn't mess him about.'

The boy ignored her. Guards eyed them suspiciously as they passed. Sonea twisted her arm, but the boy's grip was strong. He pulled her into a side street.

'Listen to me,' she said. 'My name is Sonea. He knows me. So does Cery.'

'Then you won't mind seeing him again,' the boy tossed over his shoulder.

The side street was crowded, and the people seemed to be in a hurry. She grabbed a lamppost and pulled him to a halt.

'I can't go with you. I have to meet my aunt. Let me go—'

The press of people ended as the crowd passed and continued down the street. Sonea looked up and groaned.

'Jonna's going to kill me.'

A line of guards stretched across the street, shields held high. Several youths paced before them, shouting insults and jibes. As Sonea watched, one threw a small object at the guards. The missile struck a shield and exploded into a cloud of red dust. A cheer erupted from the youths as the guards backed away a few steps.

Several paces back from the youths stood two familiar figures. One was taller and bulkier than she remembered, standing with his hands on his hips. Two years of growth had erased Harrin's boyish looks but from his stance, she guessed that little else had changed. He had always been the undisputed leader of the gang, quick to smarten up anyone with a well-placed fist.

Beside him was a youth almost half his size. Sonea could not help smiling. Cery had not grown at all since she had last seen him, and she knew how much that would annoy him. Despite his small stature, Cery had always been respected in the gang because his father had worked for the Thieves.

As the watcher pulled her closer, she saw Cery lick a finger and hold it high, then nod. Harrin gave a shout. The youths pulled small bundles from their clothes and hurled them at the guards. A cloud of red billowed from the shields, and Sonea grinned as the men began to curse and cry out in pain.

Then, from an alley behind the guards, a lone figure stepped into the street. Sonea looked up and her blood froze.

'Magician!' she gasped.

The boy at her side drew in a sharp breath as he too saw the robed figure. 'Hai! Magician!' he shouted. The youths and guards straightened and turned towards the newcomer.

Then all staggered back as a hot gust of wind battered them. An unpleasant smell filled Sonea's nostrils, and her eyes began to sting as the red dust was blown into her face. The wind ceased abruptly, and all was silent and still.

Rubbing tears away, Sonea blinked at the ground hoping for some clean snow to ease the sting. Only mud surrounded her, smooth and unbroken by footprints. But that couldn't be right. As her vision cleared, she saw it was marked with fine ripples – all radiating out from the magician's feet.

'Go!' Harrin bellowed. At once the youths sprang away from the guards and fled past Sonea. With a yelp, the watcher pulled her around and dragged her after them.

Her mouth went dry as she saw that another line of guards waited at the end of the street. This was the trap! *And I've gone and got myself caught with them!*

The watcher pulled her along, following Harrin's gang as the youths raced toward the guards. As they drew close, the guards lifted their shields in anticipation. A few strides from the line, the youths veered into an alleyway. Following on their heels, Sonea noted a pair of uniformed men lying slumped against a wall by the entrance.

'Duck!' a familiar voice shouted.

A hand grabbed her and pulled her down. She winced as her knees struck the cobblestones under the mud. Hearing cries behind her, she looked back to see a mass of arms and shields filling the narrow gap between the buildings, a cloud of red dust billowing around them.

'*Sonea?*'

The voice was familiar and full of amazement. She looked up, and grinned as she saw Cery crouching beside her.

'She told me the guards were planning an ambush,' the watcher told him.

Cery nodded. 'We knew.' A smile spread slowly across

his face, then his eyes flickered past her to the guards, and the smile vanished. 'Come on, everyone. Time to go!'

He took her hand, pulled her to her feet and led her between the youths bombarding the guards. As they did, a flash of light filled the alley with a blinding whiteness.

'What was that?' Sonea gasped, trying to blink away the image of the narrow street which seemed to hang before her eyes.

'The magician,' Cery hissed.

'Run!' Harrin bellowed nearby. Half blind, Sonea stumbled forward. A body slammed into her back and she fell. Cery grasped her arms, pulled her to her feet, and guided her onward.

They leapt out of the alley and Sonea found herself back on the main street. The youths slowed, lifting hoods and hunching their backs as they spread amongst the crowd. Sonea followed suit, and for several minutes she and Cery walked in silence. A tall figure moved to Cery's side and peered around the edge of his hood to regard her.

'Hai! Look who it is!' Harrin's eyes widened. 'Sonea! What are you doing here?'

She smiled. 'Getting caught in your mischief again, Harrin.'

'She heard the guards were planning an ambush and came looking for us,' Cery explained.

Harrin waved a hand dismissively. 'We knew they'd try something, so we made sure we had a way out.'

Thinking of the guards slumped in the alley entrance, Sonea nodded. 'I should've guessed you knew.'

'So where have you been? It's been . . . years.'

'Two years. We've been living in the North Quarter. Uncle Ranel got a room in a stayhouse.'

'I hear the rent stinks in those stayhouses – and everything costs double just 'cause you're living inside the city walls.'

'It does, but we got by.'

'Doing what?' Cery asked.

'Mending shoes and clothes.'

Harrin nodded. 'So that's why we haven't seen you for so long.'

Sonea smiled. *That, and Jonna wanted to keep me from getting mixed up with your gang*. Her aunt had not approved of Harrin and his friends. Not at all . . .

'Don't sound too exciting,' Cery muttered.

Looking at him, she noted that, though he hadn't grown much in the last few years, his face was no longer boyish. He wore a new longcoat with threads dangling where it had been cut short, and probably loaded with a collection of picks, knives, trinkets and sweets hidden in pockets and pouches within the lining. She had always wondered what Cery would do when he grew out of picking pockets and locks.

'It was safer than hanging about with you lot,' she told him.

Cery's eyes narrowed. 'That's Jonna talking.'

Once, that would have stung. She smiled. 'Jonna's talking got us out of the slums.'

'So,' Harrin interrupted. 'If you've got a room in a stayhouse, why are you here?'

Sonea scowled and her mood darkened. 'The King's putting out the people in stayhouses,' she told him. 'Says he don't want so many people living in one building – that it's not clean. Guards came and kicked us out this morning.'

Harrin frowned and muttered a curse. Glancing at Cery, she saw that the teasing look in his eyes had died. She looked away, grateful, but not comforted, by their understanding.

With one word from the Palace, in one morning, everything that she and her aunt and uncle had worked for had been taken away. There had been no time to think about what this meant as they had grabbed their belongings before being dragged out into the street.

'Where are Jonna and Ranel, then?' Harrin asked.

'Sent me ahead to see if we can get a room in our old place.'

Cery gave her a direct look. 'Come see me if you can't.'

She nodded. 'Thanks.'

The crowd slowly spilled out of the street into a large paved area. This was the North Square, where small local markets were held each week. She and her aunt visited it regularly – *had* visited it regularly.

Several hundred people had gathered in the square. While many continued on through the Northern Gates, others lingered inside in the hope of meeting their loved ones before entering the confusion of the slums, and some always refused to move until they were forced to.

Cery and Harrin stopped at the base of the pool in the centre of the square. A statue of King Kalpol rose from the water. The long-dead monarch had been almost forty when he routed the mountain bandits, yet here he was portrayed as a young man, his right hand brandishing a likeness of his famous, jewel-encrusted sword, and his left gripping an equally ornate goblet.

A different statue had once stood in its place, but it had been torn down thirty years before. Though several statues had been erected of King Terrel over the years, all but one had been destroyed, and it was rumoured that even the surviving statue, protected within the Palace walls, had been defaced. Despite all else he had done, the citizens of Imardin would always remember King Terrel as the man who had started the yearly Purges.

Her uncle had told her the story many times. Thirty years before, after influential members of the Houses had complained that the streets were not safe, the King had ordered the guard to drive all beggars, homeless vagrants and suspected criminals out of the city. Angered by this, the strongest of the expelled gathered together and, with weapons provided by the wealthier smugglers and thieves, fought back. Faced with street battles and riots, the King turned to the Magicians' Guild for assistance.

The rebels had no weapon to use against magic. They were captured or driven out into the slums. The King was so pleased by the festivities the Houses had held to celebrate that he declared the city would be purged of vagrants every winter.

When the old King had died five years past, many had hoped that the Purges would stop, but Terrel's son, King Merin, had continued the tradition. Looking around, it was hard to imagine that the frail, sick-looking people about her could ever be a threat. Then she noticed that several youths had gathered around Harrin, all watching their leader expectantly. She felt her stomach clench with sudden apprehension.

'I have to go,' she said.

'No, don't go,' Cery protested. 'We've only just found each other again.'

She shook her head. 'I've been too long. Jonna and Ranel might be in the slums already.'

'Then you're already in trouble.' Cery shrugged. 'You still 'fraid of a scolding, eh?'

She gave him a reproachful look. Undeterred, he smiled back.

'Here.' He pressed something into her hand. Looking down, she examined the little packet of paper.

'This is the stuff you guys were throwing at the guards?'

Cery nodded. 'Papea dust,' he said. 'Makes their eyes sting and gives 'em a rash.'

'No good against magicians, though.'

He grinned. 'I got one once. He didn't see me coming.'

Sonea started to hand back the packet, but Cery waved his hand.

'Keep it,' he said. 'It's no use here. The magicians always make a wall.'

She shook her head. 'So you throw stones instead? Why do you bother?'

'It feels good.' Cery looked back towards the road, his eyes a steely grey. 'If we didn't, it would be like we don't mind the Purge. We can't let them drive us out of the city without some kind of show, can we?'

Shrugging, she looked at the youths. Their eyes were bright with anticipation. She had always felt that throwing anything at the magicians was pointless and foolish.

'But you and Harrin hardly ever come into the city,' she said.

'No, but we ought to be able to if we want.' Cery grinned. 'And this is the only time we get to make trouble without the Thieves sticking their noses in.'

Sonea rolled her eyes. 'So that's it.'

'Hai! Let's go!' Harrin bellowed over the noise of the crowd.

As the youths cheered and began to move away, Cery looked at her expectantly.

'Come on,' he urged. 'It'll be fun.'

Sonea shook her head.

'You don't have to join in. Just watch,' he said. 'After, I'll come with you and see you get a place to stay.'

'But—'

'Here.' He reached out and undid her scarf. Folding it into a triangle, he draped it over her head and tied it at her throat. 'You look more like a girl now. Even if the guards decide to chase us – which they never do – they won't think you're a troublemaker. There,' he patted her cheek, 'much better. Now come on. I'm not letting you disappear again.'

She sighed. 'All right.'

The crowd had grown, and the gang began to push forward through the crush of people. To Sonea's surprise, they received no protest or retaliation in return for their elbowing. Instead, the men and women she passed reached out to press rocks and over-ripe fruit into her hands, and to whisper encouragement. As she followed Cery past the eager faces, she felt a stirring of excitement. Sensible people like her aunt and uncle had already left the North Square. Those who remained wanted to see a show of defiance – and it didn't matter how pointless it was.

The crowd thinned as the gang reached its edge. At one side Sonea could see people still entering the square from a side street. On the other, the distant gates rose above the crowd. In front . . .

Sonea stopped and felt all her confidence drain away. As Cery moved on, she took a few steps back and stopped behind an elderly woman. Less than twenty paces away stood a row of magicians.

Taking a deep breath, she let it out slowly. She knew they would not move from their places. They would ignore the crowd until they were ready to drive it out of the square. There was no reason to be frightened.

Swallowing, she forced herself to look away and seek out the youths. Harrin, Cery and the others were moving further forward, strolling amongst the dwindling stream of latecomers joining the edge of the crowd.

Looking up at the magicians again, she shivered. She had never been this close to them before, or had an opportunity to take a good look at them.

They wore a uniform: wide-sleeved robes bound by a sash at the waist. According to her uncle Ranel, clothes like these had been fashionable many hundreds of years ago but now it was a crime for ordinary people to dress like magicians.

They were all men. From her position she could see nine of them, standing alone or in pairs, forming part of a line that she knew would encompass the square. Some were no older than twenty, while others looked ancient. One of the closest, a fair-haired man of about thirty, was handsome in a sleek, well-groomed way. The rest were surprisingly ordinary-looking.

In the corner of her eye she saw an abrupt movement, and turned in time to see Harrin swing his arm forward. A rock flew though the air toward the magicians. Despite knowing what would happen, she held her breath.

The stone smacked against something hard and invisible and dropped to the ground. Sonea let out her breath as more of the youths began hurling stones. A few of the robed figures looked up to watch the missiles pattering against the air in front of them. Others regarded the youths briefly, then turned back to their conversations.

Sonea stared at the place where the magicians' barrier hung. She could see nothing. Moving forward, she took out one of the lumps in her pockets, drew her arm back and hurled it with all her strength. It disintegrated as it hit the invisible wall, and for a moment, a cloud of dust hung in the air, flat on one side.

She heard a low chuckle nearby and turned to see the old woman grinning at her.

'That's a good 'un,' the woman cackled. 'You show 'em. Go on.'

Sonea slipped a hand into a pocket and felt her fingers close on a larger rock. She took a few steps closer to the magicians and smiled. She had seen annoyance in some of their faces. Obviously they did not like to be defied, but something prevented them from confronting the youths.

Beyond the haze of dust came the sound of voices. The well-groomed magician glanced up, then turned back to his companion, an older man with grey in his hair.

'Pathetic vermin,' he sneered. 'How long until we can get rid of them?'

Something flipped over in Sonea's belly, and she tightened her grip on the rock. She pulled it free and gauged its weight. A heavy one. Turning to face the magicians, she gathered the anger she felt at being thrown out of her home, all her inbred hate of the magicians, and hurled the stone at the speaker. She traced its path through the air, and as it neared the magicians' barrier, she willed it to pass through and reach its mark.

A ripple of blue light flashed outward, then the rock slammed into the magician's temple with a dull thud. He stood motionless, staring at nothing, then his knees buckled and his companion stepped forward to catch him.

Sonea stared, her mouth agape, as the older magician lowered his companion to the ground. The jeers of the youths died away. Stillness spread outward like smoke through the crowd.

Then exclamations rang out as two more magicians sprang forward to crouch beside their fallen companion. Harrin's friends, and others in the crowd, began to cheer. Noise returned to the square as people murmured and shouted out what had happened.

Sonea looked down at her hands. *It worked. I broke the barrier, but that's not possible, unless . . .*

Unless I used magic.

Cold rushed through her as she remembered how she had focused all her anger and hate on the stone, how she had followed its path with her mind and willed it to break through the barrier. Something in her stirred, as if it were eager for her to repeat those actions.

Looking up, she saw that several magicians had gathered around their fallen companion. Some crouched beside him, but most had turned to stare out at the people in the square, their eyes searching. *Looking for me*, she thought suddenly. As if hearing her thought, one turned to stare at her. She froze in terror, but his eyes slid away and roved on through the crowd.

They don't know who it was. She gasped with relief. Glancing around, she saw that the crowd was several paces behind her. The youths were backing away. Heart pounding, she followed suit.

Then the older magician rose. Unlike the others, his eyes snapped to hers without hesitation. He pointed at her and the rest of the magicians turned to stare again. As their hands rose, she felt a surge of terror. Spinning around, she bolted towards the crowd. In the corner of her eye, she saw the rest of the youths fleeing. Her vision wavered as several quick flashes of light lit the faces before her, then screams tore through the air. Heat rushed over her and she fell to her knees, gasping.

'STOP!'

She felt no pain. Looking down, she gasped in relief to find her body whole. She looked up; people were still running away, ignoring the strangely amplified command that still echoed through the square.

A smell of burning drifted to her nose. Sonea turned to see a figure sprawled face-down on the pavement a few steps away. Though flames ate at the clothing hungrily, the figure lay still. Then she saw the blackened mess that had once been an arm, and her stomach twisted with nausea.

'DO NOT HARM HER!'

Staggering to her feet, she reeled away from the corpse. Figures passed her on either side as the youths fled. With an effort, she forced herself into a staggering run.

She caught up with the crowd at the Northern Gate and pushed her way into it. Fighting her way forward, clawing past those in her way, she forced herself deep within the crowd of bodies. Feeling the stones still weighing down her pockets, she clawed them out. Something caught her legs, tripping her over, but she dragged herself to her feet and pushed on.

Hands grabbed her roughly from behind. She struggled and drew a breath to scream, but the hands turned her around and she found herself staring up at the familiar blue eyes of Harrin.

CHAPTER 2

THE MAGICIANS' DEBATE

Though he had entered the Guildhall countless times since graduating over thirty years before, Lord Rothen had rarely heard it echo with so many voices.

He regarded the sea of robed men and women before him. Circles of magicians had formed, and he noted the usual cliques and factions. Others roamed about, leaving one circle and joining another. Hands flashed in expressive gestures, and the occasional exclamation or denial rose above the din.

Meets were usually dignified, orderly affairs, but until the Administrator arrived to organise them, the participants usually milled about in the centre of the room, talking. As Rothen started toward the crowd, he caught fragments of conversations which seemed to be emanating from the roof. The Guildhall amplified sounds in odd and unexpected ways, particularly when voices were raised.

The effect was not magical, as ungifted visitors often assumed, but an unintended result of the building's conversion into a hall. The first and oldest Guild construction, it had originally contained rooms to house magicians and their apprentices as well as spaces for lessons and meetings. Four centuries later, faced with a rapidly growing membership, the Guild had constructed several new buildings. Not wanting to demolish their first home, they removed the internal walls and added seating, and since then, all Guild Meets, Acceptance and Graduation ceremonies and Hearings had been held there.

A tall, purple-robed figure stepped out of the crowd and strode toward Rothen. Noting the younger magician's eager expression, Rothen smiled. Dannyl had complained more than once that nothing particularly exciting happened in the Guild.

'Well, my old friend. How did it go?' Dannyl asked.

Rothen crossed his arms. 'Old friend indeed!'

'Old fiend, then.' Dannyl waved a hand dismissively. 'What did the Administrator say?'

'Nothing. He just wanted me to describe what happened. It appears I'm the only one who saw her.'

'Lucky for her,' Dannyl replied. 'Why did the others try to kill her?'

Rothen shook his head. 'I don't think they meant to.'

A gong rang out above the buzz of voices, and the Guild Administrator's amplified voice filled the hall.

'Would all magicians take their seats, please.'

Glancing behind, Rothen saw the huge main doors at the back of the hall swing shut. The mass of robes parted as magicians began moving toward seats on either side of the room. Dannyl nodded toward the front.

'We have some rare company today.'

Rothen followed his friend's gaze. The Higher Magicians were taking their places. To mark their position and authority within the Guild, their seats were arranged in five tiers at the front of the hall. The raised seats were reached by two narrow stairways. At the centre of the highest row stood a large chair embellished with gold and embroidered with the King's incal: a stylised night bird. The chair was empty, but the two seats flanking it were occupied by magicians wearing gold sashes tied about their waists.

'The King's Advisers,' Rothen murmured. 'Interesting.'

'Yes,' Dannyl replied. 'I wondered if King Merin would regard this Meet important enough to attend.'

'Not important enough to come himself.'

'Of course not.' Dannyl smiled. 'Then we'd behave ourselves.'

Rothen shrugged. 'It makes no difference, Dannyl. Even if the advisers weren't here, none of us would say anything we wouldn't say in the presence of the King. No, they're here to make sure we do more than merely talk about the girl.'

Reaching their usual seats, they sat down. Dannyl leaned back in his chair and surveyed the room. 'All this for one grubby street urchin.'

Rothen chuckled. 'She has caused quite a stir, hasn't she?'

'Fergun hasn't joined us,' Dannyl narrowed his eyes at the rows of seats against the opposite wall, 'but his followers are here.'

Though Rothen did not approve of his friend expressing dislike of another magician in public, he couldn't help smiling. Fergun's officious manner did not endear him to others. 'From what I remember of the Healer's report, the blow caused considerable confusion and agitation. He felt it wise to prescribe Fergun a sedative.'

Dannyl gave a quiet crow of delight. 'Fergun's *asleep*! When he realises he has missed this meeting he'll be furious!'

A gong rang out and the room began to quieten.

'And, as you can imagine, Administrator Lorlen was *most* disappointed that Lord Fergun could not give his version of the events,' Rothen added in a murmur.

Dannyl choked back a laugh. Looking across at the Higher Magicians, Rothen saw that all had taken their places. Only Administrator Lorlen remained standing, a gong in one hand, a striker in the other.

Lorlen's expression was uncharacteristically grave. Rothen sobered as he realised that this crisis was the first the magician had faced since being elected. Lorlen had proven to be well suited to dealing with everyday issues within the Guild, but there must be more than a few magicians wondering how the Administrator would tackle a crisis like this.

'I have called this Meet so that we may discuss the events which occurred in the North Square this morning,' Lorlen began. 'We have two matters of the most serious nature to address: the killing of an innocent, and the existence of a magician outside of our control. To begin, we will tackle the first and most serious of these two matters. I call upon Lord Rothen as witness to the event.'

Dannyl looked at Rothen with surprise, then smiled. 'Of course. It must be years since you stood down there. Good luck.'

Rising, Rothen gave his friend a withering look. 'Thanks for reminding me. I'll be fine.'

Faces turned as the assembled magicians watched Rothen descend from his seat and cross the hall to stand before the Higher Magicians. He inclined his head to the Administrator. Lorlen nodded in reply.

'Tell us what you witnessed, Lord Rothen.'

Rothen paused to consider his words. When addressing

the Guild, a speaker was expected to be concise and avoid elaboration.

'When I arrived at the North Square this morning, I found Lord Fergun already in place,' he began. 'I took my position beside him and added my power to the shield. Some of the younger vagrants began throwing stones but, as always, we ignored them.' Looking up at the Higher Magicians, he saw that they were watching him closely. He suppressed a twinge of nervousness. It *had* been a long time since he had addressed the Guild.

'Next, I saw a flash of blue light in the corner of my eye and felt a disturbance in the shield. I caught a glimpse of an object coming toward me, but before I could react it struck Lord Fergun on the temple, rendering him unconscious. I caught him as he fell, lowered him to the ground and made sure his injury was not serious. Then, as others came to assist, I searched for the stone's thrower.'

Rothen smiled wryly as he remembered. 'I saw that, while most of the youths looked confused and surprised, one young woman was staring at her hands with amazement. I lost sight of her as my colleagues arrived, and when they could not locate the stone thrower they called on me to point her out.'

He shook his head. 'When I did, they mistakenly believed I was pointing to a youth standing next to her and . . . and they retaliated.'

Lorlen gestured for Rothen to stop. He looked at the magicians in the row of seats below him, his eyes settling on Lord Balkan, the Head of Warriors.

'Lord Balkan, what have you discovered from questioning those who struck the youth?'

The red-robed magician rose. 'All nineteen magicians

involved believed that one of the boys in the crowd was the attacker, as they thought it unlikely that a girl would be trained as a rogue magician. Each intended to stun the boy, not harm him. From the description of the strikes from witnesses, I have been convinced that this is, indeed, what happened. I have also concluded from these reports that some of the stunstrikes had combined to form an unfocused firestrike. It was this that killed the boy.'

A memory of a smouldering form flashed into Rothen's mind. Sickened, he looked down at the floor. Even had the strikes not combined, the battering from nineteen stunstrikes would have shocked the boy's body excessively. He could not help feeling responsible. If only he had taken action himself, before the others could react . . .

'This raises difficult questions,' Lorlen said. 'It is unlikely that the public will believe us if we tell them we simply made a mistake. An apology is not enough. We must make some attempt at reparation. Shall we compensate the family of the youth?'

Several of the Higher Magicians nodded, and Rothen heard murmurs of approval behind him.

'If they can be found,' one of the Higher Magicians added.

'I fear compensation will not repair the damage we have done to our reputation.' Lorlen frowned. 'How can we regain the respect and trust of the people?'

Murmuring followed, then a voice called out: 'Compensation is enough.'

'Give it time – people will forget,' said another.

'We've done all we can.'

And quieter, to Rothen's right: '—just a slum boy. Who cares?'

Rothen sighed. Though the words did not surprise him, they roused in him a familiar anger. The Guild existed by law to protect others – and that law made no distinction between rich and poor. He had heard magicians claim that slum dwellers were all thieves and didn't deserve the Guild's protection.

'There is little more we can do,' Lord Balkan said. 'The higher classes will accept that the boy's death was an accident. The poor will not, and nothing we do or say will change their minds.'

Administrator Lorlen looked at each of the Higher Magicians in turn. All nodded.

'Very well,' he said. 'We will review this matter again during the next Meet, when we have had time to gauge the effects of this tragedy.' He drew in a deep breath, straightened, and swept his eyes around the hall. 'Now for the second matter: the rogue magician. Did anyone apart from Lord Rothen see this girl, or witness her throw the stone?'

Silence followed. Lorlen frowned, disappointed. Most discussion in the Guild Meets was dominated by the three Heads of Disciplines: Lady Vinara, Lord Balkan and Lord Sarrin. Lady Vinara, Head of Healers, was a practical and stern woman, but could be surprisingly compassionate. The robust Lord Balkan was observant and careful to explore all sides to an issue, yet was unflinching in the face of difficult or rapid decisions. The oldest of the trio, Lord Sarrin, could be harsh in his judgements but always acknowledged the others' views as valid.

It was these Higher Magicians that Lorlen considered now. 'We must begin by examining those facts that are clear and confirmed by witnesses. There is no doubt that, remarkable as it may sound, a mere stone penetrated a magical shield. Lord Balkan, how is this possible?'

The Warrior shrugged. 'The shield used to repel stones in the Purge is a weak one: strong enough to stop missiles, but not magic. It is clear from the blue flash, and the sense of disturbance described by those holding the shield, that magic was used. However, for magic to break through a shield it must be shaped to that purpose. I believe the attacker used a strike – a simple one – sent with the stone.'

'But why use a stone at all?' Lady Vinara asked. 'Why not just strike with magic?'

'To conceal the strike?' Lord Sarrin suggested. 'If the magicians had seen a strike coming, they may have had time to strengthen the shield.'

'That is possible,' Balkan said, 'but the force of the strike was used only to break through the barrier. If the attacker's intent had been malicious, Lord Fergun would have more than a bruised temple.'

Vinara frowned. 'So this attacker did not expect to do much harm? Why do it, then?'

'To demonstrate her power – to defy us, perhaps,' Balkan replied.

Sarrin's wrinkled face creased into a disapproving frown. Rothen shook his head. Catching the movement, Balkan looked down and smiled. 'You do not agree, Lord Rothen?'

'She didn't expect to do anything at all,' Rothen told him. 'By her expression, she was clearly shocked and surprised by what she had done. I believe she is untrained.'

'Impossible.' Sarrin shook his head. '*Someone* must have released her powers.'

'And trained her to control them, we hope,' Vinara added. 'Or we have a serious problem of a different kind.'

At once, the hall began to hum with speculation. Lorlen lifted a hand and the voices fell silent.

'When Lord Rothen told me what he witnessed, I called Lord Solend to my room to ask if he, in the course of studying the Guild's history, had read of magicians whose powers had developed without assistance.' Lorlen's expression was grave. 'It appears that our assumption that a magician's power can only be released by another magician is wrong.

'It has been recorded that in the early centuries of the Guild's existence, some of the individuals who sought training were using magic already. Their powers had developed naturally as they physically matured. Since we accept and initiate novices at a young age, natural development of power no longer occurs.' Lorlen gestured to the seats at one side of the hall. 'I have asked Lord Solend to gather what he knows of this phenomenon and now call him before us to relate what he has learned.'

An aged figure rose from the rows of robed men and women and started down the stairs. All waited in silence as the old historian reached the floor and shuffled to Rothen's side. Solend nodded stiffly to the Higher Magicians.

'Until five hundred years ago,' the old man began in a querulous voice, 'a man or woman seeking to learn magic would approach individual magicians for apprenticeship. They were tested and chosen according to their strength, and how much they could pay. Because of this tradition, some apprentices were quite mature by the time they began their training, as it could take many years of work, or a generous inheritance, before they were able to pay for the training.

'Sometimes, however, a young man or woman would appear whose powers were already "loosed", as they termed it in those times. Those people, known as "naturals" were never turned away. There are two reasons for this. Firstly, their powers were always very strong. Secondly, they had to be taught Control.' The old man paused, and his voice rose in pitch. 'We already know what happens when novices are unable to master Control. If this young woman is a natural, we should expect her to be more powerful than our average novice, possibly even more powerful than the average magician. If she is not found and taught Control, she will be a considerable danger to the city.'

A short silence followed, then a buzz of alarm spread through the hall.

'*If* her powers have, indeed, surfaced on their own,' Balkan added.

The old man nodded. 'There is a possibility, of course, that she has been trained by someone.'

'Then we must find her – *and* those who have taught her,' a voice declared.

The Hall filled with discussion again, but Lorlen's voice rose above it. 'If she is a rogue, we are bound by law to bring her and her teachers to the King. If she is a natural we must teach her Control. Either way, we must find her.'

'How?' a voice called.

Lorlen looked down. 'Lord Balkan?'

'A systematic search of the slums,' the Warrior replied. He turned to look up at the King's Advisers. 'We'll need help.'

Lorlen's brows rose and he followed the Warrior's gaze. 'The Guild formally requests the assistance of the City Guard.'

The Advisers exchanged glances and nodded.

'Granted,' one replied.

'We should begin as soon as possible,' Balkan said. 'Tonight, preferably.'

'If we want the Guard's assistance, it will take time to organise. I suggest we start tomorrow morning,' Lorlen replied.

'What of classes?' a voice called.

Lorlen looked at the magician seated beside him. 'I think an extra day of private study will not affect the novices' progress.'

'A day won't make much difference.' The sour University Director, Jerrik, shrugged. 'But will we find her in a day?'

Lorlen pursed his lips. 'We will meet here again tomorrow night if we have not found her, to discuss who shall continue the search.'

'If I might make a suggestion, Administrator Lorlen?'

Rothen started in surprise at the voice. He turned to see Dannyl standing amongst the watching magicians.

'Yes, Lord Dannyl?' Lorlen replied.

'The slum dwellers are sure to hamper our search, and the girl will probably hide from us. We may have a better chance of success if we enter the slums in disguise.'

Lorlen frowned. 'What disguise would you suggest?'

Dannyl shrugged. 'The less conspicuous we are, the better our chances of success. I'd suggest that at least some of us dress as they do. They may be able to tell who we are when we speak, but—'

'Definitely not,' Balkan growled. 'How would it be if one of us was discovered dressed as a grovelling beggar? We would be ridiculed throughout the Allied Lands.'

Several voices rose in agreement.

Lorlen nodded slowly. 'I agree. We, as magicians, have the authority to enter any house in this city. Our search will be hampered if we do *not* wear the robes.'

'How will we know what we're looking for?' Vinara asked.

Lorlen looked at Rothen. 'Can you remember what she looked like?'

Rothen nodded. Taking a few steps back, he closed his eyes and called up a memory of a small, skinny girl with a thin, childlike face. Drawing on his power, he opened his eyes and exerted his will. A glow appeared in the air before him, and quickly sharpened to form a slightly transparent face. As his memory filled in the rest, her rough clothing appeared: a colourless scarf around her head, a thick hooded shirt, trousers. The illusion complete, he looked up at the Higher Magicians.

'*That's* who attacked us?' Balkan muttered. 'She's barely more than a child.'

'A small package with a big surprise inside,' Sarrin said dryly.

'What if this is not the attacker?' Jerrik asked. 'What if Lord Rothen is mistaken?'

Lorlen looked at Rothen and smiled faintly. 'For now we can only assume he is correct. We shall know soon enough if the city gossips agree, and witnesses may be found among the public.' He nodded at the illusion. 'That will be enough, Lord Rothen.'

Rothen waved a hand and the illusion vanished. When he looked up again he found Lord Sarrin looking at him appraisingly.

'What are we going to do with her once we've found her?' Vinara asked.

'If she is a rogue we will apply the law,' Lorlen replied. 'If she is not, we will teach her to control her powers.'

'Of course, but afterwards? What then?'

'I think the question Lady Vinara is asking is: should we make her one of us?' Balkan said.

At once the hall filled with voices.

'No! She's probably a thief!'

'She attacked one of us! She should be punished, not rewarded!'

Rothen shook his head and sighed as the protests continued. While there was no law forbidding the testing of children from the lower classes, the Guild sought magic in the children of the Houses only.

'The Guild hasn't taken a novice from outside the Houses for centuries,' Balkan said quietly.

'But if Solend is correct, she may be a powerful magician,' Vinara reminded him.

Rothen suppressed a smile. Most women magicians became Healers, and he knew Lady Vinara would happily overlook the girl's origins if it gained her another powerful helper.

'"Strength is no blessing if a magician proves corrupt,"' Sarrin quoted. 'She could be a thief, or even a whore. What influence would someone with that background have on the other novices? How can we know if she would value our pledge?'

Vinara's brows rose. 'So you would show her what she is capable of, then bind her powers and send her back into poverty?'

Sarrin nodded. Vinara looked at Balkan, who shrugged. Biting back a protest, Rothen forced himself to remain silent. From the row above, Lorlen regarded the three magicians silently, his expression betraying no opinion.

'We should give her a chance at the very least,' Vinara said. 'If there is any possibility that she will conform to our rules and become a responsible young woman, then we should offer her the opportunity.'

'The further her powers develop, the harder it will be to bind them,' Sarrin reminded her.

'I know,' Vinara leaned forward, 'but it is not impossible. Consider how we will be regarded if we take her in. A little generosity and kindness will go a lot further toward redressing the damage we did to our reputation this morning than blocking her powers and returning her to the slums.'

Balkan's brows rose. 'True, and it may save us the trouble of a search if we make it known that she will be welcomed among us. Once she learns that she could become a magician, with all the position and wealth that entails, she will come to us.'

'And the loss of that wealth may be all the deterrent she will need should she consider returning to any distasteful ways she once had,' Sarrin added.

Lady Vinara nodded. She looked around the hall, then her gaze slid to Rothen and her eyes narrowed. 'What do you think, Lord Rothen?'

Rothen grimaced. 'I'm wondering if she would believe anything we told her after this morning.'

Balkan's expression darkened. 'Hmm, I doubt it. We will probably need to capture her first and explain our good intentions afterwards.'

'Then there is little point in waiting to see if she will come to us,' Lorlen concluded. 'We will begin our search tomorrow as planned.' He pursed his lips, then turned to face the seat above him.

Rothen looked up. Between the Administrator's and King's seats was a single chair reserved for the Guild's leader: the High Lord Akkarin. The black-robed magician had not spoken throughout the Meet, but that was not unusual. Though Akkarin had been known to alter the course of a debate with a few mild words, he generally remained silent.

'High Lord, have you any reason to suspect there are rogue magicians in the slums?' Lorlen asked.

'No. There are no rogues in the slums,' Akkarin replied.

Rothen was close enough to see the quick glance that passed between Balkan and Vinara. He smothered a smile. The High Lord was rumoured to have particularly fine senses, and nearly all the magicians were at least a little in awe of him. Nodding, Lorlen turned back to face the hall. He struck the gong, and as its peal echoed through the hall, the buzz of voices dropped to a faint murmur.

'The decision whether to teach the girl or not shall be deferred until she is found and her temperament assessed. For now, we will focus on the task of finding her. The search will begin here at the fourth hour tomorrow. Those of you who feel you have valid reason to remain in the Guild, please prepare a request and present it to my assistant tonight. I now declare this Meet ended.'

The Hall filled with the rustling of robes and the clatter of booted feet. Rothen stepped back as the first of the Higher Magicians stepped down from his seat and strode toward the side doors of the hall. Turning, he waited as Dannyl wove through the rest of the magicians and hurried to meet him.

'Did you hear Lord Kerrin?' Dannyl asked. 'He wants the girl punished for attacking his dear friend, Fergun. Personally, I don't think the girl could have found a nicer magician to knock out.'

'Now Dannyl—' Rothen began.

'—and now they've got us sorting through rubbish down in the slums,' a voice said behind him.

'I don't know what's the greater tragedy: that they killed the boy or that they missed the girl,' another replied.

Appalled, Rothen turned to stare at the speaker, an old Alchemist who was too busy looking glumly at the floor to notice. As the magician shuffled away, Rothen shook his head.

'I was about to lecture you about being uncharitable, Dannyl, but there's little point, is there?'

'No,' Dannyl agreed, stepping aside as Administrator Lorlen and the High Lord passed.

'What if we don't find her?' the Administrator asked his companion.

The High Lord gave a low laugh. 'Oh, you'll find her, one way or the other – though I'd say by tomorrow most will be in favour of the more spectacular, less fragrant alternative.'

Rothen shook his head again as the two Higher Magicians moved away.

'Am I the only one who cares what happens to this poor girl?'

He felt Dannyl's hand pat his shoulder.

'Of course not, but I hope you're not thinking of lecturing *him*, old friend.'

CHAPTER 3

OLD FRIENDS

'She's a tag.'

The voice was male, young and unfamiliar. *Where am I?* Sonea thought. Lying on something soft, for a start. A bed? *I don't remember getting into a bed—*

'Not a chance.'

This voice was Harrin's. She realised he was defending her, and then the significance of what the stranger had said sank in and she felt a belated relief. A tag was a spy in the slang of the slums. If Harrin had agreed, she would be in trouble . . . But a spy for who?

'What else could she be?' the first voice retorted. 'She's got magic. Magicians have to be trained for years and years. Who does that stuff 'round here?'

Magic? Memories came back in a rush: the square, the magicians . . .

'Magic or no magic, I've known her as long as I've known Cery,' Harrin told the boy. 'She's always been right-sided.'

Sonea barely heard him. In her mind she saw herself throwing the stone, saw it flash though the barrier and strike the magician. *I did that*, she thought. *But that's not possible . . .*

'But you said yourself, she's been gone for a few years. Who knows who she's been hanging about with.'

Then she remembered how she had drawn upon

something inside her – something that she should not possess . . .

'She's been with her family, Burril,' Harrin replied. 'I believe her, Cery believes her, and that's enough.'

. . . *and the Guild knows I did it!* The old magician had seen her, had pointed her out to the others. She shuddered as the memory of a smoking corpse flashed through her mind.

'I warned you.' Burril was unconvinced, but sounded defeated. 'If she squimps on you, don't forget who warn—'

'I think she's waking up,' murmured another familiar voice. Cery. He was somewhere close.

Harrin sighed. 'Out, Burril.'

Sonea heard footsteps moving away, then a door closing.

'You can stop pretending to be asleep now, Sonea,' Cery murmured.

A hand touched her face and she blinked her eyes open. Cery was leaning over her, grinning.

Sonea pushed herself up onto her elbows. She was lying on an old bed in an unfamiliar room. As she slid her legs down to the floor, Cery gave her an assessing look.

'You look better,' he said.

'I feel fine,' she agreed. 'What happened?' She looked up as Harrin moved to stand before her. 'Where am I? What time is it?'

Cery laughed. 'She's fine.'

'You don't remember?' Harrin crouched so that he could stare into her eyes.

Sonea shook her head. 'I remember walking through the slums but . . .' She spread her hands. 'Not how I got here.'

'Harrin carried you here,' said a female voice. 'He said you just fell asleep while you were walking.'

Sonea turned to see a young woman sitting in a chair behind her. The girl's face was familiar.

'Donia?'

The girl smiled. 'That's right.' She tapped a foot on the floor. 'You're in my father's bolhouse. He let us put you here. You slept right through the night.'

Sonea looked around the room again, then smiled as she remembered how Harrin and his friends used to bribe Donia into stealing mugs of bol for them. The brew was strong and had made them giddy.

Gellin's bolhouse was close to the Outer Wall, among the better built houses in the part of the slums called Northside. The inhabitants of this area called the slums the Outer Circle in defiance of the inner-district attitude that the slums were not part of the city.

Sonea guessed she was in one of the rooms Gellin let out to guests. It was small, the space taken up by the bed, the tattered chair Donia sat in and a small table. Old, discoloured paper screens covered the windows. From the faint light shining through them, Sonea guessed it was early morning.

Harrin turned to Donia and beckoned. As the girl pushed herself out of the chair, Harrin hooked a hand around her waist and pulled her close. She smiled at him affectionately.

'Think you could fish us up something to eat?' he asked.

'I'll see what I can do.' She sauntered over to the door and slipped out of the room.

Sonea sent Cery a questioning look and received a smug grin in reply. Dropping into the chair, Harrin looked up at Sonea and frowned. 'Are you sure you're better? You were out of it last night.'

She shrugged. 'I feel good, actually. Like I've slept really well.'

'You *have*. Almost a whole day.' He shrugged, then gave her another appraising look. 'What happened, Sonea? It was you who threw that stone, wasn't it?'

Sonea swallowed, her throat suddenly dry. She wondered for a moment if he would believe her if she denied it.

Cery put a hand on her shoulder and squeezed. 'Don't worry, Sonea. We won't tell anybody anything if you don't want us to.'

She nodded. 'It was me but . . . I don't know what happened.'

'Did you use magic?' Cery asked eagerly.

Sonea looked away. 'I don't know. I just wanted the stone to go through . . . and it did.'

'You broke through the magicians' wall,' Harrin said. 'That would have to take magic, wouldn't it? Stones don't usually go through it.'

'And there was that flash of light,' Cery added.

Harrin nodded. 'And the magicians sure got fired.'

Cery leaned forward. 'Do you think you could do it again?'

Sonea stared at him. 'Again?'

'Not the same thing, of course. We couldn't have you throwing stones at magicians – they don't seem to like it much. Something else. If it works, you'll know you can use magic.'

She shuddered. 'I don't think I want to know.'

Cery laughed. 'Why wouldn't you? Think of what you could do! It'd be fantastic!'

'No-one would ever give you any rub, for a start,' Harrin told her.

She shook her head. 'You're wrong. They'd have more reason to.' She scowled. 'Everyone hates the magicians. They'd hate me, too.'

'Everyone hates *Guild* magicians,' Cery told her. 'They're all from the Houses. They only care about themselves. Everyone knows you're a dwell, just like us.'

A *dwell*. After two years in the city, her aunt and uncle had stopped referring to themselves by the term the slums dwellers gave themselves. They had made it out of the slums. They had called themselves crafters instead.

'The dwells would love having their own magician,' Cery persisted, 'especially when you start doing good things for them.'

Sonea shook her head. 'Good things? Magicians never do anything good. Why would the dwells think I'd be any different?'

'What about healing,' he said. 'Doesn't Ranel have a bad leg? You could fix it!'

She caught her breath. Thinking of the pain her uncle suffered, she suddenly understood Cery's enthusiasm. It *would* be wonderful if she could fix her uncle's leg. And if she helped him, why not others?

Then she remembered how Ranel regarded the 'curies' who had treated his leg. She shook her head again. 'People don't trust curies, why would they trust me?'

'That's 'cause people think the curies make them sick as much as they make them well,' Cery told her. 'They're scared they'll get sicker.'

'They're scared of magic even more. They'd think I might have been sent by the magicians to get rid of them.'

Cery laughed. 'Now that's silly. Nobody'll think that.'

'What about Burril?'

He made a face. 'Burril's a dunghead. Not everyone thinks like him.'

Sonea snorted, unconvinced. 'Even so, I don't know anything about magic. If everyone thinks I can heal them, I'll have people chasing me around but I won't be able to do anything to help them.'

Cery frowned. 'That's true.' He looked up at Harrin. 'She's right. It could get really bad. Even if Sonea wanted to try magic again, we'd still have to keep it a secret for a while.'

Harrin pursed his lips, then nodded. 'If anyone asks if you can do magic, Sonea, we'll tell them you didn't do anything – that the magicians must've lost their concentration or something, and the stone got through that way.'

Sonea stared at him, the possibility filling her with hope. 'Maybe that's what happened. Maybe I didn't do anything.'

'If you can't use magic again, you'll know for sure.' Cery patted her on the shoulder. 'If you can, we'll make sure that no-one finds out. In a few weeks, everyone will think the magicians just made a mistake. Give it a month or two and they'll forget all about you.'

A rapping on the door made Sonea jump. Rising, Harrin opened the door and let Donia in. The girl carried in a tray laden with mugs and a large plate of bread.

'Here,' she said, placing the tray on a table. 'A mug of bol each to celebrate the return of an old friend. Harrin, Father wants you to go out for him.'

'Better see what he wants.' Harrin picked up a mug and drained it. 'I'll see you around, Sonea,' he said. He caught

Donia about the waist and pulled her, giggling, out of the room. Sonea shook her head as the door closed.

'How long has *that* been going on?'

'Those two?' Cery asked, his mouth full of bread. 'Almost a year, I think. Harrin says he's going to marry her and inherit the inn.'

Sonea laughed. 'Does Gellin know?'

Cery smiled. 'Hasn't chased Harrin off yet.'

She picked up a piece of the dark bread. Made from curren grains, it was dusted with spices. As she bit into it, her stomach made it known that she had been neglecting it for over a day, and she found herself eating ravenously. The bol was sour, but welcome after the salty bread. When they had finished, Sonea dropped into the chair and sighed.

'With Harrin busy keeping an inn, what will you do, Cery?'

He shrugged. 'This and that. Steal bol from Harrin. Teach his children to pick locks. At least we'll be warm this winter. What've you got planned?'

'I don't know. Jonna and Ranel said – Oh!' She leapt to her feet. 'I didn't meet them. They don't know where I am!'

Cery waved a hand dismissively. 'They'll be around.'

She groped for her money pouch, and found it hanging full and heavy at her waist.

'Nice bit of savings you've got there,' Cery noted.

'Ranel said we should each carry a bit and head for the slums on our own. We'd be so unlucky to all be searched by the guards.' She narrowed her eyes at him. 'I know how much went in there.'

He laughed. 'So do I, and it's all there. Come on, I'll help you find them.'

Rising, he ushered her through the door and out into a short corridor. Sonea followed him down a narrow flight of stairs into a familiar drinking room. As always, the air was thick with bol fumes, laughter and a constant flow of chatter and amiable swearing. A large man slouched over the bench where the thick liquor was served.

'Morning Gellin,' Cery called.

He narrowed his eyes at Sonea short-sightedly, then grinned.

'Hai! This is little Sonea, eh?' Gellin strolled over and clapped her on the shoulders. 'All grown up, too. I remember when you used to swipe bol from me, girl. A dainty little thief, you were.'

Sonea grinned and cast a glance at Cery. 'And it was all my idea, too, wasn't it, Cery?'

Cery spread his hands and blinked innocently. 'What do you mean, Sonea?'

Gellin chuckled. 'That's what comes of hanging about with Thieves. How are your parents, then?'

'You mean Aunt Jonna and Uncle Ranel?'

He waved a hand. 'That's them.'

Sonea shrugged and quickly described her family's eviction from the Stayhouse. Gellin nodded sympathetically at their misfortune.

'They're probably wondering where I got to,' she told him. 'I—'

Sonea jumped as the door of the inn slammed. The room quietened and all looked toward the entrance. Harrin stood leaning against the frame, his chest heaving and his brow slick with sweat.

'Take care of my door,' Gellin yelled.

Harrin looked up. As he saw Sonea and Cery he paled

and started forward. Hurrying across the room, he caught Sonea's arm and pulled her through a door into the inn's kitchen, with Cery following closely.

'What is it?' Cery whispered.

'The magicians are searching the slums,' Harrin panted.

Sonea stared at him with horror.

'They're *here*?' Cery exclaimed. 'Why?'

Harrin gave Sonea a meaningful glance.

'They're looking for me,' she breathed.

Harrin nodded grimly, then turned to Cery. 'Where should we go?'

'How close are they?'

'Close. They started from the Outer Wall, working outwards.'

Cery whistled. '*That* close.'

Sonea pressed a hand to her chest. Her heart was beating too fast. She felt sick.

'We've only got a few minutes,' Harrin told them. 'We have to get out of here. They're searching every building.'

'Then we'll have to put her somewhere they've already been.'

Sonea leaned against the wall, her knees losing all strength as a memory of a blackened corpse rose before her eyes.

'They're going to kill me!' she gasped.

Cery looked at her. 'No, Sonea,' he told her firmly.

'They killed that boy . . .' she shuddered.

He gripped her shoulders. 'We're not going to let that happen, Sonea.'

His gaze was direct, and his expression uncharacteristically stern. She stared back, looking for doubt and not finding it.

'Do you trust me?' he asked.

She nodded. He gave her a quick smile.

'Come on, then.'

He pulled her away from the wall and propelled her through the kitchen, Harrin following close behind. Passing through another door, they stepped out into a muddy alley. Sonea shivered as the chill winter air quickly seeped into her clothes.

Stopping near the end of the alley, Cery told them to stay back while he checked to see if the way was clear. He paused only a moment at the entrance then hurried back, shaking his head. With a wave, he sent them hurrying back down the alley again.

Midway, he stopped and lifted a small grille set into a wall. Harrin gave his friend a doubtful look, then flattened himself to the ground and slithered through. Sonea followed and found herself in a dark passageway. As Harrin helped her to her feet and pulled her to one side, Cery slid through the opening. The grille closed silently, suggesting a regular oiling of the hinges.

'Are you sure about this?' Harrin whispered.

'The Thieves will be too busy trying to stop the magicians from finding their stuff to worry about us,' Cery told him. 'Besides, we won't be down here long. Keep your hand on my shoulder, Sonea.'

She obeyed, taking hold of his coat. Harrin's hand rested firmly on her shoulder. As they started down the passage she stared into the darkness ahead, heart racing.

From Harrin's question, she knew they had entered the Thieves' Road.

Using the underground network of tunnels without prior approval was forbidden, and she had heard frightening stories of the punishment the Thieves dealt out to those who trespassed.

For as long as she could remember, people had jokingly called Cery a friend of the Thieves. There had always been a hint of both fear and respect in their teasing. His father had been a smuggler, she knew, so it was possible that Cery had inherited privileges and contacts. She had seen no proof, however, and had always suspected he had encouraged speculation to keep his place of importance as Harrin's second in the gang. For all she knew, he had no connection to the Thieves at all and she was hurrying to her death.

Better to chance a meeting with the Thieves than face certain death above ground. At least the Thieves weren't searching for her.

The way darkened even further until Sonea could see nothing but varying shades of blackness, then gradually lightened again as they approached another grille. Cery turned into another passage, then changed direction into the total darkness of a side passage. They continued on for several turns before Cery stopped.

'They should have been here already,' Cery murmured to Harrin. 'We'll stay long enough to buy something, then move on. You should get the others and make sure they haven't told anyone about Sonea. People might think they can get something out of us by threatening to tell the magicians where we are.'

'I'll round 'em up,' Harrin assured him. 'Find out if they talked and tell them to keep their mugs shut.'

'Good,' Cery replied. 'Now we're here to buy some iker powder, that's all.'

Faint sounds echoed in the dark, then a door opened,

and they stepped out into bright daylight – and a pen filled with rassook.

At the sight of invaders, the birds lifted their tiny, useless wings and screeched loudly. The sound bounced off the four walls of a small courtyard. A woman appeared in a nearby doorway. Seeing Sonea and Harrin in her pen, her face creased into a scowl.

'Hai! Who're you?'

Sonea turned to Cery, and found him squatting behind her, running his hand over the dusty ground. He rose and grinned at the woman.

'Come to pay you a visit, Laria,' he said.

The woman peered down at him. Her scowl vanished and was replaced by a wrinkly smile. 'Ceryni! Always good to see you. These your friends? Welcome! Welcome! Come in my house and have some raka.'

'How's trade?' Cery asked as they stepped out of the pen and followed Laria through the door into a tiny room. A narrow bed filled one half of the room, and a stove and table took up most of the rest.

Her brow creased. 'Busy day. Had some visitors less than an hour ago. Very nosy they were.'

'Robed visitors?' Cery asked.

She nodded. 'Scared me witless, they did. Looked everywhere, but didn't see anything, if you know what I mean. The guards did, though. I'm sure they'll be back, but when they do there'll be nothing to find.' She chuckled. 'Too late then.' She paused as she set water boiling on the stove. 'What you here for, then?'

'The usual.'

A wicked gleam entered Laria's eyes. 'Planning a few late nights, then? How much you offering?'

He smiled. 'You owe me a favour, if I remember.'

The woman pursed her lips, her sharp eyes narrowing. 'Stay there.'

She disappeared out the door. With a sigh, Cery dropped down onto the bed, which creaked loudly. 'Relax, Sonea,' he told her. 'They've been here. They won't look again.'

She nodded. Her heart was still racing and her stomach was uneasy. Taking a deep breath, she let herself lean back against the wall. As the water boiled Cery helped himself to a jar of dark powder and heaped spoonfuls into the cups Laria had set out. A reassuringly familiar, pungent aroma filled the room.

'Guess we know for sure, Sonea,' Harrin said as Cery handed him a cup.

She frowned. 'Know what?'

'What you did must've been magic.' He grinned. 'They wouldn't be searching if they didn't think it was, would they?'

With an impatient gesture, Dannyl banished the moisture from his robes. Puffs of steam billowed from the cloth. The guards shied away, then, as an icy gust of wind swept away the mist, the four men returned to their places.

They walked in formation – two beside him, two behind. A ridiculous precaution. The dwells weren't stupid enough to attack them. Besides, if they did, Dannyl knew it would be the guards who would look to him for protection.

Catching a pensive glance from one of the men, Dannyl felt a twinge of guilt. At the beginning of the day, they had been nervous and deferential. Knowing he would have to put up with this for the rest of the day, Dannyl had made an effort to be approachable and friendly.

To them this was like a holiday – infinitely more entertaining than standing at one of the gates for hours on end or patrolling the city streets. Despite their eagerness to break into smuggler's stores and whorehouses, they hadn't been much help in the search. He didn't need anybody to force locked doors or open shipping boxes, and the slum dwellers had been co-operative, even if reluctantly.

Dannyl sighed. He'd seen enough to know that many of these people were well accustomed to hiding what they didn't want found. He had also seen many smothered smiles on the faces that watched him. What chance did a mere hundred magicians have of finding one ordinary-looking girl amongst thousands of slum dwellers?

None at all. Dannyl clenched his jaw as he remembered Lord Balkan's words from the previous evening.

How would it be if one of us was discovered dressed as a grovelling beggar? We would be ridiculed throughout the Allied Lands.

He snorted. *And we're not making fools of ourselves now?*

A pungent stench filled Dannyl's nostrils. He glared at the sewage-choked gutter. The people standing beside it shrank away hastily. With an effort, he made himself take a deep breath and school his expression.

He did not like to frighten people. Impress them? Yes. Inspire awe? Even better. But not terrify. It disturbed him how these people always shied off the road when he approached, then stared at him as he passed. The children were bolder, following him around, but quick to run away if he looked at them. Men and women, old and young, regarded him warily. All looked hard and cunning. He wondered how many worked for the Thieves . . .

Dannyl stopped.

The Thieves . . .

The guards skidded to a halt and looked at him questioningly. He ignored them.

If the stories were true, the Thieves knew more about the slums than anyone else. Did they know the location of this girl? If they didn't could they find her? Would they be willing to help the Guild? Perhaps, if the rewards were attractive . . .

How would the other magicians react if he suggested bargaining with the Thieves?

They'd be horrified. Outraged.

He looked at the shallow, stinking trench that served as a gutter. The magicians might look more favourably on the idea after a few days of roaming through the slums. Which meant that the longer he waited before proposing it, the better his chances of gaining their approval.

Yet, every hour that passed gave the girl more time to hide herself. Dannyl pursed his lips. It wouldn't hurt to see if the Thieves were willing to bargain *before* he presented the idea to the Guild. If he waited for the Guild's approval first, and the Thieves then proved uncooperative, he'd have wasted a lot of time and effort.

He turned to face the eldest of the guards.

'Captain Garrin. Do you know how the Thieves may be contacted?'

The captain's brows rose so high they disappeared under his helmet. He shook his head. 'No, my lord.'

'I do, my lord.'

Dannyl turned to regard the youngest of the four guards, a lanky young man named Ollin.

'I used to live here, my lord,' Ollin admitted, 'before I joined the Guard. There's always people about who can get messages to the Thieves, if you know where to look.'

'I see.' Dannyl chewed the inside of his cheek while he considered. 'Find one of these people for me. Ask if the Thieves would be willing to work with us. Report directly back to me – and no other.'

Ollin nodded, then looked at the captain. The older man's mouth tightened with disapproval, but he nodded, then jerked his head to one of the other guards. 'Take Keran.'

Dannyl watched the pair stride back down the street then turned away and continued walking, his mind absorbed with possibilities. A familiar figure stepped out of a house a little further down the street. Dannyl smiled and lengthened his stride.

—Rothen!

The man stopped, the wind catching his robe so it swirled out around him.

—Dannyl? Rothen's sending was faint and uncertain.

—I'm here. Dannyl sent a quick image of the street to the other magician, and a sense of nearness. Rothen turned toward him, then straightened as he saw Dannyl. Drawing closer, Dannyl saw that Rothen's blue eyes were wide and haunted.

'Any luck?'

'No.' Rothen shook his head. He looked at the makeshift houses to one side. 'I had no idea what it was like out here.'

'It's like a harrel warren, isn't it?' Dannyl chuckled. 'A real mess.'

'Oh, yes, but I meant the people.' Rothen gestured at the crowds around them. 'Conditions are so bad . . . I couldn't have imagined . . .'

Dannyl shrugged. 'We haven't got a hope of finding her, Rothen. There just aren't enough of us.'

Rothen nodded. 'Do you think the others have fared better?'

'If they had, we would have been contacted.'

'You're right.' Rothen frowned. 'It occurred to me today: how do we know she's still in the city? She could have fled into the country.' He shook his head. 'I fear you are right. I've finished here. Let's go back to the Guild.'

CHAPTER 4

THE SEARCH CONTINUES

Early morning sunlight bathed the frost-coated windows with gold. The air inside the room was deliciously warm, heated by a glowing sphere hovering behind a clouded glass panel set into the wall. Tying the sash of his robe, Rothen stepped out into the guest room to greet his friends.

A second panel allowed the heat globe to warm the bedroom and guest room simultaneously. An elderly magician stood in front of this, holding his hands to the glass. Though well into his eighties, Yaldin was still robust and sharp witted, enjoying the longevity and good health that came with magical ability.

A taller and younger magician stood beside Yaldin. Dannyl's eyes were half closed, and he looked as if he was ready to fall asleep.

'Good morning,' Rothen said. 'Looks like the weather is going to clear today.'

Yaldin smiled crookedly. 'Lord Davin thinks we'll have a few warm days before winter sets in.'

Dannyl scowled. 'Davin has been saying that for weeks.'

'He didn't say *when* it would happen.' Yaldin chuckled. 'Just that it *would* happen.'

Rothen smiled. There was an old saying in Kyralia: 'The sun seeks not to please Kings, nor even magicians.' Lord

Davin, an eccentric Alchemist, had begun a study of the weather three years ago, determined to prove otherwise. He had been supplying the Guild with 'predictions' recently, though Rothen suspected his rate of success had more to do with chance than genius.

The main door to the room opened and Rothen's servant, Tania, entered. She carried a tray to the table and set it down. On it was a set of small cups decorated with gold and a plate piled high with sweet, elaborately decorated cakes.

'Sumi, my lords?' she asked.

Dannyl and Yaldin nodded eagerly. As Rothen ushered them to seats, Tania measured spoonfuls of dried leaves into a gold pot and added hot water.

Yaldin sighed and shook his head. 'To be honest, I don't know why I volunteered to go today. I wouldn't have if Ezrille hadn't insisted. I said to her, "With only half of us out there, what chance do we have?" She replied, "Better than if none of you went."'

Rothen smiled. 'Your wife is a sensible lady.'

'I'd have thought more of us would be interested in helping after the King's Advisors announced that, if she isn't a rogue, he wants her trained,' Dannyl said.

Yaldin grimaced. 'I suspect some withdrew their support in protest. They don't want a slum girl in the Guild.'

'Well, they have no choice now. And we've gained one new helper,' Rothen reminded them as he accepted a cup from Tania.

'Fergun.' Dannyl made a rude noise. 'The girl should have thrown harder.'

'Dannyl!' Rothen shook a finger at the younger magician. 'Fergun is the only reason we still have half the Guild looking for her. He was very persuasive at last night's Meet.'

Yaldin smiled grimly. 'I doubt he'll stay that way for long. I went straight to the baths when we finally came in yesterday, but Ezrille said she could still smell the slums on me afterwards.'

'I hope our little runaway magician doesn't smell that bad,' Dannyl sent Rothen a crooked grin, 'or I think the first lesson we'll have to teach her is how to wash.'

Remembering the girl's starved, dirty face, eyes wide with realisation, Rothen shivered. All night he had dreamed of the slums. He had roamed through thin-walled hovels, watched by sick-looking people, or old men shivering in their rags, or skinny children eating half-rotten food, twisted cripples . . .

A polite knock interrupted his thoughts. He turned toward the door and gave a mental command. It swung inward and a young man in the garb of a messenger stepped into the room.

'Lord Dannyl.' The messenger bowed low to the younger magician.

'Speak,' Dannyl ordered.

'Captain Garrin sent a message for you, my lord. He said to tell you that the guards Ollin and Keran were found robbed and beaten. The man you were seeking does not wish to speak to magicians.'

Dannyl stared at the servant, then frowned as he considered the news. As the silence lengthened the young man shuffled his feet uneasily.

'Are they badly injured?' Rothen asked.

The messenger shook his head. 'Bruised, my lord. Nothing broken.'

Dannyl waved a hand dismissively. 'Thank the captain for his message. You may go.'

The messenger bowed again and left.

'What was that all about?' asked Yaldin when the door had closed.

Dannyl pursed his lips. 'It seems the Thieves are not well disposed towards us.'

Yaldin snorted softly, and reached for a cake. 'I should think not! Why would they—?' The old magician stopped and narrowed his eyes at the younger magician. 'You didn't . . .'

Dannyl shrugged. 'It was worth trying. After all, they're supposed to know everything that goes on in the slums.'

'You tried to contact the *Thieves*!'

'I didn't break any laws that I know of.'

Yaldin groaned and shook his head.

'No, Dannyl,' Rothen said, 'but the King and the Houses will hardly look kindly on the Guild conducting business with the Thieves.'

'Who said we were conducting business?' Dannyl smiled and took a sip from his cup. 'Think about it. The Thieves know the slums far better than we could ever hope to. They're in a better position to find the girl than we – and I'm sure they'd prefer to look for her themselves than have us snooping around in their domain. We have only to make it appear to the King that we have persuaded or intimidated the Thieves into turning the girl over and we'll have all the approval we need.'

Rothen frowned. 'You'll have a long and difficult time convincing the Higher Magicians to agree.'

'They don't have to know for now.'

Rothen crossed his arms. 'Yes they do,' he said firmly.

Dannyl winced. 'I suppose they do, but I'm sure they would forgive me if it worked, and I gave them a way to justify it to the King.'

Yaldin snorted. 'Perhaps it's just as well it didn't work.'

Rising, Rothen walked to a window. He wiped a little frost away and peered through at the neatly laid out, carefully maintained gardens. He thought of the shivering, hungry people he had seen. Was that how she lived? Had their search driven her out of the dubious shelter of some hovel and into the streets? Winter was coming, and she could easily die from cold or starvation long before her powers grew unstable and dangerous. He drummed his fingers on the window sill.

'There are several groups of Thieves, aren't there?'

'Yes,' Dannyl replied.

'Does this man you tried to contact speak for all of them?'

'I don't know,' Dannyl admitted. 'Perhaps not.'

Rothen turned to regard his friend.

'It wouldn't hurt to find out, would it?'

Yaldin stared at Rothen, then slapped a hand to his forehead. 'You two are going to get us all in trouble,' he groaned.

Dannyl patted the old man's shoulder. 'Don't worry, Yaldin. Only one of us need go.' He grinned at Rothen. 'Leave it to me. In the meantime, let's give the Thieves a reason to help us. I'd like to have a closer look at those underground passages we found yesterday. I'd wager that they'd prefer we had no reason to be snooping around down there.'

'I don't like these underground rooms,' Donia said. 'They got no windows. Makes me feel all creepy.'

Sonea frowned and scratched at the tiny bites that she had gained during the night. Her aunt regularly washed their beds and blankets with an infusion of herbs to rid them of bugs, and for once Sonea missed her aunt's fastidious ways. She sighed and looked around the dusty room.

'I hope Cery won't get in any rub for hiding me here.'

Donia shrugged. 'He's been doing stuff for Opia and the girls at the Dancing Slippers for years. They don't mind you staying in their storeroom for a few days. His ma worked here, y'know.' Donia placed a large wooden bowl on the table in front of Sonea. 'Put your head down.'

Sonea obeyed, and winced as icy cold water rushed over her head. After several rinses, Donia took the bowl away, now full of cloudy green water. She rubbed at Sonea's hair with a threadbare towel before standing back and examining her work critically.

'Hasn't done a thing,' Donia said, shaking her head.

Sonea lifted a hand to touch her hair. It was still sticky from the paste Donia had applied. 'Nothing?'

Donia leaned closer and plucked at Sonea's hair. 'Well, it's a bit lighter, but not that you'd see straight away.' She sighed. 'It's not like we can cut it much shorter. But . . .' she stepped back and shrugged. 'If the magicians are out for a girl, like people are saying, they might not pick you, anyhow. You look like a boy with your hair like that, at least at the first look.' She put her hands on her hips and stepped back. 'Why'd you cut it so short, then?'

Sonea smiled. 'So I look like a boy. I don't get hassled so much.'

'In the stayhouse?'

'No. I did most of the picking up and delivering for Jonna and Ranel. Ranel's leg made him slow, and Jonna was better at the work. I hated being stuck in the stay-house all the time, so I went instead.' Sonea grimaced. 'The first time I had to deliver stuff to a merchant, I saw a couple of crafters and stablemen hassling a baker girl. I didn't want to put up with that, so I started dressing and acting like a boy.'

Donia's brows rose. 'And it worked?'

'Most of the time.' Sonea smiled wryly. 'Sometimes it doesn't pay to look like a boy, either. I had a maid in love with me once! Another time I was cornered by a gardener and I was sure he'd worked out I was a girl, until he grabbed me. He nearly fainted, then he got all red-faced and made me promise not to tell. There's all kinds out there.'

Donia chuckled. 'The girls here call those men gold mines. Opia charges more for boys, because if the guard found out they'd hang her. No law against girls, though. Remember Kalia?'

Sonea nodded as she recalled the thin girl who had served in a bolhouse near the market.

'Turned out her father's been selling her to customers for years,' Donia said, shaking her head. 'His own daughter! Last year she ran away and started up with Opia. Says at least she sees some of the money this way. Makes you realise how lucky you are, doesn't it? Father makes sure nobody hassles me more than what's polite. The worst I've—'

She stopped and looked at the door, then hurried to the keyhole and peered through. A smile of relief lit her face and she opened the door.

Cery slipped into the room and handed Donia a bundle. He eyed Sonea critically.

'You don't look any different.'

Donia sighed. 'The dye didn't work. Kyralian hair don't change easy.'

He shrugged, then nodded at the bundle. 'Brought you some clothes, Sonea.' He moved back to the door. 'Knock when you're done.'

As the door closed behind him, Donia picked up the bundle and unwrapped it.

'More boy's clothes,' she sniffed, tossing a pair of trousers and a high-collared shirt to Sonea. She unfurled a long swathe of heavy black cloth and nodded. 'Good cloak, though.'

Sonea changed into the clothes. As she swung the cloak about her shoulders, there was a rap on the door.

'We're leaving,' Cery told them as he strode into the room. Harrin followed carrying a small lamp. Seeing their grim expressions, Sonea felt her heart skip a beat.

'They're searching already?'

Cery nodded, then moved to an old wooden cupboard at the back of the room. Opening it, he pulled at the shelves inside. They swung forward smoothly, their contents shaking slightly. The back of the cupboard hinged inward to reveal a rectangle of darkness.

'They've been searching for a few hours,' Harrin told Sonea as she stepped through the hidden doorway into the passage.

'Already?'

'It's easy to lose track of time down here,' he explained. 'It's mid-morning outside.'

Cery shooed Harrin and Donia through the doorway. Sonea heard the faintest squeak and a sliver of light escaped Harrin's lamp to reveal the damp walls of the passage. Cery pulled the cupboard together, closed the secret door, and turned to Harrin.

'No light. I know my way better in the dark.'

The passage vanished as Harrin closed the shutter.

'No talking, either,' Cery told them. 'Sonea, grab hold of my coat and put your other hand on the wall.'

She reached out and grasped the rough material of his longcoat. A hand touched her shoulder lightly. Their footsteps echoed in the passage as they started forward.

Not a ray of light illuminated their way as they groped through several turns. The faint echo of dripping water came and went, and returned again. Opia's brothel was near the river, Sonea remembered, so the passages were probably below the level of the water. It was not a comforting thought.

Cery stopped and his longcoat slipped out of Sonea's grip as he suddenly moved upwards. She reached out and touched a rough, wooden board, then another. Anxious that she would lose Cery if she hesitated too long, she scurried up the ladder only to be rewarded by a kick from his boot. She bit back a curse and continued with more care. Behind her, she could hear Harrin and Donia's shoes scuffing the wood faintly as they followed.

A paler square of black appeared above. She followed Cery through a trapdoor into a long, straight passage. Faint light filtered in through the occasional crack in the wall on one side. They walked along this for over a hundred paces when, just as they had almost reached the turn in the passage, Cery came to an abrupt halt.

The passage ahead had begun to glow, lit by a source of light somewhere beyond the turn. She could see Cery silhouetted against the wall. A distant voice, male and cultured, drifted to their ears.

'Ah! *Another* hidden passage. Come, we shall see how far it extends.'

'They're in the passages!' Donia breathed.

Cery span around and waved frantically at Sonea. Not needing any urging, she turned to see Harrin and Donia tip-toeing back down the passage.

Though they walked as silently and quickly as they could, their footsteps sounded loud in the narrow space. Sonea strained her ears, expecting to hear a shout behind them any moment. Looking down, she saw her own shadow growing more distinct as the light behind them approached the turn.

The passage ahead extended into an infinite darkness. She glanced back. The light behind them was now so bright, she was sure the magician must be about to reach the turn. In a moment he would see them . . .

She gasped as hands grabbed her shoulders and jerked her to a halt. Cery pushed her against the wall and pressed on her shoulders. The brickwork seemed to collapse behind her, and she stumbled backwards.

Her back struck another wall. Cery shoved her to one side, against a side wall, then moved into the tiny alcove beside her. She felt his bony elbow poking into her side and heard a dry scraping sound of bricks sliding against each other and clicking into place.

In the cramped space, the sound of their breathing was thunderous. Heart pounding, Sonea strained her ears until the muffled sound of voices began to penetrate the bricks. Light appeared through cracks in the brickwork. Leaning forward, Sonea peered through one of the openings.

A glowing ball of light floated in the air just before her. Fascinated, she watched it drift forward until it passed out of sight, leaving red blotches in her vision. Then a pale hand appeared, followed by a wide, purple-coloured sleeve and the chest of a man – a man dressed in robes – a *magician*!

Her heart raced. He was so close – within arm's reach. Only a thin wall of old bricks stood between them.

And he had stopped.

'Wait a moment.' The magician sounded puzzled. He stood still and silent, then slowly turned to face her.

She froze in horror. He was the magician from the North Square – the one who had seen her. The one who had tried to point her out to the rest. His expression was distracted, as if he was listening to something, and he appeared to be staring right through the wall and into her eyes.

Her mouth was dry and felt full of dust. Swallowing hard, she fought a rising terror. The pounding of her heart seemed loud enough to betray her. Could he hear that? Or could he hear the sound of her breathing?

Perhaps he can hear the thoughts in my head.

Sonea felt her legs go weak. It was said they could do such things. She closed her eyes tightly. *He can't see me*, she told herself. *I don't exist. I'm not here. I'm nothing. No-one can see me. No-one can hear me . . .*

A strange sensation stole over her, as if a blanket had been wrapped about her head, muffling her senses. She shivered, disturbed by the certainty that she had done something – but this time to herself.

Or perhaps the magician has worked some kind of magic on me, she thought suddenly. Appalled, she opened her eyes and found herself staring into darkness.

The magician, and his light, had gone.

Dannyl regarded the building before him with distaste. The most recent of the Guild structures, it lacked the grandeur and beauty that he admired in the older buildings. While some praised the modern style, Dannyl considered this building to be as ridiculously pretentious as its name.

The Seven Arches was a flat rectangle, fronted with seven plain, undecorated arches. Inside were three rooms: the Day Room, where important guests were received, the Banquet Room and the Night Room, where magicians gathered informally each Fourday evening to relax, sip expensive wine and gossip.

It was to this last room that he and Rothen were heading. It was a chilly evening, but a little cold air had never kept Night Room regulars away. Dannyl smiled as he entered. Once inside, he could forget the architectural blunder that had brought about the building's existence, and enjoy the tasteful decorations within.

He looked around, enjoying a new appreciation of the room's luxuries after enduring a second day in the damp, cold passages of the slums. Dark blue and gold patterned screens covered the windows. Luxurious cushioned chairs were arranged around the room. The walls were decorated with paintings and carvings by the best artists of the Allied Lands.

More than the usual number of magicians were present, he noted. As he and Rothen strolled deeper into the crowd, he recognised a few less social magicians. Then Dannyl's eyes caught a splash of black and he stopped.

'The High Lord has graced us with his presence tonight,' he murmured.

'Akkarin? Where?' Rothen glanced around the room and his eyebrows rose as he located the black-robed figure. 'Interesting. How long has it been? Two months?'

Dannyl nodded as he took a glass of wine from a passing servant. 'At least.'

'Is that Administrator Lorlen with him?'

'Of course,' Dannyl said, pausing to sip from his glass. 'Lorlen's talking to someone, but I can't see who it is.'

Lorlen looked up and around the room. His gaze rested on Dannyl and Rothen. A hand rose.

—Dannyl. Rothen. I would like to speak to you.

Surprised, and a little apprehensive, Dannyl followed Rothen across the room. They stopped behind the chair that had blocked Dannyl's view of Lorlen's other companion. A cultured voice reached their ears.

'The slums are an ugly stain on this city. They are a nest of crime and disease. The King should never have let them grow so large. This is the perfect opportunity to rid Imardin of them.'

Dannyl schooled his expression and looked down at the chair's occupant. Immaculately combed blonde hair gleamed from the light of the room. The man's eyes were half closed, his legs crossed and pointing toward the High Lord. A small square bandage had been stuck to his temple.

'How do you propose he do that, Lord Fergun?' Lorlen asked mildly.

Fergun shrugged. 'It would not be hard to clear the area. The houses are not particularly well made, and it would take little effort to collapse the tunnels beneath them.'

'But every city grows and expands,' Lorlen pointed out. 'It is only natural that people build outside the walls when there is no longer room inside them. There are some areas in the slums that look little different to the quarters. The buildings are well made and the streets have effective drainage. The occupants of these areas have started referring to the slums as the Outer Circle.'

Fergun leaned forward. 'But even those houses have hidden passages beneath them. I assure you, their occupants are the most suspicious people. Any house built on top of such tunnels should be assumed to be part of a criminal conspiracy and torn down.'

Akkarin's brows rose slightly at this. Lorlen glanced at the High Lord and smiled. 'If only the problem of the Thieves could be solved so easily.' He looked up at Rothen and smiled. 'Good evening, Lord Rothen and Lord Dannyl.'

Fergun looked up. His eyes slid from Dannyl to Rothen, and his mouth stretched into a smile. 'Ah, Lord Rothen.'

'Good evening High Lord, Administrator,' Rothen replied, inclining his head to the Higher Magicians. 'And Lord Fergun. Are you feeling better?'

'Yes, yes,' Fergun replied, lifting a hand to touch the bandage on his forehead. 'Thank you for enquiring.'

Dannyl kept his expression neutral. It was rude, but not unusual, for Fergun to 'forget' to greet him. That he had done so in the High Lord's presence, however, was surprising.

Lorlen folded his hands together. 'I noticed that you both stayed in the slums longer than most others today. Did you discover any clues to this girl's whereabouts?'

Rothen shook his head, and began describing their attempts to follow the underground passages of the slums. Remaining silent, Dannyl looked at the High Lord and felt a familiar twinge of nervousness. *Ten years since I graduated, but I still react to him as if I were a novice*, he mused.

Dannyl's duties and interests rarely brought him in contact with the Guild's leader. As always, he felt a mild surprise at Akkarin's youthfulness. He thought of the arguments that had risen, five years before, at the election of a young magician to the position of High Lord. Guild leaders were selected from the strongest of the magicians, yet older magicians were usually chosen over younger ones due to their greater experience and maturity.

While Akkarin had demonstrated powers far stronger than any other magician's, it was the knowledge and diplomatic skills that he had gained while travelling abroad that had convinced the Guild to elect him. A Guild leader was expected to have qualities of strength, skill, dignity and authority, and Akkarin had all of these in abundance. As many had pointed out at the time of Akkarin's choosing, age mattered little to the role. Important decisions were always made by vote, and the everyday running of the Guild was left to the Guild Administrator.

While this sounded reasonable, Dannyl suspected that questions about the High Lord's age still lingered. He had noted that Akkarin now wore his hair in the old fashioned and distinguished style favoured by older men – long and tidily knotted at the back of his neck. Lorlen, too, had adopted the style.

Dannyl turned to regard the Administrator, who was listening to Rothen intently. The High Lord's closest friend, Lorlen had become the former Guild Administrator's assistant at Akkarin's suggestion. When the Administrator retired, two years past, Lorlen had taken his place.

Lorlen had proven to be well-suited to the position. He was efficient, authoritative, and, most importantly, approachable. It was not an easy role, and Dannyl did not envy Lorlen the long hours involved. Of the two positions, it was the most demanding.

Lorlen shook his head as Rothen finished his account of their day. 'From the descriptions I've heard of the slums, I can't see how we'll ever find her.' He sighed. 'The King has ordered that the Port be opened tomorrow.'

Fergun frowned. 'Already? What if she escapes on a ship?'

'I doubt if the embargo would have stopped her from leaving Imardin if she really wanted to.' Lorlen looked up at Rothen and smiled wryly. 'As Lord Rothen's former guardian used to say: "Kyralia would run itself very well if ruling was declared a crime".'

Rothen chuckled. 'Yes, Lord Margen was a source of many such remarks. I don't believe we have explored all our options, however. Dannyl pointed out to me this morning that the people who have the best chance of finding this girl are the slum dwellers themselves. I think he's right.'

Dannyl stared at his friend. Surely Rothen was not going to reveal their intention to contact the Thieves!

'Why would they help us?' Lorlen asked.

Rothen glanced at Dannyl and smiled. 'We could offer a reward.'

Dannyl slowly let out the breath he had been holding. *You should have warned me, old friend!*

'A reward!' Lorlen exclaimed. 'Yes, that might work.'

'An excellent idea,' Fergun agreed. 'And we should fine those who hinder us, too.'

Lorlen gave Fergun a reproachful look. 'A reward will be sufficient. Mind you, nothing shall be given until she is found, or the entire population of the slums will claim to have seen her.' He frowned. 'Hmm, we'll also want to discourage people from trying to catch her themselves . . .'

'We could post a description of her and terms of the reward at street corners, with a warning that she should not be approached,' Dannyl suggested. 'We should encourage people to report sightings of her, too, as they could give us some indication of the areas she frequents.'

'We could have a map of the slums drawn up so we can keep track of sightings,' Fergun suggested.

'Hmm, that *would* be useful,' Dannyl said, pretending to be begrudgingly surprised at the suggestion. Remembering the maze of passages and streets, he knew a task like that would keep Fergun out of their way for months. Rothen narrowed his eyes at Dannyl, but said nothing.

'The posting of a reward,' Lorlen glanced up at Dannyl, 'you'll arrange it?'

'Tomorrow.' Dannyl inclined his head.

'I will inform the rest of the searchers of this tomorrow morning,' Lorlen said. He looked up at Rothen and Dannyl and smiled. 'Any more ideas?'

'This girl must have a presence,' the High Lord said quietly. 'She is untrained, and would not know how to hide it – or even that she has one. Has anyone looked for it yet?'

For a moment, all were silent, then Lorlen chuckled ruefully. 'I can't believe I hadn't thought of that. No-one has mentioned looking for her presence.' He shook his head. 'It seems we've all forgotten what we are – and what she is.'

'A presence,' Rothen said quietly. 'I think I . . .'

Lorlen frowned as Rothen did not finish his sentence. 'Yes?'

'I'll organise a mental search for tomorrow,' Rothen offered.

Lorlen smiled. 'Then you two have a busy day ahead.'

Rothen inclined his head. 'We'd best have an early night, then. Good night Administrator, High Lord, Lord Fergun.'

The three magicians nodded in reply. Dannyl followed as Rothen hurried toward the Night Room doors. As they stepped out into the chilly air, Rothen let out an explosive breath.

'*Now* I realise!' He slapped a hand to his forehead.

'Realise what?' Dannyl asked, bemused.

'Today, while I was following one of the passages, I *felt* something. As if somebody was watching me.'

'A presence?'

'Perhaps.'

'Did you investigate?'

Rothen nodded. 'It didn't make sense. What I was detecting would have to have been right next to me, yet there was nothing but a brick wall.'

'Did you look for a hidden door?'

'No, but . . .' Rothen hesitated, and frowned, '. . . it stopped.'

'It stopped?' Dannyl looked perplexed. 'How could it just stop? A presence doesn't just stop – not unless it has been hidden. She hasn't been trained to do that.'

'Or has she?' Rothen smiled grimly. 'If it was her, then either she has been taught by someone, or she has worked it out for herself.'

'It's not difficult to learn,' Dannyl pointed out, 'and we teach it by playing games of hideaway.'

Rothen nodded slowly as he considered the possibility,

then shrugged. 'I guess we'll know tomorrow. I had better go back in and see if I can round up some help. I expect many of those who don't want to enter the slums again will be happy to help with a mental search. I want you to join us, Dannyl. You've got particularly fine senses.'

Dannyl shrugged. 'If you put it that way, how can I refuse?'

'We'll begin early, I think. You'll want to have those reward notices printed and sent out as soon as possible.'

'Agh.' Dannyl grimaced. 'Not another early morning.'

CHAPTER 5

THE REWARD

'Cery?'

Lifting his head from the table, Cery blinked his eyes. It was morning, he guessed, though it was always hard to tell when you were underground. Straightening, he looked over to the bed. The candle had burned low and its light didn't reach far, but he could just make out the glimmer of Sonea's eyes.

'I'm awake,' he said, stretching to loosen his stiff shoulders. Lifting the candle from the table, Cery carried it over to the bed. Sonea lay with her arms pillowing her head, staring up at the low ceiling. Seeing her, he felt a strange, compelling uneasiness. He could remember feeling that way two years ago, just before she had stopped meeting the gang. After she had disappeared, he had realised too late that he had known all along that she was going to leave them one day.

'Good morning,' he said.

She managed a smile, but it didn't chase away the haunted look in her eyes. 'Who was that boy in the square – the one who died?'

He sat down on the end of the bed and sighed.

'His name was Arrel, I think. Didn't really know him. The son of a woman who used to work at the Dancing Slippers, I think.'

She nodded slowly. For a long time she was silent, then her brows knitted together.

'Have you seen Jonna and Ranel since yesterday?'

He shook his head. 'No.'

'I miss them.' She laughed suddenly. 'Never thought I would so much, really. You know,' she turned on her side and looked at him directly, 'I miss them more than my mother. Isn't that strange?'

'They've looked after you most of your life,' Cery reminded her. 'And your mother has been dead a long time.'

She nodded. 'I sometimes see her in dreams, but when I wake up I can't remember what she looked like. I can remember the house where we lived, though. It was amazing.'

'Your house?' He hadn't heard this before.

She shook her head. 'Mother and father were servants for one of the Families, but they were thrown out when father was accused of stealing something.'

Cery smiled. 'Did he?'

'Probably.' She yawned. 'Jonna blames him for everything I do that she thinks is wrong or bad. She doesn't approve of theft, even if it's from someone rich and mean.'

'Where is your da now?'

She shrugged. 'He left when mother died. Came back once when I was six. Gave Jonna a bit of money then left again.'

Cery picked some of the run wax off the candle. 'The Thieves killed my da when they found out he was cheating them.'

Her eyes widened. 'Oh, that's awful! I knew he was dead, but you never told me *that*.'

He shrugged. 'It's not smart to let people know your da was a squimp. He took stupid risks and got caught. That's what Ma says, anyway. He taught me lots of stuff, though.'

'The Thieves' Road.'

He nodded.

'We've been using it, haven't we?'

He nodded again.

She grinned. 'So it's true then? You *are* a Thieves' man.'

'Nah,' he replied, looking away. 'My da showed me the Road.'

'So, you've got permission?'

He shrugged. 'Yes and no.'

Sonea frowned but said no more.

Looking down at the candle, Cery thought back to a day, three years before, when he had slipped into the passages to escape a guard who had taken offence at having his pockets explored. A shadow had appeared in the darkness, taken Cery by the collar and dragged him to a room off the tunnel and locked him in. Despite all Cery's lock-picking skills, he hadn't been able to free himself. Several hours later, the door had opened and he had been dazzled by a lamp burning so bright he could only make out the silhouette of the man holding it.

'Who're you?' the stranger had demanded. 'What's your name?'

'Ceryni,' he had squeaked.

There had been a pause, and then the light came closer.

'So you are,' the stranger had remarked, amusement in his tone. 'A familiar little rodent, too. Ah, I've got you tagged, now. Torrin's son. Hmm, you know the price for using the Road without the Thieves' say-so?'

Terrified, Cery had nodded his head.

'Well then, little Ceryni. You be in a lot of rub, you know, but I think I can give you a bit of space. Don't use the Road regular-like – but if you have to, use it. If anyone asks, tell 'em Ravi said you could. But remember, you owe me. If I ask you for something, you'll give it to me. If you give me boot, you don't get to use *any* road again. We right?'

Cery had nodded again, too frightened to speak.

The stranger had chuckled. 'Good. Now get yourself gone.' The light had disappeared and Cery had been hauled by unseen hands to the nearest exit from the Road and tossed outside.

Since then, he had rarely set foot on the Thieves' Road. The few times he had returned to the maze, he had been surprised to find his memory of its ways hadn't faded. He had occasionally passed other travellers, but they had never stopped or questioned him.

In the last few days, however, he had flouted the Thieves' rule far more than he was comfortable with. If someone confronted him, he would have to trust that Ravi's name still held some influence. However, he was not about to tell Sonea that. It would frighten her too much.

Looking down at her, he felt that strange uneasiness again. He had always hoped she would come back one day, but had never believed it. She was different. Special. He'd always known she would get out of the slums one day.

She *was* special, but in a way he could not have guessed. She had magic! But she also had very bad timing. Why couldn't she have discovered it while making a cup of raka, or polishing shoes? Why do it in front of the Magicians' Guild?

She had, however, and now he must do all he could to keep her from them. At least that left them plenty of time together. Even if that did mean risking his understanding with Ravi, it was worth it. But he hated seeing her looking so worried . . .

'Don't worry. So long as the magicians are snooping in the tunnels the Thieves won't pay any mind to—'

'Shhh!' she interrupted, lifting a hand to silence him.

He stared at her as she climbed off the bed and walked into the centre of the room. Turning full circle, she stared at the walls intently, her eyes roving about. He strained his ears, but could hear nothing unusual.

'What is it?'

She shook her head, then suddenly flinched. A look of surprise and terror crossed her face. He leapt to his feet, alarmed.

'What is it?' he repeated.

'They're searching,' she hissed.

'I can't hear anything.'

'No, you wouldn't,' she said, her voice shaking. 'I can *see* them, but it's not like seeing. It's more like hearing, but it isn't because I can't tell what they're saying. It's more like . . .' She sucked in a breath and whirled about, her eyes roving after something beyond his senses. 'They're searching with their minds.'

Cery stared at her helplessly. If he still had doubts that she had magical powers, this cast them aside forever.

'Can they see you?'

She gave him a frightened look. 'I don't know.'

He clenched and unclenched his fists. He had been so sure he could keep her from them, but there was no place he could take her – no walls that would hide her – from *this*.

Sucking in a breath, he stepped forward and grabbed her hands.

'Can you stop them seeing you?'

She spread her hands. 'How? I don't know how to use magic.'

'Try!' he urged. 'Try something. Anything!'

She shook her head, then tensed and drew in a sharp breath. He watched her face turn white.

'That one seemed to look right at me . . .' She turned to look at Cery. 'But it went past. They keep looking past me.' A smile slowly spread across her face. 'They can't see me.'

He searched her eyes. 'Are you sure?'

She nodded. 'Yes.'

Pulling her hands from his, she sat down on the bed, her expression thoughtful. 'I think I did something yesterday, when that magician nearly got us. I kind of made myself invisible. I think he would have found me if I hadn't.' She looked up suddenly, then relaxed and grinned. 'It's like they're blind.'

Cery allowed himself a sigh of relief. He shook his head. 'You really had me worried, Sonea. I can hide you from magicians' eyes, but I'm afraid hiding from magicians' minds is a bit much to ask. I think I better move you again. I've a place in mind off the Road that might do for a few days.'

The Guildhall was silent except for the whisper of breathing. Rothen opened his eyes and looked up at the rows of faces.

As always, he felt a vague embarrassment watching other magicians absorbed in mind work. He could not help feeling as if he was spying on them, that he was peeking at a private moment.

Yet he also got a childish amusement from their different expressions. Some magicians frowned, others looked puzzled or surprised. Most might have been asleep, their faces smooth and serene.

Catching a soft snore, Rothen smiled. Lord Sharrel leant back in his chair, his bald head drooping slowly toward his chest. Obviously the exercises to calm and focus his mind had been too effective.

—He's not the only one not keeping his mind on the job, eh Rothen?

Dannyl opened an eye and smiled. Shaking his head in disapproval, Rothen scanned the faces to see if his friend had disturbed the concentration of the others. Dannyl gave the slightest shrug and closed his eye again.

Rothen sighed. They should have found her by now. He looked up at the rows of magicians and shook his head. Another half-hour, he decided. Closing his eyes, he drew in a deep breath and started his mind-calming exercise once again.

By late morning the mist shrouding the city had been burned away by cheerful sunlight. Standing at the window, Dannyl took a moment to enjoy the silence. The printing machines, while more efficient than scribes, made a din of whirring and thumping that always set his ears ringing.

He pursed his lips. Now that the last batch of reward notices had been printed and sent out, he was free. The mental search had failed, and Rothen was already in the slums. Dannyl wasn't sure if he should be pleased that he was going out in the fine weather, or dismayed that he must roam about in the hovels again.

'Lord Dannyl,' a voice said, 'there is a large gathering of people at the Guild Gates who wish to speak to you.'

Startled, Dannyl turned to find Administrator Lorlen standing in the doorway.

'*Already?*' he exclaimed.

Lorlen nodded, his lips curling into a bemused smile. 'I don't know how they got there. They've avoided two sets of Gate Guards and passed into the Inner Circle before arriving here – unless they're vagrants we missed in the Purge.'

'How many?'

'About two hundred,' Lorlen replied. 'The guards say they all claim to know where the missing girl is.'

Picturing that many thieves and beggars amassed at the gates, Dannyl pressed a hand to his forehead and groaned.

'Exactly,' Lorlen said. 'What are you going to do now?'

Dannyl leaned against the table and considered. It had been no more than an hour since he had sent the first messengers out with copies of the reward. Those at the gates were the first of a hoard of informers that was sure to follow.

'We need somewhere to question them,' he mused aloud.

'Not in the Guild,' Lorlen replied, 'or people will make up stories just for the chance to have a look at us.'

'Somewhere in the city then.'

Lorlen drummed his fingers softly on the doorframe. 'The Guard have several halls around the city. I will arrange to have one of them prepared for our use.'

Dannyl nodded. 'Could you ask for some guards to remain to keep order, as well?'

The Administrator nodded. 'I'm sure they'll be quite anxious to stay.'

'I'll see if I can find some volunteers to help question the informers.'

'It sounds like you have everything in hand.' Lorlen took a step back from the doorway.

Dannyl smiled and inclined his head. 'Thank you, Administrator.'

'If you need anything else, just send a messenger to me.' Lorlen nodded then strode away.

Crossing the room, Dannyl gathered up the implements he had used to draft the reward notice and placed them in the ornate writing box. He entered the corridor and hurried toward his quarters, stopping as a novice stepped out of a nearby classroom and began to stroll toward the stairs.

'You there,' Dannyl called. The youth froze before spinning around. His eyes met Dannyl's, then slid to the floor as he bowed. Dannyl swept down the corridor and thrust the box into the boy's arms.

'Take these to the Magicians' Library and tell Lord Jullen that I will collect them later.'

'Yes, Lord Dannyl,' the novice replied, nearly dropping the box as he bowed again. He turned and hurried away.

Continuing to the end of the corridor, Dannyl started down the stairs. Several magicians stood within the Entrance Hall, all staring through the huge doors of the University toward the gates. Larkin, a young Alchemist who had recently graduated, looked up as Dannyl neared the bottom of the stairs.

'These are your informers, Lord Dannyl?' he asked, grinning.

'Reward seekers,' Dannyl said dryly.

'You're not bringing them in here,' a gruff voice said.

Recognising the sour tone of the University Director, Dannyl turned to regard the magician.

'Would you like me to, Director Jerrik?' Dannyl asked.

'Absolutely not!'

From behind, Dannyl heard Larkin utter a soft bark of amusement and he resisted the temptation to smile. Jerrik never seemed to change. He had been the same disapproving, sour old man when Dannyl had been a novice.

'I'm sending them to a Guard hall,' Dannyl told the old magician. He turned away, wove between the other magicians milling around in the hall, then started down the stairs.

'Good luck,' Larkin called.

Dannyl raised a hand in reply. Ahead, a dark crowd of milling bodies was pressed against the ornate bars of the Guild Gates. Dannyl grimaced, and sought a mind familiar to him.

—Rothen!

—Yes?

—Look. Dannyl sent a mental image of the scene. He felt alarm from the other magician, which quickly changed to amusement as Rothen realised who the people were.

—Informers already! What are you going to do?

—Tell them to come back later, Dannyl replied, *and that we won't be tossing money to anyone until we have the girl*. As quickly and clearly as mental communication allowed, he explained that Administrator Lorlen was organising a place in the city to interview the 'informers'.

—Shall I come back to help?

—I couldn't keep you away if I tried.

He sensed amusement from the older magician, then Rothen's presence faded beyond his detection.

Drawing closer to the gate, Dannyl could see people pressing against the bars and jostling each other. A bewildering clamour of voices reached his ears as they all began to call to him at once. The guards regarded Dannyl with a mixture of relief and curiosity.

He stopped about ten paces from the gates. Straightening his back to take full advantage of his height, he crossed his arms and waited. Slowly the noise dwindled. When the crowd had quietened, Dannyl worked the air before him to amplify his voice.

'How many of you are here with information regarding the girl we are seeking?'

A clamour of voices rose in reply. Dannyl nodded and lifted a hand to silence them again.

'The Guild welcomes your assistance in this matter. You will be given an opportunity to speak to us individually. We are arranging for a Guard hall to be prepared for this purpose. The location of this hall will be posted on these and the city gates in an hour. In the meantime, we ask that you return to your homes.'

A few grumbling voices rose in the back of the crowd. Dannyl lifted his chin and put a note of warning in his voice.

'No reward will be given until the girl is secure within our protection. Only then will the reward be paid, and only to those who have given us useful information. Do not approach the girl yourself. She may be da—'

'*She's here!*' a voice shrieked.

Despite himself, Dannyl felt a thrill of hope. A disturbance stirred the crowd and people grumbled as someone pushed their way forward.

'Let her through,' he commanded.

The crowd parted and a shrivelled woman pressed up against the gate. A bony hand thrust through the bars and beckoned to him. The other held the arm of a thin, young girl dressed in dirty, threadbare clothes.

'This is her!' the woman declared, her huge eyes staring at him.

Dannyl looked closely at the girl. Short, unevenly cut hair surrounded a thin, hollow-cheeked face. The girl was pitifully thin and her clothes hung loosely from her formless body. As Dannyl's eyes fell on her, she burst into tears.

Doubts crept over him, then, as he realised he could not remember the face of the girl Rothen had projected in the Guildhall.

—Rothen?

—Yes?

He sent the magician an image of the girl.

—It's not her.

Dannyl sighed in relief. 'She is not the one,' he announced, shaking his head. He turned away.

'*Hai!*' the woman protested. He turned back to find her glaring at him. He held her gaze, and she quickly lowered her eyes. 'Are you sure, my lord?' she wheedled. 'You've not looked at her close.'

The sea of faces watched him expectantly and he realised that they wanted some kind of visible proof. Unless he convinced them that he could not be deceived, others would bring young girls in the hope of gaining the reward – and he couldn't keep asking Rothen to identify every girl that was brought to him.

He approached the gate slowly. The girl had stopped

crying, but as Dannyl drew closer she turned white with terror.

Dannyl reached out a hand to her and smiled. The girl stared at it and shrank away, but the woman beside her grabbed her arm and pushed it through the bars of the gate.

Taking it, Dannyl sent a mental inquiry to her mind. He immediately sensed a well of power lying dormant. Surprised, he hesitated a moment before releasing her hand and stepping back.

'She is not the one,' he repeated.

The informers began shouting again, but there was less urgency and demand in the din. He moved away a few paces and lifted his arms. They shied back.

'Go!' Dannyl called. 'Return this afternoon.'

He turned quickly so his robes swirled around him dramatically and strode away. A low exclamation of awe rose from the crowd. Smiling, he lengthened his stride.

But his smile vanished as he considered the power he had sensed in the beggar girl. She had not been particularly strong. If she had been a daughter of a House, it was unlikely that she would have been sent to the Guild for training. She would have been more valuable to her family as a bride who would strengthen the magical bloodlines in her House. If she'd been a second or third son, however, they would have been delighted. Even a weak magician brought prestige to a family's name.

Dannyl shook his head as he neared the University. It was merely a coincidence that the one slum dweller that he had tested possessed magical potential. Perhaps she was the daughter of a prostitute who had conceived a magician's child. Dannyl had no illusions about other magicians' habits.

Then he remembered Lord Solend's words: '*If this young woman is a natural, we should expect her to be more powerful than our average novice, possibly even more powerful than the average magician.*' The girl they were seeking might be at least as strong as him. She might even be stronger . . .

He shivered. Suddenly it was easy to imagine the existence of thieves and murderers secretly wielding powers that only the magicians of the Guild were meant to possess. It was a frightening thought, and he knew that he was not going to feel so completely invulnerable next time he walked the streets of the slums.

The air in the attic was deliciously warm. Late afternoon light streamed through two small windows and painted bright squares on the walls. The smell of reber wool and smoke fought for dominance in the room. Here and there small groups of children sat bundled in blankets, talking quietly.

Sonea watched them from the corner she had claimed for herself. When the trapdoor to the attic opened she looked up eagerly, but the boy that climbed into the room was not Cery. The other children greeted the newcomer eagerly.

'Have you heard?' he said, dropping onto a bundle of blankets. 'The magicians say they'll give a reward to anyone who shows them where that girl is.'

'A reward!'

'Really?'

'How much?'

The boy opened his eyes wide. 'A hundred gold.'

A murmur of excitement ran through the children. They gathered around the newcomer, forming a circle of eager faces. A few cast thoughtful glances in Sonea's direction.

She forced herself to watch them, keeping her expression neutral. They had given her more than a few curious looks since she'd arrived. The attic was a refuge for homeless children. It lay in the area where the slums met the markets, and a view of the Marina could be seen from the tiny windows. She was too old to be admitted, but Cery knew the owner – a kind retired merchant called Norin – and had promised a favour in return.

'The magicians really want to get this girl, don't they?' one of the girls said.

'They don't let anyone have magic 'cept themselves,' a stocky boy replied.

'Lot of people be looking for her now,' the newcomer said, nodding wisely. 'That's a lot of money.'

'It's blood money, Ral,' the girl replied, her nose wrinkling.

'So?' Ral replied. 'Some people won't care. They just want the money.'

'Well, I wouldn't turn her in,' she said. 'I hate the magicians. My cousin was burned by them, years ago.'

'Really?' another girl asked, her eyes bright with curiosity.

'It's true.' The first girl nodded. 'In the Purge. Gilen was playing around, though. He probably fished for it. One of those magicians got him with his magic. He was burned all down one side of his face. There's a big, red scar there now.'

Sonea shivered. Burned. A memory of a charred body flashed into her mind. She looked away from the children. The attic no longer seemed cosy. She wanted to get up and leave, but Cery had been firm about her staying put and not drawing attention to herself.

'My uncle tried to rob a magician once,' a girl with long, knotted hair said.

'You're uncle was stupid,' murmured a boy at her side. She scowled at him, and aimed a kick at his shin that he evaded easily.

'He didn't know it was a magician,' the girl explained. 'The man wore a big cloak over his robes.'

The boy snorted, and the girl raised her fist. 'You were saying?' he asked innocently.

'He tried to cut his purse,' the girl continued, 'but the magician had magicked it so he'd know if anyone touched it. Well, the magician turned around real quick and hit him with his magic and broke his arms.'

'Both arms?' one of the younger boys asked.

She nodded. 'Without even touching him. He just put up his hands like this . . .' she raised her hands so her palms faced them, 'and the magic hit my uncle like someone had thrown a wall at him. That's how he told it, my uncle did.'

'Hai!' the boy breathed. The room was silent for a few minutes, then a new voice lifted out of the quiet.

'My sister was killed because of the magicians.'

Every face turned toward a skinny boy who sat cross-legged at the edge of the rough circle.

'We were in a crowd,' he told them. 'The magicians started their flashing lights in the street behind us and everyone began to run. Ma dropped my little sister, but she couldn't stop because there were so many people running. Da went back and found her. I heard him cursing them, saying that it was their fault that she died. The magicians' fault.' He narrowed his eyes and glared at the floor. 'I *hate* them.'

Several of the heads around the circle nodded. A thoughtful silence followed, then the first girl made a satisfied noise.

'See,' she said, 'would you help the magicians? Not me. That girl showed 'em, she did. Maybe next time she'll get more of 'em.'

The children grinned and nodded at each other. Sonea let out a silent sigh of relief. She heard the creak of the hatch as it opened, and smiled as Cery climbed into the attic. He moved to her side and sat down, grinning.

'We've been betrayed,' he murmured. 'The house is about to be searched. Follow me.'

Her heart skipped. Staring at him, she saw that the grin did not reach his eyes. He climbed to his feet again, and she leapt up to follow. A few children watched her pass them, but she avoided their eyes. She could feel their interest growing as Cery stopped and opened the doors of a large cabinet at the back of the room.

'There's a secret door to the passages here,' he murmured, reaching inside. He tugged at something gently, then frowned and pulled harder. 'It's been blocked from the other side.' He cursed under his breath.

'Are we trapped?'

He glanced back at the room. Most of the children were watching them now. He closed the cabinet door then moved across to one of the windows.

'No use in pretending now. How are your climbing skills?'

'It's been a while . . .' She looked up. The windows had been set into the roof, which sloped down almost to the floor.

'Give me a leg up.'

Linking her hands, she grimaced as he stepped onto them. She staggered as Cery climbed up onto her shoulders. Grabbing a roof beam, Cery steadied himself, pulled a knife out of his coat and began to work at the window.

From somewhere below the attic Sonea heard the sound of a door slamming, then the muffled sound of raised voices. Sonea felt a stab of fear as the trapdoor sprang open, but the face that appeared was that of Norin's niece, Yalia.

The woman took in the children, Sonea, and Cery poised on top of her shoulders, in one glance.

'The door?' she asked.

'Blocked,' he told her.

She scowled, then looked down at the children.

'The magicians are here,' she told them. 'They're going to search the house.'

The children began asking questions. Above Sonea, Cery muttered a colourful curse. Sonea almost dropped him as he shifted his weight abruptly.

'Hai! You're not being a very good ladder, Sonea.'

His weight suddenly lifted from her hands. Cery's foot kicked out, hitting her in the chest. Sonea bit back a sour retort as she ducked out of the way of his swinging legs.

'They won't harm us,' Yalia was telling the children. 'They wouldn't dare. They'll see straight away that you're all too young. They're more interested in—'

'Hai! Sonea!' Cery whispered harshly.

She looked up to see that Cery had slipped his legs though the window frame and was dangling down, reaching for her.

'Come on!'

She reached up and grasped his hands. With surprising

strength, Cery lifted her up until she could grasp the sill. She hung for a moment, then edged around the frame until she held the high side. Swinging her legs up, she caught the edge of the frame with the toe of her boot, then stepped through.

Gasping from the exertion, she lay flat against the cold tiles. The air was icy and the cold immediately began to seep though her clothes. Lifting her head, she saw a sea of roofs. The sun hung low in the sky.

Cery reached out to close the window and froze. The sound of the attic trapdoor opening reached them, then the children began murmuring in awe and fear. Sonea lifted her head and peered inside.

A man in red robes stood beside the open trapdoor, staring with unblinking rage around the room. His hair was pale and combed back against his scalp. A small red scar marked his temple. She pressed herself against the roof again, heart racing. There was something familiar about him but she was not going to risk a second glance.

His voice reached their ears.

'Where is she?' he demanded.

'Who do you mean?' Yalia replied.

'The girl. I was informed that she was here. Where have you hidden her?'

'I haven't hidden anybody,' stated an aged voice.

Norin, Sonea guessed.

'What's this place then? Why are these beggars here?'

'I let them stay here. They have nowhere else to go during the winter.'

'Was the girl here?'

'I don't ask their names. If this girl you seek was among them then I wouldn't know.'

'I think you're lying, old man,' the magician's tone darkened.

A wailing began as a few of the children began to cry. Cery grabbed her sleeve and tugged it.

'I am telling you the truth,' the old merchant replied. 'I have no idea who they are, but they are always children—'

'Do you know what the penalty is for hiding enemies of the Guild, old man?' the magician snapped. 'If you do not show me where you have hidden this girl I will have your house taken down, stone by stone, and—'

'*Sonea*,' Cery whispered.

She turned to stare at him. He beckoned urgently, then began edging across the roof. Sonea forced her arms and legs to move, following.

She dared not slide too quickly, afraid the magician would hear her. The end of the roof drew slowly closer. Reaching it, Sonea looked back to find that Cery had disappeared. Catching a fleeting movement, she saw a pair of hands grasping the guttering below her.

'Sonea,' he hissed. 'You've got to get down here with me.'

Slowly, she bent her legs and slid down until she was lying along the gutter. Looking over the edge, she saw that Cery was hanging two storeys from the ground. He nodded to a single storey house built close to the merchants' home.

'We're going there,' he told her. 'Watch me, then do what I do.'

Reaching out to the wall, Cery grasped hold of a pipe that ran from the gutter, down the wall to the ground. As he let it take his entire weight the pipe creaked alarmingly, but Cery scurried down quickly, using the clamps that attached it to the wall as a ladder. He stepped across to the other roof, then looked up and beckoned to her.

Taking a deep breath, Sonea grasped the gutter and let herself roll off the roof. She hung for a moment, her hands protesting, then reached out to grasp the pipe. Climbing down as quickly as she could, she stepped onto the roof of the other house.

Cery grinned. 'Easy?'

She rubbed her fingers, which were red from the sharp edge of the clamps, and shrugged. 'Yes and no.'

'Come on. Let's get away from here.'

They carefully picked their way across the roof, bracing themselves against the bitterly cold wind. Reaching the neighbouring house, they climbed up onto its roof. From there, they slid down another drainage pipe into a narrow alley between the houses.

Putting a finger to his lips, Cery started along the alley. He stopped halfway along and, after glancing behind to check that they were still alone, lifted a small grille in the side of a wall. He dropped to his belly and quickly wiggled through. Sonea followed.

They paused to rest in the darkness. Slowly her eyes adjusted until she could see the walls of a narrow brick passage. Cery was staring into the darkness, toward Norin's house.

'Poor Norin,' Sonea whispered. 'What will happen to him?'

'I don't know, but it sounds bad.'

Sonea felt a pang of guilt. 'All because of me.'

He turned to stare at her.

'No,' he growled. 'Because of the *magicians* – and

whoever betrayed us.' He scowled back down the passage. 'I'd go back and find out who it was, but I've got to get you somewhere safe.'

Looking at him closely, she saw a hardness in his expression that she had never seen before. Without him she would have been captured days ago, would probably be dead.

She needed him, but what was it going to cost him to help her? He had already promised or used owed favours for her and he risked the disapproval of the Thieves by using the tunnels.

And what if she was found by the magicians? If Norin suffered the ruin of his house for being suspected of hiding her, what would the magicians do to Cery? *'Do you know what the penalty is for hiding enemies of the Guild, old man?'* She shivered and caught his arm.

'Make me a promise, Cery.'

He turned to stare at her, eyes wide. 'A promise?'

She nodded. 'Promise that, if they ever catch us, you'll pretend that you don't know me.' He opened his mouth to protest, but she did not wait for him to speak. 'If they do see that you're helping me, then run away. Don't let them catch you as well.'

He shook his head. 'Sonea, I wouldn't—'

'Just say you will. I . . . I couldn't bear it if they killed you because of me.'

Cery's eyes widened, then he placed a hand on her shoulder and smiled.

'They won't catch you,' he told her. 'And even if they do, I'll get you back. I promise you that.'

CHAPTER 6

UNDERGROUND ENCOUNTERS

The sign on the bolhouse read: The Bold Knife. Not an encouraging name, but a quick look inside had revealed a quiet room. Unlike the occupants of all the other bolhouses Dannyl had entered, the customers were subdued and talked in low voices.

Pushing open the door, he stepped inside. A few of the drinkers looked his way, but most ignored him. This, too, was a welcome change. He felt a twinge of uneasiness. Why was this place so different to the others he had visited?

He had never entered a bolhouse until this day, and had never wanted to, but the guard he had sent to find the Thieves had given him specific instructions: go to a bolhouse, tell the owner who you wanted to talk to, and pay the fee when a guide appeared. That, apparently, was the way it was done.

Of course, he couldn't walk into a bolhouse dressed in robes and expect the sort of co-operation he needed, so he had disobeyed his peers and changed into the plain garb of a merchant.

He had chosen his disguise carefully. No amount of dressing down was going to hide his unusual height, obvious health and cultured voice. The story he had invented told a tale of unlucky investment and bad debts. Nobody would loan him money. The Thieves were a last resort. A merchant in that situation would be as out of his depth as Dannyl was, though a great deal more frightened.

Taking a deep breath, Dannyl made his way across the room to the serving bench. The server was a thin man with high cheekbones and a grim expression. Streaks of grey ran through his black hair. He regarded Dannyl with hard eyes.

'What will it be?'

'A drink.'

The man took a wooden mug and filled it from one of the casks behind the bench. Dannyl took a copper and silver coin from his purse. Hiding the silver, he dropped the copper into the man's outstretched hand.

'You'll be after a knife then?' the server asked in a quiet voice.

Dannyl looked at the man in surprise.

The server smiled grimly. 'What else would you be at The Bold Knife for, then? You done this before?'

Dannyl shook his head, thinking quickly. By the man's tone, it seemed he should want some secrecy in the acquiring of this 'knife'. There was no law against owning blades, so 'knife' must be a word used for an illegal object – or service. He had no idea what it might be, but this man had already indicated he was expecting shady dealings and that seemed as good a start as any.

'I don't want a knife,' Dannyl gave the man a nervous smile. 'I want to contact the Thieves.'

The man's brows rose. 'Oh?' He narrowed his eyes at Dannyl. 'It takes a bit of colour to get them interested in talking, you know.'

Dannyl opened his hand to reveal the silver coin, then

closed his fingers again as the server reached for it. The man snorted, then turned slightly.

'Hai, Kollin!'

A boy appeared in a doorway behind the bench. He looked at Dannyl, his sharp eyes moving from boots to hair.

'Take this man to the slaughterhouse.'

Kollin looked at Dannyl, then beckoned. As Dannyl moved behind the bench, the server blocked his path and opened his hand.

'There's a fee. Silver.'

Dannyl frowned at the extended hand doubtfully.

'Don't worry,' the server said. 'If they found out I was cheating those who went looking for their help, they'd flay me and hang my skin off the rafters as a lesson to others.'

Wondering if he was being duped, Dannyl pressed the silver coin into the server's palm. The man stepped aside, allowing Dannyl to follow Kollin through the doorway.

'Follow me but don't say nothing,' the boy said. He entered a small kitchen, then opened another door and checked the alley outside before stepping out.

The boy moved quickly, leading Dannyl through a maze of narrow streets. They passed doorways from which wafted the smell of baking, or cooked meat and vegetables, or the tang of oiled leather. The boy stopped and gestured to the entrance of an alley. The narrow street was filled with litter and mud, and came to a dead-end after twenty paces.

'Slaughterhouse. You go there,' the boy said, pointing down the alley. He turned and hurried away.

Dannyl regarded the alley dubiously as he walked down it. No doors. No windows. Nobody stepped out to greet him. Reaching the end of the alley, he sighed. He *had* been duped. Considering the name of the place, he had suspected an ambush at least.

Shrugging, he turned around and found three heavily built men standing in the alley's entrance.

'Hai! Looking for someone?'

'Yes.' Dannyl strode toward them. All wore heavy long-coats and gloves. The one at the centre bore a scar down one cheek. They returned his stare coldly. *Just your average thug*, Dannyl mused. Perhaps this *was* an ambush.

He stopped a few paces away, then glanced back down the alley and smiled. 'So this is the slaughterhouse. How appropriate. Are you my escort now?'

The middle thug held out his hand.

'For a price.'

'I gave my money to the man at *The Bold Knife*.'

The thug frowned. 'You want a knife?'

'No.' Dannyl sighed. 'I want to talk to the Thieves.'

The man looked at his companions, who were grinning. 'Which one?'

'The one with the widest influence.'

The thug at the centre chuckled. 'That'd be Gorin.' One of his companions smothered a laugh. Still grinning, the leader gestured for Dannyl to follow him. 'Come with me.'

The other two stepped aside. Dannyl followed his new guide to the entrance of a wider street. Glancing back, he saw that the others were watching him, still smiling broadly.

A series of twisting streets and alleys followed. Dannyl began to wonder if the back of every baker, leather-merchant, tailor and bolhouse looked the same. Then he recognised a sign, and stopped in his tracks.

'We've been here before. Why are you leading me in circles?'

The thug turned and regarded Dannyl, then turned and moved to the nearby wall. Bending down, he grasped the edge of a ventilation grille and pulled. It swung forward.

The thug gestured to the hole. 'You first.'

Dannyl crouched and looked inside. He could see nothing. Resisting the temptation to create a globe light, he put a leg into the hole, but found only emptiness where he expected the floor to be. He looked up at his guide.

'The street's 'bout chest height,' the thug told him. 'Go on.'

Grasping the edge of the hole, Dannyl climbed through. He found a ledge to brace himself on, then drew his other leg through and lowered it until his foot reached the floor. Stepping back, his shoulder met a wall. The thug slipped into the passage with practiced ease. Unable to see much more than the man's shape within the dim light, Dannyl kept his distance.

'Follow my footsteps,' the man said. As he started down the passage, Dannyl walked a few paces behind, trailing his hands along the walls on either side. They walked for several minutes, taking numerous turns, then the footsteps in front of Dannyl stopped and he heard a rapping from somewhere close by.

'You've got a long way to go,' the thug said. 'You sure 'bout this? You can change your mind now and I'll take you back.'

'Why would I want to do that?' Dannyl asked.

'You just might, that's all.'

A sliver of light appeared, then widened beside them.

Within it stood a silhouette of another man. In the glare Dannyl could not make out the man's face.

'This one's for Gorin,' the thug said. He looked at Dannyl, made a quick gesture, then turned and disappeared into the shadows.

'Gorin, eh?' the man in the doorway said. The voice could have belonged to a man anywhere between twenty and sixty years. 'What is your name?'

'Larkin.'

'What is your profession?'

'I sell simba mats.' Mat-making houses had sprung up all over Imardin in the last few years.

'A competitive market.'

'You're telling me?'

The man grunted.

'Why you want to talk to Gorin?'

'That's for Gorin to know.'

'Of course.' The man shrugged, then reached up to the inner wall of the room.

'Turn away from me,' he ordered. 'From here, you go blindfold.'

Dannyl hesitated, before reluctantly turning around. He had expected something like this. A piece of cloth dropped over his eyes, and he felt the man knot it behind his head. The faint light of the lamp revealed only the thick weave of the material.

'Follow my footsteps, please.'

Once again, Dannyl walked with his hands trailing along the walls. His new guide travelled fast. Dannyl counted his steps, thinking that, as soon as he had the opportunity, he would measure how far a thousand strides would normally take him.

Something, probably a hand, was suddenly pressed on his chest, and he halted. He heard a door open, and he was pushed forward. The smell of spices and flowers filled his senses, and he felt a softness under his boots which suggested carpet.

'Stay here. Don't remove your blindfold.'

The door closed.

The faint sounds of voices and footsteps came from above, and he guessed he was under one of the rowdier bolhouses. He listened to the sounds, then began counting his breaths. When that bored him, he lifted his hands to the blindfold. He heard a soft thud behind him, like the sound a bare heel makes on a carpeted floor. He turned and grasped the blindfold to remove it, then froze as he heard the door handle turning. Straightening, he quickly let go of the material.

The door didn't open. He waited, and concentrated on the silence within the room. Something drew his attention. Something more subtle than the faint sound he had heard before.

A presence.

It hovered behind him. Taking in a deep breath, he stretched his arms out and pretended to be feeling for walls. As he turned about, the presence moved away.

Someone was in the room with him. Someone who didn't want to be noticed. The carpet muffled the tread of their feet, and the bolhouse noise covered any involuntary sounds. The flowery perfume that hung in the air would hide the small scents of a body. Only the senses unique to him as a magician had detected the stranger.

It was a test. He doubted if the owner of the presence was being tested on their ability to remain unnoticed. No, this test was for him. To see if he detected anything. To see if he was a magician.

Casting his senses out, he detected another faint presence. This one was stationary. Stretching his arms out, he started forward again. The first presence darted around him, but he ignored it. After ten steps he encountered a wall. Keeping his hands on the rough surface, he began moving around the room in the direction of the other presence. The first one moved away, then suddenly rushed toward him. He felt a faint breeze against his neck. Ignoring it, he continued on.

His fingers met the door frame, then a sleeve and arm. The blindfold was lifted from his eyes, and he found himself staring at an old man.

'I apologise for keeping you waiting,' the man said. Recognising the voice, Dannyl knew this was his guide. Had the man left the room at all?

Offering no explanation, the guide opened the door. 'If you would follow me now, please.'

Dannyl glanced around the now-empty room, then stepped into the passage.

They continued the journey at a more relaxed pace, the lamp swinging in the old man's hand. The walls were well made. At each turn a small panel was set into the bricks, engraved with strange symbols. It was impossible to guess what time it was, but he knew that many hours must have passed since he had entered the first bolhouse. He was pleased with himself for realising he was being tested. Would they have taken him to the Thieves if he had proven to be a magician? He doubted it.

There might be more tests – he would have to be careful. He did not know how close he was to speaking with Gorin.

In the meantime, he should find out as much as he could about the people he wanted to negotiate with. He regarded his companion speculatively.

'What is a "knife"?'

The old man grunted. 'An assassin.'

Dannyl blinked, then smothered a smile. The Bold Knife was truly an appropriate name, then. How did the owner get away with advertising so blatantly?

He could wonder about that later. For now there were more useful things to learn.

'Are there any other alternative names I should know about?'

The old man smiled. 'If someone sends you a messenger, you'll be getting either a threat, or they'll be carrying out that threat.'

'I see.'

'And a squimp is someone who betrays the Thieves. You don't want to be one of those. They live short lives.'

'I'll keep that in mind.'

'If all goes well, you'll be called a client. Depends what you're here for.' He stopped and turned to regard Dannyl. 'Guess it's time to find out.'

He knocked on the wall. Silence followed, then the bricks collapsed inward in two sections. The old man gestured towards the opening.

The room Dannyl entered was small. A table fit snugly between the walls, effectively blocking access to the huge man sitting in the chair behind it. A pair of doors stood partly open behind him.

'Larkin the mat-seller,' the man said. His voice was startlingly deep.

Dannyl inclined his head. 'And you are?'

The man smiled. 'Gorin.'

There was no chair for visitors. Dannyl moved closer to the table. Gorin was not an attractive man, but his bulk was more muscle than fat. His hair was thick and curly, and a woolly beard covered his jaw. He truly lived up to his namesake, the huge beasts that hauled punts up the Tarali river. Dannyl wondered if this was a joke of the thug's – perhaps Gorin was the man with the *widest* influence among the Thieves.

'You lead the Thieves?' Dannyl asked.

Gorin smiled. 'Nobody leads the Thieves.'

'Then how do I know if I'm talking to the right person?'

'You want to make a deal? You make it with me.' He spread his hands. 'If you break the deal, I punish you. Think of me like something between a father and a king. I'm helping you out, but if you betray me, I'll kill you. Does that make sense?'

Dannyl pursed his lips. 'I was thinking of something a bit more balanced. Father to father, perhaps? I wouldn't presume to suggest king to king, though I like the sound of it.'

Gorin smiled again, but it didn't extend to his eyes. 'What you want, Larkin the mat-seller?'

'I want you to help me find somebody.'

'Ah.' The Thief nodded. He pulled over a small block of paper, a pen and an inkwell. 'Who?'

'A girl. Fourteen to sixteen. Small build, dark hair, skinny.'

'Ran away did she?'

'Yes.'

'Why.'

'A misunderstanding.'

Gorin nodded sympathetically. 'Where you think she might have gone?'

'The slums.'

'If she is alive, I'll find her. If she is not, or we have not found her within a time – we'll agree on how long – your obligations to me end. What's her name?'

'We don't know her name yet.'

'You don't—' Gorin looked up, then narrowed his eyes. 'We?'

Dannyl allowed himself to smile. 'You need to devise a better test.'

Gorin's eyes widened slightly. He swallowed, then leaned back in his chair. 'Is that so?'

'What did you intend to do with me if I hadn't passed?'

'Lead you somewhere far from here.' He licked his lips, then shrugged. 'But you are here. What do you want?'

'As I said: we want you to help us find the girl.'

'And if we don't?'

Dannyl let the smile fall from his face. 'Then she will die. Her own powers will kill her, and destroy part of the city too – though I cannot tell you how much as I do not know her strength.' He stepped forward, placed his hands on the table and held the Thief's gaze. 'If you help us, it doesn't have to be a profitless arrangement – though you must understand that there are limits to what we can be seen to be doing.'

Gorin stared at him in silence, then put pen and paper aside. He leaned back in his seat and turned his head slightly.

'Hai, Dagan! Bring our visitor a chair.'

The room was dark and musty. Shipping boxes were stacked

against one wall, many of them broken. Pools of water had gathered in the corners, and a thick layer of dust covered everything else.

'So this is where your father used to hide his stuff?' Harrin asked.

Cery nodded. 'Da's old storeroom.' He wiped dust off one of the boxes, and sat down.

'There's no bed,' Donia said.

'We'll put something together,' Harrin replied. Walking over to the boxes, he began rummaging through them.

Sonea had stopped in the doorway, dismayed at the prospect of spending the night in such a cold and unpleasant place. Sighing, she sat on the lowest stair. They had moved three times during the night to avoid reward-seekers. She felt as if she hadn't slept for days. Closing her eyes, she allowed herself to drift. Harrin's conversation with Donia grew distant, as did the sound of footsteps from the passage behind her.

Footsteps?

Opening her eyes, she looked back and saw a distant light swaying in the darkness.

'Hai! Someone's coming.'

'What?' Harrin strode across the room and stared into the passage. He listened for a moment, then pulled Sonea to her feet and pointed at the far side of the room. 'Get over there. Keep out of sight.'

As Sonea moved away from the door, Cery rose to join Harrin. 'Nobody comes here,' he said. 'The dust on the stairs wasn't marked.'

'Then they must have been following us.'

Cery stared up the passage, cursing. He turned to Sonea. 'Cover your face. They might be after something else.'

'We're not leaving?' Donia asked.

Cery shook his head. 'No way out. There used to be a passage, but the Thieves closed it years ago. That's why I didn't bring us here before.'

The footsteps were more audible within the room now. Harrin and Cery backed away from the door and waited. Pulling up the hood of her cloak, Sonea joined Donia at the far side of the room.

Boots appeared within the passage, then trousers, chests, and faces as the newcomers descended the stairs. Four boys stepped through the doorway. They looked at Harrin and Cery then, as they located Sonea, they exchanged eager looks.

'Burril,' Harrin said. 'What you doin' here?'

A stocky youth with muscular arms swaggered forward to face Harrin. Sonea felt a chill. This was the boy who had accused her of being a spy.

Looking at the other youths, she felt a shock as she recognised one. She remembered Evin as one of the quieter boys of Harrin's gang. He had taught her how to cheat at tiles. There was no friendship in his gaze now as he twirled a heavy iron bar in one hand. Sonea shivered and looked away.

The other two boys carried lengths of rough wood. They had probably picked up the makeshift cudgels along the way. Sonea considered the odds. Four against four. She doubted that Donia had ever learned to fight, or that either of them would be equal to one of Burril's allies. They might be able to tackle one together, however. She reached down and picked up a wooden slat from one of the broken shipping boxes.

'We're here for the girl,' Burril said.

'Turned squimp, have we Burril?' Harrin's voice was dark with contempt.

'I was thinking of asking *you* that,' Burril replied. 'We haven't seen you in days. Then we hear about the reward and it all makes sense. You wanta keep the money for yourself.'

'No, Burril,' Harrin said firmly. He looked at the other youths. 'Sonea's a friend. I don't sell my friends.'

'She's no friend of ours,' Burril replied, glancing at his companions.

Harrin crossed his arms. 'So, that's how it is. It didn't take long before you got a fancy for taking charge. You know the rules, Burril. You're either with me or out.' He looked at Burril's allies again. 'Same for you lot. You wanta follow this squimp?'

Though they remained in place, the youths glanced at Burril, then at Harrin, then at each other. Their expressions were guarded.

'A hundred gold,' Burril said quietly. 'You wanta give up that much money just so you can follow this fool around? We could live like kings.'

The youths' expressions hardened.

Harrin's eyes narrowed. 'Get out, Burril.'

A knife flashed into Burril's hand, and he pointed it at Sonea. 'Not without the girl. Give her over.'

'No.'

'Then we'll have to take her.'

Burril took a step toward Harrin. As Burril's companions fanned out to surround him, Cery moved to his friend's side, eyes steely, hands in his pockets.

'Come on Harrin,' Burril crooned. 'We don't have to do this. Give her up. We'll share the money, just like old times.'

Harrin's face twisted with anger and contempt. A knife flashed into his hand and he lunged forward. Burril dodged and slashed out with his blade. Sonea caught her breath as the knife sliced open Harrin's sleeve and left a line of red. As Evin lashed out with the iron bar, Harrin dodged out of reach.

Donia grabbed her arm. 'Stop them, Sonea,' she whispered urgently. 'Use your magic!'

Sonea stared at the girl. 'But . . . I don't know how!'

'Just try something. Anything!'

As the other two youths approched him, Cery drew out two daggers from his pockets. The boys hesitated when they saw them. Sonea noted the straps holding the daggers firmly against his palms so he could still use his hands to grab and push without losing the blades. She could not help smiling. He really hadn't changed a bit.

As the heavier one lunged, Cery caught the boy's wrist and pulled him forward, using the boy's momentum to unbalance him. The boy staggered forward, his wooden cudgel clattering to the floor as Cery twisted his wrist. Swinging his arm around and up, Cery dealt the boy a stunning blow to the head with the pommel of a dagger.

The youth staggered to his knees. Cery ducked away as his second attacker swung a cudgel at him. Behind him, Harrin dodged another thrust from Burril. As the two pairs of fighters separated for a moment, Evin slipped past them and started toward Sonea.

His hands were empty, Sonea noted with relief. She had no idea where the iron bar had gone. Perhaps it was tucked into his coat . . .

'Do something!' Donia yelped, her grip on Sonea's arm tightening.

Looking down at the slat in her hands, Sonea realised that attempting to repeat what she had done in the North Square would be pointless now. There was no magicians' shield to get past, and she doubted that throwing the slat at Evin was going to stop him.

She had to try something else. Perhaps she could will the slat to hit harder? *Could I?* She looked up at Evin. *Should I? What if I do something really awful to him?*

'Do it!' Donia hissed, backing away as Evin drew closer.

Taking a deep breath, Sonea threw the slat at Evin, willing it to knock him back. He batted it aside without checking his stride. As he reached toward Sonea, Donia stepped in front of her.

'How can you do this, Evin?' she demanded. 'You used to be our friend. I remember you and Sonea playing tiles together. Is this—'

Evin grabbed Donia's shoulders and shoved her to one side. Sonea lunged forward and punched him in the stomach with all her strength. He spluttered and staggered back a step, warding off her blows as she struck again, this time aiming for his face.

A strangled cry filled the room. She looked up to see Cery's opponent backing away, one hand clutching his arm. Then something slammed into her chest and she fell backwards. As she landed on the floor she twisted, trying to roll out of Evin's reach, but he threw his weight across her and held her down.

'Get off her!' Donia screamed. The girl stood over Evin, a wooden slat in her hands. It smashed down on Evin's head and he yelled. He rolled aside, and Donia's second swing caught his temple. He went limp and sagged back onto the floor.

Donia brandished her weapon at the unconscious youth, then relaxed and grinned at Sonea. Extending a hand, she helped Sonea back to her feet. They turned to find Burril and Harrin still fighting. Cery was looking down at the other two youths, one clutching his side, the other sagging against a wall with a hand pressed to his head.

'Hai!' Donia exclaimed. 'I think we're winning!'

Burril stepped back from Harrin and glanced at her. He reached into a pocket, then made an abrupt gesture. Red mist filled the air about Harrin's head.

Harrin swore loudly as the papea dust began to sting his eyes. Blinking rapidly, he backed away from Burril.

As Donia started toward Harrin, Sonea grabbed the girl's arm and pulled her back.

Harrin dodged as Burril lunged forward again but not quickly enough. An exclamation of pain followed and Harrin's knife clattered to the floor. Cery leapt toward Burril, who turned just in time to meet the attack. Still wiping at his eyes, Harrin dropped into a crouch and groped for his knife.

Pushing Cery away, Burril reached into his coat, made another abrupt gesture and again, a stream of red dust flew from his hands. Cery ducked too late. His face contorted with pain, he staggered backwards as Burril advanced on him.

'He'll kill them!' Donia cried.

Reaching down, Sonea grabbed another wooden slat. She closed her eyes a moment, trying to remember what she had done in the North Square. Gripping it tightly, she gathered all her anger and fear. Concentrating on the slat, she hurled it at Burril with all her strength.

He grunted at it struck his back and turned to glare at

her. Then he threw up his arms as Donia began to throw anything she could get hold of.

'Use your magic,' Donia urged as Sonea joined her.

'I tried. It's not working.'

'Try again,' Donia panted.

Burril reached into his pocket and pulled out a tiny packet. Recognising it, Sonea felt a surge of anger. She braced herself to throw the slat in her hands, then hesitated.

Perhaps she was concentrating too much on throwing hard. Magic was not a physical thing. She watched as Donia hurled a box at Burril. No need to throw anything herself . . .

Focussing on the box, she gave it a mental push, willing it to shoot forward and strike Burril hard enough to knock him out.

She felt something loosen inside her mind.

A flash of light lit the room and the box burst into flame. Burril yelled as it roared toward him, then ducked out of the way. It clattered across the floor and came to rest in a puddle, the water sizzling as it evaporated.

The packet of papea dust fell to the floor. Burril stared at her. Smiling, Sonea stooped to pick up another slat, straightened, then narrowed her eyes at him.

All colour drained from his face. Sparing no glance at his allies, he leapt for the door and staggered away.

Sonea heard a thin noise beside her, and turned to find Evin standing, conscious, only a few paces away. He took two steps backwards, then darted for the door. Seeing their companions leaving, the other two youths scrambled to their feet and followed.

As their footsteps faded, Harrin's laughter filled the

room. He rose, swayed, then walked carefully to the doorway. 'What's the problem?' he shouted. 'Did you think she'd just *let* you take her?'

Grinning, he turned to blink at Sonea. 'Hai! Well done!'

'Nice finish,' Cery agreed. He rubbed at his eyes and grimaced. Slipping a hand into his coat, he pulled out a small flask and began washing his eyes with the contents. Donia hurried to Harrin's side and examined his wounds.

'You need these dressed. You hurt Cery?'

'No.' Cery handed her the flask.

Donia began washing Harrin's face. His skin was red and blotchy. 'You'll be sore for days. Do you think you could heal him, Sonea?'

Sonea frowned and shook her head. 'I don't know. That wood wasn't supposed to start burning. What if I try to heal Harrin and burn him instead?'

Donia looked at Sonea with wide eyes. 'That's an awful thought.'

'You need to practice,' Cery said.

Sonea turned to regard him. 'I need time to practice, and a place where I won't get anyone's attention when I do.'

He pulled a cloth out of his coat and wiped his daggers clean. 'Once this gets around, people will be too scared to try and catch you. That'll give us some rope.'

'It won't,' Harrin said. 'You can bet Burril and the others won't tell anyone about this. Even if they do, some will think they can do better.'

Cery frowned, then cursed.

'Then we better get away from here real quick,' Donia said. 'Where next, Cery?'

He scratched his head, then smiled. 'Who's got money?'

Harrin and Donia looked at Sonea.

'It's not mine,' she protested. 'It's Jonna and Ranel's.'

'I'm sure they wouldn't mind you spending it to save your life,' Donia told her.

'And they'd think you stupid if you didn't,' Cery added.

Sighing, Sonea reached inside her shirt for the buckle of her money pouch. 'I suppose, if I ever get out of this mess, I can pay them back.' She looked at Cery. 'You better find them soon.'

'I will,' he assured her. 'Just as soon as you're safe. For now, I think we should split up. We'll meet again in an hour. I have a place in mind where no-one will think to look for you. We can only stay for a few hours, but it will give us a chance to figure out where to go next.'

CHAPTER 7

DANGEROUS ALLIANCES

Returning from the stables alone, Rothen slowed as he reached the gardens. The air was cold, but not uncomfortably so, and the stillness was welcome after the bustle of the city. He drew in a deep breath and sighed.

Though he had interviewed countless informers, few had given useful information. Most informers had come in the hope that some piece of information, no matter how irrelevant, would lead to her capture and their reward. A few had come simply to air whatever grievance they had with the Guild.

Others, however, had reported seeing lone girls hiding from sight. After a few journeys into the slums, it became clear that there were plenty of street urchins hiding away in dark corners. Conversations with the other magicians who were interviewing the informers revealed many similar disappointments.

It would be so much easier if the reward notices had included a likeness of the girl. He thought wistfully of his late mentor, Lord Margen, who had tried without success to invent a way to transfer mental images to paper. Dannyl had taken up the challenge, but had made little progress.

He wondered how Dannyl was faring. A brief mental conversation with his friend had revealed that the younger magician was alive and unharmed, and would return at sunset. They could not refer to the true purpose behind Dannyl's visit to the slums, as it was always possible that other magicians would overhear their conversation. Nevertheless, Rothen had sensed a promising smugness in his friend's communication.

'. . . know . . . Rothen . . .'

Hearing his own name spoken, Rothen looked up. The thick foliage of the garden hedges hid the speaker, but Rothen was sure he had recognised the voice.

'. . . these things cannot be hurried.'

This voice belonged to Administrator Lorlen. The pair were drawing closer to Rothen's position. Guessing that they would pass close by, Rothen moved into one of the small courtyards in the gardens. He sat down on a bench seat and listened carefully as the conversation became clearer.

'I have noted your claim, Fergun,' Lorlen said patiently. 'I can do no more. When she is found the matter will be dealt with in the usual manner. For now, I am only concerned with her capture.'

'But must we go through all this . . . this *bother*? Rothen was not the first to know of her powers. *I* was! How can he have any case against me?'

The Administrator's voice was smooth as he replied, but his stride was hurried. Rothen smiled to himself as the pair passed.

'It is not *bother*, Fergun.' Lorlen replied sternly. 'It is the law of the Guild. The law says—'

'"The first magician to recognise magical potential in another has the right to claim their guardianship",' Fergun recited rapidly, '*I* was the first to feel the effects of her power, not Rothen.'

'Nevertheless, the matter cannot be dealt with until the girl is found . . .'

The pair were well past Rothen now, and their voices faded beyond comprehension. He rose from the bench and began to stroll slowly toward the Magicians' Quarters.

So Fergun intended to claim guardianship of the girl. When Rothen had offered to take responsibility for her training, he had thought no other magician would want the task. Certainly not Fergun, who had always appeared to regard the lower classes with disdain.

He smiled to himself. Dannyl was not going to be pleased. His friend had harboured a dislike for Fergun since they were both novices. When he heard the news, Dannyl would be even more determined to find the girl himself.

It had been years since Cery had visited a bathhouse, and he had never seen the inside of the expensive private rooms. Scrubbed, warm for the first time in days and clothed in a thick wrap, he was in a good mood as he followed the towel girl into an airy drying room. Sonea sat on a length of simba matting, her thin body swamped by a heavy wrap and her face glowing from the attentions of the bathhouse girls. Seeing her looking so relaxed improved his mood even more.

He grinned at her. 'Hai! What a treat! I'm sure Jonna would approve!'

Sonea winced, and Cery immediately regretted his words.

'Sorry, Sonea.' He grimaced apologetically. 'I shouldn't have reminded you.' He folded himself down onto the mat beside her, then leaned back against the wall. 'If we talk quietly, we should be safe,' he added in a low voice.

She nodded. 'What now? We can't stay here.'

'I know. I've been thinking about that.' He sighed. 'Things are bad, Sonea. Keeping you hidden from the magicians would have been easy, but the reward changed that. I can't trust anyone now. I can't call in favours and . . . and I've run out of places to hide you.'

Her face paled. 'What will we do, then?'

He hesitated. After the fight he had realised that she had only one option left. She would not like it. Neither did he, for that matter. If only there was someone he could trust. He shook his head and turned to meet her gaze.

'I think we should get help from the Thieves.'

Sonea's eyes widened. 'Are you mad?!'

'Only if I keep trying to hide you myself. Sooner or later someone's going to turn you in.'

'What about the Thieves? Why wouldn't they?'

'You've got something they want.'

She frowned, then her expression darkened. 'Magic?'

'That's right. I bet they'd love to have their own magician.' He ran his fingertips over the matting. 'Once you have their protection nobody will touch you. No-one crosses the Thieves. Not even for a hundred gold.'

She closed her eyes. 'Jonna and Ranel always told me that you can never get free of the Thieves. They keep their hooks in you. Even after a deal's over, you're never really out of their debt.'

Cery shook his head. 'I know you've heard bad stories. Everyone has. You just have to stick to their rules and they'll treat you fair. That's what my da used to say.'

'They killed your da.'

'He was stupid. He squimped.'

'What if . . .?' She sighed and shook her head. 'What

choice do I have? If I don't, the Guild will find me. I guess being a slave to a Thief is better than death.'

Cery grimaced. 'It won't be like that. Once you've learned to use your powers, you'll be important and powerful. They'll give you a lot of rope. They'll have to. After all, if you decide you don't want to do something, how will they make you?'

She looked at him, searching his face for an unbearably long time. 'You're not sure about it, are you?'

He forced himself to meet her eyes. 'I'm sure that it's your only choice. I'm sure they'll treat you fairly.'

'Then?'

He sighed. 'I'm not sure what they'll get you to do for them in return.'

She nodded, then leaned back and stared at the far wall for several minutes.

'If you think it's what I should do, then I'll do it, Cery. I'd rather be stuck with the Thieves than give in to the Guild.'

Looking at her white face, he felt the now-familiar uneasiness return, only this time it felt more like guilt. She was frightened, but she would face the Thieves with her usual unflinching determination. That only made him feel worse. Though he could not delude himself about his ability to protect her, taking her to the Thieves felt like a betrayal. He did not want to lose her again.

But he had no other choice.

Rising, he walked to the door.

'I'm going to find Harrin and Donia,' he told her. 'You be fine?'

She did not look up at him, just nodded.

The towel girl stood in the passage outside the room.

He asked for Harrin and Donia, and the girl nodded towards the door of the next room. Biting his lip, he knocked.

'Come in,' Harrin called.

Both Harrin and Donia were sitting on simba mats. Donia was rubbing her hair with a towel.

'I've told her, and she's agreed.'

Harrin frowned. 'I'm still not sure. What if we take her out of the city?'

Cery shook his head. 'I don't think we'd get far. You can be sure the Thieves know all about her by now. They'll have found out where she's been and lived. They'll know what she looks like, who her parents were, where her aunt and uncle are. It won't be hard to find out from Burril and his lot that she's—'

'If they know so much,' Donia interrupted, 'why haven't they just come and taken her?'

'That's not how they do things,' Cery told her. 'They like making bargains, then most of the people working for them are happy, and won't cause trouble later. They could come to us and offer protection, but they haven't. That makes me think they're not sure she's got magic. If we don't go to them, they'll let one of their own turn her in. That's why we'd never get her out of the city.'

Donia and Harrin exchanged a glance.

'What does she think?' Donia asked.

Cery grimaced. 'She's heard the stories. She's scared, but she knows she's got no other choice.'

Harrin stood. 'You sure about this, Cery?' he asked. 'I thought you had a shine on her. You might not see her again.'

Cery blinked in surprise, and felt his face warming. 'You think I'd see her again if the magicians got her?'

Harrin's shoulders sagged. 'No.'

Cery began pacing. 'I'll go with her. She'll need someone familiar around. I can make myself useful.'

Harrin reached out and grabbed Cery's arm. He stared at Cery, searching his eyes, and let him go.

'So we won't be seeing much of you any more, then?'

Cery shook his head. He felt a pang of guilt. Harrin had been deserted by four members of his gang, and was unsure of the rest of them. Now his closest friend was leaving. 'I'll come by when I can. Gellin already thinks I work for the Thieves, anyway.'

Harrin smiled. 'All right, then. When will you take her?'

'Tonight.'

Donia placed a hand on Cery's arm. 'But what if they don't want her?'

Cery smiled grimly. 'They'll want her.'

The corridor of the Magicians' Quarters was silent and empty. Dannyl's footsteps echoed as he made his way to Yaldin's door. He knocked and waited, hearing faint voices from the room beyond. A woman's voice rose above the others.

'He did *what*?'

A moment later the door opened. Ezrille, Yaldin's wife, smiled distractedly and stepped back so Dannyl could enter the room. Several cushioned chairs were arranged around a low table, and Yaldin and Rothen sat in two of them.

'He ordered the Guard to evict the man from his home,' Yaldin said.

'Just for letting children sleep in his attic? That's awful!' Ezrille exclaimed, waving Dannyl toward a chair.

Yaldin nodded. 'Good evening, Dannyl. Would you like a cup of sumi?'

'Good evening,' Dannyl replied as he dropped into a chair. 'Sumi would be very welcome, thank you. It's been a long day.'

Rothen looked up and raised his eyebrows questioningly. Smiling, Dannyl shrugged in reply. He knew that Rothen would be impatient to know how matters had gone with the Thieves, but first Dannyl wanted to know what had stirred Ezrille, who was normally so placid and forgiving, to anger.

'What have I missed?'

'Yesterday one of our searchers followed an informer to a house in the better part of the slums,' Rothen explained. 'The owner was letting homeless children sleep in his attic, and the informer claimed that an older girl was hiding there. Our colleague claims that the girl and her companion escaped just before he arrived, with the help of the owner. So he ordered the Guard to evict the man and his family.'

Dannyl frowned. 'Our colleague? Who . . .?' He narrowed his eyes at Rothen. 'Would this happen to be a certain Warrior by the name of Fergun?'

'It would.'

Dannyl made a rude noise, then smiled as Ezrille handed him a steaming cup of sumi. 'Thank you.'

'So what happened?' Ezrille asked. 'Was the man evicted?'

'Lorlen countermanded his order, of course,' Yaldin replied, 'but Fergun had already disrupted much of the house – looking for hiding places, he said.'

Ezrille shook her head. 'I can't believe Fergun would be so . . . so . . .'

'Vindictive?' Dannyl snorted. 'I'm surprised he didn't decide to interrogate the poor man.'

'He wouldn't dare,' Yaldin said scornfully.

'Not now,' Dannyl agreed.

Rothen sighed and leaned back in his chair. 'There's more. I overheard something interesting tonight. Fergun wants her guardianship.'

Dannyl felt his blood turn cold.

'Fergun?' Ezrille frowned. 'He's not a strong magician. I thought the Guild discouraged weaker magicians from taking on the guardianship of novices.'

'We do,' Yaldin replied. 'But there is no rule against it.'

'What chance does he have of winning his claim?'

'He says he was the first to know of her powers because he *felt* the effects of them first,' Rothen told her.

'Is that a good argument?'

'I hope not,' Dannyl muttered. This news disturbed him. He knew Fergun well. Too well. What did Fergun, with his contempt for the lower classes, want with a slum girl anyway?

'Perhaps he's planning to take revenge for his humiliation in the North Square?'

Rothen frowned. 'Now Dannyl—'

'You have to consider the possibility,' Dannyl injected.

'Fergun isn't going to all this trouble over a small bruise, even if it did hurt his ego,' Rothen said firmly. 'He just wants to be the one to capture her – and he doesn't want people to forget it afterwards.'

Dannyl looked away. The older magician had never understood that his dislike for Fergun was more than just a grudge left over from their days as novices. Dannyl had experienced too well how single-minded Fergun could be when it came to revenge.

'I can see quite a fight coming out of this.' Yaldin chuckled. 'The poor girl has no idea how much she has stirred up the Guild. It's not often we have two magicians competing for a novice's guardianship.'

Rothen snorted softly. 'I'm sure that's the least of her concerns. After what happened in the North Square, she's probably convinced that we intend to kill her.'

Yaldin's smile faded. 'Unfortunately we can't convince her otherwise until we've found her.'

'Oh, I don't know about that,' Dannyl said quietly.

Rothen looked up. 'Do you have a suggestion, Dannyl?'

'I expect my new Thief friend has his own way of sending information around the slums.'

'Friend?' Yaldin gave an incredulous laugh. 'Now you're calling them *friends*.'

'Associates.' Dannyl smiled mischievously.

'I gather you had some success?' Rothen raised an eyebrow.

'A little. Just a beginning.' Dannyl shrugged. 'I spoke to one of their leaders, I believe.'

Ezrille's eyes were wide. 'What was he like?'

'His name was Gorin.'

'Gorin?' Yaldin frowned. 'That's a strange name.'

'It seems the leaders name themselves after animals. I guess they choose a title according to their stature, because he certainly looks like his namesake. He's enormous and woolly. I almost expected to see horns.'

'What did he say?' Rothen asked eagerly.

'Made no promises. I told him how dangerous it was to be around a magician who hadn't been taught to control her powers. He seemed more concerned with what the Guild would give him in exchange for finding her.'

Yaldin frowned. 'The Higher Magicians won't agree to exchanging favours with the Thieves.'

Dannyl waved a hand dismissively. 'Of course not. I told him that and he understood. I think he'd accept money.'

'Money?' Yaldin shook his head. 'I don't know . . .'

'Since we're already offering a reward, it will hardly matter if it goes to one of the Thieves.' Dannyl spread his hands. 'Everybody knows that the money will go to someone from the slums anyway, so they must expect that person to be someone of questionable nature.'

Ezrille rolled her eyes. 'Only you could make something like that sound perfectly reasonable, Dannyl.'

Dannyl grinned. 'Oh, it gets better. If we present this carefully, everyone will be patting themselves on the back for persuading the Thieves to do a good service for the city.'

Ezrille laughed. 'I hope the Thieves don't realise this, or they'll refuse to help you.'

'Well, it must remain a secret for now,' Dannyl told them. 'I don't want to stir things up here until I know whether Gorin is willing to help us or not. Can I rely on your silence?'

He looked at the others. Ezrille nodded enthusiastically. Rothen bowed his head once. Yaldin frowned, then shrugged.

'Very well. But be careful, Dannyl. It's not just your skin you're risking here.'

'I know.' Dannyl smiled. 'I know.'

* * *

Travelling along the Thieves' Road by lamplight was faster and more interesting than groping along in the dark. The walls of the passages were made of a seemingly endless variety of bricks. Symbols were carved into the walls and signs marked some of the intersections.

The guide stopped at a juncture of passages and set the lamp on the floor. He pulled a handful of black cloth from his coat.

'You must go blind from here.'

Cery nodded, and stood silently as the man bound a strip of cloth around his eyes. The man moved behind Sonea and she closed her eyes as the rough material was wrapped tightly around her face. She felt a hand rest on her shoulder, then another grasped her wrist and began pulling her along the passage.

Though she tried to memorise the turns, she soon lost count of them. They shuffled through darkness. Faint sounds reached them: voices, footsteps, dripping water, and a few noises she could not identify. The blindfold made her skin itch, but she dared not scratch herself in case the guide thought she was peeking.

When the guide stopped again she gave a sigh of relief. Fingers pulled the blindfold away. She glanced at Cery. He smiled back at her reassuringly.

Taking a polished stick from his coat, the guide pushed it into a hole in the wall. After a pause, a section of the wall swung inward and a large, muscular man stepped out.

'Yes?'

'Ceryni and Sonea to see Faren,' the guide stated.

The man nodded, opened the door wider and jerked his head at Sonea and Cery.

'Go on in.'

Cery hesitated, then turned to the guide. 'I asked to see Ravi.'

The man smiled crookedly. 'Then Ravi must want you to see Faren.'

Cery shrugged, then moved through the doorway. Following him, Sonea wondered if a Thief named after a poisonous eight-legged insect was more dangerous than a Thief named after a rodent.

They entered a small room. Two more heavily built men eyed them from chairs on either side. The first closed the passage door, then opened a door on the opposite side of the room and gestured for them to continue through.

Lamps hung from the walls of the next room, throwing warm-yellow circles up onto the ceiling. The floor was covered with a large carpet which was fringed with gold-tipped tassels. At the far side of the room, sitting behind a table, was a dark-skinned man in black, slim-fitting clothes. Startling pale yellow eyes examined them closely.

Sonea stared back. The Thief was a Lonmar, a member of the proud desert race whose lands lay a long way to the north of Kyralia. Lonmar were uncommon in Imardin; few liked to live outside their rigid culture. Theft was considered a great evil to the Lonmar, as they believed that when one stole something, no matter how small, one lost a portion of their soul. Yet here was a Lonmar Thief.

The man's eyes narrowed. Realising that she was staring, Sonea quickly looked down. He leaned back in his chair, smiled and pointed a long brown finger at her.

'Come closer, girl.'

Sonea moved forward until she stood in front of the table.

'So you are the one the Guild is looking for, eh?'

'Yes.'

'Sonea, isn't it?'

'Yes.'

Faren pursed his lips. 'I was expecting something more impressive.' He shrugged, then leaned forward and placed his elbows on the table. 'How am I to know you are what you say you are?'

Sonea glanced over her shoulder. 'Cery said you'd know I was the one, that you would have been watching me.'

'Oh he did, did he?' Faren chuckled and his gaze slid to her friend. 'A smart one, this little Ceryni, like his father. Yes, we've been watching you – both of you – but Cery longer. Come here, Cery.'

Cery moved to Sonea's side.

'Ravi sends his regards.'

'From one rodent to the other?' Cery's voice betrayed a slight quaver.

White teeth flashed, but Faren's grin quickly faded and his yellow eyes slid back to Sonea.

'So you can do magic, can you?'

Sonea swallowed to wet her throat. 'Yes.'

'Have you used it since your little surprise in the North Square?'

'Yes.'

Faren's brows rose. He ran his hands through his hair. A few grey strands were visible at his temple, but his skin was smooth and unlined. Several rings, many set with large stones, burdened his fingers. Sonea had never seen stones that large on the hands of a slum dweller before – but this man was no ordinary dwell.

'You chose a bad moment to discover your powers, Sonea,' Faren told her. 'The magicians are anxious to find you now. Their search has caused us a great deal of inconvenience – and the reward is, no doubt, causing *you* a great deal of inconvenience. Now you want *us* to hide you from *them*. Wouldn't it be far better for us to turn you in and collect the reward? The searches end. I get a little richer. The annoying magicians go away . . .'

She glanced at Cery again. 'Or we could make a deal.'

Faren shrugged. 'We could. What do you offer in exchange, then?'

'My father said you owed him—' Cery began.

The yellow eyes snapped to Cery. 'Your father lost all that was due him when he deceived us,' Faren snapped.

Cery bowed his head, then lifted his chin and met the Thief's eyes. 'My father taught me a lot,' he began. 'Perhaps I can—'

Faren snorted and waved a hand. 'You might be useful to us one day, little Ceryni, but, as yet, you don't have the friends your father had – and this is a great favour you ask. Did you know that the penalty for hiding a rogue magician from the Guild is death? There is nothing the King likes less than the idea of a magician sneaking about doing things that he didn't order.' His eyes slid to Sonea and he smiled slyly. 'But it is an interesting idea. One I like a great deal.' He folded his hands together. 'What have you used your powers for since the Purge?'

'I made something catch fire.'

Faren's eyes gleamed. 'Really? Have you done anything else?'

'No.'

'Why don't you demonstrate something now.'

She stared at him. 'Now?'

He gestured to one of the books on the table. 'Try to move this.'

Sonea looked at Cery. Her friend nodded slightly. Biting her lip, she reminded herself that, the moment she had agreed to seek the Thieves' help, she had resigned herself to using magic. She had to accept it, no matter how uneasy it made her feel.

Faren leaned back in his chair. 'Go on.'

Taking a deep breath, Sonea stared at the book and willed it to move.

Nothing happened.

Frowning, she thought back to the North Square and the fight with Burril. She had been angry both times, she recalled. Closing her eyes, she thought of the magicians. They had wrecked her life. It was their fault she was selling herself to the Thieves for protection. Feeling anger rising, she opened her eyes and projected her resentment at the book.

The air crackled and a flash of light lit the room. Faren jumped back with a curse as the book burst into flame. Grabbing the glass, he hastily poured the contents over the book to extinguish the fire.

'I'm sorry,' Sonea said hastily. 'It didn't do what I wanted last time, either. I'll—'

Faren lifted a hand to silence her, and grinned.

'I think you might have something worth protecting, young Sonea.'

CHAPTER 8

MESSAGES IN THE DARK

Looking around at the crowded Night Room, Rothen realised he had made a mistake arriving early. Instead of talking to a crowd, he had been questioned by small groups or individuals, forced to answer the same questions over and over.

'I'm beginning to sound like a novice repeating formulas,' he muttered to Dannyl irritably.

'Perhaps you should write a report on your progress every evening and nail it to your door.'

'I don't think that would help. I'm sure they'd feel they'd miss out on some snippet of information if they didn't question me personally.' Rothen shook his head and looked around at the knots of conversing magicians. 'And they all want to hear it from *me* for some reason. Why don't they ever bother you?'

'Respect for your obvious seniority,' Dannyl replied.

Rothen narrowed his eyes at his friend. 'Obvious?'

'Ah, here's some wine to wet your poor, tired vocal cords.' Dannyl beckoned to a servant carrying a tray.

Accepting a glass, Rothen sipped appreciatively. Somehow, he had become the unofficial organiser of the search for the girl. All except Fergun and his friends looked to Rothen for instruction. This had forced him to spend less time actively searching, and he was being interrupted many times a day by mind communication from those who wanted him to identify the girls they had found.

Rothen winced as a hand touch his shoulder. Turning, he found Administrator Lorlen standing at his side.

'Good evening Lord Rothen, Lord Dannyl,' Lorlen said. 'The High Lord wishes to speak to you.'

Rothen looked across the room to see the High Lord taking his preferred seat. The murmur of voices had changed to a buzz of interest as Akkarin's presence was noted. *Seems I'm going to be repeating myself again*, Rothen mused as he and Dannyl started toward the Guild leader.

The High Lord looked up as they approached, and acknowledged them with an almost imperceptible nod. His long fingers were curled around a wineglass.

'Please sit down.' Lorlen waved to two empty chairs. 'Tell us how your search is progressing.'

Rothen settled into a seat. 'We have interviewed over two hundred informers. Most haven't given us any useful information. A few had locked up ordinary beggar girls, despite our warning not to approach her. Some were convincingly disappointed when the place where they believed she was hiding turned out to be empty. That, unfortunately, is all I can report so far.'

Lorlen nodded. 'Lord Fergun believes she is being protected by someone.'

Dannyl's lips pressed into a thin line, but he said nothing.

'The Thieves?' Rothen suggested.

Lorlen shrugged. 'Or a rogue magician. She did learn to hide her presence quickly.'

'A rogue?' Rothen glanced at Akkarin, remembering the High Lord's assertion that no rogue magicians existed in the slums. 'Do you think there's reason to suspect we have one now?'

'I have sensed someone using magic,' Akkarin said quietly. 'Not much, and not for long. I believe she is experimenting alone, since a teacher would have instructed her to hide her activities by now.'

Rothen stared at the High Lord. That Akkarin could sense such weak magical events in the city was astounding, even disturbing. As the man's dark eyes rose to meet his, Rothen quickly looked down at his hands.

'That is . . . interesting news,' he replied.

'Could you . . . Could you trace her?' Dannyl asked.

Akkarin pursed his lips. 'She is using magic in short bursts, sometimes a single occurrence, sometimes several over an hour. You would sense them if you were waiting and alert to them, but you would not have time to find and capture her unless she used her power for a longer period.'

'We can get a little closer every time she uses it, though,' Dannyl said slowly. 'We could spread ourselves throughout the city and wait. Each time she experiments we can move a little closer until we know her location.'

The High Lord nodded. 'She is in the northern section of the Outer Circle.'

'Then we'll begin there tomorrow.' Dannyl drummed his fingers together. 'But we'll have to be careful that our movements don't warn her of our strategy. If someone is protecting her, they may have helpers on the lookout for magicians.' He lifted an eyebrow at the High Lord. 'Our chances of success will be greater if we disguise ourselves.'

The corner of Akkarin's mouth curled upward. 'Cloaks should hide your robes sufficiently.'

Dannyl nodded quickly. 'Of course.'

'You'll only have one chance,' Lorlen warned. 'If she learns that you can sense her using magic, she will evade you by moving to a new location after each experiment.'

'Then we must work quickly – and the more magicians we have, the faster we can locate her.'

'I will call for more volunteers.'

'Thank you Administrator.' Dannyl inclined his head.

Lorlen smiled and leaned back in his chair. 'I must say, I never thought I'd be happy to learn that our little runaway has started to use her powers.'

Rothen frowned. *Yes*, he thought, *but each time she does she comes closer to losing control of them completely.*

The parcel was heavy, despite its small size. It made a satisfying thud when Cery dropped it on the table. Faren picked it up and tore off the paper wrapping, revealing a small wooden box. As he opened it, tiny discs of reflected light scattered over the Thief and the wall behind him.

Looking down, Cery's chest tightened when he saw the polished coins. Faren drew out a wooden block with four pegs set into it. Cery watched as the Thief began stacking coins onto the pegs. The holes in the coins fit corresponding pegs: gold onto the round peg, silver on the square, and large coppers onto the triangular. The last peg, for the large coppers, which Cery was most familiar with, remained empty. As the stack of gold reached ten coins high, Faren transferred it to a 'cap', a single wooden stick with stoppers at both ends, and set it aside.

'I have another job for you, Ceryni.'

Dragging his eyes reluctantly from the wealth stacking

up in front of him, Cery straightened, then frowned as Faren's words sank in. How many more 'jobs' must he do before he would be allowed to see Sonea? It had been over a week since Faren had taken her in. Swallowing his annoyance, he nodded at the Thief.

'What is it?'

Faren leaned back in his chair, his yellow eyes bright with amusement. 'This may be more suited to your talents. A couple of thugs have taken to robbing shops around the inner Northside – shops belonging to men I have arrangements with. I want you to find out where this pair live and deliver a message in such a way they will be certain I am watching them closely. Can you do this?'

Cery nodded. 'What do they look like?'

'I've had one of my men question the shopkeepers. He will fill you in. Take this.' He handed Cery a small, folded piece of paper. 'Wait in the room outside.'

Cery turned, then hesitated. He looked back at Faren and considered whether it would be an appropriate moment to ask after Sonea.

'Soon,' Faren said. 'Tomorrow, if all goes well.'

Nodding, Cery strode to the door and stepped through. Though the burly guards eyed him suspiciously, Cery smiled back. Never make enemies of someone's lackeys, his father had taught him. Better still, make them like you a lot. This pair looked so similar they had to be brothers, though a distinctive scar across one man's cheek made it easy to tell them apart.

'I'm to wait here,' he told them. He gestured to a chair. 'Taken?'

The scarred one shrugged. Cery sat down and looked around the room. His eyes were drawn to a strip of bright green cloth hanging from a wall, an incal stitched in gold at the tip.

'Hai! Is that what I think?' he asked, rising again.

The scarred man grinned. 'It is.'

'A saddle-ribbon from Thunderwind?' Cery breathed. 'Where'd you get it?'

'My cousin is stable hand at House Arran,' the man replied. 'Got it for me.' He reached out and caressed the cloth. 'Won me twenty gold, that horse.'

'Sired good racers, they say.'

'Never be one like him again.'

'Did you see the race?'

'Nah. You?'

Cery grinned. 'Snuck past the feemasters. Was no easy trick. Didn't know it was going to be Thunderwind's day. Just lucky.' The guard's eyes misted over as he listened to Cery describe the race.

A knock at the door interrupted them. The silent guard opened the door, admitting a tall, wiry man with a sour expression in a black longcoat.

'Ceryni?'

Cery stepped forward. The man examined him, his brows rising, then gestured for Cery to follow. Nodding to the guards, Cery started down the passage.

'I'm to fill you in,' the man said.

Cery nodded. 'What do the thugs look like?'

'One's my height, but heavier, the other's smaller and skinny. They've got short black hair – cut it themselves from the sounds of it. The bigger one's got something odd with one of his eyes. One shopkeeper said it was coloured funny, another said it looked oddways. Elsewise, they're regular dwells.'

'Weapons?'

'Knives.'

'Know where they live?'

'No, but one of the shopkeepers seen them in a bolhouse tonight. You're going there now, so you can track them. They're sure to take the long way home, so be sly about it.'

'Of course. What's their style?'

The man glanced back, his expression unreadable. 'Rough. Beat up the shopkeepers and some family. Didn't stop to play, though. Just got out when they had what they came for.'

'What did they take?'

'Coin, mostly. A bit of drink if it was around. We're almost there.'

They emerged from the passages into a dark street. The guide extinguished the lamp and led Cery to a larger thoroughfare, then stopped in the shadows of a doorway. The sounds of revelry from across the road drew his attention to a bolhouse.

His companion made a quick gesture, his hands forming a silent query. Following the man's gaze, Cery caught a movement in a nearby alley.

'They're still there. We wait.'

Cery leaned against the door. His companion remained silent, watching the bolhouse intently. Rain began to fall, pattering on roofs and forming puddles. While they waited the moon rose above the houses and flooded the street with light, before reaching the grey clouds and becoming a ghostly glow in the sky.

Men and women left the bolhouse in small groups. As a large group of men stepped out into the street, laughing and staggering drunkenly, Cery's companion tensed. Looking closer, Cery saw two figures slip past the revellers. The watcher in the alley made another movement with his hands and Cery's companion nodded.

'That's them.'

Nodding, Cery stepping out into the rain. He kept in the shadows as he followed the two men down the street. One was clearly drunk; the other navigated the puddles with confidence. Letting them gain some distance, he listened as the drunk man berated his companion for drinking too little.

'Nothin'll 'appn, Tull'n,' he slurred. 'We t' smar' fr them.'

'Shut it, Nig.'

The pair took a circular journey through the slums. From time to time, Tullin stopped and looked about. He never saw Cery standing in the shadows. Finally, exasperated by his friend's chatter, he took a straight route of several hundred paces across the slums, and arrived at an abandoned shop.

Once the pair had disappeared inside, Cery crept closer, examining the building. A sign lay on the ground outside. He recognised the word for raka. Placing a hand on his chest, he considered the message waiting in his pocket.

Faren wanted it delivered in such a way that would frighten the thugs. The pair had to be shown that the Thieves were aware of everything: who they were, where they were hiding, what they had done, and how easily the Thieves could kill them. Cery bit his lip, considering.

He could slip the note under their door, but that was too easy. It wouldn't frightened the thugs as much as discovering that someone had been inside their hideout.

He would have to wait until they went out again, then slip inside.

Or would he? Returning home to find a message in their hideout was going to scare them, but not as much as waking up and realising that someone had been there while they were asleep.

Smiling, Cery considered the hideout. It was part of a row of shops, each sharing a wall with the next. That left only the front and back for entry. Moving to the end of the street, Cery entered the alley which ran behind them. It was filled with empty shipping crates and piles of garbage. He counted doors, and knew he had found the thugs' shop by the stinking bags of rotting raka leaves piled against the wall. Dropping into a crouch, he peered through the keyhole of the shop's back door.

A lamp burned in the room beyond. Nig lay in a bed to one side, snoring softly. Tullin paced about, rubbing his face. When he turned into the lamplight, Cery could see his twisted eye and deep shadows under it.

The big man hadn't been sleeping well – probably worried about the Thieves dropping in for a visit. As if reading Cery's thoughts, Tullin suddenly strode toward the back door. Cery tensed, ready to slip away, but Tullin didn't reach for the handle. Instead, his fingers closed around something in mid-air and traced it's path upward, out of sight. String, Cery guessed. He didn't need to see what was suspended above the door to guess that Tullin had laid a trap for unwanted visitors.

Satisfied, Tullin moved to a second bed. He pulled a knife from his belt and placed it on a nearby table, then topped up the oil in the lamp. Taking one last look around the room, he stretched out on the bed.

Cery considered the door. Raka arrived in Imardin as stalks of beans, wrapped in their own leaves. The beans were stripped off the stalks by the shop owners and roasted. The leaves and stalks were usually dropped into a chute leading to a tub outside and the tubs were collected by boys who then sold their contents to farmers near the city.

Moving along the wall, Cery located the outer flap of the chute. It was locked from the inside with a simple bolt – not difficult to open. He drew a tiny flask from his coat, and a slim, hollow reed. Sucking a little oil into the reed, he carefully oiled the bolt and the hinges of the flap. Putting flask and reed away again, he drew out a few picks and levers, and began manipulating the bolt.

It was slow work, but gave Tullin plenty of time to fall into a deep sleep. When the flap was free, Cery opened it carefully and considered the tiny space within. Pocketing the picks, he drew out a piece of polished metal wrapped in a square of finely woven cloth. Reaching through the chute, he used this to examine Tullin's trap.

He almost laughed aloud at what he saw. A rake was suspended over the door. The end of the handle was tied with string to a hook above the door frame. The iron spikes were balanced on a rafter, probably hooked into place over a nail. A piece of string stretched from the spikes to the door handle.

Too easy, Cery mused. He checked for other traps but found none. Sliding his arm out of the chute, he returned to the door and brought out his oiling tools again. A quick inspection of the lock revealed that it had been broken, probably by the thugs when they first entered the shop.

Taking a tiny box out of his coat, he opened it and selected a thin blade. From another pocket he took a hinged tool, part of the inheritance he had gained from his father. Clamping this tool to the blade, he slipped it through the keyhole and probed for the door handle. Finding it, he worked his way along the neck of it until he felt the slight resistance of the string. He pressed on it firmly.

Moving back to the chute, he saw with the mirror that the string now hung harmlessly down from the rafters. Satisfied, he packed his tools away, wrapped some cloth around his boots, and drew in a deep breath to steady himself.

Cery opened the door silently. Slipping inside, he regarded the sleeping men.

His father had alway said that the best way to sneak up on someone was to *not* try to sneak up on them. He considered the thugs. Both were asleep, the drunk one snoring softly. Walking across the room, Cery examined the front door. A key protruded from the lock. Turning back, he considered the two men again.

Tullin's knife glinted in the darkness. Pulling out Faren's message, Cery moved to the thug's side. He picked up the knife, and carefully pinned the paper to the table with it.

That should do it. Smiling grimly, he moved back to the door and grasped the key. As he turned it, the lock clicked. Tullin's eyelids fluttered, but his eyes did not open. Cery opened the door and stepped outside, then slammed the door closed.

A shout came from inside. Darting to the shadowed doorway of the next shop, Cery turned back to watch. After a moment the door of the thugs' shop opened and Tullin stared out into the night, his face pale in the muted moonlight. From within the house came a protesting voice, then an exclamation of horror. Tullin scowled and ducked back into the shop.

Smiling, Cery slipped away into the night.

Sonea cursed Faren under her breath.

A short stick lay on the hearth before her. After experimenting with various objects, she had settled on wood as the safest material to work with when experimenting with magic. It wasn't cheap – timber was cut in the northern mountains and floated down the Tarali River – but despite this, it was expendable and there was plenty of it in the room.

She regarded the block dubiously, then looked around the room to remind herself that the frustration was worth it. Polished tables and cushioned chairs surrounded her. In the adjoining rooms were soft beds, plenty of food stores and a generous supply of liquor. Faren was treating her like an honoured guest of one of the great Houses.

But she felt like a prisoner. The hideout had no windows, as it was entirely underground. It could only be reached by the Road, and was guarded day and night. Only Faren's most trusted people, his 'kin', knew of it.

Sighing, she let her shoulders slump. Safe from both magicians and enterprising dwells, she now struggled to evade boredom. After six days of looking at the same walls, even the room's luxuries no longer distracted her, and, though Faren stopped by from time to time, she had little to do but experiment with magic.

Perhaps that was Faren's intention. Looking down at the stick, she felt another stab of frustration. Though she had called on her powers several times a day since coming to the hideout, they never worked in the way she intended.

When she wanted to burn something, it moved. When she told it to move, it exploded. When she willed it to break, it burned. When she admitted this to Faren, he just smiled and told her to keep practising.

With a grimace, Sonea turned her attention back to the stick again. Taking a deep breath, she stared intently at the piece of wood. Narrowing her eyes, she willed it to roll across the stones of the hearth.

Nothing happened.

Patience, she told herself. It often took several attempts before magic worked. Drawing all her will together into an imagined force, she commanded the stick to move.

It remained perfectly still.

She sighed and sat back on her heels. Every time the magic had worked she had been angry, whether from frustration or hate for the Guild. While she could draw those emotions up by thinking about something which angered her, doing so was exhausting and depressing.

But the magicians did this all the time, she reminded herself. Did they keep a store of anger and hate inside to draw upon? She shuddered. What kind of people were they?

Staring at the piece of wood, she realised that she was going to have to do just that. She would have to hoard her anger and gather her hate, storing them up for the times she needed to use magic. If she didn't, she would fail and Faren would abandon her to the Guild.

Wrapping her arms around herself, she felt a smothering desperation rush over her. *I'm trapped*, she thought. *I have two choices: either I become one of them, or I let them kill me.*

A soft snapping sound reached her ears, a noise like a

length of material being thrown into the air and quickly jerked back again. She jumped and turned around.

Bright orange flames curled across the surface of a small table between two of the chairs. She leapt up and away, her heart racing.

Did I do that? she thought. *But I wasn't angry.*

The fire began to crackle as the flames multiplied. Sonea edged closer, unsure what to do. What would Faren say when he discovered his hideout has been burnt? Sonea snorted. He'd be irritated, and a little disappointed that his pet magician had died.

Smoke was pouring upwards and curling along the roof. Creeping forward on hands and knees, Sonea grabbed a leg of the table and dragged it forward. The fire flared with the movement. Flinching at the heat, Sonea lifted the table and threw it into the fireplace. It settled against the grate and continued to burn.

Sonea sighed and watched the fire consume the table. She had discovered something new, at least. Tables don't burst into flames on their own. It seemed desperation was an emotion that would rouse magic as well.

Anger, hate and desperation, she mused. *What fun it is to be a magician.*

'Did you sense that?' Rothen asked, his voice tense with excitement.

Dannyl nodded. 'Yes. It's not what I was expecting. I always thought that sensing magic was like *feeling* someone singing. This felt more like a cough.'

'A cough of magic.' Rothen chuckled. 'That's an interesting way of describing it.'

'If you don't know how to sing or speak, would you

make rough noises instead? Perhaps this is what magic sounds like when it is uncontrolled.' Dannyl blinked, then stepped away from the window and rubbed his eyes. 'It's late, and I'm getting far too abstract for comfort. We should get some sleep.'

Rothen nodded, but didn't move from the window. He gazed out at the last few lights glinting in the city.

'We've been listening for hours. There's nothing to be gained by doing so any longer,' Dannyl told Rothen. 'We know we can sense her now. Get some sleep, Rothen. We'll need to be alert tomorrow.'

'It seems incredible to think she's so close to us, but we haven't been able to find her,' Rothen said softly. 'I wonder what she tried to do.'

'Rothen,' Dannyl said sternly.

The older magician sighed and turned from the window. He smiled wanly.

'Very well. I will try to sleep.'

'Good.' Satisfied, Dannyl walked to the door. 'I'll see you tomorrow.'

'Good night, Dannyl.'

Looking back as he closed the door, Dannyl was pleased to see his friend walking toward the bedroom. He knew Rothen's interest in finding the girl had gone past duty. As he started down the corridor, he smiled to himself.

Years before, when Dannyl was a novice, Fergun had circulated rumours about him in revenge for a prank. Dannyl hadn't expected anyone to take Fergun seriously, but when the teachers and novices began treating him differently and he realised he could do nothing to regain their regard, he had lost all respect for his peers. The enthusiasm he'd had for his lessons fled, and he fell further and further behind.

Then Rothen had taken him aside and, with seemingly endless determination and optimism, had turned Dannyl's mind back to magic and learning. It seemed he could not help wanting to help rescue youngsters in strife. Though Dannyl was sure his friend was as determined as ever, he could not help wondering if Rothen was truly prepared to take on the education of this girl. There had to be a big difference between a sullen novice and a slum girl who probably hated magicians.

One thing was sure: life was going to get very interesting when she was found.

CHAPTER 9

AN UNWELCOME VISITOR

A chill wind whipped the rain into flurries and clawed at winter coats. Cery pulled his longcoat tighter and hunched deeper into the folds of his scarf. He grimaced as the rain beat at his face then resolutely leant into the wind.

It had been seductively warm in the bolhouse with Harrin. Donia's father had been in a generous mood, but even free bol could not tempt Cery to stay – not when Faren had finally allowed him to visit Sonea.

Cery grunted as a tall man pushed past him. He glowered at the back of the stranger as the man strode on down the road. A merchant, Cery guessed, from the way the rain glistened on new cloak and boots. He muttered an insult and trudged on.

When Cery had returned from the thugs' shop, Faren had questioned him about the night's work. The Thief had listened to Cery's report, expressing neither praise nor disapproval, then simply nodded.

He's testing my usefulness, Cery mused. *Wants to know what my limits are. I wonder what he'll ask me to do next.*

Looking up, he scanned the street. A few dwells hurried through the rain. Nothing unusual in that. Ahead, the merchant had stopped and was standing beside a building for no reason Cery could see.

Continuing down the road, Cery glanced up at the

merchant as he passed him. The stranger's eyes were closed and he was frowning as if in concentration. Stepping into the next alley, Cery looked back just in time to see the man's head snap up and his eyes focus on the road.

No, Cery thought, his skin crawling, *beneath the road.*

He looked closer, examining the merchant's clothes. The man's shoes were both familiar and unusual. A small symbol gleamed in the dull light . . .

Cery's heart skipped. Turning, he broke into a run.

Through the rain, Rothen could see the shape of a tall cloaked man standing on the street corner opposite him.

—*We're close*, Dannyl sent. *She's somewhere below these houses.*

—*All we have to do is find a way in*, Rothen replied.

It had been a slow and frustrating day. Sometimes the girl had used magic several times in a row, and they made good progress. Other times they waited hours only to find she made a single attempt, then stopped.

He had noted quickly that his cloak, while hiding his robes, still marked him as someone too well dressed for the slums. He had also realised that several cloaked men loitering in one area were going to attract attention so, as the magicians drew closer to the girl, he had ordered most of them to move away.

A buzz at the edge of his mind snatched his attention back to the girl. Dannyl moved from his position and entered an alleyway. Checking with the other searchers, Rothen decided that the girl must be somewhere below the house to his left.

—*I think there's an entrance to the passages here*, Dannyl

sent. *A ventilation grille in the wall, like we've seen before.*

—This is as close as we're going to get without revealing ourselves, Rothen sent to the searchers. *It's time. Makin and I will watch the front entrance. Kiano and Yaldin keep an eye on the back door. Dannyl and Jolen will enter the passage first, since that's the way she'll probably try to escape.*

When all had reported that they were in position, he instructed Dannyl and Jolen to go. As Dannyl opened the grille, he started sending images to them all.

Climbing through the opening, Dannyl dropped to the floor of the passage. He created a globe of light, and watched as Lord Jolen followed. They separated, each disappearing into the dark passage on either side.

After a hundred paces or so, Dannyl stopped and sent his light forward. It continued for several paces before reaching a turn.

—This goes under the street, I think. I'm going back.

A moment later, Lord Jolen sent an image of a narrow descending staircase. He started down, then stopped as a man stepped out in front of him. The newcomer stared at Jolen's globe light, then turned and fled into a side passage.

—We've been spotted, Jolen sent.

—Keep going, Rothen replied.

Dannyl had stopped sending images so that Rothen could follow Jolen's progress. Reaching the bottom of the stairs, Jolen started striding down a narrow passage. As he reached a turn, dust, noise and a sense of alarm battered Rothen's senses. Confusion followed, as all of the magicians started sending questions.

—They've caved in the passage. Jolen replied, sending an image of a wall of rubble. *Dannyl was behind me.*

Rothen felt a stab of apprehension. *Dannyl?*

Silence followed, then a faint mental voice.

—Buried. Wait . . . I'm free. No harm done. Go on ahead, Jolen. They obviously meant to stop us getting past here. Go on and find her.

—Go, Rothen repeated. Jolen turned from the wall of rubble and hurried down the passage.

A bell chimed. Sonea looked up from the fireplace and climbed to her feet. A panel in the wall slid open and Faren stepped through. Dressed in black, with his striking eyes gleaming, he looked suitably insect-like and dangerous. He smiled and handed her something wrapped in material and fastened with cord.

'This is for you.'

She turned it over in her hands. 'What is it?'

'Open it,' Faren urged, folding his long limbs into one of the chairs.

Sitting opposite hom, Sonea untied the string. The material fell open to reveal an old book with a leather cover. A large section of pages had come free from the binding. She looked up at Faren and frowned.

'An old book?'

He nodded. 'Look at the title.'

Sonea glanced down, then looked up at him again.

'I can't read.'

He blinked in surprise. 'Of course.' He shook his head. 'I'm sorry, I should have realised. It's a book on magic. I had someone look in all the pawn shops and scavengers' dens. Apparently, the magicians burn their old books but, according to the shop's owner, this one was sold by an enterprising and disobedient servant. Look inside.'

Opening the cover, she found a folded piece of paper.

Picking it up, she immediately noticed the thickness of the parchment. A sheet of paper this well made usually cost more than a meal for a large family or a new cloak. Unfolding it, she looked at the black characters curling in perfect lines across the page, then she drew in a breath as she saw the symbol stamped onto a corner. A diamond with a 'Y' dividing it – the symbol of the Guild.

'What is it?' she breathed.

'A message,' Faren replied. 'For you.'

'Me?' She looked up at him.

He nodded.

'How did they know how to get it to me?'

'They didn't, but they gave it to someone they knew had connections with the Thieves, and he passed it on.'

She held it out to him.

'What does it say?'

He took the paper from her. 'It reads: "To the young lady with magical powers. As we cannot speak to you in person, we are sending this message through the Thieves in the hope that they will be able to reach you. We wish to assure you that we do not intend to harm you in any way. Be assured, as well, that we did not intend to hurt you or the young man on the day of the Purge. His death was a tragic accident. We only wish to teach you how to control your power, and to offer you the opportunity to join the Guild. You are welcome among us." It is signed: "Lord Rothen of the Magicians' Guild."'

Sonea stared at the message with disbelief. The Guild wanted her, a slum girl, to *join* them?

It must be a trick, she decided, an attempt to draw her out of hiding. Remembering the magician who had invaded the attic refuge, she recalled how he had called her an enemy of the Guild. He hadn't known that she was listening. That, more likely, was the truth.

Folding the parchment, Faren slipped it into a pocket. Seeing his sly smile, Sonea felt a twinge of suspicion. How did she know whether what he had read out was truly what the message said?

But why would he make it up? He wanted her to work for him, not go running off to join the magicians. Unless he was testing her . . .

The Thief lifted an eyebrow. 'What do you think, young Sonea?'

'I don't believe them.'

'Why not?'

'They'd never take a dwell.'

He rubbed the arm of his chair. 'What if you were to discover that they did want you join them? Many ordinary people dream of becoming a magician. Perhaps the Guild is anxious to redeem itself in the eyes of the public.'

Sonea shook her head. 'It's a trick. It was a mistake that they got the wrong dwell, not that they killed one.'

Faren nodded slowly. 'That is what most witnesses say. Well, we shall decline the Guild's invitation and get onto more important business.' He pointed at the book in her lap. 'I don't know if that will be useful. I will have to get someone to read it to you. It might be better if you learned to read yourself.'

'My aunt taught me a little,' Sonea told him, flicking through the pages. 'But it was a long time ago.' She looked up. 'Will I be able to see Jonna and Ranel soon? I'm sure Jonna could teach me to read.'

He shook his head. 'Not until the magicians stop—'

He frowned and tilted his head slightly. A faint ringing reached her ears.

'What's that?'

Faren rose. 'Wait here,' he said and disappeared into the darkness behind the panel.

Sonea put the book aside and moved to the fireplace. The panel slid open again and Faren stepped back into the room.

'Quickly,' he snapped, 'follow me – and keep silent.'

He strode past her. Sonea stared at him for a heartbeat before following him across the room.

Drawing a small object from a pocket, Faren ran it back and forth over the panelling. Sonea drew closer and saw a knot in the wood slide forward until it protruded half a finger length into the room. Faren grasped this and pulled.

A section of the wall swivelled inward. Taking her arm, Faren pulled her into the shadows. After pushing the knot flush with the panel again, he closed the door.

They stood in darkness. As her eyes adjusted, she saw that five tiny holes were spaced across the door at shoulder height. Faren's eye hovered close to one.

'There are faster ways out of the room,' he told her, 'but since we had the time, I thought it better to choose the door that is near impossible to open. Look.'

He moved away from the peephole. She blinked as a flame suddenly lit the darkness. Faren lifted a tiny lamp and slid the shutter across until only a thin ray of light spilled into the passage. Holding it up, he pointed out several metal bolts and complicated looking gears on the back of the door.

'So what's going on?' she asked.

Faren's yellow eyes glinted in the dim light as he slid

the bolts into place. 'Only a handful of magicians are still searching for you. My spies now know what they look like, their names, their movements.' Faren chuckled. 'We've been sending false informers to them, keeping them busy.

'Today they've been acting strangely. More came into the slums than usually do, and they wore cloaks over their robes. They took positions all around the slums and seemed to be waiting for something. I don't know what, but they kept moving to new positions. Each time they did, they came closer to this place. Then, just now, Ceryni told me that he thought the magicians were tracking you. He said they must be able to sense you using magic. I didn't believe it until . . .'

Faren paused, then the sliver of light from the lamp suddenly vanished and darkness filled the passage. Sonea heard him move to the wall. She crept forward and put her eye to one of the little holes.

The entrance to the room stood open, a rectangle of darkness. At first Sonea thought the hideout was empty, then a figure suddenly strode into sight from one of the side rooms, his green robes swaying as he stopped.

'My people managed to stop them by caving in the passage,' Faren whispered, 'but one got through. Don't be alarmed. No-one can get through this door. It's . . .' He sucked in a quiet breath. 'Interesting.'

Sonea put her eye back to the hole and felt her heart skip. The magician appeared to be staring right at her.

'Can he hear us?' Faren murmured. 'I tested the walls many times.'

'Perhaps he can see the door,' Sonea suggested.

'No, he'd have to look very closely. Even if he did start

looking for doors, there are five exits leading from this room. Why would he choose this one?'

The magician walked toward them and stopped. He stared at the wood, then closed his eyes. Sonea felt an all-too familiar sensation pass over her. When the magician opened his eyes again, his frown was gone and he was staring directly at Faren.

'How does he know?' Faren hissed. 'Are you doing magic right now?'

'No,' Sonea replied, surprised at the confidence in her own voice. 'I can hide myself from him. It's you. He's sensing you.'

'*Me?*' Faren turned his head from the hole and stared at her.

Sonea shrugged. 'Don't ask me why.'

'Can you hide me?' Faren's voice was strained. 'Can you hide us both?'

Sonea drew away from the hole. Could she? She couldn't hide what the magician was sensing without detecting it herself. She looked at Faren, then she *looked* at Faren. It was as if she had extended her senses – no, another sense that wasn't sight or hearing – and could feel a *person* there.

Faren uttered an oath.

'Stop whatever your doing!' he gasped. Something brushed against the wall. Faren backed away.

'He's trying to open it,' he told her. 'I was afraid he'd try to blast it down. That gives us some time.' He opened the lamp's shutter and gestured for her to follow him.

They had only taken a few steps when the sound of a bolt sliding across wood halted them. Faren turned and swore. He raised the lamp until its light illuminated the wall.

One by one the bolts were sliding back, apparently on their own. Sonea saw the cogs of the door mechanism begin to turn, then the passage plunged into darkness as the lamp clattered to the floor.

'Run!' Faren hissed. 'Follow me!'

Throwing out a hand to the passage wall, Sonea chased the rapping of Faren's shoes on the ground. She had run no more than twenty paces when a wedge of light leapt past her, throwing her shadow across the floor. The sound of booted footsteps echoed down the passage behind her.

Bright light suddenly filled the passage and her shadow began to shrink rapidly. Heat flashed against her ear and she shied as a bright ball of light overtook her. It shot past Faren and flashed outward to form a glowing barrier.

Skidding to a halt, Faren span about to face their pursuer, his face pale in the white light. Reaching his side, Sonea turned. A robed figure strode toward them. Heart pounding, Sonea backed away until she could feel the vibration and heat of the barrier behind her.

Faren made a growling noise deep in his throat, then clenched his fists and started back down the passage toward the magician. Surprised, Sonea could only stare at him with amazement.

'You!' Faren pointed at the magician. 'Who do you think you are? This is *my* domain. You're *trespassing*!'

His voice echoed in the passage. The magician slowed and regarded the Thief with wary eyes.

'The law says we may go where we must,' the magician told him.

'The law also says you may not harm people or their property,' Faren retorted. 'I'd say you've done enough of both in the last few weeks.'

The magician stopped and raised his hands in a placating gesture.

'We did not mean to kill that boy. It was a mistake.' The magician looked at Sonea and she felt a chill run down her spine. 'There is much we must explain to you. You must be taught how to control your powers—'

'Don't you understand?' Faren hissed. 'She doesn't want to become a magician. She doesn't want anything to do with you. Just *leave her alone*.'

'I can't do that,' the magician shook his head. 'She must come with us—'

'No!' Faren shouted.

The magician's eyes turned cold, sending a chill through Sonea.

'Don't, Faren!' she called. 'He'll kill you.'

Ignoring her, Faren braced his legs and placed his hands on the walls on either side of the passage.

'If you want her,' he growled, 'you'll have to come through me.'

The magician hesitated, then took a step forward, his palms turning toward Faren. A metallic clang filled the passage.

The magician threw out his arms and vanished.

Baffled, Sonea stared at the floor where the magician had been standing. A dark square had appeared.

Dropping his arms, Faren threw back his head and began to laugh. Heart still pounding, Sonea crept forward until she stood beside him. Looking down, she saw that the square of darkness was a large hole in the floor.

'Wh-what happened?'

Faren's laughter subsided to a chuckle. He reached up and swivelled out a brick in the wall. Reaching into the gap beyond, he grasped something and, with a grunt of effort, pulled it forward. A trapdoor slowly swivelled up and clicked into place, covering the hole. Faren kicked some of the dust on the floor over it.

'That was far too easy,' he said, wiping his hands on a nosecloth. He grinned at Sonea, and sketched a quick bow. 'Did you like my performance?'

Sonea felt a smile starting to pull at her lips. 'I'm still awake, I guess.'

'Ha!' Faren's brows rose. '*You* seemed to think it was convincing. "Don't, Faren! He'll kill you!",' he said in a high-pitched voice. He placed a hand over his heart and smiled. 'I'm so touched at your concern for my safety.'

'Enjoy it,' she told him. 'It might not last.' She touched the trapdoor with her toe. 'Where does it go?'

He shrugged. 'Oh, straight down into a pit filled with iron spikes.'

Sonea stared at him. 'You mean . . . he's dead?'

'Very.' Faren's eyes flashed.

Sonea looked down at the trapdoor. Surely not . . . but if Faren said . . . though the magician might have managed to . . .

Suddenly she felt sick and cold. She had never considered that any of the magicians might be killed. Injured, perhaps, but not *killed*. What would the Guild do when they learned that one of their magicians was dead?

'Sonea.' Faren placed a hand on her shoulder. 'He's not dead. The trap leads to a sewage pool. It's meant as an escape route. He'll wade out of there smelling worse than the Tarali River, but he'll be alive.'

Sonea nodded, relieved.

'But consider what he would have done to *you*, Sonea.

One day *you* may have to kill for your freedom.' Faren lifted an eyebrow. 'Have you thought about that?'

Without waiting for an answer, he turned and regarded the barrier of light and heat that still blocked the passage. He shook his head and began to walk back down the passage toward the hideout. Sonea stepped nervously across the trapdoor and followed him.

'We can't go back,' he mused aloud as he walked, 'in case the other magicians have found another way in. We'll have to . . .' He moved closer to the wall to inspect it. 'Ah, here it is.' He touched something on the wall.

She gasped as the floor fell away from under her feet. Something hard slapped her backside, then she was sliding down a steep, smooth surface. The air began to warm rapidly and gain a distinctly unpleasant odour.

She was airborne suddenly, then plunging into wet darkness. Water filled her ears and nose, but she kept her mouth tightly closed. Kicking out, she discovered the floor and pushed herself up to the surface of the water. She opened her eyes in time to see Faren fly from a tunnel and splash into the pool. He thrashed around, pushing himself up to the water's surface with a curse.

'Argh!' he roared. He wiped his eyes and swore again. 'Wrong trapdoor!'

Sonea crossed her arms. 'So where *did* the magician end up?'

Faren looked up and an evil light filled his yellow eyes. 'The garbage chute of the bol brewhouse a few houses away,' he breathed. 'After he wades out of there he'll stink of fermented tugor mash for a week.'

Sonea snorted and began to wade to the edge of the pool. 'That's worse than this?'

He shrugged. 'Perhaps for a magician. From what I hear, they hate the stuff.' He followed her out of the pool then gave her a speculative look. 'I think I owe you a bath and a change of clothing, eh?'

'For nearly failing to protect me?' Sonea shrugged. 'It'll do, but you'll have to think of something better for dropping me in a sewer.'

He grinned. 'I'll see what I can do.'

CHAPTER 10

TAKING SIDES

Though the air was crisp with the gathering winter cold, and the sky was heavy with grey cloud, Rothen's mood lifted when he stepped outside. It was a Freeday. For most magicians, the fifth and last day of the week was a day of leisure. For novices, it was, in part, dedicated to study, and for teachers it allowed time to review and prepare lessons.

Rothen usually spent an hour walking in the gardens, then returned to his rooms to work on lessons. He had nothing to prepare this week, however. Officially designated as the organiser of the search, his duties as a teacher had been delegated to another magician.

He spent most of his time co-ordinating the volunteers. It was an exhausting task – for himself *and* the volunteers. They had spent the last three weeks, including Freedays, searching. Rothen knew that some would withdraw their help if the demands on their time continued, so he had decided to call the search off for a day.

As he turned a corner, the Guild's Arena came into sight. Eight spires curved up from the circular base, providing a framework for a powerful shield which protected everything outside from the forces thrown about during Warrior classes. Four novices stood within, but today no spectacular show of power was in progress.

Instead, the novices stood in pairs, swinging swords in controlled, synchronised movements. A few paces away stood Fergun, sword in hand, observing the novices closely.

Watching them, Rothen struggled not to disapprove. Surely the novices' time would be better spent on study than pursuing this redundant martial art?

Sword fighting was not part of the University's studies. Those novices who were determined to learn the art gave up their spare time to do so. It was a hobby, and Rothen knew it was healthy for the youngsters to have an interest that didn't involve magic and got them out of their stuffy rooms.

However, he had always believed that robes and swords did not go together well. There were already too many ways a magician could harm another person. Why add a non-magical one to the list?

Two magicians stood on the steps surrounding the Arena, watching intently. Rothen recognised Fergun's friend, Lord Kerrin, and Lord Elben, a teacher of Alchemy. Both were from the powerful House Maron, as was Fergun. He smiled to himself. Novices and magicians were expected to leave House alliances and enmities behind them when they joined the Guild, but few ever did.

As he watched, Fergun called one of the novices over to him. Teacher and novice saluted each other and dropped into a crouch. Rothen caught his breath as the novice advanced, sword flashing in a confident attack. Fergun stepped forward, his weapon all but vanishing in a blur of movement. The novice froze and looked down to find Fergun's weapon pressing against his chest.

'Tempted to join Lord Fergun's classes?' asked a familiar voice behind him.

Rothen turned. 'At my age, Administrator?' He shook his head. 'Even if I were thirty years younger, I wouldn't see the value in it.'

'It sharpens the reflexes, I'm told, and is useful in teaching discipline and concentration,' Lorlen said. 'Lord Fergun has some support for it now, and has asked us to consider including sword fighting in the University studies.'

'That would be for Lord Balkan to decide, wouldn't it?'

'Partly. The Head of Warriors must present the addition to the Higher Magicians for vote. When and if he does that is up to him.' Lorlen spread his hands. 'I heard you had decided to give the searchers a rest for the day.'

Rothen nodded. 'They've been working long hours, sometimes late into the night.'

'It has been a busy four weeks for you all,' Lorlen agreed. 'Are you making any progress?'

'Not much,' Rothen admitted. 'Not since last week. Every time we sense her, we find she has moved to another location.'

'As Dannyl predicted.'

'Yes, but we've been looking for repetitions in her movements. If she is returning to some of these hiding places, we might be able to locate them in the same way we did the first time, but over a longer period.'

'And what of this man that helped her escape? Do you think he was one of the Thieves?'

Rothen shrugged. 'Perhaps. He accused Lord Jolen of invading his territory, which suggests he was, but I find it hard to believe that one of the Thieves is a Lonmar. The man may simply be a protector and his accusation designed to lure Jolen over the trapdoor.'

'So there's a possibility she is not involved with the Thieves?'

'A possibility, yes, but it is unlikely. I doubt she has the money to pay for protectors. The men Jolen encountered in the tunnel, and the comfortable rooms she was staying in, suggest that someone well organised and funded is looking after her.'

'Either way, not good news.' Lorlen sighed and looked at the novices in the Arena. 'The King is not happy about this, and he won't be until we have her under our control.'

'Neither will I.'

Lorlen nodded. He pursed his lips, then regarded Rothen again. 'There is another matter I should discuss with you.'

'Yes?'

Lorlen hesitated, as if considering his words carefully. 'Lord Fergun wishes to claim guardianship of her.'

'Yes, I know.'

Lorlen's eyebrows rose. 'You are unexpectedly well informed, Lord Rothen.'

Rothen smiled. 'Unexpectedly, yes. I learned of this by accident.'

'Do you still intend to claim her guardianship yourself?'

'I haven't decided yet. Should I?'

Lorlen shook his head. 'I do not see the need to tackle that issue until she is found. But you understand that I must call a Hearing when she has been, if you both still intend to claim her?'

'I understand.' Rothen hesitated. 'May I ask a question of you?'

'Of course,' Lorlen replied.

'Does Fergun have a strong argument to support his claim?'

'Perhaps. He says that, since he experienced the consequences of the girl's magic, he was the first to know of her powers. You reported that you saw her *after* she used her powers, and that you guessed it was her from her expression, which means you never saw or sensed her use her powers. It is unclear how the law should be applied in this case, and when it comes down to bending a law to suit a situation, the simplest interpretation often wins the vote.'

Rothen frowned. 'I see.'

Gesturing for Rothen to follow, Lorlen began walking toward the Arena, his strides slow and measured. 'Fergun is determined,' he said quietly, 'and has much support, but many would support you, too.'

Rothen nodded, then sighed. 'It is not an easy decision. Would you prefer if I did not stir up the Guild by contesting his claim? It would cause you less trouble.'

'What would *I* prefer?' Lorlen chuckled and gave Rothen a direct look. 'It would cause me no less trouble either way.' He smiled crookedly, then inclined his head. 'Good day, Lord Rothen.'

'Good day,' Rothen replied. They had reached the edge of the stairs surrounding the Arena. The novices were paired now, practising moves on each other. Rothen stopped and watched, bemused, as Lorlen descended toward the pair of magicians watching the lesson. Something in the way Lorlen had looked at him hinted that the Administrator had been suggesting something more.

The two watchers started as Lorlen appeared beside them.

'Greetings, Lord Kerrin, Lord Elben.'

'Administrator.' The pair inclined their heads, then quickly looked at the Arena again as one of the novices gave a yell of surprise.

'A fine teacher,' Lord Elben said enthusiastically, gesturing to the Arena. 'We were just saying that Lord Fergun would make a worthy guardian for this slum girl. After a few months of his strict guidance, she'd be as refined and disciplined as the best of us.'

'Lord Fergun is a responsible man,' Lorlen replied. 'I can offer no good reason why he should not guide the training of a novice.'

Yet he hasn't shown any interest until now, Rothen thought. Turning away, he continued his stroll through the gardens.

Guardianship was not common. A few novices were favoured each year, but only those that had demonstrated exceptional talent or power. No matter what strength or aptitude the slum girl proved to have, she would need help and support as she adjusted to living in the Guild. By becoming her guardian he could ensure that she would receive that help.

He doubted Fergun's reasons for wanting her guardianship were the same. If Lord Elben's words were an indication, Fergun intended to discipline the unruly vagrant girl into a meek and obedient novice. He would receive a certain amount of praise and admiration if he succeeded.

How Fergun was going to achieve that would be interesting, since her powers were probably particularly strong and his were weak. He would not be able to stop her if she took it into her mind to disobey him.

For that reason, and others, magicians were discouraged from taking on the guardianship of novices with stronger powers. Weak magicians rarely became guardians at all since, if they claimed a novice with powers less than their own, it only drew attention to their own shortcomings – and the novice's lack of strength.

But the vagrant girl was different. Nobody would care if Fergun's limitations handicapped her learning. As far as most were concerned, she was lucky to have any training at all.

And if he failed, who would blame Fergun? He could always use her origins as an excuse . . . and if he neglected her training, nobody would question it . . .

Rothen shook his head. Now he was starting to think like Dannyl. Fergun was willing to help the girl, which was noble enough in itself. Unlike Rothen, who had been a guardian of two novices already, Fergun had a measure of glory to gain – and there was nothing wrong with that. Lorlen obviously didn't think there was.

Or did he? What *had* Lorlen said? *'It would cause me no less trouble either way.'*

Rothen chuckled as Lorlen's meaning finally came to him. If he was right, then Lorlen believed that letting Fergun win his claim would cause as much trouble as the fight over her guardianship – and that fight was sure to cause him no small amount of trouble.

Which meant that Lorlen had given Rothen a rare indication of his support.

As always, Sonea's guards were silent as they guided her through the passages. Apart from the weeks she had spent in the first hideout, she had been almost constantly on the move since the Purge. The welcome difference now was that she felt no lurking fear of discovery as she travelled.

The lead guard stopped at a door and knocked. A familiar, dark face appeared in the doorway.

'Stay and guard the door,' Faren ordered. 'Come in, Sonea.'

Stepping into the room, her heart leapt as she saw the smaller figure standing behind him.

'Cery!'

He grinned and gave her a quick hug. 'How are you?'

'Well,' she told him. 'You?'

'Happy to see you again.' He searched her face. 'You look better.'

'Haven't come face to face with a magician for, hmm, at least a *few* days,' she said, looking sidelong at Faren.

The Thief chuckled. 'We do seem to have outwitted them.'

The room was small, but cosy. A generous fire burned within one wall. Faren directed them to chairs. 'Any progress, Sonea?'

She winced. 'No, nothing yet. I try over and over, but it never does what I want it to.' She frowned. 'Though it nearly always does *something* now. Before it would take a few tries before anything happened.'

Faren leaned back and smiled. 'There, that *is* progress. Have the books helped?'

She shook her head. 'I don't understand them.'

'Is the scribe not clear?'

'No, it's not that. His reading is fine. It's just, well, there are too many strange words, and some things make no sense.'

Faren nodded. 'If you had more time to study them, perhaps you would find their meaning. I am still looking for more books.' Pursing his lips, he regarded them both speculatively. 'I'm looking into some rumours. It's been said for years that a certain Thief has cultivated a friendship with a man who knows something about magic. I've always thought it was an invention to ensure the rest of us stayed polite but I'm looking into it, regardless.'

'A magician?' Cery asked.

Faren shrugged. 'I don't know. I doubt it. Most likely he is nothing more than a man who performs tricks that appear to be magic. If he has any knowledge of real magic, however, he may be useful. I will tell you when I know more.' He smiled. 'That is all the news I have, but I believe Cery has more.'

Cery nodded. 'Harrin and Donia found your aunt and uncle.'

'They did!' Sonea moved to the edge of her seat. 'Where are they? Are they well? Did they find a good place to stay? Did Harrin—?'

Cery waved his hands. 'Hai! One question at a time!'

Grinning, Sonea leaned toward him eagerly. 'Sorry. Tell me what you know.'

'Well,' he began, 'it seems they didn't get a room where they used to live, but found a better one a few streets away. Ranel's been searching for you every day. They'd heard that the magicians were looking for a girl, but didn't think it could be you.'

He chuckled. 'Jonna said a few things when Harrin told her you'd joined them in the Purge, but then he said what you did. They didn't believe it at first. He told them how we tried to hide you, and about the reward, and that you were being protected by the Thieves. Harrin says they weren't as wild about it as he thought they'd be – not when he explained everything.'

'Did they give him any message for me?'

'They said to tell you to look after yourself, and be careful who you trust.'

'That last bit would be Jonna.' Sonea smiled wistfully. 'It's so good to hear they found a place – and they know I didn't just run off on them.'

'I think Harrin was scared that Jonna might flay him for inviting you to join us in the Purge. He says they're going to keep coming past the inn for news. Got any messages for them?'

'Just that I'm well and safe.' She looked at Faren. 'Will you bring them to see me?'

He frowned. 'Yes, but not until I'm sure it is safe. It's possible – though doubtful – that the magicians know who they are, and will find you through them.'

Sonea drew in a sharp breath. 'What if they do know who they are, and threaten to hurt them if I don't give myself up?'

The Thief smiled. 'I don't think they would. Certainly not publicly. If they tried to do so secretly . . .?' He nodded at Cery. 'We would find a way around it, Sonea. Don't worry about things like that.'

Cery smiled faintly. Surprised by the implied partnership, Sonea looked at her friend closely. His shoulders were tense, and a crease appeared between his brows whenever he looked at Faren. She would not have expected him to be relaxed in the presence of a Thief, but he looked a little too anxious.

She turned to regard the Thief.

'Can Cery and I have some time to talk?' she asked. 'Just us?'

'Of course.' He rose and moved to the door, then looked

back. 'Cery, I have something for you when you are done. Nothing urgent. Take your time. See you tomorrow, Sonea.'

'Tomorrow,' she replied, nodding.

When the door had closed behind the Thief, Sonea turned to Cery.

'Am I safe here?' she asked, her voice low.

'For now,' he said.

'And later?'

He shrugged. 'That depends on your magic.'

She felt a stab of alarm. 'What if I never work it out?'

He leaned forward and took her hand. 'You will. You just need to practice. If it was easy, there wouldn't be a Guild, would there? From what I've heard, it takes novices five years before they're good enough to be called "Lord" so-and-so.'

'Does Faren know this?'

He nodded. 'He'll give you time.'

'Then I'm safe.'

He smiled. 'Yes.'

Sonea sighed. 'What about you?'

'I'm making myself useful.'

She gave him a direct look. 'Making yourself Faren's slave?'

He looked away.

'You don't have to be here,' she told him. 'I'm safe. You said so. Go. Get away before they get their hooks in you.'

Shaking his head, he stood, letting go of her hand.

'No, Sonea. You need someone familiar around. Someone you can trust. I won't leave you alone with them.'

'But you can't become Faren's slave just so I have a friend to talk to. Go back to Harrin and Donia. I'm sure Faren will let you visit now and then.'

He paced to the door, then turned to face her.

'I want to do this, Sonea.' His eyes were bright. 'Everyone's been talking as if I worked for the Thieves as long as I can remember. Now I have a chance to make it real.'

Sonea stared at him. Was this really what he wanted? Would someone as nice as Cery choose to become . . . what? A ruthless, money-hoarding murderer? She looked away. That was Jonna's opinion of the Thieves. Cery had always said that the Thieves were about helping and protecting as much as they were involved in smuggling and thievery.

She couldn't – shouldn't – stop him from doing what he had always wanted to do. If the work turned out to be less than he'd hoped, he was smart enough to get out. She swallowed, her throat suddenly tight.

'If it's what you want,' she said. 'Just be careful.'

He shrugged. 'I always am.'

She smiled. 'It will be wonderful to have you dropping by all the time.'

He grinned. 'Nothing would keep me away.'

The brothel was in the darkest, dirtiest part of the slums. Like most, the lower floor was a bolhouse, and the upstairs rooms were for the prettier girls. All other commerce took place in stalls situated in the back of the building.

As Cery entered he thought of Faren's words. '*He knows most of the faces. He won't know you, though. Pretend you're new at it. Give him a good price for what he's got. Bring the goods back to me.*'

Several girls sidled up to him as he crossed the room. They looked pale and tired. A sickly fire which gave off little heat burned in a hearth to one side of the room. A server slouched behind the bar, talking to a pair of male customers. Cery smiled at the girls, looking each one over as if considering, then, as he had been instructed, he approached a plump Elyne girl with a tattoo of a feather on her shoulder.

'Want some fun?' she asked.

'Perhaps later,' he told her. 'I heard you got a room for meeting people.'

Her eyes widened, and she nodded quickly. 'Yes, that's right. Upstairs. Last on the right. I'll take you.'

She took his hand and led him to the stairs. There was a slight tremble in her light grasp. As he climbed the stairs he glanced down and found that many of the girls were watching him, their eyes fearful.

Disturbed, he looked around cautiously as he reached the top of the stairs and started down the corridor. The tattooed girl let go of his hand and waved toward the rooms at the end.

'It's the last door.'

He pressed a coin into her hand, and continued on. Opening the door cautiously, Cery peered inside. The room was tiny, containing only a small table and two chairs. Stepping inside, Cery inspected everything quickly. A few spy holes had been drilled into the walls. He suspected there was a hatch under the worn simba matting on the floor. A small window offered a view of a wall, and little else.

He opened the window and considered the wall outside. The brothel was unusually quiet for such an establishment. A door opened nearby, then footsteps moved down the corridor, drawing nearer. Returning to the table, Cery schooled his face into a wary expression. A man stepped into the doorway.

'You're the gutter?' the man asked in a gravelly voice.

Cery shrugged. 'What I do.'

The man's eyes darted all over. His face might have been handsome, if it were not so thin, or the light in the man's eyes not so wild and cold.

'Got something to sell,' the man said. His hands, which had been thrust deep into his pockets, emerged. One was empty, the other held a glittering necklace. Cery drew in a sharp breath, not having to fake his surprise. Such a piece could only have belonged to a rich man or woman – *if* it was real.

Cery reached out to take the necklace but the man snatched it away.

'I have to check it's not fake,' Cery pointed out.

The man frowned, his eyes hard with distrust. He pursed his lips, then reluctantly spread the necklace out on the table.

'Look,' he said. 'But don't touch.'

Cery sighed, then bent to examine the stones. He had no idea how to tell the difference between real or fake gems – something he would have to attend to – but he had seen pawnshop owners examining jewellery before.

'Turn it over,' he ordered.

The man flipped the necklace over. Looking close, Cery saw a name engraved on the setting. 'Hold it up so the light goes through the stones.'

Holding the necklace up by one hand, the man watched Cery squinting at it.

'What you think?'

'I'll take it for ten silver.'

The man dropped his hand. 'It's worth at least fifty gold!'

Cery snorted. 'Who's going to give you fifty gold in the slums?'

The man's mouth twitched.

'Twenty gold,' he said.

'Five,' Cery countered.

'Ten.'

Cery grimaced. 'Seven.'

'On the table.'

Reaching into his coat pocket, Cery counted coins with his fingertips, then drew out half of them. Producing more coins from the other places he had stowed Faren's money, he made six stacks of coins equal to one gold each, then sighed and drew a glinting gold coin from his boot.

'Put the jewels down,' Cery said.

The necklace dropped down onto the table beside the money. As the man reached for the coins Cery picked up the necklace and slipped it into his coat. The man looked down at the small fortune in his hands and grinned, his eyes bright with glee.

'A good deal, boy. You'll do well at this.' He backed out of the room, then turned and hurried away.

Cery moved to the door and watched the man stride to one of the other doors and step through. As he stepped in to the corridor he heard a girl squeak with surprise.

'We never be apart now,' the gravelly voice said.

As Cery passed the room he glanced inside. The tattooed girl sat on the end of a bed. She glanced up at Cery, her eyes wide with fear. The man stood behind her, looking down at the coins in his hands. Continuing on, Cery headed back down to the lower floor.

He affected a sullen, disappointed look as he descended into the bolhouse. Reading his expression, the girls let him be. The male customers eyed him, but did not call out or approach.

It was only slightly colder outside. Thinking of the lack of customers in the brothel, he felt a small stirring of pity for the whores as he crossed the street and stepped into the shadows of the alley.

'You look bored, little Ceryni.'

Cery span about. It took a disconcertingly long time before he found the dark-skinned man in the shadows. Even when he had located Faren, he was disturbed to find he could see only a pair of yellow eyes, and the occasional flash of teeth.

'Have you got what I sent you for?'

'Yes.' Cery drew out the necklace and held it out in Faren's general direction. He felt gloved fingers brush his, then the jewellery lifted from his hand.

'Ah, that is the one.' Faren sighed and looked back at the brothel. 'Tonight's work is not done, Cery. There is something else I want you to do.'

'Yes?'

'I want you to go back and kill him.'

Cery felt a chill rush through his belly, a sensation too much like what he imagined it would feel like to have a knife slicing through his insides. He could not think for a moment, then his mind began to work rapidly.

This was another test. Faren merely wanted to see how far he could push his new man.

What should he do? Cery had no idea what would happen if he refused. And he wanted to refuse. Badly. The realisation was both a relief and a worry to him. Not wanting to kill did not mean that he could not do it . . . yet when he considered walking across the street and sinking his knife into a man's vital organs, he could not make himself move.

'Why?' As he spoke, he knew he had failed one test already.

'Because I need him killed,' Faren replied.

'W-why do you want him killed?'

'Do you need me to justify it?'

Cery gathered his courage. *Let's see how far I can push this.*

'Yes.'

Faren made a small noise of amusement. 'Very well. The man you traded with is named Verran. He was employed by another Thief from time to time, but sometimes used what he learned from his work to gain a bit of money on the side. The Thief tolerated it until a few nights ago, when Verran chose to visit a particular house uninvited. The house belonged to a rich merchant who had an arrangement with the Thief. When Verran entered the house, it was occupied by the merchant's daughter and a few servants.' Faren paused, and Cery heard a hiss of anger. 'The Thief has given me the right to punish Verran. Even had she lived, he would be a dead man.'

The yellow eyes turned to regard Cery. 'Of course, you would have to wonder if I'm making this up. You have to make up your mind whether you trust me.'

Cery nodded, then looked across at the brothel. Whenever he needed to make a decision without being certain of the truth, he turned to his instincts. What did they tell him now?

He thought of the cold, wild look in the man's gaze, and the fear in the plump girl's eyes. Yes, that man was capable of evil deeds. Then he thought of the other whores;

the tension in the air; the lack of customers. The only two men in the establishment had been talking to the owner. Were they Verran's friends? Something else was going on there.

And Faren? Cery considered everything that he had learned of the man. He suspected that the Thief could be merciless if driven to it but in all else, Faren had been fair and honest. And there had been anger in his voice when he had spoken of Verran's crime.

'I've never killed anyone before,' Cery admitted.

'I know.'

'Don't know if I can.'

'You would if someone threatened Sonea. Am I right?'

'Yes, but this is different.'

'Is it?'

Cery narrowed his eyes at the Thief.

Faren sighed. 'No, I do not mean that. It is not how I work. I am testing you. You must know that. You don't have to kill that man. It matters more that you learn to trust me and that I know your limits.'

Cery's heart skipped a beat. He had expected tests. But Faren had given him so many different tasks that Cery had begun to wonder what the Thief was looking for. Did he have something in mind for him? Something different?

Perhaps this was a test Cery would face again, when he was older. If he was unable or reluctant to kill, he might endanger himself or others when the need was urgent. And if that other was Sonea . . .

Suddenly all hesitation and indecision was gone.

Faren looked across the street at the brothel and sighed. 'I really do want that man killed. I'd do it myself, except . . . Never mind. We'll find him again.' He turned and took a few steps further down the alley, then stopped as he realised that Cery hadn't followed.

'Cery?'

Reaching into his coat, Cery drew out his daggers. Faren's eyes flicked to the blades as they caught the faint light from the brothel windows. He took a step back.

Cery smiled. 'I'll be right back.'

CHAPTER 11

SAFE PASSAGE

After half an hour the stink of bol became almost pleasant. The aroma had a cosy warmth to it that promised comfort. Dannyl eyed the mug before him.

Remembering stories of unhygienic brewhouses and casks of bol with drowned ravi floating in them, he hadn't been able to persuade himself to try the syrupy brew. This evening, however, he had been bothered by darker suspicions. If the dwells *had* worked out what he was, what was to stop them from poisoning his drink?

His fears were probably unfounded. He had exchanged his robes for merchant garb again, taking care to look a little shabby. The other customers had given him one appraising glance, mostly directed at the wallet at his hip, then ignored him.

Despite this, Dannyl could not shake the feeling that every man and woman in the crowded room knew who and what he was. They were a sullen lot, bored and listless. Seeking shelter from the storm outside, they lurked in every corner of the room. Sometimes he heard them cursing the weather, other times they cursed the Guild. This had amused him at first. It seemed that the dwells felt it safer to blame the Guild than the King for their troubles.

One dwell, a man with a scarred face, kept staring at

him. Dannyl straightened and stretched his shoulders, then looked around the room. As he steeled himself to meet the starer's gaze, the man became more interested in the fit of his gloves. Dannyl noted the man's gold-brown skin colouring and broad face before turning back to his drink.

He had seen men and women of all races in the bolhouses he had visited. The short Elynes were most common, their homeland being Kyralia's closest neighbour. The brown-skinned Vindo were more numerous in the slums than in the rest of the city, as many of them travelled abroad looking for work. The athletic, tribal Lan and the dignified Lonmar were rarer.

This was the first Sachakan he had seen in years. Though Sachaka was a neighbour to Kyralia, a high mountain range and the desert wasteland beyond it discouraged travel between the two lands. Those few merchants that did try the route had reported stories of barbaric people fighting to survive in the wasteland, and a corrupt city with little to offer in trade.

It had not always been so. Many centuries before, Sachaka had been a great empire ruled by sophisticated magicians. A war lost against Kyralia and the newly formed Guild had changed that.

A hand touched Dannyl's shoulder. Turning, he found a swarthy man standing behind him. The man shook his head, then moved away.

Sighing, Dannyl rose and sidestepped through the crowd to the door. Once outside, he trudged through the puddles that filled most of the alleyway. Three weeks had passed since the Guild had tracked the girl to the underground hideout and Lord Jolen had been tricked by the

Lonmar. Since then, Gorin had declined Dannyl's request for an audience four times.

Administrator Lorlen was reluctant to accept that the Thieves were protecting the girl. Dannyl understood why. Nothing upset a King more than the presence of a rogue magician in his realm. The Thieves were tolerated. They kept the criminal underground in check, and they never presented a greater threat than the loss of taxes to smuggling. Even if the King managed to find and remove them, he knew others would take their place.

But the King would be willing to raze the slums to the ground – and lower – if he knew beyond a doubt that there was a rogue magician in the city.

Dannyl wondered if the Thieves realised this. He had not spoken of the possibility during his talks with Gorin, not wanting to appear unreasonable or threatening. Instead, he had warned the Thief of the danger the girl presented.

Reaching the end of the alley, he hurried across a wider street into the narrow space between two buildings. From there, the slums wove into a maze. The wind shivered down each narrow alley, whimpering like a hungry child. Occasionally it died away completely, and in one of these pauses Dannyl heard the sound of footsteps behind him. He turned around.

The alley was empty. Shrugging, he continued on.

Though he tried to ignore it, his imagination would not let go of the idea that he was being followed. In the pause between his own steps he would hear the crunch of another footfall or, looking back, he sometimes caught the flicker of movement around a corner. As the conviction became stronger, Dannyl grew exasperated with himself.

Turning a corner, he quickly manipulated the lock of a door and slipped into a building.

To his relief, the room inside was unoccupied. Peering through the door's keyhole, he snorted softly as he saw that the alley outside was still empty. Then a figure stepped into view.

He frowned as he recognised the scars on the man's broad face. The Sachakan's eyes flickered about, searching. Dannyl caught a glimmer and, looking down, he saw a vicious-looking knife in the man's gloved hand.

Dannyl chuckled quietly. *Fortunate for you that I heard you following*, he thought. He considered tackling the mugger and dragging him to the nearest Guard Hall, but decided against it. Night was approaching, and he was eager to get back to the warmth of his own rooms.

The Sachakan examined the ground, then doubled back. Dannyl counted to a hundred, then slipped through the door again and continued on his way. It seemed his fear that the dwells knew what he was had been unfounded. No dwell was foolish enough to attack a magician with a mere knife.

Sonea was bent over a large book when Cery entered the hideout. She looked up and smiled.

'How's the magic going?' he asked.

Her smile disappeared. 'The usual.'

'The book's not helping?'

She shook her head. 'It's been five weeks since I started practising, but the only thing I'm getting better at is reading. I can't read in exchange for Faren's protection.'

'You can't hurry what you're doing,' he told her. *Not when she could only practise once a day*, he added silently.

Since her near-capture, there had been a group of magicians patiently closing in on each of Faren's hideouts each time she used magic, forcing him to find new ones. Cery knew Faren was calling in favours from all around the slums. He also knew that the Thief believed Sonea was worth every coin and favour he spent.

'What do you think you need to get your magic to work?' he asked.

She rested her chin in one hand. 'I need someone to *show* me.' She lifted an eyebrow at Cery. 'Has Faren said anything about that person he was going to find out about?'

Cery shook his head. 'Nothing to me. I've overheard something but it didn't sound good.'

She sighed. 'I don't suppose *you* know of any friendly magician who's willing to reveal the Guild's secrets to the Thieves? Perhaps you could kidnap one of them for me.'

Cery laughed, then stopped as an idea began to form. 'Do you think—'

'Shh!' Sonea hissed. 'Listen!'

Cery leapt to his feet as he heard the faint tapping from the floor.

'The signal!'

Cery hurried to the street-side window and peered into the shadows below. Instead of the sentry, an unfamiliar figure paced in the shadows. He grabbed Sonea's cloak from the back of a chair and tossed it at her.

'Shove it down your shirt,' he told her. 'And follow me.'

He grabbed a bucket of water sitting beside her table and threw its contents on the few embers still lingering in the fireplace. The wood hissed and steam billowed up the chimney. Pulling the grate out, he ducked inside and began to climb the chimney, setting the toes of his boots into the cracks between the rough, hot bricks.

'You've got to be joking,' Sonea muttered from below.

'Come on,' he urged. 'We're going across the roofs.'

Muttering a curse, she began to climb.

As the sun emerged from behind storm clouds, the rooftops were bathed in golden light. Cery moved into the shadow of a chimney.

'It's too bright,' he said. 'We'll be seen for sure. I think we should stay here 'til it gets dark.'

Sonea settled beside him. 'Are we far enough away?'

He glanced back toward the hide. 'I hope so.'

She looked around. 'We're on the High Road, aren't we? Those rope and wood bridges – the handholds.' She smiled as Cery nodded. 'That brings back memories.'

He grinned at the wistful look in her eyes. 'It seems like such a long time ago.'

'It was. Most time I can't believe we actually did some of the things we did.' She shook her head. 'Wouldn't have the guts now.'

He shrugged. 'We were just kids.'

'Kids sneaking into houses and lifting things.' She smiled. 'Remember that time we got into that woman's room and she had all those wigs? You curled up on the floor and we put them all over you. When she came in you made groaning noises.'

Cery laughed. 'She sure could scream.'

Her eyes gleamed in the light of the setting sun. 'I got into so much rub when Jonna worked out I was sneaking out at night to join you.'

'Didn't stop you,' he reminded her.

'No. You'd taught me how to pick locks by then.'

He looked at her closely. 'Why *did* you stop coming out with us?'

She sighed and pulled her knees to her chest. 'Things changed. Harrin's lot started treating me differently. It was like they had remembered I was a girl, and thought I was hanging out with them for other stuff. It wasn't fun any more.'

'I didn't treat you different . . .' he hesitated, gathering his courage. 'But you stopped wanting to come out with me, too.'

She shook her head. 'It wasn't you, Cery. I think I got tired of it. I had to grow up and stop pretending. Jonna was always saying how honesty was valuable, and stealing was wrong. I didn't think that stealing when you had no choice was wrong, but that wasn't what we were doing. I was almost glad when I moved into the city, because it meant I didn't have to think about all that any more.'

Cery nodded. Perhaps it had been better that she had left. The boys in Harrin's gang hadn't always been nice to the young women they encountered.

'Was it better working in the city?'

'A little. You can still get in a lot of rub if you're not careful. The guards are the worst, cause no-one stops them hassling you.'

He frowned as he tried to imagine her fending off over-interested guards. Was there anywhere safe? Shaking his head, he wished that he could take her somewhere where no guards or magicians would bother them.

'We lost the book, didn't we?' Sonea said suddenly.

Remembering the tome lying on the table back at the hide, Cery cursed.

'Wasn't real useful, anyhow.'

There was no regret in her voice. Cery frowned. There had to be another way for her to learn magic. He bit his lip gently as the idea she had given him returned.

'I'd like to get you out of the slums,' he said. 'The magicians are going to be everywhere tonight.'

She frowned. 'Out of the slums?'

'Yes,' he replied. 'You'll be safer in the city.'

'The *city*? You sure?'

'Why not?' He smiled. 'It's the last place they'd look.'

She considered that and shrugged. 'But how will we get there?'

'The High Road.'

'But it won't get us past the gates.'

Cery grinned. 'We don't have to use 'em. Come on.'

The Outer Wall loomed high over the slums. Ten strides deep, it was well maintained by the city guard, though it had been many centuries since Imardin had faced the threat of invasion. A road ran around the outside, keeping the buildings of the slum at bay.

Not far from this road, Sonea and Cery descended from the rooftops into an alley. Taking her arm, Cery led her to stacks of boxes and slipped between them. The air smelled tangy inside, a mix of young wood and old fruit.

Cery squatted and tapped on the ground. To Sonea's surprise the sound was metallic and hollow. The ground shifted and a large disc hinged upwards. A wide face appeared, framed by a circle of darkness. From around the head drifted a nauseating stench.

'Hello, Tul,' Cery said.

The man's face wobbled into a grin.

'How ya' doin', Cery?'

Cery grinned. 'Fine. Wanta work off a debt?'

'Sure.' The man's eyes gleamed. 'Passage?'

'For two,' Cery said.

The man nodded and descended into the rank air. Cery smiled at Sonea and gestured to the hole.

'After you.'

She extended a foot into the hole and found the top rung of a ladder. Taking one last breath of clean air, she slowly descended into the murk. The sound of running water echoed in the darkness and the air was heavy with damp. As her eyes adjusted to the gloom, she saw that she was standing on a narrow ledge on the side of an underground sewage tunnel. The roof was so low she had to stoop.

The fat face of the man they had spoken to belonged to an equally wide body. Cery offered his thanks and handed the man something that brought a wide smile to his face.

Leaving Tul at his post, Cery led her down the passage in the direction of the city. After several hundred paces, another figure and a ladder came in sight. The man might once have been tall, but his back was hunched over as if it had grown to fit the curve of the tunnel. He looked up and watched them approach with large, heavy-lidded eyes.

The man turned abruptly to stare behind him. From further down the tunnel came a faint ringing noise.

'Quickly,' he rasped at them. Cery grabbed Sonea's arm and dragged her into a run.

Taking something from beneath his coat, the man began to strike it with an old spoon. The sound was deafening in the tunnel.

As they reached the ladder, he stopped and they heard

more ringing sounds behind them. He grunted then began flapping his arms.

'Up! Up!' he cried.

Cery clambered up. There was a metallic clunk, then a hole of light appeared. Cery scrambled though it and disappeared. As Sonea followed she heard a distant, low noise in the tunnel. The hunchback climbed out behind her and pulled the ladder up.

Sonea looked around. They stood in a narrow alleyway, hidden by the gathering darkness. Hearing the low noise again, she turned back to the tunnel. The sound grew rapidly louder, becoming a deep roar that was muffled suddenly as the hunchback carefully closed the lid of the tunnel. A moment later she felt a faint vibration under her feet. Cery leaned close so that his mouth brushed her ear.

'The Thieves have been using these tunnels for years to get past the Outer Wall,' he murmured. 'When the city guard found out, they started flushing the pipes. Not a bad idea, really – it keeps them clean. Of course, the Thieves figured out when they did it and business continued as usual. That's when the guard started flushing them randomly.'

He beckoned for her to crouch down beside the lid, then carefully lifted it. Water rushed by a few inches from her face and the roar spilled loudly into the street. Cery quickly closed the lid again.

'That's why they ring the bells,' she breathed.

Cery nodded. 'A warning.' He turned away and handed the hunchback something, then led her down the alley to a dark corner where raised bricks in a wall allowed them to climb to the roof of a house. The air was growing colder, so Sonea drew out her cloak and wrapped it about her shoulders.

'I hoped to get us a little closer than this,' Cery murmured, 'but . . .' He shrugged. 'Good view from up here, eh?'

She nodded. Though the sun had dropped below the horizon, the sky was still glowing. The last of the storm clouds hovered over the Southern Quarter, but were slowly retreating toward the East. The city spread before her, bathed in orange light.

'You can even see a bit of the King's Palace,' Cery pointed out.

Over the tall Inner Wall, the high towers of the Palace and the top of a glittering dome were visible.

'Never been there,' Cery breathed. 'But I will one day.'

Sonea laughed. 'You? In the King's Palace?'

'It's something I've promised myself,' he told her, 'that I'll get inside all the big places in the city at least once.'

'So where have you gone so far?'

He pointed to the gates of the Inner Circle. Through the entrance she could see walls and roofs of the mansions within, lit by the yellow glow of street lamps.

'Couple of the big houses.'

She snorted in disbelief. When running errands for Jonna and Ranel, she had occasionally needed to enter the Inner Circle. The streets were patrolled by guards who questioned anyone who was not richly dressed or clad in the servant's uniform of a House. Customers had given her a small token that indicated she had legitimate business in the area.

Each visit had revealed wonders. She remembered seeing extraordinary houses of fantastic colours and shapes, some with terraces and towers so thin and fine that they looked as if they should collapse under their own weight. Even the servants' quarters had been luxurious.

The plainer houses that surrounded her were more familiar. Merchants and lesser families lived in the North Quarter. They had few servants, and used the services of crafters for all else. Jonna and Ranel had gathered a small group of regular customers in the two years they had worked there.

Sonea looked down at the painted screens covering the windows around her. Through some she could see the shadows of people. She sighed as she thought of the customers her aunt and uncle had lost when the guards evicted them from the stayhouse. 'Where now?'

He smiled. 'Follow me.'

They continued on across the rooftops. Unlike the residents of the slums, those of the city did not always oblige the Thieves by leaving bridges or handholds in place. Cery and Sonea were often forced to descend to the ground when they reached an alley or street. The larger roads were patrolled by guards, so they had to wait for the men to march by before hurrying across.

After an hour they stopped for a rest, then continued on when a thin sliver of moonlight rose above the horizon. Sonea followed Cery in silence, concentrating on keeping her footing in the faint light. When he finally stopped again, a wave of weariness swept over her and she sat down with a groan.

'We better get there soon,' she said. 'I'm almost done.'

'Not far now,' Cery assured her. 'Just through here.'

She followed him over a wall into a large, neat garden. The trees were tall and symmetrical. He led her along in the shadows of a wall which seemed to go on forever.

'Where are we?'

'Wait and see,' Cery replied.

Something caught her foot and she stumbled against a tree. The roughness of the bark surprised her. She looked up and around. Endless trees stood like sentries before her. In the dark they looked strange and sinister, a forest of clawed arms.

A forest? She frowned, then a chill seized her. *There aren't any gardens in the North Quarter, and there is only one forest in Imardin . . .*

Her heart began to race. She hurried after Cery and grabbed his arm.

'Hai! What are you doing?!' she gasped. 'We're in the *Guild*!'

His teeth flashed. 'That's right.'

She stared at him. He was a black silhouette in the moonlit forest, and she could not see his expression. A frightening suspicion stole over her. Surely he hadn't . . . he wouldn't . . . Not Cery. No, he would *never* turn her over to the magicians.

She felt his hand on her shoulder. 'Don't worry, Sonea. Think about it. Where are the magicians? In the slums. You're actually safer here than there.'

'But . . . don't they have guards?'

'A few at the gates, that's all.'

'Patrols?'

'No.'

'What about a magical wall?'

'No.' He laughed quietly. 'Guess they think people are too scared of them to trespass.'

'How do you know if there's a wall or guards?'

He chuckled. 'Been here already.'

She drew in a sharp breath. '*Why?*'

'After I decided I would visit every place in the city, I came here and snooped around a bit. Couldn't believe how easy it was. I didn't try to get inside any of the buildings, of course, just watched the magicians through the windows.'

Sonea stared at his shadowed face in disbelief. 'You *spied* on the Guild?'

'Sure. It was real interesting. They've got places where they teach the new magicians, and places where they live. I saw the Healers working last time. *That* was something to see. There was this boy with cuts all over his face. When the healer touched him they all went away. Amazing.'

He paused and she saw his head turn toward her in the faint light. 'Remember how you said you wanted someone to show you how to use magic? Perhaps if you watch them, you'll see something that will help you learn.'

'But . . . the *Guild*, Cery.'

He shrugged. 'I wouldn't bring you here if I knew it was real dangerous, would I?'

Sonea shook her head. She felt awful for doubting him. If he had intended to turn her in, he would have let the magicians catch her back at the hide. But he would never betray her. Though his explanation *was* incredible.

If this is a trap, I'm already doomed.

She pushed the thought away and turned her mind to what Cery was proposing.

'You really think we can do this?'

'Sure.'

'It's madness, Cery.'

He laughed. 'At least come and look. We'll go as far as the road and you can see for yourself how easy it is. If you don't want to try it, we'll go back. Come on.'

Swallowing her fear, she followed him through the trees. The forest thinned a little, and through it she saw walls. Keeping to the shadows, Cery crept forward until he was less than twenty paces from a road, then darted forward and stood behind the trunk of a large tree.

Sonea hurried after and pressed her back against another tree. Her legs seemed to have lost most of their strength and she felt light-headed and dizzy. Cery grinned, then pointed through the trees.

She looked up at the building before her and gasped.

CHAPTER 12

THE LAST PLACE THEY'D LOOK

It was so tall, it seemed about to touch the stars.

At each corner was a tower. Between them, white walls glowed softly in the moonlight. At the front stone arches spanned the width of the building, one above the other, and from each arch hung a curtain of stone. A wide staircase led up to a pair of grand doors, which stood open.

'It's beautiful,' Sonea breathed.

Cery laughed softly. 'It is, isn't it? See those doors? They're about four times as tall as a man.'

'They must be very heavy. How do they close them?'

'With magic, I suppose.'

Sonea tensed as a figure in blue robes appeared in the doorway. The man paused, then strode down the stairs and walked away toward a smaller building to the right.

'Don't worry. They can't see us,' Cery assured her.

Sonea let out the breath she was holding and dragged her eyes away from the distant figure. 'What's inside?'

'Classrooms. That's the University.'

Three rows of windows ran down the side of the building. The bottom two rows were mostly obscured by a line of trees but she could see warm yellow light through gaps in the foliage. A large garden was on the left of the building. Cery pointed to a building on the far side of this.

'That's where the novices live,' he said. 'There's another building just like it on the other side of the University where the magicians live. Over there,' he pointed to a circular building several hundred paces to their left, 'is the place where the Healers do their work.'

'What's that?' Sonea asked, pointing to a collection of curved masts rising up from somewhere within the garden.

Cery shrugged. 'I don't know,' he admitted. 'Never found out.'

He gestured to the road in front of them. 'This goes to the servants' houses down there,' he pointed to the left, 'and the stables that way,' he pointed to the right. 'There are a few other buildings behind the University, and another garden in front of the magicians' building. Oh, and there are more houses for magicians up the hill a bit.'

'So many buildings,' she breathed. 'How many magicians *are* there?'

'Over a hundred living here,' he told her. 'There's more that don't. Some live in the city, some out in the country, and lots more in other countries. About two hundred servants live here too. They've got maids, stablemen, cooks, scribes, gardeners, even farmers.'

'Farmers?'

'They have fields down near the servants' houses.'

Sonea frowned. 'Why wouldn't they just buy their food?'

'I've heard they grow all sorts of plants to make medicines from.'

'Oh.' Sonea looked at Cery, impressed. 'How did you find out so much about the Guild?'

He grinned. 'I asked a lot of questions, especially after I went looking around last time.'

'Why?'

'I was curious.'

'Curious?' Sonea snorted. 'Just *curious?*'

'Everybody wonders what they do in there. Don't *you?*'

Sonea hesitated. 'Well . . . sometimes.'

'Of course you do. You've got more reason than most. So, do you want to spy on a few magicians?'

Sonea looked up at the buildings. 'How are we going to look inside without them seeing us?'

'The garden goes right up to the walls of the buildings,' Cery told her. 'There are paths going back and forth, and beside them are trees with hedges on either side. You can walk between the hedges and nobody can see you.'

Sonea shook her head. 'Only you would do something this crazy.'

He smiled. 'But you know I don't take stupid risks.'

She bit her lip, still ashamed that she had suspected him of betraying her. He had always been the cleverest of Harrin's gang. If it was possible to spy on the Guild, he would know how to do it.

She knew she should tell him to take her back to Faren. If someone discovered them . . . It was too frightening to think about. Cery was watching her expectantly. *It would be a shame not to try*, a voice in the back of her mind whispered, *and I might see something helpful*.

'All right.' She sighed. 'Where first?'

Cery grinned and pointed toward the Healers' building. 'We'll get into the gardens down there, where the road's dark. Follow me.'

He scampered back into the forest and wove his way through the trees. After a few hundred paces, he moved back toward the road and stopped beside a tree.

'The magicians are busy training right now,' he

murmured. 'Or they've gone to their rooms. We've got until the night classes finish, then we'll dig down and hide. For now, we just have to watch out for servants. Stuff your cloak in your shirt. It'll only get in the way.'

She obeyed. Cery took her hand and started toward the road. Sonea looked up at the windows of the University dubiously.

'What if they look out? They'll see us.'

'Don't worry,' he told her. 'Their rooms are full of light, so they can't see anything outside unless they go right up to the windows and they're too busy doing what they do to look outside.'

Taking her arm, he pulled her across the road. She held her breath and searched the windows above them for watchers, but no human shapes appeared in them. As they entered the shadows of the garden, she breathed a sigh of relief.

Dropping to his belly, Cery wriggled through the base of a hedge. Following him, Sonea found herself crouching under a dense net of foliage.

'It's grown a bit since I was here last,' Cery murmured. 'We'll have to crawl.'

Moving forward on their hands and knees, he led her through a tight tunnel of vegetation. Every twenty paces or so they had to squeeze past the trunk of a tree. After crawling for several hundred paces, he stopped.

'We're in front of the Healer's building,' he told her. 'We cross a path, then go into the trees against the wall. I'll go first. Check to make sure the path is clear, then follow.'

Dropping to his belly again, he pushed his way out of the hedge and disappeared. Moving to the hole he had made, Sonea peered out. A path ran along the hedge. She could see the gap where Cery had pushed into the hedge on the other side.

Crawling out, she hurried across and pushed her way into the foliage. She found Cery sitting in the space behind, resting his back against the trunk of a large tree, facing a wall.

'You think you could climb this?' Cery asked quietly, patting the wall. 'You'll have to go to the second floor. That's where they have their lessons.'

Sonea examined the wall. It was made of large stone bricks. The mortar between was old and crumbling. Two ledges ran around the building, forming the base of the windows. Once she had reached a window she would be able to rest on the ledge while she looked inside.

'Easy,' she whispered.

His eyes narrowed, then he began searching his pockets. Bringing out a small jar, he opened it and began smearing dark paste on her face.

'There. Now you look like Faren.' He grinned, then grew serious again. 'Stay behind the trees. If I see someone coming, I'll hoot like a mullook. You stay put and keep real still and quiet.'

Nodding, she turned to the wall and carefully set her toes into a crack. Digging her fingers into the crumbling mortar, she sought the next foothold. Soon she was clinging to the wall, her feet level with Cery's head. She looked down at him and saw his teeth flash as he grinned.

Her muscles protested as she hauled herself up but she did not stop until she had reached the second ledge. Pausing to catch her breath, she turned her head toward the nearest window.

It was the size of a doorway and filled with four large panes of glass. She cautiously slid along the ledge until she could see into the room beyond.

A large group of brown-robed magicians sat inside, all gazing intently at something in a far corner of the room. She hesitated, fearing that one would look up and see her, but none glanced her way. Heart racing, she edged forward until she could see what they were staring at.

A man with dark green robes stood at the far corner. He held in his hands a carving of an arm with coloured lines and words scrawled over it. The magician was using a short stick of wood to point at the different words.

Sonea felt a thrill of excitement. The magician's voice was a little muffled by the glass, but she could make out his words if she listened carefully.

As she did, a familiar frustration grew. Strange words and phrases made up much of the magician's lecture. It made as much sense to her as another language. She was about to give in to the ache in her fingers and return to Cery when the speaker turned and called out loudly: 'Bring Jenia in.'

The novices turned toward the open door. A young woman entered the room, accompanied by an old servant. Her arm was bandaged and hung from a sling tied behind her neck.

The woman smiled boldly and laughed at something one of the novices said. With a stern look from the teacher, the class quietened.

'Jenia broke her arm this afternoon when she fell off her horse,' he told them. He gestured for the young woman to take a chair. As he began to unwrap her bandages the smile fled from her face.

A bruised and swollen forearm was uncovered. The teacher picked two novices from the class. The pair ran their hands gently over the bruised arm, stepped back and gave their assessment. The teacher nodded, pleased.

'Now,' his voice rose to include the class, 'first we must stop the pain.'

At a signal from the teacher, one of the novices took the woman's hand. He closed his eyes and the room was silent for a moment. A look of relief passed over the woman's face. The novice released her and nodded at the teacher.

'It is always better to let the body heal itself,' the magician continued, 'but we can mend it to the point where the bones join and the swelling is relieved.'

The other novice slowly ran his palm along the woman's arm. The bruises faded under his touch. When the youth drew away, the young woman smiled and tentatively wriggled her fingers.

The teacher examined her arm, then replaced the sling, which the woman regarded with obvious disdain. He instructed her sternly not to use her arm for two weeks. One of the novices said something and the rest laughed.

Sonea drew away from the window. She had just seen the magicians' legendary healing powers at work, something that few dwells ever witnessed. It was as amazing as she had imagined.

But she had learned nothing of how they had done it.

This must be a class for skilled novices, she reasoned. New novices would not know how to treat an injury like that. If she found a class for new novices, she might be able to understand it.

She climbed down. As her feet touched the ground Cery grabbed her arm.

'Did you see any healing?' he whispered.

She nodded.

Cery grinned. 'Told you this was easy, didn't I.'

'For you, maybe,' she said, rubbing her hands. 'I'm out of practice.' Moving to the next tree, she forced her tired fingers between the bricks, and hauled herself up again.

The teacher in the next classroom was a woman, and she was also wearing green robes. She was silent, watching her novices as they bent over their desks, frantically writing on sheets of paper and leafing through well-worn leather books. Sonea gave in to the ache in her arms and returned to the ground.

'Well?' Cery asked.

She shook her head. 'Nothing much.'

The next window revealed a class of novices mixing liquids, dried powders and pastes in small jars. The window after contained a single young man in green robes, his head resting on the open pages of his book as he dozed.

'The rest of the rooms don't have lights,' Cery told her when she reached the ground again. 'I guess that's all you'll see here.' He turned to point at the University. 'There are more classes to watch over there.'

She nodded. 'Let's go.'

Squeezing out of the hedge, they dashed across the path and pushed into the foliage on the other side. Halfway across the garden, Cery stopped and pointed to a gap in the hedge.

Looking out between the leaves, Sonea saw they had reached the strange masts she had seen rising above the gardens. They curved inward, as if bowing to each other, and tapered to a point at the top. They were spaced evenly around a large circular slab of stone which had been set into the ground.

Sonea shivered. A vaguely familiar vibration tainted the air. Disturbed, she put a hand on Cery's back.

'Let's move on.'

Cery nodded and, glancing one more time at the tall masts, led her away.

They crossed two more paths before reaching the wall of the University. Cery placed a hand on the stone.

'You won't be able to climb this one,' he whispered. 'But there's plenty of windows at the ground level.'

Sonea touched the wall. The stone was covered with rivulets and ripples running up and down the surface. She could not see any cracks or seams. It was as if the entire building had been made from one huge block of stone.

Moving behind a tree, Cery linked his fingers together. She rose and placed a foot in his hands. Stepping up, she peered over the window ledge and into the room beyond.

A man in purple robes was writing with sticks of charcoal on a board. The sound of his voice drifted to her ears, but she could not make out what he said. The drawings on the board were as incomprehensible as the speech of the Healer. With a pang of disappointment and frustration she signalled for Cery to let her down.

They crept along the building to the next window. The scene inside was as mysterious as the first. Novices sat rigidly in their seats with their eyes closed. Behind each seated novice stood another who pressed his palms against his fellow's temples. The teacher, a stern looking man in red robes, watched them in silence.

Sonea was about to move away when he spoke suddenly.

'Come away now.' His tone was unexpectedly soothing for a man with such a hard visage. The novices opened their eyes. Those who had been standing rubbed their own temples and grimaced.

'As you can see, it is impossible to see into somebody else's mind without their good will,' the teacher told them. 'Well not *impossible*, as our own High Lord has proven, but far out of the reach of ordinary magicians such as you and I.'

His eyes flicked towards the window. Sonea quickly ducked out of view. Cery let her down, and she crouched under the window ledge, pressing her back against the wall and gestured to Cery to do the same.

'Were you seen?' Cery whispered.

Sonea pressed a hand to her heart, which was pounding rapidly. 'I'm not sure.' Was the magician hurrying through the University now, intending to investigate the gardens? Or was he standing at the window, waiting for them to step out from under the ledge?

She swallowed, her mouth dry. She turned to Cery, ready to suggest they run for the forest, then stopped. Behind her, in the room, the muffled sound of the teacher's voice had begun again. She closed her eyes and sighed with relief.

Cery leaned forward and cautiously peered up at the window. He looked at her and shrugged.

'Keep going?'

She drew in a deep breath and nodded. Rising, they moved down the building and stopped under the next window. Linking his hands together, Cery lifted Sonea up.

Flashes of movement met her eyes as she peered through the window. She stared at the scene in amazement. Several novices were dodging and ducking about, doing their best to avoid a tiny point of light that flew around the room. Standing on a chair in one corner, a red-robed magician followed the progress of the speck with an outstretched hand. He roared at the novices: 'Hold still! Stand your ground!'

Four of the novices were already standing still. When the bright speck came close to them it was propelled away like a swatted fly. Gradually more of the novices followed the others' example, but the spark was quick. A few of the less skilled youths bore tiny red marks on their arms and faces.

Suddenly the spark vanished. The teacher leapt off the chair and landed lightly. The novices relaxed and grinned at each other. Afraid that they would glance her way, Sonea dropped to the ground.

At the next window she watched a purple-robed magician demonstrating to his class a strange experiment with coloured liquids. In another she watched a group of novices working with floating globules of molten glass, shaping the glowing masses into intricate, glowing sculptures. Then in the next, she listened to a gentle-looking man dressed in red robes giving a speech on making fire.

A deep chime suddenly echoed through the Guild. The magician looked up in surprise and the novices began to rise from their seats. Sonea ducked away from the window.

Cery lowered her to the ground. 'That bell marks the end of classes,' he told her. 'We'll stay quiet now. The magicians will leave the University and go to their rooms.'

They huddled close to the trunk of a tree. For several minutes all was quiet, then Sonea heard the sound of footsteps beyond the hedge.

'. . . a long day,' a woman was saying. 'We're stretched very thin with this winter cough taking hold. I hope the search ends soon.'

'Yes,' a second woman agreed. 'But the Administrator has been reasonable. He has given most of the work to the Warriors and Alchemists.'

'True,' the first woman replied. 'Now tell me, how is Lord Makin's wife? She must be over eight months now . . .'

The women's voices faded away and were replaced by boyish laughter.

'. . . had you fooled. He practically thrashed you, Kamo!'

'It was just a trick, merely,' a boy with a thick Vin accent replied. 'It will not work a second time.'

'Ha!' a third boy retorted. 'This *is* the second time!'

The boys burst into laughter but Sonea could hear another set of footsteps approaching from her left. The boys fell silent.

'Lord Sarrin,' they murmured respectfully as the footsteps reached them. When the steps had moved well past them, the boys' voices rose again as they continued teasing each other. They moved out of her hearing.

Several more groups of magicians passed. Most were silent. Gradually, the activity around the Guild dwindled and then ceased. By the time Cery pushed his head through the hedge to check the path, they had been hidden for almost an hour.

'We'll head back to the forest now,' he told her. 'There won't be any more classes for you to see.'

She followed as he pushed his way out onto the path and into the next hedge. They travelled through the garden and scampered back across the road into the forest. Crouching under a tree Cery grinned at her, his eyes glittering with excitement.

'That was easy, wasn't it?'

Sonea looked back at the Guild and felt a smile spread over her face.

'Yes!'

'See. Just think: while the magicians are hunting around out in the slums we've been snooping around *their* territory.'

They chuckled quietly, then Sonea drew in a deep breath and sighed.

'I'm glad we're done,' she admitted. 'Can we go back now?'

Cery pursed his lips. 'There's something else I wanted to try, since we're here.'

Sonea eyed him suspiciously. 'What?'

Ignoring her question, he rose and moved away through the trees. She hesitated, then hurried after him. As they travelled further into the forest, it grew darker and Sonea stumbled several times on hidden roots and branches. Cery turned to the right and, feeling a different surface under her feet, she realised they were crossing the road again.

From there, the ground began to slope upwards. After several hundred paces they crossed a narrow path and the slope grew steeper. Cery stopped and pointed.

'Look.'

A long, two-storey building was visible through the trunks.

'The novices' building,' Cery told her. 'We're behind it. Look, you can see inside.'

Through one of the windows she could see part of a room. A plain, sturdy bed stood against one wall, and a narrow table and chair along another. Two brown robes hung from hooks on the wall.

'Not very fancy.'

Cery nodded. 'They're all like that.'

'But they're rich, aren't they?'

'I guess they don't get to choose their own stuff until they become full magicians.'

'What are the magicians' rooms like?'

'Fancy.' His eyes gleamed. 'Want to see?'

Sonea nodded.

'Come on then.'

He moved deeper into the trees and up the slope. When they drew close to the edge of the forest again Sonea saw that several buildings and a wide paved courtyard lay behind the University. One of the structures curved down the slope like a long stairway, glittering softly as if it were made entirely out of molten glass. Another looked like a huge upturned bowl, smooth and white. The whole area was illuminated by two rows of large, round lamps, set high on iron poles.

'What are all these buildings for?' Sonea asked.

Cery stopped. 'I'm not sure. I think that glass one is the baths. The others . . .?' He shrugged. 'I could find out.'

He moved on through into the forest. When they came in sight of the Guild again, they had passed the courtyard and were standing closer to the magicians' building. Cery crossed his arms and frowned.

'They've all got screens over their windows,' he said. 'Hmm, perhaps if we go around the side we'll see something.'

By the time they returned to the edge of the trees, Sonea's legs were aching. Though the forest grew closer to the building at the side, she could only see a glimpse of furniture through the open window Cery pointed out. Suddenly more tired than curious, she dropped to the ground.

'I don't know how I'm going to make it back to the slums,' she moaned. 'My legs won't take me another step.'

Cery grinned and squatted beside her. 'You've sure got soft these last few years.'

She gave him a withering look. He chuckled and looked down at the Guild.

'Sit down and rest for a while,' he told her, rising to his feet. 'There's something I want to do. I'll be quick.'

Sonea frowned. 'Where are you going?'

'Closer. Don't worry. I'll be back soon.' He turned and disappeared into the shadows.

Too tired to be annoyed, she stared at the forest. Between the trunks she could see something flat and grey. She blinked in surprise as she realised she was sitting no more than forty paces from a small, two-storey building.

Rising, she moved closer to the structure, wondering why Cery hadn't pointed this building out to her. Perhaps he hadn't noticed it. Made of a different, darker stone than the other Guild buildings, it was all but invisible in the shadows of the trees.

Like the University, a hedge ran around the outside. A few steps further and Sonea felt the hard stone of a path beneath her feet. Dark windows invited her closer.

Glancing back, she wondered how long Cery would be. If she didn't dally too long, she could take a look through the building's windows and be back before he returned.

Creeping down the path, she moved behind the hedge and peered through the first window. The room inside was dark and she could see little. Some furniture, nothing more. She moved to the next, and the next, but the view was the same. Disappointed, she turned to go, then froze as she heard footsteps behind her.

Ducking down behind the hedge, she watched a figure step around the side of the building. Though she could make out little more than a silhouette, she could see that the man was not wearing robes. A servant?

The man moved to the side of the house and opened a door. Hearing the latch close behind him Sonea breathed a sigh of relief. She braced her hands to haul herself off the ground, then paused as she heard a tinkling somewhere close by.

Looking around, she saw a small grille set into the wall just above the ground. Dropping to her hands and knees, she bent down to examine it. The tiny air vent was cluttered with dirt, but through it she could see a stairway spiralling down to an open door.

Beyond the doorway was a room lit by the yellow glow of an unseen light. As she watched, a man with long hair and a heavy black cloak strode in sight. A pair of shoulders blocked her view for a moment as another figure entered the stairway and descended to the room. Sonea caught a glimpse of servant's clothing before the newcomer moved beyond her vision.

She heard a voice, but could not make out the words. The cloaked man nodded.

'It's done,' he said, plucking at the clasp and pulling the cloak from his shoulders.

Sonea's breath caught in her throat as she saw what was underneath. The man was wearing the ragged garments of a beggar.

And they were splattered with blood.

The man looked down at himself and an expression of distaste crossed his face.

'Did you bring my robes?'

The servant murmured an answer. Sonea choked back a gasp of surprise and horror. The man was a magician.

He grasped the bloodstained shirt and pulled it over his head, revealing a leather belt strapped to his waist. A large dagger sheath hung from the belt.

Removing the belt, he tossed it and the shirt onto a table, then pulled a large bowl of water and a towel into sight. The magician dipped the towel into the water and quickly scrubbed the red stains from his bare chest. Each time he rinsed the towel, the water turned a darker shade of pink.

Then an arm came into view, holding a bundle of black material. The magician took the cloth and moved out of sight.

Sonea sat back on her haunches. Black robes? She had never seen a black-robed magician before. None of the magicians in the Purge had worn black. His position in the Guild must be unique. Bending down again, she considered the blood-stained clothes. Perhaps he was an assassin.

The magician moved into view again. He was wearing the black robes now and had combed and bound his dark hair into a tail. Reaching for the belt, he unclipped the lid of the dagger pouch.

Sonea drew in a quick breath. The dagger's handle glittered in the light. Gems set within it sent out glints of red and green. The magician examined the long, curved blade closely, then carefully wiped it on the towel. He looked up at the hidden servant.

'The fight has weakened me,' he said. 'I need your strength.'

She heard a murmured reply. The servant's legs moved into view, then all but his head appeared as he dropped to one knee and held out his arm. The magician grasped the man's wrist.

Turning it upward, the magician ran the dagger lightly across the man's skin. Blood welled and the magician pressed his hand over the wound as if he intended to heal it.

Then something began to flutter in her ears. Straightening, Sonea shook her head, thinking that an insect had crawled into her ears, but the buzzing continued. She stopped, then felt a chill steal over her as she realised that the noise was coming from somewhere *inside* her head.

The sensation stopped as suddenly as it had begun. Bending to the grille, Sonea saw that the magician had released the servant. He was turning slowly about, his eyes roaming around the walls as if searching for something.

'Strange,' he said. 'It's almost as if . . .'

He's not searching for something on the walls, Sonea thought suddenly. *He's searching for something* beyond *them*.

Fear rushed over her. Rising to her feet, she slipped out of the hedge and backed away from the house.

Don't run, she told herself. *Don't make any noise*. Resisting the urge to bolt for the trees, she forced herself to creep away carefully. She increased her pace as she reached the path, wincing every time a twig snapped under her feet. The forest seemed darker than before, and she felt a rising panic as she realised she was not sure where she had been sitting when Cery had left her.

'Sonea?'

She jumped as a figure stepped out of the shadows. Recognising Cery's face, she gasped with relief. In his arms was something large and heavy.

'Look,' he said, lifting his burden.

'What is it?'

He grinned. 'Books!'

'Books?'

'Books on magic.' His grin faded. 'Where have you *been*? I just got back and—'

'I was there.' She pointed at the house and shivered. It seemed darker now, like a creature lurking at the edge of the gardens. 'We have to go! Now!'

'*That* place!' Cery exclaimed. 'That's where their leader lives – the High Lord.'

She grabbed his arm. 'I think one of his magicians heard me!'

Cery's eyes widened. He glanced over her shoulder, then turned and started through the forest, away from the shadowy building.

CHAPTER 13

A POWERFUL INFLUENCE

Only twenty or so magicians had gathered in the Night Room when Rothen entered. Finding that Dannyl had not yet arrived, he started toward a set of chairs.

'The window was open. Whoever it was came though the window.'

Hearing the distress in the voice, Rothen paused and looked for the speaker. He found Jerrik standing nearby, talking to Yaldin. Curious to know what could have upset the University Director, he walked over to the two men.

'Greetings.' Rothen nodded politely. 'You look displeased about something, Director.'

'There's a resourceful thief among our novices,' Yaldin explained. 'Jerrik has lost a few valuable books.'

'A thief?' Rothen repeated, surprised. 'Which books?'

'*The Lore of the Southern Magicians, Arts of the Minken Archipelago* and the *Handbook of Firemaking*,' Jerrik said.

Rothen frowned. 'A strange combination of books.'

'Expensive books,' Jerrik grieved. 'Twenty gold pieces it cost me to have those copies made.'

Rothen whistled softly. 'Then your thief has an eye for value.' He frowned. 'Books of that rarity would be hard to hide. They are large volumes, I seem to remember. You could authorise a search of the Novices' Quarters.'

Jerrik grimaced. 'I was hoping to avoid that.'

'Perhaps somebody borrowed them,' Yaldin suggested.

'I've asked everyone.' Jerrik sighed and shook his head. 'Nobody has seen them.'

'You didn't ask me,' Rothen pointed out.

Jerrik looked up sharply.

'No, I didn't take them.' Rothen laughed. 'But you may have missed others as well. Perhaps you could ask everyone at the next Meet. It's only two days away, and the books might surface before then.'

Jerrik winced. 'I suppose I better do that first.'

Catching sight of a familiar, tall figure entering the Night Room, Rothen excused himself. He strode to Dannyl's side and drew the magician into a quiet corner of the room.

'Any luck?' he asked quietly.

Dannyl shrugged. 'No, no luck, but at least I wasn't followed by knife-wielding foreigners this time. You?'

Rothen opened his mouth to reply but closed it again as a servant stopped to offer a tray of wine-filled glasses. He reached out to take one, then froze as a black-sleeved arm extended toward the tray from behind Dannyl. Akkarin selected a glass and stepped around Dannyl to face Rothen.

'How does the search progress, Lord Rothen?'

Dannyl's eyes widened as he turned to face the High Lord.

'We came closest to catching her two weeks ago, High Lord,' Rothen replied. 'Her protectors used a decoy. By the time we realised we had the wrong girl, she had escaped. We found a book on magic, as well.'

The High Lord's expression darkened. 'That is not good news.'

'It was old and outdated,' Dannyl added.

'Nevertheless, we cannot allow such books outside the Guild,' Akkarin replied. 'A search of pawn shops should reveal if many have made their way into the city. I will speak to Lorlen about it, but in the meantime . . .' he looked at Dannyl. 'Have you had any success re-establishing contact with the Thieves?'

Dannyl's face turned white, then flushed red.

'No,' he replied in a constricted voice. 'They have declined my requests for audience for many weeks.'

A half-smile curled Akkarin's mouth. 'I assume you attempted to impress on them the dangers of having an untrained magician in their midst?'

Dannyl nodded. 'Yes, but they did not seem concerned.'

'They will be soon. Continue your attempts to meet with them. If they refuse to see you personally, send messages. Detail the problems she will encounter as her magic becomes uncontrollable. It will not be long before they realise that you speak the truth. Keep me informed on your progress.'

Dannyl swallowed. 'Yes, High Lord.'

Akkarin nodded to them both. 'Have a good evening.' He turned and walked away, leaving the two magicians staring at his retreating back. Dannyl let out an explosive breath.

'How did he know?' he whispered.

Rothen shrugged. 'It is said that he knows more about the affairs of the city than the King himself, but then, perhaps Yaldin told someone.'

Dannyl frowned and looked across the room at the aging magician. 'That's not like Yaldin.'

'No,' Rothen agreed. He smiled and patted Dannyl on

the shoulder, 'It doesn't look like you got yourself into any trouble, however. In fact, it looks like you just received a personal request from the High Lord.'

Sonea curled the edge of the page and sighed. Why couldn't these Guild writers use normal, *sensible* words! This one seemed to have enjoyed arranging his sentences in ways that bore no resemblance to normal speech. Even Serin, the middle-aged scribe who was teaching her to read, could offer little explanation for many of the terms and phrases.

Rubbing her eyes, she leaned back in her chair. She had been staying in Serin's basement for several days. It was a surprisingly comfortable room, with an ample fireplace and sturdy furniture, and she knew she would be disappointed when she had to leave it.

After her near capture, the night Cery had taken her to the Guild, Faren had taken her to Serin's home in the North Quarter. He had decided she should stop practicing magic until he could arrange for new, better situated hiding places. In the meantime, he said, she would spend her time studying the books Cery had 'found'.

She looked down at the page again and sighed. A word lay before her – an alien, strange, annoying word which refused to make any sense. She stared at it, knowing the meaning of the whole sentence revolved around this infuriating word. She rubbed her eyes again, then jumped at a rapping on the door.

Rising, she peered through the spy hole, smiled and unlocked the door.

'Good evening,' Faren said as he slipped into the room. He handed her a bottle. 'I brought you a little token of encouragement.'

Sonea uncorked the bottle and sniffed. 'Pachi wine!' she exclaimed.

'That's right.'

Moving to a cupboard, Sonea took out two mugs. 'I don't think these are right for Pachi wine,' she said. 'But that's all I have – unless you want to ask Serin for something better.'

'They'll do.' Faren drew a chair up to the table and sat down. Accepting a mug of the clear green liquor, he took a sip, sighed contentedly and leaned back in his chair. 'Of course, it's better spiced and warmed.'

'I wouldn't know,' Sonea said. 'I've never tasted it before.' Taking a sip, she smiled as a sweet, fresh flavour filled her mouth. Faren chuckled at her expression.

'I thought you'd like it.' He stretched and leaned back in the chair. 'I've also got news for you. Your aunt and uncle are expecting a child.'

Sonea stared at him. 'They are?'

'You'll have a little cousin soon,' he told her. Taking another sip, he gave her a speculative look. 'Cery told me that your mother died when you were a child, and your father left Kyralia soon after.' He paused. 'Did either of your parents show signs of having magic in their blood?'

She shook her head. 'Not that I know of.'

He pursed his lips. 'I had Cery ask your aunt. She says she has never seen any magical talent in either your parents or grandparents.'

'Does it matter?'

'Magicians like to trace their bloodlines,' he told her. 'My mother had magic in hers. I know because her brother – my uncle – is a magician, and my grandfather's brother is, too – if he is still alive.'

'You have *magicians* in your family?'

'Yes, though I've never met either of them, and probably never will.'

'But . . .' Sonea shook her head. 'How can that be?'

'My mother was the daughter of a wealthy Lonmar merchant,' he replied. 'My father was a Kyralian sailor, working for a ship captain who regularly transported wares for my mother's father.'

'How did they meet?'

'By chance first, then in secret. The Lonmar, as you know, keep their women from sight. They don't test them for magic, as the only place they can learn to use it is the Guild, and the Lonmar believe it is unseemly for women to be far from home – or even speak to men other than those in their family.' Faren paused to take another mouthful of wine. Sonea watched expectantly as he swallowed. He smiled briefly.

'When her father discovered that my mother had been seeing a sailor, she was punished,' he continued. 'They whipped her and then imprisoned her in one of their towers. My father left his ship and stayed in Lonmar, seeking a way to free her. He did not have to wait long, for when her family discovered she was with child, they cast her out in disgrace.'

'Cast her out? Surely they would just find a home for the child?'

'No.' Faren's expression darkened. 'They considered her spoiled, and a disgrace to her family. Their traditions required her to be marked so that other men would know her crime, then she was sold in a slave market. She had two long scars on each cheek, and one down the centre of her forehead.'

'That's awful,' Sonea exclaimed.

Faren shrugged. 'Yes, to us it seems awful. The Lonmar, however, believe they are the most civilised of the world's peoples.' He took another sip of wine. 'My father bought her and passage for both of them back to Imardin. Their troubles did not end there. He had caused the ship captain to lose an important customer, as my mother's family would not trade through him any more. And no other ship owner would hire my father, so my parents grew poorer. They built a house in the slums and my father took a job in a gorin slaughterhouse. I was born soon after.'

He drained his mug. Looking at her, he smiled. 'See? Even a lowly thief can have magic in his blood.'

'A *lowly* thief?' Sonea snorted.

She had never seen Faren so talkative. What else might he tell her? Pouring more wine, she gestured impatiently. 'So, how did a slaughterman's son become a leader of the Thieves?'

Faren lifted the mug to his lips. 'My father died in the battles after the first Purge. To have enough money to feed us, my mother became a dancer in a whorehouse.' He grimaced. 'Life was hard. One of her customers was an influential man among the Thieves. He liked me, and took me in as his son. When he retired, I replaced him then worked my way up from there.'

Sonea pursed her lips. 'So anyone can become a Thief? You just have to make friends with the right person.'

'It takes more than just being good company.' He smiled. 'Do you have plans for your friend then?'

She frowned in mock puzzlement. 'Friend? No, I was thinking of myself.'

He threw back his head and laughed, then raised his mug to her.

'Here's to Sonea – a woman of small ambitions. First magician, then Thief.'

They drained their mugs together, then Faren looked down at the table. Reaching out, he turned the book around to face him.

'Is this making any more sense yet?'

She sighed. 'Even Serin can't work out some of it. It's written for someone who knows more than I do. I need a book for a beginner.' She looked up at Faren. 'Cery had any luck?'

He shook his head. 'It might have been better if you'd kept practising. It would have kept the Guild busy. In the last week, they've checked every pawn shop inside and outside of the walls. If there were any books on magic in the city, they aren't there any more.'

Sonea sighed and pressed her hands to her temples. 'What are they doing now?'

'They're still snooping around the slums,' he told her. 'Waiting for you to use your magic.'

Sonea thought of her aunt and uncle, and the child they were expecting. Until the magicians stopped searching, she would not be able to see them. How she longed to talk to them. She looked down at the book and felt a surge of frustration and anger. 'Don't they *ever* give up?'

She jumped as a loud bang echoed through the room, followed by a light patter of something scattering over the floor. Looking down, Sonea saw fragments of a white ceramic vase.

'Now Sonea,' Faren said, shaking his finger at her. 'I don't think this is a nice way to repay Serin for –' He stopped abruptly, then slapped his forehead and groaned. 'They'll know you're in the city.' He swore, then frowned at her disapprovingly. 'There's more than one reason why I told you to avoid using magic while you're here, Sonea.'

Sonea flushed. 'I'm sorry Faren, but I didn't mean it.' She reached down and picked up one of the fragments. 'First I can't make it happen when I want to, and now it happens when I'm not even thinking about it.'

Faren's expression softened. 'Well, if you can't help it, you can't help it.' He waved a hand, stiffened and turned to stare at her.

'What?' she asked.

He swallowed and looked away. 'Nothing. Just . . . a thought. The magicians won't have been close enough to us to work out your location, though they'll probably be all over the North Quarter tomorrow. I don't think I need to move you yet – just try not to use your magic again.'

Sonea nodded. 'I'll try.'

'Larkin the merchant?'

Dannyl turned to see a bolhouse worker standing beside him. He nodded. The man jerked his head to indicate that Dannyl should follow him.

For a moment, Dannyl stared at the man, unable to believe that he was finally getting somewhere, then hastily rose from the stool. Following the man through the crowd, he considered the contents of his letter to Gorin. What had made the Thief agree to see him this time?

Snow was falling outside. The guide hunched his shoulders and drew his coat tighter, then started down the street at a rapid pace. As they reached the entrance of a nearby alley, a cloaked figure stepped out in front of Dannyl, blocking his path.

'Lord Dannyl. What a surprise! Or should I say, what a *disguise*?'

Fergun was smiling broadly. Dannyl stared at the magician, his disbelief rapidly turning to annoyance. Remembering other times, many years before, when he had been pursued and taunted by a younger Fergun, an uneasiness began to nag at him – then he became annoyed with himself. Straightening his shoulders, he drew a little petty satisfaction out of being a head taller than the other magician.

'What do you want, Fergun?'

Fergun's fine brows rose. 'To know why you're wandering about the slums in such a state, *Lord* Dannyl.'

'And you expect me to tell you?'

The warrior's shoulders rose. 'Well, if you don't, I'll be forced to speculate, won't I? I'm sure my friends will be happy to help me guess your reasons.' He put a finger to his lips. 'Hmm, obviously you don't wish it to be known why you are here. Is there a scandal you are hiding? Are you involved in something so embarrassing that you must dress like a beggar to avoid discovery? Ah!' Fergun's eyes widened. 'Are you visiting the brothels?'

Dannyl looked over Fergun's shoulder. As he had expected, the guide had disappeared.

'Oh, was he the one then?' Fergun asked, glancing behind. 'A bit rough looking. Not that I have any idea what your *specific* tastes are.'

Anger rushed over Dannyl like icy water. It had been years since Fergun had confronted him like this, but the hatred the jibe provoked was as strong as it had ever been. 'Get out of my way, Fergun.'

Fergun's eyes flashed with pleasure. 'Oh, no,' he said, his voice no longer mocking. 'Not until you tell me what you're up to.'

It would not be hard to knock Fergun off his feet, Dannyl mused.

Dannyl controlled his anger with an effort. 'Fergun, you couldn't keep your mouth shut or out of the gutter if you wanted to – and everybody knows it. Nobody will believe a word you say. Now get out of my way before I'm forced to report you.'

The Warrior's eyes became steely. 'I'm sure the Higher Magicians will be more interested in *your* actions. From what I remember, there's a rather strict law concerning magicians and where they must wear robes. Do they know you're breaking it?'

Dannyl smiled. 'It's not entirely unknown.'

A flicker of doubt broke Fergun's gaze. 'They're letting you?'

'They – or I should say *he* – instructed me to,' Dannyl replied. He let his gaze become distant, then shook his head. 'I've never been able to tell if he's watching or not. He'll need to know about this. I will have to tell him when I get back.'

Fergun's face had turned a shade whiter. 'No need! I will talk to him myself.' He stepped aside. 'Go. Finish your work.' Taking another step back, he turned and hurried away.

Smiling, Dannyl watched the Warrior disappear into the thickening snow. He doubted that Fergun would speak a word to the High Lord.

His satisfaction died as he found himself alone in an empty street. He searched the shadows where the guide had disappeared. Fergun would *have* to show up when the Thieves had finally agreed to a meeting. Sighing, Dannyl started back along the street toward the North Road and the Guild.

Hurried footsteps crunched the fresh snow behind him. He glanced back and blinked in surprise as he saw the guide approaching. Stopping, he let the man catch up.

'Hai! What was that about?' the man asked.

'One of our searchers got a little over-curious.' He smiled. 'I guess you'd call him a nosy tag.'

The man grinned, revealing stained teeth. 'I get you.' He gave a little shrug, then a tilt of his head to indicate that Dannyl should follow. Checking to make sure Fergun hadn't hung about to watch, Dannyl started through the falling snow again.

'"Gradually increase the amount of power until the heat melts the glass",' Serin read.

'But that's nothing like how it works!' Sonea exclaimed. She rose and paced the room. 'It's more like a . . . a water skin with a tiny hole in it. If you squeeze the bag, the water squirts out, but you can't aim it, or make it—'

She stopped as a knock sounded on the door. Serin rose and checked the spy hole before opening the door.

'Sonea,' Faren said, waving the scribe out of the room. 'I have some visitors for you.'

He stepped inside, grinning. Behind him was a stocky man with sleepy eyes and a short woman with a heavy scarf draped over her head.

'Ranel!' Sonea cried. 'Jonna!' She dashed around the table and hugged her aunt.

'Sonea.' Jonna gave a little gasp. 'We were so worried

about you.' Holding Sonea at arm's length, she nodded approvingly. 'You look well enough.'

To Sonea's amusement, Jonna narrowed her eyes at Faren. The Thief leaned against the back wall, smiling. Sonea moved to Ranel and hugged him.

He gave her a searching look. 'Harrin told us you've been doing magic.'

Sonea grimaced. 'That's right.'

'And the magicians are looking for you.'

'Yes. Faren's hiding me from them.'

'For what price? Your magic?'

Sonea nodded. 'That's right. Not that it's doing him much good at the moment. I'm not very good at it.'

Jonna snorted softly. 'You can't be that bad at it, or he wouldn't be hiding you.' She looked around the room and nodded. 'Not as bad as I thought.' Moving to a chair, she sat down, pulled off her scarf and exhaled a long breath.

Sonea dropped to her haunches beside the chair. 'I heard you were starting a new trade.'

Her aunt frowned. 'New trade?'

'Making cousins for me, I think.'

Her aunt's frown softened and she patted her belly. 'Ah, so the news reached you. Yes, there'll be another member in our little family next summer.' Jonna looked up at Ranel, who smiled broadly.

Looking at them, Sonea felt a surge of affection and longing. A familiar sensation slipped through her mind, and she drew in a sharp breath. Rising, she cast about, but saw nothing out of place.

'What?' Faren asked.

'I did something.' She flushed as she realised that her aunt and uncle were staring at her. 'Well, it felt like I did.'

The Thief looked around the room, then shrugged. 'Perhaps you moved a bit of dirt behind the walls.'

Jonna looked puzzled. 'What do you mean?'

'I used magic,' Sonea explained. 'I didn't intend to. It happens sometimes.'

'And you don't know what you did?' Jonna's hand tightened on her belly.

'No.' Sonea swallowed and looked away. The alarm in her aunt's gaze saddened her, but she understood why Jonna feared. The thought that she might accidentally harm . . .

No, she thought. *Don't think about it*. She took a deep breath and let it out slowly.

'Faren, I think you should take them away. Just in case.'

He nodded. Jonna rose, her face lined with anxiety. She turned to Sonea and opened her mouth to speak, then shook her head and held out her arms. Sonea gave her aunt a tight hug before drawing away.

'I'll see you again,' she told them. 'When all this has sorted itself out.'

Ranel nodded. 'Take care of yourself.'

'I will,' she promised.

Faren ushered the couple out of the room. Turning away, Sonea listened to their footsteps ascending the stairs. An unfamiliar patch of colour on the floor caught her attention. Her aunt's scarf.

Picking it up, she hurried to the door and up the stairs. As she climbed, she saw that her aunt and uncle were standing with Faren in Serin's kitchen, staring at something in the room. Reaching them, she saw what had captured their attention.

The floor had once been covered by large stone slabs.

Now it was a jagged jumble of stone and dirt. A heavy wooden table had dominated the room, but all that remained was twisted, splintered wood.

Sonea felt her mouth go dry, then her mind shifted again and the table suddenly burst into flame. Faren turned to her and seemed to struggle with himself for a moment before speaking.

'As I said,' he said. 'She's probably just going through a difficult phase. Sonea, go back downstairs and pack your bag. I'll take your visitors home and get someone to put out the fire. Everything will be fine.'

Nodding, Sonea handed her aunt the scarf and fled back down the stairs to the basement.

CHAPTER 14

AN UNWILLING ALLY

Pausing to rest in an alley, Rothen closed his eyes and drew up a little power to chase away his weariness.

He opened his eyes and considered the snow piled against the side of the buildings. The milder weather of the previous weeks was a distant memory now that the winter blizzards had reached Imardin. Checking that his robes were well covered by his cloak, he prepared to step out into the street.

He paused as a familiar buzzing began at the back of his head. Closing his eyes, he cursed under his breath as he realised how far away he was from the source. Shaking his head, he stepped out into the street.

—*Dannyl?*

—*I heard her. She's a few streets away from me now.*

—*Has she moved?*

—*Yes.*

Rothen frowned. If she had fled, why was she still using her powers?

—*Who else is near?*

—*We're closer*, Lord Kerrin called. *She must be no more than a hundred paces from us.*

—*Sarle and I are about the same distance away*, Lord Kiano sent.

—*Move closer*, Rothen told them. *Don't approach her alone.*

Rothen crossed the street and hurried down an alley. An old beggar stared blindly as he passed.

—*Rothen?* Dannyl called. *Look at this.*

An image flashed into Rothen's mind of a house clothed in orange flames, smoke billowing into the sky. A feeling of suspicion and dread came with the image.

—*Do you think she's . . .?*

—*We'd see something more dramatic than this*, Rothen replied.

At the end of the alley, Rothen stepped into a wider street. He checked his stride as he saw the burning house. People were already gathering to watch, and as he drew closer he saw the occupants of the neighbouring homes emerging, their arms laden with belongings.

A tall shadow detached itself from the darkness of another alley and approached him.

'She'll be close,' Dannyl said. 'If we . . .'

They both stiffened as a stronger, shorter buzz hit their senses.

'Behind that building,' Rothen said, pointing.

Dannyl started forward. 'I know this area. There's an alley beside that house that meets with two others.'

They strode into the darkness between two buildings. Rothen checked his stride as he felt another sharp vibration a hundred paces to the left of the previous one.

'She's moving fast,' Dannyl muttered, breaking into a jog.

Rothen hurried after. 'Something's not right,' he panted. 'Silence for weeks, then this week every day – and why is she still using her powers?'

'Perhaps she can't help it.'

'Then Akkarin was right.'

Rothen sent out a mental call.

—*Kiano?*

—*She's moving toward us.*

—*Kerrin?*

—*She crossed our path a moment ago, heading south.*

—*We have her surrounded,* Rothen told them. *Be careful. She may be losing control of her powers. Kiano and Sarle, move in slowly. Kerrin and Fergun, keep to her right. We'll come in on her—*

—*I've found her,* Fergun sent.

Rothen frowned.—*Fergun, where are you?*

There was a pause.

—*She's in the tunnels beneath me. I can see her through a grille in the wall.*

—*Stay there,* Rothen ordered. *Do not approach her alone.*

A moment later Rothen felt another vibration, and then several more. He sensed the other magicians' alarm and lengthened his stride.

—*Fergun? What's happening?*

—*She saw me.*

—*Don't approach her!* Rothen warned.

The buzz of magic stopped abruptly. Dannyl and Rothen exchanged a glance, then hurried on. Reaching a crossroads, they saw Fergun standing in one of the alleys, looking through a grille in a nearby wall.

'She's gone,' he told them.

Dannyl hurried to the grille, opened it and looked inside the passage.

'What happened?' Rothen asked.

Fergun replied. 'I was waiting for Kerrin to meet me when I heard noises through the grille.'

Dannyl rose to his feet. 'So you went in by yourself and frightened her off.'

Fergun narrowed his eyes at the tall magician. 'No. I remained here, as ordered.'

'Did she see you watching and become frightened?' Rothen asked. 'Was that why she started using her powers?'

'Yes.' Fergun shrugged. 'Until her friends knocked her out and ran.'

'You didn't follow them?' Dannyl asked.

Fergun brows rose. 'No. I stayed here, as ordered,' he repeated.

Dannyl muttered something under his breath and stalked back down the alley. As the other magicians arrived, Rothen walked forward to meet them. He explained what had happened, then sent them and Fergun back to the Guild.

He found Dannyl sitting on a doorstep, shaping a handful of snow into a ball.

'She's losing control.'

'Yes,' Rothen agreed. 'I'll have to call off the search. A chase or a confrontation will probably undo the little control she has.'

'What can we do, now?'

Rothen looked at his friend pointedly. 'Negotiate.'

The smell of smoke was heavy and rough in Cery's lungs. He hurried along the passage, dodging half-seen shapes of other men travelling the Road. Coming to a stop outside a door, he paused to catch his breath.

The guard that opened the door nodded as he recognised Cery. Hurrying up the narrow wooden stairs beyond, Cery pushed open the trapdoor at the top and climbed into a dimly lit room.

He quickly took in the three bulky guards lurking in

the shadows, the dark-skinned man standing at the window, and the figure lying asleep in a chair.

'What happened?'

Faren turned to regard him.

'We gave her a drug to put her to sleep. She was worried she would do more damage.'

Moving to the chair, Cery bent to examine Sonea's face. A dark, swollen bruise marked her temple. Her skin was pale and her hair slick with sweat. Looking down, he saw that the hem of her sleeve was charred, and her hand was bandaged.

'The fire is spreading,' Faren observed.

Rising, Cery joined the Thief at the window. Three of the houses across the street were afire, flames making glowing eyes out of the windows and rising like wild orange hair where the roofs had once been. Smoke had begun to billow out of the windows of another house.

'She said she was dreaming – a nightmare,' Faren told him. 'When she woke up there were fires in her room. Too many to put out. The more frightened she became, the more fires started.' Faren sighed. For a long time they remained silent, then Cery took a deep breath and turned to regard the Thief.

'What will you do now?'

To his surprise, Faren smiled. 'Introduce her to the friend of an old acquaintance of ours.' He turned and pointed to one of the men lurking in the shadows. 'Jarin, carry her.'

A large, muscular man moved out of the shadows and into the orange light cast by the fires. He bent to pick up Sonea, but as he grasped her shoulders her eyes fluttered open. Snatching his hands back, Jarin quickly backed away.

'Cery?' she murmured.

Cery hurried to her side. She blinked slowly, her eyes struggling to focus on him.

'Hello,' he said, smiling.

Her eyes closed again. 'They didn't follow, Cery. They let us go. Isn't that strange?'

She opened her eyes again and her gaze shifted over her shoulder. 'Faren?'

'You're awake.' Faren observed. 'You should have slept for at least another two hours.'

She yawned. 'I don't feel awake.'

Cery chuckled. 'You don't look real awake either. Go back to sleep. You need the rest. We're going to take you somewhere safe.'

She nodded and closed her eyes, and her breathing returned to the slow rhythm of sleep. Faren looked at Jarin, then nodded at the unconscious girl.

The big man reluctantly gathered her into his arms. Sonea's eyes fluttered once, but she remained asleep. Picking up a lamp, Faren strode to the trapdoor, kicked it open and started down the stairs.

They wove through the passages in silence. Looking up at Sonea's face, Cery felt his heart twist. The old, familiar uneasiness had become something more powerful than anything he had ever felt before. It kept him awake at night and tormented him through the day, and he found it hard to remember a time when he didn't feel sick with it.

Mostly he feared for her, but lately he had begun to fear being around her. The magic within her had slipped beyond her grasp. Every day, sometimes every hour, something near her exploded into flames or shattered. She had laughed about it that morning, joking that she was getting plenty of practise extinguishing fires and dodging flying objects.

Each time her magic slipped out, magicians came running from all over the city. Constantly on the move, spending more times in the passages than in Faren's hideouts, she was exhausted and miserable.

Lost in his thoughts, Cery paid little attention to the journey. At one point they descended down a steep staircase, then passed under an enormous slab of stone. Recognising the base of the Outer Wall, he knew they were entering the North Quarter, and he wondered who Faren's mysterious friend was.

Not long after, Faren stopped and ordered the guard to set Sonea down. She woke, and this time, she seemed more aware of her surroundings. Faren took off his coat and, with Jarin's help, slipped Sonea's arms into the sleeves and pulled up the hood.

'Do you think you can walk?' he asked her.

She shrugged. 'I'll try.'

'If we meet anyone, try to keep out of sight,' he told her.

At first she needed assistance, but within a few minutes she had regained her balance. They walked for another half an hour, gradually encountering more people in the passages. Faren stopped before a door and knocked. A guard opened it and let them into a small room, before knocking on a second door.

A small, swarthy man with a pointy nose opened the door and regarded the Thief.

'Faren,' he said. 'What brings you?'

'Business,' Faren answered.

Cery frowned. There was something familiar about the voice. The man's beady eyes narrowed.

'Come in then.'

Faren stepped into the doorway, then paused and pointed at his guards.

'You stay,' he said. He pointed at Cery, then Sonea. 'You both come with me.'

The man frowned. 'I don't . . .' He hesitated, narrowed his eyes at Cery, then smiled. 'Ah, it's little Ceryni. So you've kept Torrin's urchin, Faren. I wondered if you would.'

Cery smiled as he realised who the man was. 'Hello Ravi.'

'Come in.'

As Cery moved into the room, Sonea followed. Glancing around, Cery's gaze was met by an old man sitting in a chair to one side, stroking his long white beard. Cery nodded, but the man did not return the polite greeting.

'And who's this?' Ravi asked, nodding at Sonea.

Faren pulled her hood down. Sonea gazed at Ravi, her pupils large and black from the effects of the drug.

'This is Sonea,' Faren said, his mouth stretching in a humourless smile. 'Sonea, meet Ravi.'

'Hello,' Sonea said softly. Ravi took a step backwards. His face had turned white.

'This is . . . *her*? But I—'

'*How dare you bring her here!*'

All turned toward the voice. The old man had pushed himself to his feet and stood glaring at Faren. Sonea gave a little gasp and staggered away.

Faren placed his hands on her shoulders and steadied her. 'Don't worry Sonea,' he soothed. 'He wouldn't dare hurt you. If he did, we'd have to tell the Guild all about him, and he wouldn't like them to discover that he's not dead, as they believe.'

Cery turned to stare at the old man, suddenly understanding why the stranger hadn't bothered to acknowledge his nod.

'You see,' Faren continued, his tone smug, 'you and he have a lot in common, Sonea. You're both protected by Thieves, you both have magic, and you both don't want the Guild to find you. And now that you've seen Senfel here, he won't have any choice but to show you how to control your magic – because if he doesn't, the magicians might find you, and you might tell them about him.'

'He's a magician?' she breathed, staring at the old man with wide eyes.

'An ex-magician,' Faren corrected.

To Cery's relief, her eyes filled with hope, not fear.

'You can help me?' she said.

Senfel crossed his arms. 'No.'

'No?' she echoed softly.

The old man frowned, then his lip curled with contempt. 'Drugging her will only make it worse, Thief.'

Sonea drew in a sharp breath. Seeing the fear return to her eyes, Cery moved to her side and grasped her hands.

'Its all right,' he whispered to her. 'It's only a sleeping drug.'

'No, it's not all right,' Senfel said. He narrowed his eyes at Faren. 'I cannot help her.'

'You have no choice,' Faren replied.

Senfel smiled. 'Don't I? Go to the Guild then. Tell them I'm here. Better that they find me than I die when she loses control of her powers.'

Feeling Sonea tense, Cery turned to face the old man. 'Stop frightening her,' he hissed.

Senfel stared at him, then his eyes flickered to Sonea.

She glared back at him defiantly. The old man's expression softened a little.

'Go to them,' he urged. 'They will not kill you. The worst they will do is bind your powers so you cannot use them. Better that than death, eh?'

She continued to glare at him. Senfel shrugged, then straightened and fixed Faren with steely eyes.

'There are at least three magicians nearby. It would take little effort to call them, and I'm sure I could prevent you from leaving while they found their way to this room. Do you still wish to reveal my presence to the Guild?'

Faren's jaw shifted as he stared back at the magician. He shook his head.

'No.'

'Go – and when she's sober repeat what I said to her. If she does not seek the Guild's help, she will die.'

'Then help her,' Cery said.

The old man shook his head. 'I cannot. My powers are too weak and she is too far gone. Only the Guild can help her now.'

Dragging a barrel out from under the table, the bolhouse owner dropped it on the bench with a grunt. He gave Dannyl a meaningful look as he began filling mugs and handing them around the table. Leaning forward, he smacked a mug down in front of Dannyl, then crossed his arms and waited.

Giving the man a distracted frown, Dannyl handed over a coin. The man's gaze did not waver. Looking down at the drink, Dannyl knew he could avoid it no longer. He was going to have to drink the stuff.

Lifting the mug, he took a tentative mouthful, then

blinked in surprise. A sweet, rich flavour filled his mouth. The taste was familiar, and after a moment he recognised it. Chebol sauce, but without the spices.

A few mouthfuls later he felt a warmth filling his belly. He raised the mug to the shop owner and received an approving nod in reply. The man did not stop watching him, however, and Dannyl was relieved when a young man stomped into the shop and started a conversation.

'How's business, Kol?'

The man shrugged. 'The usual.'

'How many barrels you want this time?'

Dannyl listened to the pair barter. When they had arranged a price, the newcomer settled onto a chair and sighed.

'Where's that strange one with the flashy ring gone?'

'The Sachakan guy?' The barman shrugged. 'He got done weeks ago. Found him in the alley.'

'Really?'

'It's true.'

Dannyl snorted softly. *A fitting end*, he mused.

'Heard about that fire last night?' the barman asked.

'I live near there. It took out a whole street. Good thing it weren't summer. Could've burned the whole slums.'

'Not that the city folk would care,' the barman added. 'Fire'd never get past the Wall.'

A hand touched Dannyl's shoulder. He looked up and recognised the thin man that the Thieves had chosen to be his guide. The man jerked his head toward the door.

Dannyl finished his bol and put down his mug. As he stood, he received a friendly nod from the owner. Smiling, Dannyl returned it, then followed the guide to the door.

CHAPTER 15

ONE WAY, OR THE OTHER . . .

Sonea watched as water, seeping through a crack high on one wall, gathered into a droplet, ran down the empty lamp hook, then dove off to splatter on the hard floor. Looking up again, she watched as another droplet formed.

Faren had chosen her latest hide wisely. An empty underground storeroom, with brick walls and a stone bench for a bed, it held nothing flammable or valuable.

Except herself.

The thought sent a ripple of fear through her mind. Closing her eyes, she quickly pushed it aside.

She had no idea how long she had been in the room. It could have been days, or merely hours. There was nothing to measure time by.

She had not felt the familiar shift within her mind since arriving. The list of emotions which could set off her powers had grown so long that she no longer kept a mental count of them. Lying in the storeroom, she had concentrated on staying calm. Each time a thought disturbed that calm, she took a deep breath and pushed it away. A comforting detachment had settled upon her.

Perhaps the drink Faren had given to her had caused that.

Drugging her will only make it worse. She shivered as she

remembered the strange dream she'd had after the fire. In it, she had visited a magician in the slums. Though her imagination had invented a helper, his words had been no comfort. Taking a deep breath, she sent the memory away.

Obviously, she had been wrong to think she had to keep a store of anger inside to call upon when she wanted to use magic. She now admired the magicians for their control, but knowing that they were emotionless beings did not give her any more reason to like them.

There was a light tapping on the door, then it began to open. Smothering a twinge of apprehension, she rose and peered through the widening crack. Cery stood there, grimacing with the effort of moving the stiff metal door. When he had pushed it open enough to slip through, he stopped and beckoned to her.

'You have to move again.'

'But I haven't done anything.'

'Perhaps you didn't realise.'

Slipping through the door, she considered what this might mean. Had the drug prevented her from feeling the magic slipping from her mind? She hadn't seen anything explode or burst into flames. Were her powers still escaping, but in a less destructive form?

The questions brought her dangerously close to feeling strong emotions, so she pushed them from her mind. Following Cery, she focused on maintaining her sense of calm. He stopped and climbed a rusty ladder set into the wall. Pushing open a hatch, he scrambled through, sending fresh snow into the passage.

Following close behind, Sonea felt chill air on her face as she emerged into the daylight. They stood in an empty alley. Cery grinned at her as she brushed snow from her clothes.

'You've got snow in your hair,' he said. He reached out to brush it off, gasped and snatched his hand back.

'Ouch! What . . .?' He reached out again and flinched. 'You've made one of those barriers, Sonea.'

'No, I haven't,' she replied, still certain that she had not used any magic. Reaching out, she felt a shock of pain as her hand met an invisible wall of resistance. Catching a movement over Cery's shoulder, she looked past him. A man had just entered the alley and was walking toward her.

'Behind you,' she warned, but Cery was looking at something above her head.

'*Magician!*' he hissed, pointing.

She looked up and sucked in a breath. A man was standing on the roof above them, staring down at her intently. She caught her breath in disbelief as he stepped over the edge of the building, but instead of falling, he floated toward the ground.

A vibration rang through the air as Cery pounded against the barrier.

'Run!' he shouted. 'Get away!'

She backed away from the descending magician. Abandoning all efforts to stay calm, she dashed down the alley. The sound of booted feet tramping in the snow behind her told her that the floating magician was on the ground.

Ahead, the alley crossed with another. Beyond the intersection another figure strode toward her. With a gasp she threw herself forward with all the strength of panic. She felt a thrill of triumph as she reached the intersection several paces before the second magician.

Skidding to a halt, she leapt down the right hand passage . . .

. . . and caught the corners of the walls to stop herself. Another man stood there, his arms crossed. With a gasp she hauled herself away from him.

Twisting around, she sprang into the only alley remaining, and slid to a stop. A fourth man stood several paces away, guarding her last retreat.

Cursing, she spun around to stare behind her. The third man regarded her intently, but he had not moved. She looked back at the fourth. He had started to walk toward her.

Her heart was beating crazily. Looking up, she considered the walls. They were the usual rough brick, but she knew that, even if she had time to climb them, the magicians could easily bring her down. A dreadful, sinking cold crept over her.

I'm trapped. There is no way out.

Looking back, she felt a stab of fear as she saw that the first two men had joined the third at the crossroads, and a familiar slipping sensation fluttered through her mind. Dust and fragments of brick rained down as part of the wall above the men shattered. Rubble bounced harmlessly off the air above their heads.

The magicians glanced at the wall, then turned calculating eyes on her. Afraid that they would think she was attacking them, and retaliate, she backed away. She felt the slipping again. A searing heat enveloped her leg. Looking down, she saw snow sizzling into a pool of water at her feet. Steam billowed up, filling the alley with warm, impenetrable mist.

They can't see me! She felt a rush of hope. *I can slip past them.*

Turning, she leapt back down the alley. The dark shadow of the man moved to block her path. She hesitated, then reached into her coat. The cold handle of her knife met her searching fingers. As the magician reached out to grab her she ducked under his outstretched hands and threw herself against him with all her weight. He staggered backwards, but did not fall. Before he could recover his balance, she stabbed the thin blade hard into his thigh.

The blade sank sickeningly deep into his leg. As he yelled in surprise and pain, she felt a cruel thrill of satisfaction. Pulling the knife free, she thrust him out of her way with all her strength. As he fell against the wall, groaning, she turned to run.

Fingers caught her wrist. With a growl she turned and tried to twist herself free. His grip tightened and began to hurt, and she felt the knife slip from her grasp.

A gust of wind chased the mist from the alley and revealed the other three magicians hurrying toward her. She felt panic rising and began to struggle uselessly, her feet skittering over the wet ground. With a grunt of effort, her captor yanked on her arm, pulling her past him toward the trio.

Terror rushed over her as she felt hands grasp her arms. Twisting about, she tried to shake herself free, but their grip was strong. Hands pushed her against the wall, holding her still. Panting, she found herself surrounded by magicians, all staring at her with bright eyes.

'She's a wild one,' one of the men said. The injured one gave a short, rueful laugh.

As she looked at the closest magician she felt a shock of recognition. This was the magician who had seen her during the Purge. He stared into her eyes intently.

'Do not fear us, Sonea,' he said. 'We will not harm you.'

One of the magicians muttered something. The older magician nodded, then the others slowly withdrew their hands.

An invisible force held her against the wall. Unable to move, she felt a wave of despair followed by the familiar sensation of magic slipping beyond her grasp. The other three magicians ducked as the wall behind them burst, showering the alley with bricks.

A man in a baker's apron stepped up to the opening, his face dark with anger. Seeing the four magicians, he hesitated, eyes widening. One of the magicians turned and made an abrupt gesture.

'Get yourself away from here,' he barked. 'And everyone else in this block.'

The man backed away, then disappeared into the darkness of the house.

'Sonea.'

The older magician was looking at her intently. 'Listen to me. We are not going to hurt you. We . . .'

A searing heat pressed against her face. Turning, she saw that the bricks nearby were glowing red. A trickle of something ran down the wall. She heard one of the magicians utter an oath.

'Sonea,' the older magician said, a sternness entering his voice. 'Stop fighting us. You will harm yourself.'

The wall behind her began to shake. The magicians threw their arms out as the tremor spread. Sonea gasped as cracks began to shoot out from the ground beneath her feet.

'Slow your breathing,' the magician urged. 'Try to calm yourself.'

She closed her eyes, then shook her head. It was no use. The magic was flowing from her like water from a broken pipe. She felt a hand touch her forehead and opened her eyes.

The magician withdrew his hand. His face was tense. He said something to the others, then looked into her eyes.

'I can help you, Sonea,' the magician said. 'I can show you how to stop this but not if you won't let me. I know you have every reason to fear and distrust us but if you don't do this now, you are going to harm both yourself and many, many people in this area. Do you understand?'

She stared at him. Help her? Why would he want to help her?

But if he had intended to kill me, she realised suddenly, *he would have done it already*.

His face began to shimmer then, and she realised that the air about her had begun to ripple with heat. It seared her face and she bit back a cry of pain. The magician and his companions appeared unaffected, but their expressions were grim.

Though a part of her rebelled at the idea, she knew something bad was about to happen if she didn't do what these magicians wanted her to do.

The older magician frowned. 'Sonea,' he said sternly. 'We don't have enough time to explain. I will attempt to show you, but you must not resist.'

The magician lifted a hand and touched her forehead. His eyes closed.

At once she became aware of a *person* at the edge of her mind. She knew instantly that his name was Rothen. Unlike the minds that she had sensed searching for her, this one could *see* her.

Closing her eyes, she concentrated on his presence.

—Listen to me. You have almost completely lost control of your powers.

Though she heard no words, the meaning was clear – and frightening. She understood at once that the power she had would kill her if she did not learn to control it.

—Look for this in your mind.

Something – a wordless thought – an instruction to search. She became aware of a place within herself that was both familiar and strange. As she focused upon it, it became clearer. A great blinding sphere of light, floating in darkness . . .

—This is your power. It has grown into a great store of energy, even with you drawing upon it. You must release it – but in a controlled way.

This was her magic? She reached toward it. Immediately, white light flashed from the sphere. Pain raced through her, and somewhere in the distance she heard a voice cry out.

—Don't try to reach for it – not until I show you how. Now, watch me . . .

He called her attention away. She followed him somewhere else, and she became aware of another sphere of light.

—Observe.

She watched as, with a flexing of his will, he *drew* power from the sphere, shaped it and let it go.

—Now you try.

Focusing on her own light, she willed a little of its energy to come forth. Magic suffused her mind. She had only to think of what she wanted it to do and it was gone.

—That's right. Now do it again, but keep drawing until you have used all the power you have.

—All?

—Do not be afraid. You are meant to be able to wield that much, and the exercise that I have shown you will use it in a way that will not cause harm.

Her chest swelled as she took a deep breath and let it out. Drawing on her power again, she began to shape and release it over and over. Once she had begun, it seemed eager to answer her will. The sphere began to shrink, slowly diminishing until it was no more than a spark floating in darkness.

—There, it is done.

She opened her eyes and blinked at the destruction surrounding her. The walls were gone, replaced with smouldering rubble for twenty paces in all directions. The magicians regarded her cautiously.

Though the wall behind her was gone, the invisible force still held her upright. As it released her she swayed on her feet, her legs shaking with weariness, then crumpled to her knees. Barely able to hold her back straight, she frowned up at the older magician.

He smiled and bent to place his hand on her shoulder.

—You are safe for now, Sonea. You have used all your energy. Rest. We will talk soon.

As he lifted her into his arms a wave of dizziness rushed over her, bringing a blackness that smothered all thought.

Panting from effort and pain, Cery slumped against the broken wall. Sonea's cry still echoed in his ears. He pressed his hands to his head and closed his eyes.

'Sonea . . .' he whispered.

Sighing, he removed his hands and belatedly heard the sound of footsteps behind him. He looked up to see that the man who had blocked his retreat from the alley had returned and was now staring at him intently.

Cery ignored him. His eyes had found a bright colour in all the dust and rubble. He crouched and touched a ribbon of red dripping along the edge of a broken brick. Blood.

Footsteps drew near. A boot appeared beside the blood – boots with buttons in the shape of the Guild symbol. Anger blazed through Cery, and he rose and struck out in one motion, aiming for the man's face.

The man caught Cery's fist neatly and twisted. Unbalanced, Cery stumbled and fell, his head striking the broken wall. Colours flashed before his eyes. Gasping, he staggered to his feet, his hands pressed to his head in an attempt to stop the world spinning. The man chuckled.

'Stupid dwell,' he said.

Running his fingers through his fine blonde hair, the magician turned on his heel and stalked away.

PART TWO

CHAPTER 16

INTRODUCTIONS

As the morning grew old, Rothen felt weariness drag at his eyes. He closed them and called upon a little Healing magic to refresh himself, then lifted his book and forced himself to read.

Before he had finished the page, he found himself looking at the sleeping girl again. She lay in a small bedroom that was part of his suite, in the bed that had once belonged to his son. Others had argued with him over his decision to keep her in the Magicians' Quarters. Though he had not shared their concerns, he had kept an eye on her – just in case.

In the darkest part of the night he had allowed Yaldin to take over the watch so that he could get some rest. But instead of sleeping, he had lain awake thinking about her. There was so much to explain. He wanted to be prepared for all the questions and accusations she was sure to have. Possible conversations had repeated themselves over and over in his mind and he had eventually abandoned his attempt to sleep and returned to her side.

She had slept most of a day. Magical exhaustion often affected the young this way. In the two months since the Purge, her dark hair had grown a little longer, but her skin was pale and clung to the bones of her face.

Remembering how light she had been to carry, Rothen shook his head. Her time with the Thieves had not improved her health. Sighing, he turned his attention to the book again.

After managing to read another page, he looked up. Dark eyes stared back at him.

The eyes dropped to his robes. In a flurry of movement, the girl struggled from the clinging sheets of the bed. Once free, she looked down in dismay at the heavy cotton nightrobe she wore.

Putting the book on the table beside the bed, Rothen stood up, taking care to keep his movements slow. She pressed her back against the far wall, eyes wide. Moving away, he opened the doors of a cupboard at the back of the room and took out a thick leisure coat.

'Here,' he said, taking it down and holding it out to her. 'This is for you.'

She stared at the coat as if it were a wild animal.

'Take it,' he urged, taking a few steps toward her. 'You must be cold.'

Frowning, she edged forward and snatched the coat from his hands. Without taking her eyes from him, she shrugged her arms into the garment and pulled it close around her thin body, backing away to the wall again.

'My name is Rothen,' he told her.

She continued to stare at him, saying nothing.

'We do not intend to harm you, Sonea,' he told her. 'You have nothing to fear.'

Her eyes narrowed and her mouth tightened into a thin line.

'You don't believe me.' He shrugged. 'Nor would I in your position. Did you get our letter, Sonea?'

She frowned, then a look of contempt crossed her face. He smothered the urge to smile.

'Of course, you wouldn't believe that, either, would you? Tell me, what do you find hardest to believe?'

Crossing her arms, she looked out the window and did not answer. He pushed aside a mild annoyance. Resistance, even this ridiculous refusal to answer, was to be expected.

'Sonea, we *must* talk to each other,' he said gently. 'There is a power in you that, whether you want it or not, you must learn to control. If you do not, it will kill you. I know you understand this.'

Her brows knitted together, but she continued staring silently out of the window. Rothen allowed himself to sigh.

'Whatever reasons you have to dislike us, you must realise that to refuse our help is foolish. Yesterday we did no more than use up the store of power inside you. It will not be long before your powers grow strong and dangerous again. Think on that,' he paused, 'but not for too long.'

Turning toward the door, he reached for the handle.

'What do I have to do?'

Her voice was high and faint. He felt a thrill of triumph, but quickly schooled his expression. Turning back, he felt his heart twist as he saw the fear in her eyes.

'You have to learn to trust me,' he told her.

The magician – Rothen – had returned to his chair. Sonea's heart was still pounding, but not as quickly now. The coat made her feel less vulnerable. She knew it was no protection against magic, it covered the ridiculous *thing* they had dressed her in.

The room she was in was not large. A tall cupboard stood at one end, the bed filled the other, and a small table fit in the middle. The furniture was made of expensive polished wood. On the table lay small combs and writing implements made of silver. A mirror hung on the wall above it and a painting graced the wall behind the magician.

'Control is a subtle skill,' Rothen told her. 'To show you I must enter your mind, but I can't if you resist me.'

The memory of Guild novices standing in a room, one of each pair pressing hands against his fellow's temples rose in Sonea's mind. The teacher instructing them had said much the same. Sonea felt an uneasy satisfaction that she knew this magician was telling the truth. No magician could enter her mind uninvited.

Then she frowned, remembering the presence that had shown her the source of her magic, and how to use it.

'You did yesterday.'

He shook his head. 'No, I pointed you toward your own power, then demonstrated how to use it with my own. This is quite different. To teach you how to control your power, I must go to the place within you where your power resides, and to get there, I must enter your mind.'

Sonea looked away. Let a magician into her mind? What would he see? Everything or only what she let him?

Did she have any choice?

'Talk to me,' the magician urged. 'Ask me any questions you wish. If you learn more about me, you will find that I am a trustworthy person. You don't have to like the entire Guild, you don't even have to like me. You just have to know me well enough to trust that I will teach you what must be taught and do nothing to harm you.'

Sonea looked at him closely. He was middle aged or older. Though his dark hair was streaked with grey, his eyes were blue and lively. Wrinkles around his eyes and mouth gave him a good-humoured expression. He looked like a gentle, fatherly man – but she was no fool. Tricksters always looked honest and appealing. If they didn't, they failed to make a living. The Guild would have arranged for her to meet their most appealing magician first.

She had to look deeper. As she stared into his eyes, he returned her gaze steadily. His confidence disturbed her. Either he was certain that there was nothing she would find objectionable about him, or he believed he could trick her into thinking so.

Either way, he had a difficult task ahead of him, she decided.

'Why should I believe anything you say?'

He lifted his shoulders. 'Why would I lie to you?'

'To get what you want. Why else?'

'And what do I want?'

She hesitated. 'I don't know yet.'

'I only want to help you, Sonea.' He sounded genuinely concerned.

'I don't believe you,' she told him.

'Why not?'

'You're a magician. They say you vow to protect people, but I've seen you kill.'

The wrinkles between his brows deepened, and he nodded slowly. 'Indeed you have. As we said in our letter to you, we did not intend to harm anybody that day – you or the boy.' He sighed. 'It was a terrible mistake. If I'd known what was going to happen I would never have pointed you out.

'There are many different ways to project magic, and the most common is the strike. The weakest of those is the stunstrike, which is designed to paralyse – to freeze up a person's muscles so they cannot move. The magicians who struck the youth all used stunstrike. Do you remember the colour of the strikes?'

Sonea shook her head. 'I wasn't watching.' *Too busy running away*, she thought, but she wasn't going to say it aloud.

He frowned. 'Then you'll have to believe me when I say that they were red, a stunstrike is red. But with so many magicians responding, some of the strikes met and combined to form a stronger firestrike. Those magicians never intended to harm anyone, only to stop the boy running away. I assure you, our mistake has caused us much anguish, and a great deal of disapproval from the King and the Houses.'

Sonea sniffed. 'Like they care.'

His eyebrows rose. 'Ah, but they do. I'll admit their reasons have more to do with keeping the Guild in line than sympathy for the boy or his family, but we *were* chastised for our mistake.'

'How?'

He smiled crookedly. 'Letters of protest. Public speeches. A warning from the King. It doesn't sound like much, but in the world of politics, words are much more dangerous than whipping sticks or magic.'

Sonea shook her head. 'Using magic is what you do. It's what you're supposed to be best at. One magician might make a mistake, but not as many as were there.'

His shoulders lifted. 'Do you think we spend our days preparing for a poor girl to attack us with magically directed stones? Our Warriors are trained in the most subtle manoeuvres and strategies of war but no situation in the Arena could have prepared them for an attack from their own people – people who they believed were harmless.'

Sonea snorted loudly. Harmless. She saw Rothen's lips tighten at the noise. *I probably disgust him*, she mused. To the magicians, the slum dwellers were dirty, ugly and a nuisance. Did they have any idea how much the dwells hated them?

'But you've done almost as bad before,' she told him. 'I've seen people with burns they got from magicians. Then there're those who get crushed when you frighten the crowd into running. But mostly they die from cold afterwards, in the slums.' She narrowed her eyes at him. 'But you wouldn't see that as being the Guild's fault, would you?'

'Accidents have happened in the past,' he admitted. 'Magicians who were careless. Where possible, those that were harmed were Healed and compensated. As for the Purge itself . . .' He shook his head. 'Many of us think it is no longer needed. Do you know why it began?'

Sonea opened her mouth to give a tart reply, then hesitated. It wouldn't hurt to know how *he* believed the Purge started. 'Tell me, then.'

Rothen's gaze became distant. 'Over thirty years ago a mountain in the far north exploded. Soot filled the sky and blocked some of the warmth of the sun. The winter that followed was so long and cold that we had no true summer before the next winter began. All over Kyralia and in Elyne, crops failed and stock died. Hundreds, perhaps thousands, of farmers and their families came to the city, but there wasn't enough work or housing for them all.

'The city filled with starving people. The King handed out food and arranged for places like the Racing Arena to be used as shelters. He sent some farmers back to their homes with enough food to last them until the next summer. There wasn't enough to feed everyone, however.

'We told people that the next winter wouldn't be so bad, but many didn't believe us. Some even thought that the world was going to freeze completely, and we would all die. They cast aside all decency and preyed on others in the belief that nobody would be alive to punish them. It became dangerous to walk the streets, even in daylight. Gangs broke into houses, and people were murdered in their beds. It was a terrible time.' He shook his head. 'One I will never forget.

'The King sent the Guard to drive these gangs from the city. When it was clear that it couldn't be done without bloodshed, he asked the Guild to help. The next winter was also harsh and when the King saw signs of similar trouble rising, he decided to clear the streets again before the situation became dangerous. So it has been ever since.'

Rothen sighed. 'Many say that the Purge should have stopped years ago, but memories are long and the slums have grown many times larger than they were during that terrible winter. Many fear what will happen if the city isn't cleared every winter, particularly now that the Thieves exist. They fear that the Thieves would use such a situation to take control of the city.'

'That's ridiculous!' Sonea exclaimed. Rothen's version of the story was predictably one-sided, but some of the reasons he gave for the first Purge were new and strange. Mountains exploding? There was no point arguing. He would just point out her ignorance of such things. But she knew something he didn't.

'It was the Purge that started the Thieves,' she told him. 'Do you think all the people you drove out were muggers and gangs? You drove out those starving farmers and their families, and people like beggars and scavengers who needed to be in the city to survive. Those people got together so they could help each other. They survived by joining the lawless ones, because they saw no reason to live by the King's laws any more. He'd driven them out when he should have helped them.'

'He helped as many as he could.'

'Not all, and not now. Do you think he's clearing the streets of muggers and gangs? No, they're good people who make a living from what rich people waste, or have a trade in the city but live in the slums. The lawless ones are the Thieves – and the Thieves aren't bothered by the Purge at all because they can get in and out of the city whenever they want.'

Rothen nodded slowly, his expression thoughtful. 'I suspected as much.' He leaned forward. 'Sonea, I don't like the Purge any more than you do – and I'm not the only magician that feels that way.'

'Why do *you* do it?'

'Because when the King asks us to do something we are bound by our oath to obey.'

Sonea snorted again. 'So you can blame the King for anything you do.'

'We are all subjects of the King,' he reminded her. 'The Guild must be seen to obey him because the people need to be reassured that we will not seek to rule Kyralia ourselves.' He leaned back in his chair. 'If we are the remorseless murderers you believe us to be, why haven't we done that, Sonea? Why haven't magicians taken over all the lands?'

Sonea shrugged. 'I don't know, but it would make no difference to the dwells. When have you ever done anything good for us?'

Rothen's eyes narrowed. 'There is much that you would not see.'

'Like what?'

'We keep the Marina clear of silt, for example. Without us, Imardin could not receive ships, and trade would move elsewhere.'

'How is that good for the dwells?'

'It creates work for Imardians of all classes. Ships bring sailors who buy board, food and goods. Workers pack and carry goods. Crafters make the goods.' He considered her, then shook his head. 'Perhaps our work is too far removed from your own life for you to see its value. If you would see us helping people directly, consider the work of our Healers. They work hard to—'

'Healers!' Sonea rolled her eyes. 'Who's got coin to spare for a Healer? The fee is ten times as much as a good Thief earns in his life!'

Rothen paused. 'Of course, you are right,' he said quietly. 'There are only so many Healers – barely enough to keep up with the number of sick that come to us for help. The high fees discourage those with minor ailments from overusing the Healers' time, and goes toward teaching non-magicians about medicines that can treat those minor ailments. These medics treat the rest of Imardin's citizens.'

'Not the dwells,' Sonea retorted. 'We have curies, but they're just as likely to kill you as cure you. I only heard of a few medics when I was living in the North Quarter and they cost a cap of gold.'

Rothen looked out of the window and sighed. 'Sonea, if I could solve the problem of class and poverty in the city, I would do so without a moment's hesitation. But there is little that we – even as magicians – can do.'

'No? If you really don't like the Purge, then refuse to go. Tell the King you'll do anything else he says but that. It's happened before.'

He frowned, obviously puzzled.

'Back when King Palen refused to sign the Alliance.' She suppressed a smile at his expression of surprise. 'Then get the King to build proper sewers and the like in the slums. His great-grandfather did it for the rest of the city, why shouldn't he do it for us too?'

His brows rose. 'You wouldn't want to move the slum people into the city?'

Sonea shook her head. 'Parts of the Outer Circle are good. The city won't stop growing. Perhaps the King should build another wall, too.'

'Walls are obsolete. We have no enemies. But the rest is . . . interesting.' He regarded her appraisingly. 'And what else would you have us do?'

'Go into the slums and heal people.'

He grimaced. 'There aren't enough of us.'

'Some's better than none. Why is the broken arm of the son of a House more important than a dwell's broken arm?'

He smiled then, and Sonea suddenly felt a disturbing suspicion that her answers were no more than an amusement to him. What did he care, anyway? He was just trying to get her to believe he sympathised with her. It would take more than that to make her trust him.

'You'll never do it,' she growled. 'You keep saying that some of you'd help if you could, but the truth is, if any magicians really cared, they'd be out there. There's no law stopping them, so why don't any go? I'll tell you why. The slums are smelly and rough, and you'd rather pretend they weren't there. Here you're real comfortable.' She gestured at the room and its fine furniture. 'Everyone knows the King pays you a lot. Well, if you're all feeling so sorry for us, then you should put some of that money into helping people but you won't. You'd rather keep it all for yourself.'

He pursed his lips, his expression thoughtful. She found herself strangely aware of the silence in the room. Realising she had allowed him to provoke her, she gritted her teeth.

'If a large amount of money was given to any of the people you know in the slums,' he said slowly, 'do you think they'd give it all up to help others?'

'Yes,' she replied.

He lifted an eyebrow. 'So none of them would be tempted to keep it to themselves?'

Sonea paused. She knew some people who wouldn't. Well, more than some.

'A few, I suppose,' she admitted.

'Ah,' he said. 'But you would not have me believe all dwells were selfish people, would you? Neither should *you* believe that all magicians are self-centred. You would also, no doubt, assure me that, for all their law breaking or rough behaviour, the people you know are mostly decent folk. It does not make sense, then, for you to judge all magicians by the mistakes of a few, or for their high birth. Most, I assure you, strive to be decent people.'

Frowning, Sonea looked away. What he said made sense, but it did not comfort her at all. 'Perhaps,' she replied, 'but I still don't see *any* magicians helping people in the slums.'

Rothen nodded. 'Because we know that the slum people would refuse our help.'

Sonea hesitated. He was right, but if the dwells refused the Guild's help, it was because the Guild had given the dwells reason to hate them.

'They wouldn't refuse money,' she pointed out.

'Assuming you are not one of those who would hoard it, what would you do if I gave you a hundred gold slips to do with as you pleased?'

'I'd feed people,' she told him.

'A hundred gold would feed some for many weeks, or many for a few days. Afterwards, those people would still be as poverty-stricken as before. You will have made little difference.'

Sonea opened her mouth, then closed it again. There was nothing she could say to that. He was right, and yet he wasn't. There had to be something wrong with not even trying to help.

Sighing, she looked down at herself and frowned at the foolish garments she was wearing. Despite knowing that changing the subject might give him the notion that he had won the argument, she plucked at the coat.

'Where are my clothes?'

He looked down at his hands. 'Gone. I will give you new ones.'

'I want my own,' she told him.

'I had them burned.'

She stared at him in disbelief. Her cloak, though dirty and charred in places, had been of good quality – and Cery had given it to her.

There was a knock on the door. Rothen rose to his feet.

'I must leave now, Sonea,' he told her. 'I will return in an hour.'

She watched him move away and open the door. Beyond, she glimpsed another luxurious room. As he closed the door she listened for the sound of a key turning, and felt a twinge of hope when it did not come.

Frowning, she stared at the door. Was it locked by magic? She took a step closer, then heard the muffled sound of voices coming from beyond the door.

No sense trying the door now but perhaps later . . .

Pain squeezed his head tightly, but he could feel something cool was dribbling down behind his ear. Opening his eyes, Cery saw a blurred face within darkness. A woman's face.

'Sonea?'

'Hello.' The voice was unfamiliar. 'About time you returned to us.'

Cery closed his eyes tightly, then opened them again. The face became clearer. Long dark hair framed exotically beautiful features. The woman's skin was dark, but not as inky as Faren's. The familiar, straight Kyralian nose added elegance to the long face. It was as if Sonea and Faren had become one person.

I'm dreaming, he thought.

'No, you're not,' the woman replied. She looked up, at something above his head. 'He must have been hit pretty hard. Do you want to talk to him now?'

'May as well try.' This voice was familiar. As Faren moved into sight, memory returned and Cery tried to sit up. The darkness swayed, and his head thundered with pain. He felt hands on his shoulders and reluctantly allowed them to push him back down onto his back.

'Hello, Cery. This is Kaira.'

'She looks like you but pretty,' Cery murmured.

Faren laughed. 'Thanks. Kaira is my sister.'

The woman smiled and moved out of sight. Cery heard a door close somewhere to his right. He stared at Faren.

'Where's Sonea?'

The Thief sobered. 'The magicians have her. They took her to the Guild.'

The words echoed over and over in Cery's mind. He felt something awful tearing at his insides. *She is gone!* How could he have believed that he could protect her? But, no. *Faren* was supposed to have kept her safe. A spark of anger flared. He drew a breath to speak . . .

No. I must find her. I must get her back. I might need Faren's help.

All anger drained out of him. Cery frowned at the Thief.

'What happened?'

Faren sighed. 'The inevitable. They caught up.' He shook his head. 'I don't know what I could have done to stop them. I had already tried everything.'

Cery nodded. 'And now?'

The Thief's lips twitched into a humourless, half smile. 'I was unable to honour my side of our bargain. Sonea, however, never had a chance to use her magic for me. We both tried hard but failed. As for you . . .' Faren's smile disappeared. 'I would like you to remain with me.'

Cery stared at the Thief. How could he abandon Sonea so easily?

'You are free to go if you wish,' Faren added.

'What about Sonea?'

The Thief frowned. 'She is in the Guild.'

'Not a hard place to break into. I've done it before.'

Faren's frown deepened. 'That would be foolish. They will guard her closely.'

'We'll distract them.'

'We'll do no such thing.' Faren's eyes flashed. He took a few steps away, then paced back to Cery's side. 'The Thieves have never pitted themselves against the Guild, and never will. We're not so stupid as to think we would win.'

'They aren't that smart. Believe me, I've—'

'NO!' Faren interrupted. He took a deep breath, then let it out slowly. 'It is not as easy as you think, Cery. Get some rest. Heal. Think about what you're suggesting. We will talk again soon.'

He moved out of sight. Cery heard the door click open, then close firmly. He tried to rise but his head felt as if it would burst from the pain. Sighing, he closed his eyes and lay flat, breathing hard.

He could try to convince Faren to rescue Sonea, but he knew he would not succeed. No. If she was to be saved, he would have to do it himself.

CHAPTER 17

SONEA'S RESOLVE

Sonea looked around the room again. Though not large, it was luxurious. She could be in any one of the homes of the Inner City, but she doubted it.

Moving to the window, she pushed aside the finely decorated screen that covered it, caught her breath and took a step backwards.

The Guild gardens stretched out before her. The University building loomed to the right, and the High Lord's house lay, half hidden behind the trees, to the left. She was on the second storey of the building Cery had called the 'magicians' building'.

The Guild was swarming with magicians. Everywhere she looked, she saw robed figures: in the garden, in windows, and strolling along the snow-edged path just below her window. Shivering, she pushed the screen back and turned away.

A bleak desperation swept over her. *I'm trapped. I'll never leave this place. I won't see Jonna and Ranel, or Cery, ever again.*

She blinked as tears blurred her sight. Catching a movement in the corner of her eye, she turned to find herself reflected in a shining oval mirror. She regarded the red-eyed face. The girl's mouth twisted in contempt.

Am I going to give up so easily? she asked the reflection. *Am I going to blubber like a child?*

No! The Guild might be filled with magicians during the day, but she had seen it at night and knew how easy it was to move around undetected. If she waited until night, and managed to slip outside, nothing would stop her returning to the slums.

Getting outside would be the hard part, of course. The magicians would probably keep her locked up. However, Rothen himself had said that magicians were not incapable of making mistakes. She would wait and watch. When the opportunity came, she would be ready to take it.

The face in the mirror was now dry-eyed and stiff with determination. Feeling better, she moved to the small table. Picking up a hair brush, she caressed the silver handle appreciatively. Something like this, traded at a pawn shop, could buy her new clothes and feed her for several weeks.

Had Rothen even considered that she might steal them? Of course, he wouldn't be worried about theft if he was confident that she couldn't escape. Snatching valuables wasn't going to do her any good while she was stuck in the Guild.

Looking around again, it struck her that this was a very strange prison. She had expected a cold cell, not comfort and luxury.

Perhaps they did truly intend to invite her to join the Guild.

She looked up at the mirror and tried to imagine herself wearing robes. Her skin crawled.

No, she thought, *I could never be one of them. It would be like betraying everyone – my friends, all the people of the slums, myself . . .*

But she had to learn to control her powers. The danger was real, and Rothen probably did intend to teach her some things – even if it was just to prevent her from making a mess of the city. She doubted he would teach her anything more, however. Remembering the frustration and horrors of the last six weeks, she shivered. Her powers had caused her enough trouble already. She would not be disappointed if she never used them again.

What would happen to her then? Would the Guild let her return to the slums? Not likely. Rothen claimed that the Guild wanted her to join them. Her? A slum girl? Not likely, either.

But why would they offer? Was there some other reason. Bribery? They might promise to teach her magic if she . . . did what? What could the Guild possibly want from her?

She frowned as the answer leapt into her mind.

The Thieves.

If she escaped would Faren still be interested in hiding her? Yes – particularly if her powers were no longer dangerous. Once she was in his confidence, it would not be hard to work against the Thief. She could use her mental powers to send the Guild information about the criminal groups of the city.

She snorted. Even if she had wanted to co-operate with the Guild, the Thieves would work it out soon enough. No dwell was stupid enough to squimp on the Thieves. Even if she managed to protect herself with magic, she would not be able to stop them harming her friends and family. The Thieves were ruthless when crossed.

But would she have a choice? What if the Guild threatened to kill her if she did not help them? What if *they* threatened to harm her friends and family? With rising alarm, she wondered if the Guild knew about Jonna and Ranel.

She pushed the thought away, still wary of any strong emotions that might loosen her hold on her magic. Shaking her head, she turned away from the mirror. A book lay on a small table beside the bed. She crossed the room and picked it up.

Flicking through the pages, she discovered that they were covered in neat lines of text. Looking closer, she was surprised to find she could understand most of the words. Serin's lessons had done more good than she had thought.

The text appeared to be about boats. After reading several lines, Sonea realised that the last word in each pair of lines ended in the same sound, like the lyrics of songs the street performers in markets and bolhouses sang.

She froze as a soft knocking came from the door. As it opened Sonea quickly placed the book back on the table. She looked up to see Rothen standing in the doorway, a cloth-covered bundle under one arm.

'Can you read?'

She considered how she should answer. Was there any reason to hide her ability? She couldn't think of one, and it would be satisfying to let him know that not all dwells were illiterate.

'A little,' she admitted.

He closed the door and gestured to the book.

'Show me,' he said. 'Read some aloud.'

She felt a little doubt creep in, but pushed it aside. Picking up the book again, she opened it and began to read.

At once, she regretted getting herself into the situation. Conscious of the magician's gaze, she found it hard to concentrate. The page she had selected was more difficult than the first, and she felt her cheeks warm as she stumbled on unfamiliar words.

'Mar*ee*na, not mar*in*er.'

Annoyed at the interruption, she closed the book and tossed it onto the bed. Smiling apologetically, Rothen dropped the bundle of cloth down next to it.

'How did you learn to read?' he asked.

'My aunt taught me.'

'And you've been practising recently.'

She looked away. 'There's always stuff to read. Signs, labels, reward notices . . .'

He smiled. 'We found a book on magic in one of the rooms you occupied. Did you understand any of it?'

A warning chill ran down her spine. He would not believe her if she denied reading the book but if she admitted it, he would ask more questions and she might accidentally reveal which other books she had read. Should he know the books Cery had stolen were missing, he would have to consider it possible that she had slipped into the Guild at night, and he would be more cautious about keeping her locked inside.

Instead of answering, she nodded at the cloth bundle on the bed.

'What's that?'

He considered her for a moment, then shrugged. 'Clothes.'

Sonea eyed the bundle dubiously.

'I'll give you time to get changed, then send my servant in with some food.' He turned to the door.

After he had left, Sonea unwrapped the bundle. To her

relief, he had not brought magicians' robes. Instead she found a pair of simple trousers, undershirt and a high-collared shirt – much the same as the clothes she had been wearing in the slums but made of soft, expensive materials.

Shrugging out of the leisure coat and night robe, she pulled on the new clothes. Though she now felt decently covered, her skin still felt strangely bare. Looking at her hands, she saw that her fingernails had been clipped and cleaned. She sniffed them and smelt a soapy fragrance.

A shiver of alarm and indignation ran through her. Somebody had washed her while she had slept. She stared at the door. Rothen?

No, she decided, tasks like that would be left to the servants. Running her hands through her hair she discovered that it, too, had been washed.

A few more minutes passed, then a softer knock came from the door. Remembering that the magician was going to send in a servant, Sonea waited for the stranger to enter. The knock came again.

'Lady?' a woman called, her voice muffled by the door. 'May I enter?'

Amused, Sonea sat down on the bed. Nobody had ever called her 'Lady' before.

'If you want,' she answered.

A woman of about thirty years entered the room. She was dressed in a plain grey smock and matching trousers, and was carrying a covered tray.

'Hello,' the woman said, smiling nervously. Her eyes flickered to Sonea's, then quickly away again.

Sonea watched the servant carry the tray to the table and set it down. As the women reached for the cover her hand shook slightly. Sonea frowned. What was the servant afraid of? Surely not a mere slum girl?

The woman adjusted a few items on the tray, then turned and bowed deeply to Sonea before retreating quickly from the room.

For several minutes, Sonea stared at the door. The woman had bowed to her. This was . . . strange. Disturbing. She could not work out what it meant.

Then the smell of hot bread and something tantalisingly spicy drew her attention to the tray. A generous bowl of soup and a plate of small, sweet cakes beckoned to her, and she felt her stomach rumble.

She smiled. The magicians were going to find that she could not be bribed into betraying Faren, but they didn't need to know that straightaway. If she played with them a little, they might treat her like this for a very long time.

And she had no qualms about taking advantage of them.

Sonea crept into the guest room with all the watchful nervousness of a wild animal emerging from a cage. Her eyes flicked about, lingering longest on the doors, before settling on Rothen.

'That leads to a small washroom,' Rothen told her, pointing. 'My bedroom is through there, and that door opens to the main corridor of the Magicians' Quarters.'

She stared at the main door, then glanced at him before moving closer to the bookshelves. Rothen smiled, pleased so see her attracted to the books.

'Take down anything that interests you,' he urged. 'I will help you read them, and explain what you do not understand.'

She glanced at him again, her brows rising, and bent

closer to the books. She lifted a finger to touch the spine of a volume, but froze as the University gong began to ring.

'That indicates to novices that it is time to return to classes,' he explained. Crossing to one of the windows, he gestured for her to look outside.

Moving to the next window along, she looked out. At once, her face stiffened with tension. Eyes darting about, she watched the magicians and novices making their way back to the University.

'What do the colours mean?'

Rothen frowned. 'Colours?'

'The robes, they are different colours.'

'Ah.' He leaned on the sill of the window and smiled. 'First I should explain about the disciplines. There are three major uses to which magic can be applied: Healing, Alchemy and Warrior Skills.' He pointed to a pair of Healers walking slowly through the gardens. 'The Healers wear green. Healing involves learning more than just the magical methods of curing wounds and disease. It also includes all knowledge of medicine, which makes it a discipline that one must dedicate one's entire life to.'

Glancing at Sonea, he noted the interest in her eyes.

'Warriors wear red,' he told her, 'and study strategy and the ways that magic can be used in battle. Some also practice traditional forms of fighting and swordplay.'

He gestured to his own robes. 'Purple represents Alchemy, which is everything else that can be done with magic. It includes chemistry, mathematics, architecture and many other uses for magic.'

Sonea nodded slowly. 'What about the brown robes?'

'They are novices.' He pointed to a pair of youths. 'Do

you see how the robes fall only to the thigh?' Sonea nodded. 'They do not receive full robes until they graduate, by which time they have chosen a discipline to follow.'

'What if they want to learn more than one?'

Rothen chuckled. 'There just isn't enough time for that.'

'How long do they study for?'

'That depends how long they take to learn the required skills. Usually five years.'

'That one.' Sonea pointed. 'He wears a different coloured belt.'

Rothen looked down to see Lord Balkan striding by, his harsh face set in a frown as if he was worrying at a difficult problem.

'Ah, very observant of you.' Rothen smiled approvingly. 'The sash is black. It indicates that the man you are looking at is the Head of his chosen discipline.'

'The Head of the Warriors.' Sonea glanced at Rothen's robes and her eyes narrowed.

'What sort of Alchemy do you study?'

'Chemistry. I also teach it.'

'What is that?'

He paused, considering how best to explain it in terms she would understand. 'We work with substances: liquids, solids and gases. We mix them together, or heat them, or subject them to other influences and see what happens.'

Sonea frowned. 'Why?'

Rothen smiled crookedly. 'To see if we can discover anything useful.'

Sonea's eyebrows rose. 'What useful things have you discovered?'

'Me, or the Chemists of the Guild?'

'You.'

He laughed. 'Not much! I guess you could call me a failed Alchemist, but along the way I did discover one important thing.'

Sonea's brows rose.

'What was that?'

'I'm a very good teacher.' Moving away from the window, he considered the bookshelf. 'If you would allow me, I could help you improve your reading skills. Would you be interested in working on them this afternoon?'

She regarded him for a long time, her expression guarded but thoughtful. Finally, she gave a stiff nod. 'What do you think I should try?'

Approaching the bookcase, Rothen ran his eyes over the volumes. He needed something easy to read, but which would hold her interest. Taking down a book, he flicked through the pages.

She was more co-operative than he had anticipated. Her curiosity was strong, and her ability to read and her interest in his books were unexpected advantages. Both indicated that she might adapt well to a life of study.

He nodded to himself. All he had to do was persuade her that the Guild was not as bad as she thought it was.

Dannyl smiled at his friend. Since joining Yaldin and his wife for the evening, Rothen had been talking without pause. Dannyl hadn't seen Rothen so animated about a potential novice before – though Dannyl rather hoped his friend had been this enthusiastic when taking on *his* training.

'You're such an optimist, Rothen. You've barely met her and already you're talking as if she'll be the prize of the University.'

He smiled as his friend's expression became defensive.

'Am I?' Rothen replied. 'If I wasn't, would I have had so many successes with novices over the years? If you give up on them, they have no reason to try.'

Dannyl nodded. He hadn't been the most co-operative novice, and had resisted Rothen's early attempts to direct his mind away from bickering with Fergun and his fellow novices. Despite all Dannyl's attempts to prove Rothen wrong, his teacher had never given up on him.

'Did you tell her that we don't intend to harm her?' Ezrille asked.

'I've explained about the death of the youth and that we want to teach her how to control her powers. Whether she believes it or not . . .' He shrugged.

'Did you tell her that she can join the Guild?'

Rothen grimaced. 'I didn't press the issue. She doesn't like us much. It's not that she holds us responsible for the state of the poor, but she feels we should be doing something about it.' He frowned. 'She says she has never seen us do anything good, which is probably true. Most of the work we do for the city does not affect her or the rest of the dwells. And then there's the Purge.'

'Then it's hardly surprising that she doesn't like the Guild,' Ezrille said. She leaned forward. 'But what is she *like*?'

Rothen considered. 'Quiet, but defiant. She's obviously frightened, but I don't think we'll be seeing any tears. I'm sure she understands that she must learn Control, so I don't think we'll see any escape attempts just yet.'

'And after she has learned Control?' Yaldin asked.

'Hopefully by then we will have convinced her to join us.'

'What if she refuses?'

Rothen drew in a deep breath and sighed. 'I'm not sure what will happen. We can't force anyone to join us, but, by law, we can't allow magicians to exist outside the Guild, either. If she refuses,' he grimaced, 'we will have no choice but to block her powers.'

Ezrille's eyes widened. 'Block them? Is that bad?'

'No. It's . . . Well, it would be distressing for most magicians because they are used to having power to call upon. In Sonea's case, we have someone who isn't used to wielding magic – not in any useful form, anyway.' He shrugged. 'She won't miss it as much.'

'How long do you think it will take to teach her Control?' Yaldin asked. 'I feel uneasy knowing there's an uncontrolled magician living only a few doors away.'

'It will take some time for me to gain her trust,' Rothen replied. 'She might take several weeks.'

'Surely not!' Yaldin exclaimed. 'It never takes more than two weeks, even for the most difficult novices.'

'She is no spoilt or nervous child from the Houses.'

'I suppose you're right.' Yaldin shook his head and sighed. 'I'll be shaking with nerves by the end of a week.'

Rothen smiled and lifted his cup to his lips. 'Ah, but the longer she takes, the more time I have to convince her to stay.'

Sitting on the bed, Sonea peered at the gardens through a narrow gap in the window screen and toyed with a slender hair pin. It was night outside and the moon had risen. The snow edging the paths glowed softly in the subtle light.

An hour earlier, the gong had rung again. As magicians and novices hurried back to their Quarters, she had watched and waited. All was quiet now apart from the occasional servant hurrying by, breath streaming behind in the chilly night air.

Rising, she crept to the door and put her ear to it. Though she listened until her neck ached, she heard no sounds coming from the room beyond.

She looked down at the handle. It was smooth, polished wood. Set into it were pieces of darker timber, forming the lines of the Guild symbol. Sonea traced the pattern, marvelling at the skill and effort spent on a mere door handle.

Slowly, quietly, she began to turn the handle. It rotated only slightly before something blocked its movement. She carefully pulled the door inwards, but the latch was still caught.

Unperturbed, she started to rotate the handle in the other direction. Once more it only moved a little before stopping. She tugged the door but it remained in place.

Bending down, she raised her hand to insert the hair pin in the lock, then paused. There was no keyhole.

Sonea sighed and sat back on her heels. She hadn't heard the sound of a key turning any of the times Rothen had left the room, and she had noticed earlier that there were no bolts on the other side of the door. The door was locked by magic.

Not that she *could* go anywhere. She had to stay until she had learned to Control her magic.

But she needed to test her boundaries. If she didn't look for ways to escape, she might never find any.

She rose and moved to the table beside the bed. The book of songs still lay there. Picking it up, she opened it to the first page. Something was written there. Moving to the table, she lit the candle Rothen had left.

'For my darling Rothen, to mark the birth of our son. Yilara.'

Sonea pursed her lips. So he was married and had at least one child. She wondered where his family was. Considering Rothen's age, his son was probably a grown man.

He seemed a decent sort of person. She had always thought herself a good judge of character – something she had learned from her aunt. Her instincts told her that Rothen was kind and well-meaning. But that didn't mean she could trust him, she reminded herself. He was still a magician, bound to do whatever the Guild wanted.

A faint high-pitched laugh came from outside, drawing her attention to the window again. Pushing aside the screen, Sonea watched as a couple strode through the garden, the green robes under their cloaks shining in the glow of a floating light. Two children ran before them, tossing snow at each other.

Sonea watched them pass, her eyes following the woman. She had never seen female magicians in the Purge. Did they choose not to go, she wondered, or was there a rule that prevented them?

She pursed her lips. Jonna had told her that the daughters of rich families were carefully watched until they married the husband their fathers chose for them. Women made no important decisions within the Houses.

In the slums no-one arranged marriages. Though women *tried* to find a man who could support a family, they usually married for love. While Jonna believed this was better, Sonea was cynical. She had noticed that women often put up with a lot when in love, but, at some stage, love tended to wear off. Better to marry a man you liked and trusted.

Were female magicians cosseted away? Were they

encouraged to leave the running of the Guild to the men? It would be frustrating to be magically powerful, but still completely under the control of others.

As the family moved out of sight, Sonea began to draw away from the window, but, as her eyes flickered across the grounds, she caught a movement in one of the windows of the University. Looking up, she saw a pale oval face.

From the neckline of the stranger's clothes, she guessed this figure was a magician. Though she could not be sure in the dark and at the distance, she had a strong suspicion that he was watching her. A chill crept up her spine and she quickly pushed the screen closed.

Unnerved, she crossed the room and blew out the candle, then lay down on the bed and curled up in the blankets. She felt drained, tired of thinking, tired of being afraid. Tired of being tired . . .

But as she stared at the ceiling, she knew that sleep was not going to come easily.

CHAPTER 18

AWAY FROM PRYING EYES

A delicate, faint light had settled on the trees and buildings of the Guild. Cery frowned. Last time he had looked, everything had been shrouded in darkness. He must have dozed off, but he couldn't even remember closing his eyes. Rubbing his face, Cery looked around and considered the long night he had just passed.

It had begun with Faren. Recovered and fed, Cery had asked again if the Thief would help him retrieve Sonea. Faren's refusal had been firm.

'If she had been captured by the Guard, or even imprisoned in the Palace, I would have snatched her back already – and enjoyed proving that I could do it.' Faren had smiled briefly, but then his expression had hardened. 'But this is the Guild, Cery. What you suggest is out of my reach.'

'It's not,' Cery had insisted. 'They don't set guards, or magical barriers. They—'

'No, Cery.' Faren's eyes flashed. 'It is not a matter of guards or barriers. The Guild has never had a good enough reason to get off their backsides and do something about us. If we stole her back from their own grounds, it might give them reason to try. Believe me, Cery, nobody wants to find out whether we could evade them or not.'

'The Thieves are afraid of them?'

'Yes.' Faren's expression had been unusually sober. 'We are. And with good reason.'

'If we made it look as if someone else rescued her . . .'

'The Guild may still believe it was us. Listen to me, Cery. I know you well enough to guess that you will try to rescue her on your own. Consider this instead: the others will kill you if they believe you are a threat. They're watching us closely.'

Cery had said nothing to that.

'Do you want to continue working for me?'

Cery had nodded.

'Good. I have another job for you, if you want it.'

Faren's job had taken Cery to the Marina, as far from the Guild as he could get. Afterwards, Cery had made his way across the city, climbed the Guild wall, and settled himself down in the forest to watch.

As activity had dwindled and the night deepened, Cery had seen a movement in one of the windows of the University. A face appeared. A man's face, staring at the magicians' building intently.

The watcher remained at his post for half an hour. Finally, a pale face had appeared in a window of the magicians' building and Cery's heart had leapt. Even from a distance, he recognised her.

Sonea had looked down at the gardens for several minutes, then she had looked up toward the watcher. Seeing him, she had quickly retreated from view.

The watcher had disappeared soon after. Though Cery had stayed all night, he had seen no other movement, either from magicians or Sonea. Now that dawn was close, he knew he should return to Faren. The Thief would not approve of Cery's spying, but Cery had planned for that.

An admission that Sonea was too well guarded would be enough to mollify the Thief. Faren had forbidden a rescue attempt, not information gathering, and he must have expected Cery to look for evidence that she was still alive.

Cery rose and stretched. He wouldn't be telling Faren what he had learned from the night's watching, however. Aside from the mysterious watcher, the magicians had set no external guard on the buildings. If Sonea was alone in that room, there was hope for her yet.

Smiling for the first time in days, Cery started through the forest toward the slums.

Sonea woke with a start to find Rothen's servant staring down at her.

'Excuse me, Lady,' the woman said hastily. 'But when I saw the bed was empty I thought . . . Why are you sleeping on the floor?'

Rising, Sonea disentangled herself from the blankets.

'The bed,' she said. 'It sinks so much. I feel like I'm going to fall right through it.'

'Sinks?' The woman blinked in surprise. 'You mean it's too soft?' She smiled brightly. 'But you've probably not slept on a reber-wool mattress before. Here.'

She pulled the sheets from the bed to reveal several layers of thick, spongy mattress. Grasping half, she pulled them from the bed.

'Do you think that would be comfortable for you?' she asked, pressing down on the remaining layers.

Sonea hesitated, then pressed on the mattress. The bed was still soft, but she could feel the wooden base underneath. She nodded.

'Wonderful,' the servant cooed. 'Now, I've brought

water for you to wash in, and – Oh! You've slept in your clothes. No matter. I've brought fresh ones. Once you've done, come out into the guest room. We'll have some cakes and sumi to start the day.'

Amused, Sonea watched the woman gather up the mattresses and bustle out of the room. When the door had closed, she sat down on the end of the bed and sighed.

I'm still here.

She ran through the previous day in her mind: the conversations with Rothen, her determination to escape, the people she had seen through the window last night. Sighing, she rose and examined the basin of water, soap and towel that the servant had brought.

With a shrug, she stripped off, washed and changed, then moved to the door. As she reached for the handle she hesitated. No doubt Rothen was waiting beyond the door. She felt a small twinge of anxiety, but no fear.

He was a magician. That ought to scare her more, but he had said he would not harm her, and she had chosen to believe him – for now.

To let him into her mind, however, was not going to be so easy. She had no idea if he could harm her that way. What if he could change the way she thought, and make her love the Guild?

What choice do I have? She was going to have to trust that he couldn't, or wouldn't, mess around with her mind. It was a risk she had to take and worrying about it would not make it any easier.

Straightening her back, she opened the door. The room beyond appeared to be the one Rothen spent most of his time in. A set of chairs were arranged around a low table in the centre of the room. Bookshelves and higher tables stood against the walls. Rothen sat in one of the cushioned chairs, his blue eyes darting back and forth over the pages of a book.

He looked up and smiled. 'Good morning, Sonea.'

The servant woman stood beside one of the side tables. Sonea settled into the chair opposite Rothen. Bringing a tray to the table, the servant placed a cup before Rothen and another in front of Sonea.

Rothen lay the book on the table. 'This is Tania,' he said, looking up at the woman. 'My servant.'

Sonea nodded. 'Hello, Tania.'

'Honoured to meet you, Lady,' the woman replied, bowing.

Feeling her face warming with embarrassment, Sonea looked away. To her relief, Tania returned to the food table.

Watching the woman arranging cakes on a tray, Sonea wondered if she was supposed to be flattered by the obeisance? Perhaps they hoped she would gain a liking for it, as well as the luxuries, and be more willing to co-operate.

Sensing Sonea's gaze, the woman looked up and smiled nervously.

'Did you sleep well, Sonea?' Rothen asked.

Looking at him, she shrugged. 'A little.'

'Would you like to continue with your reading lessons today?'

She looked at the book that he had been reading and frowned as she realised that it was familiar.

He followed her gaze. 'Ah, *Fien's Notes on Magic Usage*. I thought I should know what you've been reading. This is an old history book, not a textbook, and the information in it may be outdated. You may—'

A knock on the door interrupted him. Rising, he

approached the main door and opened it slightly. Knowing that he could easily stop her from escaping, she realised he was deliberately stopping her from seeing the visitor – or was he preventing the visitor from seeing her?

'Yes? Lord Fergun. What can I do for you?'

'I wish to see the girl.'

The voice was smooth and cultured. Sonea started as Tania draped a dining napkin over her lap. The servant frowned at Rothen's back before moving away.

'It is too early for that,' Rothen replied. 'She is . . .' He hesitated, then stepped through the door and closed it behind him. From behind the door, Sonea could hear the faint murmur of voices as the discussion continued.

She looked up as Tania approached again, this time holding a platter of sweet cakes. Sonea chose one, and took an experimental sip from the cup in front of her.

A bitter taste filled her mouth and she grimaced. Tania's eyebrows rose, and she nodded towards the drink in Sonea's hand.

'I'd wager that means you don't like sumi,' she said. 'What would you like to drink?'

'Raka,' Sonea replied.

The servant looked genuinely apologetic. 'We don't stock raka here, I'm sorry. Can I get you some pachi juice instead?'

'No, thanks.'

'Water then?'

Sonea gave her an incredulous look.

Tania smiled. 'The water here is clean. Here, I'll get you some.' She returned to the table at the back of the room, filled a glass from a jug and brought it to Sonea.

'Thank you,' Sonea said. Lifting the glass, she was amazed to find the liquid was clear. Not even the tiniest particle floated in it. Taking a sip, she tasted nothing but a faint sweetness.

'See?' Tania said. 'I'll tidy your room now. I'll be gone for a few minutes but if you need anything, don't hesitate to call.'

Sonea nodded and listened to the servant's footsteps as she walked away. She smiled as the bedroom door closed. Taking the glass, Sonea gulped the water down and dried the inside quickly with the dining napkin. Stepping quietly to the door, she placed it against the wood and rested her ear on the base.

'. . . to keep her in there. It is dangerous.'

This voice belonged to the stranger.

'Not until she regains her strength,' Rothen replied. 'Once that happens I can show her how to spend her power safely, as we did yesterday. There is no danger to the building.'

There was a pause. 'Nevertheless, there is no reason to keep her isolated.'

'As I told you, she is easily frightened, and not a little confused. She doesn't need a crowd of magicians telling her the same thing in a dozen different ways.'

'Not a crowd, just myself – and I only wish to make her acquaintance. I'll leave all the teaching to you. Surely there is no harm in that?'

'I understand, but there will be time for that later, when she has gained some confidence.'

'There is no Guild law saying that you can keep her from me, Rothen,' the stranger replied, a warning tone entering his voice.

'No, but I believe most would understand my reasoning for it.'

The stranger sighed. 'I have as much concern for her wellbeing as you, Rothen, and I have searched for her as long and hard as well. I think many would agree that I have earned a voice in the matter.'

'You will have your opportunity to meet her, Fergun,' Rothen replied.

'When?'

'When she is ready.'

'And only you shall decide that.'

'For now.'

'We'll see about that.'

Silence followed, then the door handle began to turn. Sonea darted back to her seat and spread the napkin over her lap again. As Rothen stepped back into the room, his expression changed from annoyance to good humour.

'Who was that?' Sonea asked.

He shrugged. 'Just someone who wanted to know how you were doing.'

Sonea nodded, then leaned forward to take another sweet cake.

'Why does Tania bow and call me Lady?'

'Oh,' Rothen dropped into his chair and reached for the cup of bitter liquid Tania had left for him. 'All magicians are addressed as Lord or Lady.' He shrugged. 'It's always been that way.'

'But I'm not a magician,' Sonea pointed out.

'Well, she is a bit premature.' Rothen chuckled.

'I think . . .' Sonea frowned. 'I think she's afraid of me.'

He frowned at her over the lip of his cup. 'She's just a little nervous of you. Being near a magician who has not learnt Control can be dangerous.' He smiled crookedly. 'It seems she's not the only one who's worried. Knowing the dangers better than most, you can imagine how some magicians feel about having you living in their own Quarters. You're not the only one who slept lightly last night.'

Thinking back to her capture, to the broken walls and rubble she had glimpsed before falling unconscious, Sonea shivered. 'How long till you can teach me Control?'

His expression became sober. 'I don't know,' he admitted. 'But don't be concerned. If your powers begin to manifest again, we can use them up as we did before.'

She nodded, but as she looked at the cake she was holding, she felt her stomach clench. Her mouth suddenly seemed too dry for such a sweet thing. Swallowing, she set it aside.

The morning had been murky and dim and by mid-afternoon, heavy clouds hung low and threatening over the city. Everything was shrouded in shadows, as if night had become too impatient to wait for the end of the day. On days like this, the faint glow from the interior walls of the University was more noticeable.

Rothen sighed as, once they were in the University corridor, Dannyl's stride lengthened. He struggled to keep pace, then gave up.

'How strange,' he said to Dannyl's back. 'Your limp appears to have disappeared.'

Dannyl turned, then blinked in surprise as he saw how far Rothen had fallen behind. As he slowed his pace, the slight hesitation in his stride returned.

'Ah, *there* it is.' Rothen nodded. 'Why the hurry, Dannyl?'

'I just want to get it over with.'

'We're only handing in our reports,' Rothen told him. 'I'll probably end up doing most of the talking.'

'*I* was the one the High Lord sent off in search of the Thieves,' Dannyl muttered. '*I'll* have to answer all his questions.'

'He's only a few years older than you, Dannyl. So is Lorlen, and *he* doesn't frighten all sense out of you.'

Dannyl opened his mouth to protest, then shut it again and shook his head. They had reached the end of the corridor.

Stepping up to the door of the Administrator's room, Rothen smiled when he heard Dannyl take a deep breath. At Rothen's knock, the door swung inward, revealing a large, sparsely furnished room. A globe light hovered above a desk at the far end, illuminating the dark blue robes of the Administrator.

Lorlen looked up and beckoned to them with his pen. 'Come in, Lord Rothen, Lord Dannyl. Take a seat.'

Rothen looked around the room. No black-robed figure reclined in any of the chairs or lurked in the dim corners. Dannyl let out a long sigh of relief.

Lorlen smiled as they settled into the chairs in front of his desk. Leaning forward, he took the leaves of paper that Rothen offered. 'I've been looking forward to reading your reports. I'm sure Lord Dannyl's will be fascinating.'

Dannyl winced but said nothing.

'The High Lord sends his congratulations.' Lorlen's eyes flickered from Rothen's to Dannyl's. 'And I offer mine as well.'

'Then we offer our thanks in return,' Rothen replied.

Lorlen nodded, then smiled crookedly. 'Akkarin is

particularly pleased that he can sleep uninterrupted now there are no crude attempts at magic waking him through the night.'

Seeing Dannyl's eyes widen, Rothen smiled. 'I guess there are drawbacks to having such fine senses.'

He tried to imagine the High Lord pacing his rooms at night, cursing the elusive slum girl. The image didn't quite suit the solemn Guild leader. He frowned. How much interest was Akkarin going to take in Sonea now that she had been found?

'Administrator, do you think the High Lord will be wanting to meet Sonea?'

Lorlen shook his head. 'No. His main concern was that we might not find her before her powers became destructive – and the King had started to question our ability to take care of our own.' He smiled at Rothen. 'I think I understand why you are asking. Akkarin can be quite intimidating, especially to the younger novices, and Sonea will be easily frightened.'

'That brings me to another point,' Rothen said, leaning forward. 'She *is* easily frightened, and also very suspicious of us. It will take time for me to overcome her fear. I'd like to keep her isolated until she has gained some confidence, then begin introducing her to people one at a time.'

'That sounds sensible.'

'Fergun asked to see her this morning.'

'Ah.' Lorlen nodded and drummed his fingers on the table. 'Hmmm. I can see all the arguments he'll use to get his way. I could rule that nobody shall see her until she is ready, but I don't think he'll be satisfied until I specify what "ready" is, and I've set a date.'

He rose and began to pace back and forth behind his

desk. 'The two guardianship claims have complicated matters, too. People accept that, since you have plenty of experience in teaching Control, you should be the one to teach that to her. But if Fergun is excluded from Sonea's early training, people will support Fergun's claim for guardianship out of sympathy.' He paused. 'Can Fergun be one of these people you introduce to her?'

Rothen shook his head. 'She is observant and quick to pick up people's feelings. Fergun has little fondness for me. If I am to convince her that we're all friendly, well-meaning people, then it won't help if she notices conflict between any of us. Also, she may mistake his determination to see her as an intention to do harm.'

Lorlen regarded him for a moment, then crossed his arms.

'Everyone wants Sonea to learn Control as quickly as possible,' he said. 'I don't think anyone will disagree if I decide that nothing shall distract her from that. How long do you think it will take?'

'I don't know,' Rothen confessed. 'I've taught uninterested, easily distracted novices, but I've never tried to teach Control to somebody who distrusts magicians as much as she does. It may take several weeks.'

Lorlen returned to his chair. 'I can't give you that much time. I'll give you two weeks, during which time you can decide who will see her. After that, I will begin visiting every few days to check how close she is to gaining an acceptable level of Control.' He paused and tapped the tabletop with a fingernail. 'If you can, introduce her to at least one other magician by then. I will tell Fergun that he may see her after she has learned Control, but remember, the longer it takes, the more sympathy he will gain.'

Rothen nodded. 'I understand.'

'People will expect the Hearing to occur during the first Meet after she has learned Control.'

'If I can convince her to stay,' Rothen added.

Lorlen frowned. 'Do you think she will refuse to join the Guild?'

'It is too early to say,' Rothen replied. 'We can't force her to say the vow.'

Leaning back in his chair, Lorlen regarded Rothen thoughtfully, his brow creased with concern.

'Is she aware of the alternative?'

'Not yet. Since I'm trying to gain her trust, I felt it better to leave that news until later.'

'I understand. Perhaps, if you choose the right moment, it will convince her to stay.' He smiled wryly. 'If she leaves, Fergun will be convinced you talked her out of staying just to spite him. Either way, you are facing some tough battles, Rothen.'

Dannyl frowned. 'He has a strong claim, then?'

'It is hard to say. Much may depend on the strength of support each of you gain. But I should not speak about it before the Hearing.' Lorlen straightened and looked from Rothen to Dannyl. 'I have no more questions. Do either of you have anything else you wish to discuss?'

'No.' Rothen rose and inclined his head. 'Thank you, Administrator.'

Once in the corridor, Rothen considered his companion. 'That wasn't so bad, was it?'

Dannyl shrugged. 'He wasn't there.'

'No.' As another magician stepped out into the corridor Dannyl checked his stride, his steps becoming halting. Rothen shook his head. 'You *are* playing up that limp!'

Dannyl looked hurt. 'It was a deep cut, Rothen.'

'Not *that* deep.'

'Lady Vinara said that it would be some days before the stiffness disappeared.'

'She did, did she?'

Dannyl's brows rose. 'And it doesn't do you any harm if I remind people what we went through to catch that girl.'

Rothen chuckled. 'I am most grateful for the sacrifice you are making to your dignity.'

Dannyl made a small noise of disgust. 'Well, if Fergun can walk around for a week with a bandage over that tiny cut on his temple, then I can have my limp.'

'I see.' Rothen nodded slowly. 'Then it's all right then.'

They reached the back doors of the University and stopped. The air outside was thick with falling snow. Exchanging mutual looks of dismay, they stepped out into the swirling whiteness and hurried away.

CHAPTER 19

LESSONS BEGIN

A week of worsening weather had buried the Guild grounds in a thick layer of snow. Lawns, gardens and roofs had vanished under a sparkling white blanket. Cosy within the protection of his own magical shield, Dannyl could appreciate the spectacle without enduring the discomfort.

Novices hovered around the University entrance. As he entered the building a trio hurried past him, their cloaks wrapped tightly around their shoulders. Part of the midwinter intake, he surmised. It took several weeks of training before the new novices learned how to ward off the cold.

Climbing the stairs, he found a small group of novices waiting outside the Alchemy room where Rothen taught his classes. Waving them through the door, he started to follow.

'Lord Dannyl.'

Recognising the voice, Dannyl suppressed a groan. He turned to find Fergun strolling along the corridor toward him, Lord Kerrin at his side.

Stopping a few paces from Dannyl, Fergun eyed the classroom door. 'Is that Rothen's class you're entering?'

'Yes,' Dannyl replied.

'You're teaching them?'

'Yes.'

'I see.' Fergun turned away, Kerrin following. In a quiet voice, pitched loud enough for Dannyl to hear, he added, 'I'm surprised they allow it.'

'What do you mean?' Kerrin asked, his voice growing fainter as the pair walked away.

'Don't you remember all the trouble he got into as a novice?'

'Oh, *that*!' Kerrin laughed, the sound echoing in the corridor. 'I suppose he might be a bad influence.'

Gritting his teeth, Dannyl turned away and found Rothen standing in the doorway.

'Rothen!' Dannyl exclaimed. 'What are you doing here?'

'I was just visiting the library.' Rothen's gaze remained on Fergun's back. 'It amazes me how long you two have kept this grudge going. Are you ever going to leave the past behind you?'

'It's not a grudge to him,' Dannyl growled. 'It's sport and he enjoys it too much to stop.'

Rothen raised his brows. 'Well, if he behaves like a spiteful novice, people will treat his words accordingly.' He smiled as three novices hurried along the corridor and darted through the classroom door. 'How are my novices doing?'

Dannyl grimaced. 'I don't know how you cope, Rothen. You're not going to abandon me to them for long, are you?'

'I don't know. Weeks. Months, maybe.'

Dannyl groaned. 'Do you think Sonea is ready to begin Control lessons yet?'

Rothen shook his head. 'No.'

'But it's been a week already.'

'*Only* a week.' Rothen sighed. 'I doubt she'd trust us if we gave her six months to settle in.' He frowned. 'It's not that she dislikes us as individuals, but that she doesn't believe the Guild means well – and she won't until she sees proof. We don't have time for that. When Lorlen visits, he'll expect us to have begun lessons already.'

Dannyl grasped his friend's arm. 'For now all you have to do is teach her Control, and for that she only has to trust *you*, Rothen. You're a likeable sort. You've got her best interests at heart.' He hesitated. 'If you can't *tell* her, then *show* her.'

Rothen frowned, then his eyes widened in understanding. 'Let her see into my mind?'

'Yes. She will *know* you've been telling her the truth.'

'It's . . . it's not necessary when teaching Control, but the circumstances are hardly usual.' Rothen frowned. 'There are some things I'll have to keep her from learning, though . . .'

'Hide them.' Dannyl smiled. 'Now, I have a classroom of your novices waiting, all eager to try out their latest pranks and teacher-torturing antics on me. Lorlen is nothing. *I* expect to hear you've made *considerable* progress when we meet tonight.'

Rothen chuckled. 'Be reasonable to them, and they'll be reasonable to you, Dannyl.'

As his friend turned away, Dannyl uttered a short, humourless laugh. Somewhere above them, a striker rang the University gong. Sighing, Dannyl straightened his shoulders and entered the classroom.

Leaning on the window sill, Sonea watched the last of the magicians and novices hurry out of sight. Not all had responded to the University gong, however. Two distant figures remained standing at the other side of the gardens.

One was a woman in green robes with a black sash – the Head of Healers. *So women* did *have some influence in the Guild*, she mused.

The other was a male dressed in blue robes. Thinking back to Rothen's explanation of the robe colours, she could not recall him mentioning blue. The colour was uncommon, so perhaps he, too, was a magician of influence.

Rothen had explained how the magicians in high positions were selected by a vote among Guild members. This method of choosing leaders by the agreement of the majority was intriguing. She had expected that the strongest magicians would rule the others.

According to Rothen, the rest of the magicians spent their time teaching, experimenting, or working on public projects. This included work that ranged from the impressive to the ridiculous. She had been surprised to learn that the magicians had built the Marina, and amused to hear how one magician had spent much of his life trying to make stronger and stronger glues.

Drumming her fingers, she looked around the room again. In the last week she had found opportunities to examine everything, even the room Rothen slept in. A careful search of all cupboards, chests and drawers had revealed clothes and everyday items. The few locks she had encountered succumbed easily to her picking skills, but old documents had been her only reward.

Catching a movement at the edge of her vision, she turned back to the window. The two magicians had parted, and the blue-robed man was now walking along the edge of the garden toward the two-storey residence of the High Lord.

Remembering the night she had peeked into that building, she shivered. Rothen had mentioned nothing of assassin magicians, but that was hardly surprising. He was trying to convince her that the Guild was friendly and useful. If the black-robed magician wasn't an assassin, then what else could he be?

A memory of a man in bloodstained clothes flashed into her mind.

'It is done,' the man had said. *'Did you bring my robes?'*

She jumped as the main door clicked open behind her. Turning, she let out a breath as Rothen strode into the room in a swirl of purple robes.

'Sorry I took so long.'

He was a magician, and yet he was *apologising* to her. Amused, she shrugged in reply.

'I've brought some books from the library.' He straightened and regarded her earnestly. 'But I thought we might start working on some mind exercises. What do you think?'

'Mind exercises?' She frowned, then felt herself go cold as she realised what he was suggesting. Did he think she trusted him after only a week?

Do I?

He was watching her closely. 'We probably won't start Control lessons,' he told her. 'But you should gain a familiarity with mental communication in preparation for the lessons.'

Thinking about the past week, she considered what she had learned of him.

He had spent most of the time teaching her to read. At first she had been suspicious, and had expected to find something in the content of the books that he might use as a lure or bribe. She had been almost disappointed to find herself reading simple adventure stories, with little reference to magic at all.

Unlike Serin, who had been anxious to avoid angering her, Rothen did not hesitate to correct her when she made a mistake. He could be quite stern, but she had found, to her surprise, that he was not at all frightening. She had even caught herself wanting to tease him a little when he was being so serious.

When he was not teaching her, he tried to chat. She knew she wasn't making this easy for him when there were so many subjects she refused to discuss. Though he was always willing to answer her questions, he hadn't tried to trick or force her into revealing anything about herself in return.

Would mental communication be like this? Would she still be able to hide parts of herself?

The only way to find out is to try it, she told herself. Swallowing, she nodded quickly. 'How do we start?'

He gave her a searching look. 'If you don't want to, we can wait a few more days.'

'No.' She shook her head. 'Now is fine.'

He nodded, then gestured to the chairs. 'Sit down. Make sure you're comfortable.'

She lowered herself into a chair, then watched as he pushed the low table aside and moved a chair forward to face hers. He would be sitting close, she noted with dismay.

'I'm going to tell you to close your eyes,' he said. 'Then I'm going to take your hands. While it's not necessary for us to touch when we speak to each other, it helps to focus the mind. Are you ready?'

She nodded.

'Close your eyes,' he instructed, 'and relax. Breath deeply and slowly. Listen to the sound of your breathing.'

She did as he said. For a long time he was silent. After a while, she realised that the rhythm of their breathing was the same, and she wondered if he had changed his breath to follow hers.

'Imagine that, with every breath, a part of you relaxes. Your toes first, then feet, then ankles. Calves, knees, upper legs. Rest your fingers, hands, wrists, arms, your back. Let your shoulders drop. Let your head hang forward a little.'

Though she felt his instructions were a little peculiar, she did as he said. As she felt the tension leave her limbs, she grew aware of a fluttering in her stomach.

'Now I'm going to take your hands,' he told her.

The hands that enclosed hers seemed much larger. She resisted the urge to open her eyes to check.

'Listen. Think about what you can hear.'

Sonea was suddenly aware that she was surrounded by constant small noises. Each noise leapt out at her and demanded to be identified: the sound of footsteps outside, the distant voices of magicians and servants coming from both inside and outside the building . . .

'Now let the sounds outside the room fade away. Instead, concentrate on the sounds within this room.'

It was quieter inside. The only sound was their breathing, now at different rhythms.

'Let those sounds fade away, too. Now listen to the sounds within your own body. The slow pounding of your heart . . .'

She frowned. Aside from her breathing, she could hear no sounds in her body.

'. . . The rush of blood circulating through your body.'

Though she was concentrating hard, she could not hear . . .

'. . . The sound of your stomach . . .'

. . . or could she? There *was* something . . .

'. . . The vibration within your ears . . .'

Then she realised that the noises he described were not heard so much as *felt*.

'. . . and now listen to the sound of your thoughts.'

For a moment Sonea was puzzled by his instruction, then she sensed a presence at the edge of her mind.

—*Hello Sonea.*

—*Rothen?*

—*That's right.*

The presence grew more tangible. The personality she could sense was surprisingly familiar. It was like recognising a voice, a voice so individual that it could never be confused with another.

—*So this is mind communication*, she mused.

—*Yes. Using it, we can speak to each other from great distances.*

She realised that she was not hearing *words*, but sensing the meaning of thoughts that he had projected toward her. They flashed into her mind, and were understood so quickly and completely that she knew with certainty exactly what he wanted her to know.

—*It's so much faster than talking!*

—*Yes, and there's less chance of a misunderstanding.*

—*Could I talk like this to my aunt? I could let her know I'm still alive.*

—*Yes and no. Only magicians can communicate mind to mind without physical contact. You could speak to your aunt, but you'd need to be touching her. There is no reason why you can't send your aunt an ordinary message, however . . .*

Which would reveal their location, she realised. Sonea felt her enthusiasm for mind communication waver. She must be careful.

—So . . . do magicians talk like this all the time?

—Not often.

—Why not?

—There are limitations to this form of communication. You sense the emotions behind the thoughts others send you. It's easy to detect when someone is lying, for example.

—That is a bad thing?

—Not in itself, but imagine if you had noticed that your friend was going bald. He would sense your amusement behind your thoughts and, while not knowing what you found so funny, he would know it was at his expense. Now imagine it was not your forgiving friend, but somebody you respected and wanted to impress.

—I see what you mean.

—Good. Now for the next part of your lesson, I want you to imagine your mind is a room – a space with walls, a floor and a ceiling.

At once she found herself standing in the centre of a room. There was something familiar about it, though she could not remember seeing one like it before. It was empty, and had no doors or windows and the walls were bare wood.

—What do you see?

—The walls are wooden, and it's empty, she replied.

—Ah, I see it. This room is the conscious part of your mind.

—So . . . you can see into my mind?

—No, you just projected an image at me. Look, I'll send it back.

An image of the room flashed through her mind. It was indistinct and hazy, the details no longer visible.

—*It's . . . different, and kind of fuzzy*, she told him.

—*That is because a little time had passed, and my memory of it had faded. The difference you sense is from my mind filling in details that were missing from my memory, such as colour and texture. Now, your room needs a door.*

At once a door blinked into existence before her.

—*Go to the door. Do you remember what your power looked like?*

—*Yes, a glowing ball of light.*

—*That is a common way to visualise it. I want you to think of how it looked both when it was strong and dangerous, and after it had faded. Can you remember?*

—*Yes . . .*

—*Now open the door.*

As the door swung open she found herself standing on the threshold of darkness. A white sphere hung before her, glowing brightly. It was impossible to judge how far away it was. One moment it seemed to hover just beyond arm's reach, the next she was sure it was a colossal size, and hung an inconceivable distance away.

—*How big is it compared to what you remember?*

—*Not as big as it was when it was dangerous.* She sent him an image of it.

—*Good. It is growing faster than I expected, but we have some time before your magic begins to surface unasked for. Close the door and return to the room.*

The door closed and vanished, and she found that she was standing in the centre of the room again.

—*I want you to imagine another door. This time it's the door to the outside, so make it larger.*

Double doors appeared in her room, and she recognised them as the main doors of the stayhouse she had been living in before the Purge.

—*When you open the doors, you'll see a house. It should look something like this.*

An image of a white house, not unlike the large merchant homes in the West Quarter, flashed through her mind. As she pushed open the double doors in her mind, she found herself facing the building. Between her room and this house was a narrow street.

—*Cross to the building.*

The house had a single red door. The scene shifted and she found herself standing in front of it. As she touched the handle, it swung inward and she stepped into a large white room.

Paintings hung from the walls and cushioned chairs were arranged neatly in the room's corners. It reminded her a little of Rothen's guestroom, but grander. The sense of his personality was strong, like a powerful perfume or the warmth of sunlight.

—*Welcome, Sonea. You are in what you might call the first room of my mind. I can show you images here. Look at the paintings.*

She approached the closest picture. In it she saw herself in magicians' robes, talking earnestly with other magicians. Disturbed, she backed away.

—*Wait, Sonea. Consider the next painting.*

Reluctantly, she moved along the wall. The next picture showed her in green robes, healing a man with an injured leg. She turned away quickly.

—*Why does this future repel you?*

—*It is not who I am.*

—But it could be, Sonea. Do you see now that I have told you the truth?

Looking back at the paintings, she suddenly understood that he *was* speaking the truth. He could not lie to her here. He was showing her *real* possibilities. The Guild truly wanted her to join them . . .

Then she found a black door that she had not seen before. As she looked at it, she knew that it was locked and she felt her suspicions return. He might not be able to lie, but perhaps he could conceal some truths.

—You are hiding things from me! she accused.

—Yes, he told her. *We all have the ability to hide those parts of ourselves we wish to keep private. Otherwise, none of us would ever permit another into our minds. I will teach you to do this, for your need for privacy is stronger than most. Watch, and I will give you a glimpse of what is behind that door.*

The door swung inward. Through it Sonea saw a woman lying on a bed, her face deathly pale. A feeling of intense grief spilled out. Without warning, the door slammed shut again.

—My wife.

—She died . . .?

—Yes. Do you understand, now, why I hide that part of me?

—Yes. I am . . . sorry.

—It was a long time ago, and I understand that you must see that I speak the truth.

Sonea turned from the black door. A gust of perfumed air had entered the room, a mix of flowers and something crisp and unpleasant. The paintings of her in robes had swelled to fill the walls, but the colours were muted.

—We have achieved much. Shall we return to your mind?

At once the room began to slide under her feet,

propelling her to the red door. Stepping outside, she looked up. The face of her house rose before her. It was a plain wooden building, a bit worn, but still sturdy – typical of the better areas of the slums. Crossing the road, she re-entered the first room of her mind. The doors swung shut behind her.

—*Now turn back and look outside.*

As she pushed the doors open again she was surprised to find Rothen standing in front of her. He looked a little younger, and perhaps shorter, too.

'Are you going to invite me in?' he asked, smiling.

Stepping back, she gestured for him to enter. As he stepped over the threshold, the sense of his presence filled the room. He looked around, and she suddenly realised that it was no longer empty.

She felt a flush of guilt as she saw that, on a table nearby, was a box. It was one that she had broken into. The lid hung open and the documents inside were clearly visible.

Then she saw that Cery was sitting cross-legged on the floor, holding three familiar books.

And in another corner stood Jonna and Ranel . . .

'Sonea.'

She turned to find that Rothen had placed his hands over his eyes.

'Put anything you don't want me to see behind doors.'

Glancing around the room, she concentrated on pushing everything away. They slid backwards through the walls and disappeared.

—*Sonea?*

Turning around, she realised that Rothen had disappeared.

—*Did I push you out too?*

—Yes. Let's try that again.

Once more she opened the door and backed away to allow Rothen into the room. Catching a movement in the corner of her eye, she looked away, but whatever she had seen sank back into the walls. Turning back, she discovered that a new room had appeared beyond the door. A door stood open on the far side of this room and Rothen now stood in the doorway.

He stepped through the door and everything shifted. There were two rooms between them, then three.

—Enough!

She felt his hands release hers. Abruptly aware of the physical world, she opened her eyes. Rothen was leaning back in his chair, grimacing and rubbing his temples.

'Are you all right?' she asked, concerned. 'What happened?'

'I'm well.' He let his hands drop and smiled wryly. 'You pushed me right out of your mind. It's a natural reaction, and one you can learn to control. Don't worry, I'm used to it. I've taught many novices before.'

She nodded and rubbed her hands. 'Do you want to try again?'

He shook his head. 'Not now. We'll rest and work on your reading. Perhaps we'll try again this afternoon.'

CHAPTER 20

THE GUILD'S PRISONER

Cery yawned. Since Sonea had been taken, sleep had become a coy thing. It evaded him when he needed it, and stalked him when he didn't. Right now, he needed to be more awake than he had ever been before.

A freezing wind whipped the trees and hedges, filling the air with noise and the occasional twig or leaf. The cold crept into his muscles, making them cramp. Shifting his weight carefully, he stretched and rubbed first one leg, then the other.

Looking up at the window again, he decided that if he thought 'look outside' any harder his head was going to explode. Obviously Sonea's talent for sensing minds didn't extend to detecting unexpected visitors outside her window.

He regarded the snowballs he had made, and doubt returned. If the threw one at her window it would have to hit it loud enough to wake her, but not loud enough to attract anyone else's attention. He had no idea if she was still in the room, or if she was alone.

A light had been on when he had first arrived, but it was extinguished soon after. The windows on the left of hers were dark, but those on the right still glowed. He looked nervously at the University building towering to his left. The windows were dark. Since the first night when he had glimpsed Sonea, Cery had seen no sign of the mysterious watcher.

Somewhere in the corner of his eye, a light blinked out. He looked up at the magicians' building. The light in the rooms beside Sonea's had vanished. Cery smiled grimly and massaged his numb legs. Just a little longer . . .

When a pale face appeared at the window he thought, for a moment, that he *had* fallen asleep and was dreaming. He watched, heart pounding, as Sonea peered down at the gardens, then looked up at the University.

Then she moved out of sight.

All weariness was gone. Cery's fingers closed around a snowball. His legs protested as he wriggled out of the hedge. He took aim and, as the snowball left his fingers, ducked back into the hedge.

The faintest thud reached his ears as the snowball struck the window. His heart sang with triumph as Sonea's face appeared again. She stared at the splash of frost on the glass, and she looked out at the garden again.

Checking the other windows, Cery saw no other watchers. He wriggled out of the hedge a little, and saw Sonea's eyes widen as she spotted him. Surprise was followed by a wide grin.

He waved, then signalled a question to her. She returned with a 'yes'. No harm had been done to her. He breathed a sigh of relief.

The Thieves' code of signals was limited to simple meanings like 'ready?', 'now', 'wait', 'get out of here', and the usual 'yes' and 'no'. There was no sign for 'I'm about to rescue you. Is the window locked?' He pointed to himself, then made climbing movements, mimed opening the window, pointed at her, then himself, and finished with the sign for 'get out of here'.

She returned with 'wait', then pointed at herself, signed 'get out of here', and shook her head.

He frowned. Though she knew more than most dwells about the Thieves' signals, she had never been as well versed as he was. She could be telling him that she wasn't allowed to leave, or that she didn't want to leave now, or that he should return later in the night. He scratched his head, then signalled 'get out of here' then 'now'.

She shook her head, then something to his left caught her attention and her eyes widened. Moving away from the window a little, she began signalling 'get out of here' over and over. Cery crouched and retreated into the hedge, hoping the wind would hide the rustle of leaves.

No footsteps reached his ears, and he began to wonder what had spooked her, then warm air slid over his skin and the hairs on the back of his neck rose.

'Come out,' a cultured voice said, uncomfortably close. 'I know you're in there.'

Looking through the hedge, Cery could see the soft folds of robes only an arm's reach away. A hand snaked through the leaves. Cery twisted away, pushing out of the hedge and pressing himself against the building, his heart racing. The magician straightened quickly. Knowing that he was in full sight, Cery bolted along the side of the building toward the forest.

Something slammed into his back and he pitched forward into the snow. A weight held him there, pressing so firmly he could hardly breathe and the chill of the snow burned his face. He heard footsteps approaching and felt panic rising.

Calm. Stay calm, he told himself. *You've never heard of*

them killing intruders . . . You've never heard of them finding *intruders either . . .*

The crushing pressure eased. As he pushed himself to his hands and knees, Cery felt a hand grip his arm. It pulled him to his feet and dragged him through the hedge to the path.

Looking up, he turned cold as he recognised the magician.

The magician's eyes narrowed. 'You look familiar . . . Ah, now I remember. The filthy dwell that tried to strike me.' He glanced back at Sonea's window and smirked. 'So Sonea has an admirer. How sweet.'

He regarded Cery thoughtfully and a gleam crept into his eyes. 'What am I going to do with you, then? I believe intruders are usually questioned and then escorted out of the Guild. We best get started then.'

Cery struggled as the magician began to pull him along the path toward the University. The magician's thin hand was surprisingly strong.

'Let me go!' Cery demanded.

The magician sighed. 'If you insist on jerking my arm like that, I will be forced to use less physical means to hold you. Please co-operate. I am as anxious to see this business finished as I am sure you are.'

'Where are you taking me?'

'Out of this noisy wind for a start.' They reached the end of the magicians' building, and started toward the University.

'Lord Fergun.'

The magician stopped and looked over his shoulder. Two robed shadows were approaching. Feeling a sudden tension in his captor's grip, Cery was not sure whether to be relieved or worried about the newcomers. Obviously, Fergun didn't welcome their intrusion.

'Administrator,' Fergun said. 'How fortunate. I was just coming to rouse you. I have discovered an intruder. He appears to have been attempting to reach the slum girl.'

'So I have been told,' the taller newcomer glanced at his companion.

'Will you question him?' Fergun sounded hopeful, yet his grip on Cery's arm tightened.

'Yes,' the tall magician replied. He made a lazy gesture, and a ball of light flared into existence above them. Cery felt warmth slide over him and the wind disappeared. Looking around, he could still see trees twisting about, but the three magicians stood undisturbed.

In the strong light, the magicians' robes were brightly coloured. The tall magician wore blue, his companion, an older man, wore purple, and Cery's captor wore red. The tall magician looked down at Cery and smiled faintly.

'Do you want to talk to Sonea, Cery?'

Cery blinked in surprise, then frowned. How did this magician know his name?

Sonea must have told him. If she had wanted to warn Cery, she would have given them another name . . . unless they had tricked it out of her, or read it from her mind, or . . .

What did it matter? They had caught him. If they intended to do him harm, he was doomed anyway. He may as well see Sonea.

He nodded. The tall magician looked at Fergun. 'Let him go.'

Fergun's grip tightened before his fingers uncurled

from Cery's arm. The blue-robed magician gestured for Cery to follow, then started toward the magicians' building.

The doors opened before them. Aware of the two magicians pacing behind like guards, Cery followed the tall magician up a short flight of stairs to the upper floor. They strode down a wide corridor to one of many plain doors. The older magician stepped forward to touch the handle, and the door swung inward.

Inside was a luxurious room with cushioned chairs and fine furniture. In one of the chairs sat Sonea. When she saw Cery, she smiled.

'Go on,' the blue-robed magician said.

Heart still racing, Cery stepped into the room. As the door closed, he looked back and wondered if he had just walked into a trap.

'Cery,' Sonea breathed. 'It's so good to see you.'

He turned to study her. She smiled again, but it quickly disappeared.

'Sit down, Cery. I asked Rothen to let me talk to you. I told him you would keep trying to rescue me unless I explained why I can't leave.' She pointed to a seat.

He sat down reluctantly. 'Why can't you leave?'

She sighed. 'I don't know if I can tell you in a way that makes sense.' She leaned back in the chair. 'Magicians have to be taught how to control magic, and only another magician can teach it, because it has to be taught mind to mind. If they don't learn to control it, the magic works whenever the magician feels something. The magic takes simple, dangerous forms, always stronger as it grows. Eventually . . .' She grimaced. 'I . . . I nearly died the day they found me, Cery. They saved me.'

Cery shivered. 'I saw it, Sonea. The buildings – they're gone.'

'It would have been worse if they hadn't found me. People would have been killed. Lots of people.'

He looked down at his hands. 'So you can't come home.'

She chuckled, a sound so unexpectedly cheerful that he stared at her in astonishment.

'I'll be fine,' she told him. 'Once I've learned Control I won't be in danger any more. I'm getting to know how things work here.' She gave him a wink. 'So where are you hanging out now?'

He grinned. 'Same old place. Best bolhouse in the slums.'

She nodded. 'And your . . . friend? Is he still giving you work?'

'Yes.' Cery shook his head. 'But maybe not once he finds out what I did tonight.'

As she considered that, the familiar lines of worry appeared between her brows. He felt something squeeze his heart so tightly it hurt. Clenching his fists, he looked away. He wanted to pour out all the guilt and fear he'd felt since her capture, but the thought that others might be listening kept the words choked within his throat.

Looking at the luxuries of the room, he consoled himself that she was being treated well, at least. She yawned. It was late, he remembered.

'I guess I had better go.' He rose, then stopped, not wanting to leave her.

She smiled, this time sadly. 'Tell everyone I'm well.'

'I will.'

He couldn't move. Her smile faded a little as he stared at her, then she waved toward the door. 'I'll be fine, Cery. Trust me. Go on.'

Somehow he made himself walk to the door and knock. It swung inward. The three magicians regarded him closely as he stepped into the corridor.

'Shall I escort our visitor to the gate?' Fergun offered.

'Yes, thank you,' the blue-robed magician replied.

A globe of light appeared above Fergun's head. He looked at Cery expectantly. Glancing back at the blue-robed magician, Cery hesitated.

'Thanks.'

The magician nodded once in reply. Turning away, Cery started toward the stairs, the blonde magician following.

He considered Sonea's words as he descended. Her signals made sense now. She had to wait until she had learned to control her magic, but once she had she would try to escape. He could do little to help her, except make sure she had a secure place to return to.

'Are you Sonea's husband?'

Cery glanced up at the magician in surprise.

'No.'

'Her, ah . . . lover, then?'

Cery felt his cheeks warming. He looked away. 'No, just a friend.'

'I see. It was very heroic of you to come here.'

Deciding that he didn't need to reply to that, Cery stepped out of the magicians' building into the cold wind, and turned toward the garden. Fergun stopped.

'Wait. Let me take you through the University. It is a warmer journey.'

His heart skipped. The University.

He had always wanted to see inside the great building. Such an opportunity would never come again once Sonea escaped. Shrugging as if it made no difference to him, he started toward the back entrance of the enormous building.

His heart began to race as they climbed the stairs. They entered a room full of elaborately decorated staircases. The magician's light vanished as he directed Cery through a side door and into a wide corridor which seemed to extend for an eternity.

Doors and passages lined the walls on either side. Looking around, Cery could not find the source of light. It was as if the walls themselves glowed.

'Sonea was quite a surprise to us,' Fergun said suddenly, his voice echoing. 'We have never found any talent in the lower classes before. It's normally restricted to the Houses.'

Fergun looked at Cery expectantly, obviously expecting conversation.

'It gave her a surprise, too,' Cery replied.

'This way.' The magician guided Cery into one of the side passages. 'Have you ever heard of other dwells with magic?'

'No.'

They turned a corner, pushed through a door into a small room, then stepped through another door into a slightly wider corridor. Unlike the earlier passages, the walls were panelled with wood, and paintings hung at regular intervals.

'It's quite a maze in here,' Fergun said, sighing a little. 'Come, I'll take you through a shortcut.'

He stopped beside a painting and reached behind it. A section of the wall slid aside, revealing a rectangle of darkness the size of a narrow doorway. Cery looked at the magician questioningly.

'I've always loved secrets,' Fergun said, his eyes bright.

'Does it surprise you that we, too, have underground passages? This one comes out in the Inner Circle – a dry, windless journey. Shall we?'

Cery looked at the doorway, then at the magician. Passages under the Guild? This was too strange. He stepped back and shook his head.

'I've seen plenty of passages before,' he said, 'and I don't mind the cold. The pretty things in this building are more interesting.'

The magician closed his eyes and nodded. 'I see.' He straightened and smiled. 'Well, it's good to know you don't mind the cold.'

Something pressed on Cery's back, forcing him toward the rectangle. He yelled and grabbed the edges of the hole, but the push was too strong and his fingers slipped on the polished wood. Falling forward, he brought his hands up in time to protect his face as he slammed into a wall.

The force held him firmly against the bricks. He could not even move a finger. Heart racing madly, he cursed himself for trusting the magicians. He heard a click behind him. The secret doorway had closed.

'Yell now if you want.' Fergun chuckled, a low, nasty sound. 'Nobody comes down here, so you won't bother anyone.'

A piece of cloth dropped over Cery's eyes and was bound tightly. His hands were pulled together behind his back, and bound with more cloth. As the pressure against his back eased, a hand gripped his collar and shoved him forward.

Cery staggered down the passage. After a few steps he reached a steep stairway. He felt his way down, then the guiding hands pushed him along a route that twisted lazily.

The temperature of the air dropped rapidly. After a few hundred steps, Fergun halted. Cery's stomach sank as he heard the sound of a key turning in a lock.

The blindfold was pulled away. Cery found himself standing at the door of a large, empty room. The cloth about his wrists was untied.

'In you go.'

Cery looked at Fergun. His hands itched for his knives, but he knew he would only lose them if he tried to fight the magician. If he didn't walk into the room himself, Fergun would push him.

Slowly, numbly, he entered the cell. The door swung shut, leaving him standing in darkness. He heard the lock turn, then the muffled sound of footsteps moving away.

Sighing, he dropped to his haunches. Faren was going to be *furious*.

CHAPTER 21

A PROMISE OF FREEDOM

As he hurried along the corridor of the Magicians' Quarters, Rothen received more than a few inquiring looks from the magicians he passed. He nodded to some, and smiled at those he was most familiar with, but did not slow his stride. Reaching the door to his rooms, he grasped the handle and willed the lock to release.

As the door opened, he heard two voices from the guestroom within.

'—my father was a servant of Lord Margen, Lord Rothen's mentor. My grandfather worked here too.'

'You must have many relations here.'

'A few,' Tania agreed. 'But many of them have left to take up positions in the Houses.'

The two women were sitting beside each other on the chairs. Seeing him, Tania leapt to her feet, her face flushed.

'Don't let me interrupt,' Rothen said, waving a hand.

Tania bowed her head. 'I have not yet finished my work, my Lord,' she told him. Her face still glowing, she hastened away into his bedroom. Sonea watched, clearly amused.

—She's not afraid of me any more, I think.

Rothen considered his servant as she reappeared with a bundle of clothes and bedding under her arm.

—No. You two are getting along well.

Pausing, Tania gave Rothen a hard look, then glanced at Sonea speculatively.

—Can she tell that we're talking like this? Sonea asked.

—She sees our expressions changing. You don't have to be around magicians for long to know this is a sure sign that a silent discussion is taking place.

'Excuse us, Tania,' Rothen said aloud. Tania's brows rose, but she gave a little shrug and dropped the bundle of clothes into a basket.

'Is that all, Lord Rothen?'

'Yes, thank you Tania.'

Rothen waited until the door had closed behind the servant, then sat down beside Sonea. 'It's probably about time I told you that it's not considered polite to communicate mind to mind while others are present, especially if they haven't the ability to join in. It's like whispering behind someone's back.'

Sonea frowned. 'Have I offended Tania?'

'No.' Rothen smiled at her expression of relief. 'However, I should also warn you that mind communication isn't as private as you may think. Mental conversations can be picked up by other magicians, particularly if they are listening for them.'

'So someone might have been listening to us just now?'

He shook his head. 'It's possible, but I doubt it. Listening in is considered to be rude and disrespectful – and it takes concentration and effort. If it didn't, the distraction of other people's conversations would probably drive us mad.'

Sonea looked thoughtful. 'If you don't hear until you are listening, how do you know when someone wants to talk to you?'

'The closer you are to a magician, the easier it is to hear them,' he told her. 'When you are in the same room you can usually detect the thoughts they project at you. When you are far away, however, they need to get your attention first.'

He placed a hand on his chest. 'If you wanted to talk to me while I was in the University, for instance, you would have to project my name loudly. While other magicians will hear, they won't reply or open their minds to listen to the conversation that follows. When I shout your name in reply you'll know I've heard you, and we can start talking. If we are skilled and familiar with each other's mind voice, we can make it harder for others to hear us by focusing our projected thoughts, but that is all but impossible over long distances.'

'Has anyone ever ignored this rule?'

'Probably.' Rothen shrugged. 'That's why you must remember that mind communication is not private. We have a saying here: secrets are better voiced, than spoken.'

Sonea snorted softly. 'That doesn't make sense.'

'Not when taken literally.' He chuckled. 'But the words "speak" and "hear" have other meanings here in the Guild. Despite the general rule of courtesy, it is amazing how often people discover that the secret they have tried so hard to hide has become the latest subject of gossip. We often forget that magicians aren't the only people who can hear us.'

Her eyes brightened with interest. 'They aren't?'

'Not all children found to have magical potential enter the Guild,' he told her. 'If the child is the eldest brother, for example, he may be of more value to his family as their heir. There are laws in most lands that discourage magicians from involving themselves in politics. A magician cannot become King, for example. For this reason, it is not wise to have a magician as the head of a family.

'Mental communication is an ability that comes with magical potential. Sometimes, though it is very rare, an individual who did not become a magician will find their ability to communicate mentally has developed naturally. These people can be taught how to truth read, which can be a very useful skill.'

'Truth read?'

Rothen nodded. 'It can't be done with an unwilling recipient, of course, so it's only useful when somebody wants to show another person what they have seen or heard. We have a law in the Guild concerning accusations. If somebody accuses a magician of falsehood or of committing a crime, they must allow themself to be truth read or withdraw their accusation.'

'That doesn't seem fair,' Sonea said. 'It was the magician who did something wrong.'

'Yes, but it does prevent false accusations. The accused, whether magician or not, can easily prevent a truth read.' He hesitated. 'There is one exception, however.'

Sonea's frowned. 'Oh?'

Rothen leaned back in his chair and linked his fingers together. 'A few years ago, a man suspected of committing particularly malicious murders was brought to the Guild. The High Lord – our leader – read his mind and confirmed his guilt. It takes great skill to get past the blocks in an unwilling mind. Akkarin is the only one of us who has managed it, though I have heard that magicians in the past could do it. He is an extraordinary man.'

Sonea absorbed this. 'But wouldn't the murderer have

simply put his secrets behind doors, like you have shown me?'

Rothen shrugged. 'Nobody really knows how Akkarin did it, but once inside the man's mind it would not have been long before his thoughts betrayed him.' He paused, then looked at her closely. 'You know yourself that it takes some practice to keep secrets behind doors. The more concerned you are that they will be revealed, the harder it is to hide them away.'

Sonea's eyes widened, then she looked away, her expression suddenly guarded.

Watching her, Rothen could guess what she was thinking. Each time he had stepped into her mind the objects and people she wanted to keep him from identifying slid into sight. She always panicked and pushed him out of her mind.

All novices reacted as she did to some extent. He did not discuss the secrets he glimpsed. The hidden concerns of the young men he had taught revolved around personal vices or physical habits – and the occasional political scandal – and were easy to ignore. By not speaking of them, he reassured the novice that their privacy was respected.

But silence was not reassuring Sonea, and time was running short. Lorlen would make his first visit at the end of the week, and would expect her to have started Control lessons. If she was ever going to learn Control, she needed to get past these fears.

'Sonea.'

Her eyes met his reluctantly. 'Yes?'

'I think we should talk about your lessons.'

She nodded.

He leaned forward and rested his elbows on his knees. 'Usually I don't talk about what a novice has shown me in his or her mind. It makes it easier for them to trust me, but that's not working for us. You know I've seen things you wanted to keep concealed, and pretending I haven't isn't helping at all.'

She stared at the table, her knuckles turning white as she tightened her grip on the chair.

'For a start,' he continued, 'I expected you to search my rooms. I would have if I was in your position. It doesn't bother me. Forget about it.'

Her cheeks reddened slightly, but she remained silent.

'Secondly, your friends and family are in no danger from us.' She looked up and met his eyes. 'You worry that we'll threaten to harm them if you do not agree to co-operate.' He held her gaze. 'We won't Sonea. To do so would break the King's law.'

She looked away again, her expression hardening.

'Ah, but you worry anyway. You have little reason to believe we respect the King's law,' Rothen acknowledged. 'Little reason to trust us. Which brings me to your third fear, that I'll discover your plans to escape.'

Her face slowly drained of colour.

'You don't need to make such plans,' he told her. 'We won't force you to stay if you don't want to. Once you have learned Control you can leave or stay as you choose. Becoming a magician involves a vow that we all must make – a vow which holds us for our entire life. It is not a vow to be made unwillingly.'

She stared at him, her mouth slightly open. 'You'll let me go?'

He nodded, then chose his next words carefully. It was

too soon to tell her that the Guild would not let her leave unless her powers were blocked first, yet she needed to know that she would lose all her magical abilities.

'Yes, but I must warn you: without training you will not be able to use your powers. What you were able to do before will no longer be possible. You will not be able to use magic at all.' He paused. 'You will be of no use to the Thieves.'

To his surprise, she looked relieved. A ghost of a smile touched her lips. 'That won't be a problem.'

Rothen looked at her closely. 'Are you sure you want to return to the slums? You'll have no means to defend yourself.'

Sonea lifted her shoulders. 'It'll be no different to before. I got along well enough.'

Rothen frowned, impressed by her confidence and yet alarmed by the idea of sending her back into poverty. 'I know you want to be reunited with your family. Joining the Guild won't mean you have to abandon them, Sonea. They can come and visit you, or you can visit them.'

She shook her head. 'No.'

He pursed his lips. 'Do you fear that they will be afraid of you, that you will be betraying all dwells by becoming what they hate?'

The quick, penetrating look she gave him revealed that he had come closer to understanding her than she had expected.

'What would it take for you to remain acceptable in their eyes?'

She snorted. 'As if the Guild – or the King – would let me do whatever I wanted to please the dwells!'

'I'm not going to deceive you into thinking it would

be easy,' Rothen replied. 'But it is a possibility you should consider. Magic is not a common gift. Many people would give all their wealth to have it. Think of what you could learn here. Think of how you could use it to help others.'

Her gaze wavered for a moment, then her expression hardened.

'Control is all I'm here for.'

He nodded slowly. 'If that is all you want, then that is all we can give. It will be a great surprise to all here when they hear you've chosen to return to the slums. Many won't understand why someone who has lived in poverty all her life would refuse such an offer. I know you well enough to see you don't place great value in wealth and luxuries.' He shrugged, then smiled. 'And I will not be the only one to admire you for doing so. However, you should know that I'm going to try very hard to convince you to join us.'

For the first time he could remember, she smiled. 'Thanks for the warning.'

Feeling pleased with himself, Rothen rubbed his palms together. 'Well, that's that. Shall we start your lessons?'

She hesitated, then pushed her chair around to face his. Bemused by her eagerness, he took her offered hands.

Closing his eyes, he slowed his breathing and sought the presence that would lead him to her mind. She was well practised at visualising now, and he instantly found himself standing before an open doorway. Moving through, he entered a familiar room. Sonea stood at the centre.

A feeling of determination imbued the air. He waited for the usual disturbance in the scene, but nothing unwanted appeared in the room. Surprised and pleased, he nodded at the image of Sonea.

—Show me the door to your power.

She looked away. Following her gaze, he found himself standing in front of a white door.

—Now open it and listen carefully. I am going to show you how to control this power of yours.

Sinking to his knees, Cery let out a hiss of frustration.

He had examined his prison thoroughly, his breath catching in his throat whenever he felt the scuttle of eight-legged faren under his hands. His search had revealed that the walls were made of large stone bricks and the floor of hard dirt. The door was a thick slab of wood with large iron hinges.

As soon as the magician's footsteps had faded beyond his hearing, he had taken a pick from his longcoat and groped for the door. Finding the keyhole, he had manipulated the lock until he heard the mechanism turn, but when he had pulled on the door it would not open.

He remembered laughing, then, as he realised that the magician hadn't locked the door. He had just picked the lock closed.

Manipulating the lock again, he found that the door was still held fast. Recalling that he had heard the sound of a key turning, he had decided that there must be another lock. He searched for another keyhole.

Finding none, he decided that the lock holding the door must only have a key hole on the outside. Taking his pick, he inserted it in the crack between the door and its frame. It had seemed to catch on something.

Feeling pleased that he had found the lock at the first try, he had tugged at the pick to remove it, only to discover that it was stuck.

It had flexed as he tried to twist or wiggle it free. Afraid he would damage it, he left the tool lodged in the crack and reached for another. This he inserted slightly higher than the first.

Before he'd had a chance to prod around to find what was holding his first tool, the second had locked into place. Cursing, Cery had pulled at it with all his strength, but he only succeeded in bending it.

Reaching into his coat for a third pick, he had slipped it in the gap between the floor and door. At once it became stuck. No matter how hard he pulled, the pick remained in place. He tried removing the others, with no success.

As dark hours passed, he had tried several times to retrieve his tools. He could think of no device that would grab and hold a pick so fast. Nothing except, of course, magic.

His legs began to cramp with the cold, so he rose to his feet. He put a hand out to the wall to steady himself as his head began to spin. His stomach growled, telling him it had been far too long since he had eaten, but his thirst was worse. He longed for a mug of bol or a glass of pachi juice, or even a little water.

He wondered, again, if he would be left to die in the cell. If the Guild had wanted him dead, however, he was sure they would have arranged it *before* hiding his body somewhere. That gave him some hope. It meant that their plans probably relied on him being alive – for now. If those plans failed, however, he might find himself getting very hungry.

Thinking of the other magician – the blue-robed one – he could not remember any signs of deceit in the man's demeanour. The magician was either skilled at projecting trustworthiness, or he had known nothing about Cery's impending captivity. If the latter was true, then this was Fergun's game.

Whether the blonde magician was the sole plotter or not, Cery could see only two reasons for his imprisonment: the Thieves or Sonea.

If the magicians intended to use Cery to manipulate the Thieves, they would be disappointed. Faren didn't need or care about Cery *that* much.

They might try torture to get information out of him. While he preferred to think that he could resist such persuasion, he was not going to fool himself. He would not know if he was capable of remaining silent until he faced such a trial.

It was possible that the magicians could read his mind anyway. If they did, they would discover he knew little that could be used against the Thieves. Once they realised that, they would probably leave him in the dark permanently.

But he doubted that the Thieves were their target. They would have questioned him by now.

No, the only questions he had been asked concerned Sonea. During his journey to the University, Fergun had asked what kind of relationship Cery had with her. If the magicians wanted to know if Cery was important to her, they probably meant to use him to blackmail her into doing something she didn't want to do.

The thought that he might have made her situation worse tormented him as much, sometimes more, than the fear of being left to die. If only he hadn't been tempted to see the University. The more Cery thought about it, the more he cursed himself for his curiosity.

Between one breath and the next he heard the sound of

footsteps in the distance. As they grew louder his anger subsided and his heart began to race.

The footsteps stopped outside the door. There was a dull metallic click, followed by the lighter patter of his tools falling to the floor. A long slice of yellow light appeared as the door opened.

Fergun slipped through, his light following. Blinking at the brightness, Cery saw the magician regard him with narrowed eyes, then look down at the floor.

'Well, look at this,' Fergun murmured. Turning to one side, he let go of the plate and bottle he was carrying. Instead of falling, they descended slowly to the floor. He spread his fingers out and the picks rose obediently to his hand.

As he examined them, the magician's eyebrows rose. He looked up at Cery and smiled.

'You didn't really think these would work, did you? I expected you to have a little experience with such things, so I took precautions.' His eyes dropped to Cery's clothes. 'Do you have any more of these hidden away somewhere?'

Cery swallowed the denial that came to his lips. Fergun would never believe it. The magician smiled and held his hand out.

'Give them to me.'

Cery hesitated. If he gave up several of the objects hidden within his clothes, he might be able to retain a few of his more valuable possessions.

Fergun stepped closer.

'Come now, what use are they to you here?' He wiggled his fingers. 'Give them to me.'

Slowly, Cery reached into his coat and pulled out a handful of his less useful tools. Glaring at the magician, he dropped them into the outstretched hand.

Fergun looked thoughtfully at the picks, then his eyes rose to meet Cery's. A malicious smile thinned his mouth.

'Do you really expect me to believe this is all you have?'

His fingers flexed. Cery felt something invisible push against his chest and he staggered backwards until he hit the wall. A force wrapped itself over him, pressing him against the bricks.

Fergun drew closer and examined Cery's coat. With a jerk, he ripped open the lining to reveal hidden pockets. He plucked out the contents, then turned his attention to the rest of Cery's clothes.

As he drew the knives out of Cery's boots, Fergun made a small grunt of satisfaction, then a more appreciative 'ah' as he found Cery's daggers. Straightening, he pulled one of the weapons out of its sheath. He examined the widest part of the blade where a rough picture of the small rodent that was Cery's namesake had been etched.

'Ceryni,' the magician said. He looked up at Cery.

Cery stared back defiantly. Fergun chuckled and stepped away. Taking a large square of cloth from his robes, he wrapped up the tools and weapons, then turned to the door.

Realising that the magician was going to leave without giving any explanation, Cery's heart skipped.

'Wait! What do you want from me? Why am I here?'

Fergun ignored him. As the door closed, the magical restraints vanished and Cery stumbled forward onto his knees. Panting with fury, he felt his coat, cursing as he confirmed that most of his tools had been taken. He regretted the daggers most, but it was hard to hide weapons of that size.

Sitting back on his heels, he let a long sigh escape him. He still had a few items. They might come in handy. He would just have to come up with a plan.

CHAPTER 22

AN UNEXPECTED OFFER

'Do I have to?'

'Yes.' Dannyl grasped Rothen's shoulders, turned him about and pushed him out of his rooms. 'If you hide yourself away you'll only add strength to what Fergun's supporters are saying.'

Rothen sighed and followed Dannyl down the corridor. 'You're right, of course. I've barely spoken to anyone for the last two weeks – and I should ask Lorlen to delay visiting for a few days. Wait . . .' Rothen looked up, his brow creasing. 'What have Fergun's supporters been saying?'

Dannyl smiled grimly. 'That she learned control in a few days, and you've been keeping her locked away so Fergun can't see her.'

Rothen made a rude noise. 'What nonsense. I'd like to see *them* suffering some of the headaches I've had in the last week.' He grimaced. 'I guess this means I can't delay Lorlen for long.'

'No,' Dannyl agreed.

They reached the entrance to the Magicians' Quarters and stepped outside. Though the snow was melted from the paths and pavement by novices each morning and evening, the courtyard was already covered in a thin white powder. It crunched under their boots as they crossed to the Seven Arches.

As they stepped into the warmth of the Night Room, several heads turned in their direction. Dannyl heard his companion give a low groan as several magicians began to move toward them. Sarrin, the Head of Alchemists, was the first to arrive.

'Good evening, Lord Rothen, Lord Dannyl. How are you both?'

'Well, Lord Sarrin,' Rothen replied.

'Any progress with the slum girl yet?'

Rothen paused as several magicians moved in to hear his answer. 'Sonea is doing well,' he told them. 'It took some time before she was able to stop pushing me from her mind. She was, as you'd expect, quite suspicious of us.'

'Doing well?' a magician in the crowd muttered. 'Few novices take as long as two weeks.'

Dannyl smiled as Rothen's expression darkened.

His friend turned toward the speaker. 'You must remember that she is not a reluctant novice sent to us by coddling parents. Until two weeks ago, she believed we intended to kill her. It has taken some time to gain her trust.'

'When did you begin Control exercises?' another magician asked.

Rothen hesitated. 'Two days ago.'

A muttering began among the magicians. Several frowned and shook their heads.

'In that case, I'd say you've made impressive progress, Lord Rothen,' said a new voice.

Dannyl turned to see Lady Vinara moving through the crowd. Magicians stepped aside respectfully as the Head of Healers approached.

'What did you see of her power?'

Rothen smiled. 'When I first saw what was contained within her I did not believe it. The strength she has is remarkable!'

The muttering among the audience grew louder. Dannyl nodded to himself. *Good*, he thought. *If she's strong people will favour Rothen as her guardian.*

An older magician near the front of the gathering gave a shrug. 'But we knew she had to be strong or her powers would not have developed on their own.'

Vinara smiled. 'Of course, strength is not the ultimate test of a novice. What talents has she displayed.'

Rothen pursed his lips. 'Her visualisation ability is good. That will help her in most disciplines. Her memory is good, too. I've found her to be an intelligent and attentive student.'

'Has she tried to use her powers at all?' asked a red-robed magician.

'Not since she arrived. She understands the danger very well.'

The questions continued. Glancing around the crowd, Dannyl caught a glimpse of a smooth blonde head in a group of approaching magicians. He shifted closer to Rothen, waiting for an appropriate moment to whisper a warning.

—Lord Dannyl.

A few magicians in the crowd blinked and looked at Dannyl. Recognising the mind voice, Dannyl searched the room and found Administrator Lorlen sitting in his usual chair. The blue-robed magician pointed to Rothen, then beckoned.

Smiling, Dannyl nodded and leaned close to Rothen's ear.

'I believe the Administrator wishes to rescue you.'

As Rothen turned to look at the Administrator, Dannyl saw that Fergun had reached the crowd. A familiar voice joined the chatter, and a few faces turned in the warrior's direction.

'Excuse me, all.' Rothen said. 'I must speak to Administrator Lorlen.' He inclined his head politely, then nudged Dannyl in Lorlen's direction.

Looking back, Dannyl's gaze locked with Fergun's for a moment. The Warrior's lips were stretched in a satisfied smile.

As they reached Lorlen's chair, the Administrator waved to neighbouring seats. 'Good evening Lord Rothen, Lord Dannyl. Sit down and tell me how Sonea is progressing.'

Rothen remained standing. 'I was hoping to have a private word to you about that, Administrator.'

Lorlen's brows rose. 'Very well. Shall we talk in the Banquet Room?'

'Please.'

The Administrator rose and led them to a nearby door. As they stepped through, a globe light flared above his head, illuminating a huge table that filled most of the room.

Lorlen pulled out one of the chairs arranged around the table and sat down. 'How is your leg, Lord Dannyl?'

Dannyl looked up, surprised. 'Better.'

'Your limp seems to have returned this evening,' Lorlen observed.

'It is the cold,' Dannyl replied.

'Ah, I see.' Lorlen nodded, then turned to Rothen. 'What is it that you would like to discuss?'

'I began Control exercises two days ago,' Rothen told

him. Lorlen frowned, but remained silent as Rothen continued. 'You wanted to check on her progress after two weeks, and asked that I introduce her to another magician before then. Because of her lack of progress, I haven't wanted to distract her with visitors, but I feel she may be ready soon. Can you put off your visit for a few days?'

Lorlen regarded Rothen steadily, then nodded. 'Only a few days, though.'

'Thank you. There is another matter, however. A possibility we will have to start considering sooner rather than later.'

Lorlen's brows rose. 'Yes?'

'Sonea does not want to join the Guild. I have . . .' He sighed. 'To gain her trust, I have told her that, if she wishes to return to the slums, she may go. We can't, after all, force her to take the vow.'

'Did you tell her that we would block her powers?'

'Not yet.' Rothen frowned. 'Though I don't think she will care. I warned her that she would not be able to use her powers at all and she seemed pleased by the prospect. I believe she would rather be rid of them.'

Lorlen nodded. 'I am not surprised. She has only experienced magic as an uncontrollable, destructive force.' He pursed his lips. 'Perhaps if you taught her a few useful tricks she would start to like it better.'

Rothen frowned. 'She should not use her power until she has full control of it, and once she has Control she will expect us to let her go.'

'She does not know the difference between a Control lesson and a magic lesson,' Dannyl pointed out. 'Just let the instruction evolve from control into magic usage. That will also give you more time to convince her to stay.'

'Not much,' Lorlen added. 'Fergun doesn't need to know exactly when she achieved Control, but you won't fool him for long. You might gain an extra week.'

Rothen looked at Lorlen expectantly. The Administrator sighed and ran a hand over his brow. 'Very well. Just make sure he doesn't find out, or I'll never hear the end of it.'

'If he does, we'll say we were testing her Control,' Dannyl said. 'She is, after all, unusually strong. We would not want her to make any mistakes.'

Lorlen gave Dannyl an appraising look. He seemed about to say something, but instead he shook his head and turned to Rothen. 'Is that all you wish to discuss?'

'Yes, thank you Administrator,' Rothen replied.

'Then I will arrange to visit in a few days. Have you considered who you will introduce her to first?'

Dannyl blinked as Rothen looked pointedly at him. 'Me?'

Rothen smiled. 'Yes. Tomorrow afternoon, I think.'

Dannyl opened his mouth to protest, then closed it again as he realised Lorlen was watching him closely.

'All right,' he said grudgingly. 'Just make sure you hide the cutlery.'

Sonea was bored.

It was too early to sleep. Tania had left with the dirty plates not long after dinner and Rothen had disappeared soon after. Having finished the book Rothen had brought for her to read that morning, Sonea paced the room, examining ornaments and the bookcase.

Finding nothing interesting or within her ability to understand, she moved to the window and looked out.

There was no moon, and the gardens were shrouded in darkness. Nothing stirred.

Sighing, she decided to go to bed early. Sliding the window screen back, she started toward the bedroom – and froze as a knock came from the main door.

She turned to stare at the door. Rothen never knocked before entering, and Tania's knock was soft and polite, not this insistent rapping. A few visitors had knocked before, but Rothen had never invited them in.

A fleeting chill prickled her skin as the visitor knocked again. Sonea crept across the room to the door.

'Who is it?'

'A friend,' came the muffled reply.

'Rothen's not here.'

'I don't want to talk to Rothen. I want to talk to you, Sonea.'

She stared at the door, her heart starting to race.

'Why?'

The reply was fainter. 'I have to tell you something important, something *he* won't tell you.'

Rothen was keeping something from her? Alarm and excitement set her heart beating even faster. Whoever this stranger was, he was willing to defy the magicians for her sake. She wished she could see through the door to see who the visitor was.

But was it a good idea to learn something disturbing about Rothen right now, when she needed to trust him?

'Sonea. Let me in. The corridor is empty, but it won't be for long. This is my only chance to talk to you.'

'I can't. The door's locked.'

'Try it again.'

She regarded the door handle. Though she had tried

it several times during her first days in the rooms, it had always been locked. Reaching out, she twisted the handle, then drew in a surprised breath as the door swung open.

A red sleeve appeared, then the full red robes of a magician. Backing away, she stared at the magician in dismay. She had expected a servant, or a rescuer disguised as a servant – unless this man had dared to don robes so he could reach her . . .

The man closed the door gently behind him, then straightened and looked at her.

'Hello, Sonea. We meet at last. I am Lord Fergun.'

'You're a magician?'

'Yes, not a magician such as Lord Rothen is.' He placed a hand on his chest.

Sonea frowned. 'You're a Warrior?'

Fergun smiled. He was much younger than Rothen, she noted, and quite attractive. His hair was pale and neatly combed, and his facial features were both fine and strong. She knew she had seen him before, but couldn't remember where.

'I am,' he said. 'But that is not the difference I speak of.' He placed a hand over his heart. 'I am on your side.'

'And Rothen isn't?'

'No, though he means well,' he added. 'Rothen is the sort of man who believes he knows what's best for others, particularly a young woman like yourself. I, however, see you as an adult who ought to be allowed to make her own choices.' He raised an eyebrow. 'Will you listen to me, or shall I leave you in peace?'

Though her heart was still racing, she nodded and gestured to the chairs. 'Stay,' she said. 'I will listen.'

Inclining his head politely, he glided to a chair. Taking the seat opposite, she looked at him expectantly.

'Firstly, has Rothen told you that you may join the Guild?' he asked.

'Yes.'

'And has he told you what you must do to become a magician?'

She shrugged. 'A little. There is a vow, and years of training.'

'And do you know what you must vow?'

She shook her head. 'No, but it doesn't matter. I don't want to join the Guild.'

He blinked. 'You don't want to join the Guild?' he repeated.

'No.'

He nodded slowly and leaned back in his chair. For a while he was silent and thoughtful, then his gaze shifted to hers again.

'May I ask why?'

Sonea considered him carefully. Rothen had told her that many of the magicians would be surprised when she refused the Guild's offer.

'I want to go home,' she told him.

He nodded again. 'Do you know that the Guild does not allow magicians to exist outside its influence?'

'Yes,' she replied. 'Everybody knows that.'

'So you know they will not just let you walk out of here.'

'I won't be able to use my powers, so I won't be a threat.'

He raised his eyebrows again. 'So Rothen has told you that the Guild will block your powers?'

Sonea frowned. *Block* her powers?

He nodded slowly. 'No, I thought not. He is only telling you part of the truth.' He leaned forward. 'The Higher Magicians will cage your powers within you so that you cannot reach for them. It's . . . not a pleasant procedure, not at all, and the cage will be there for the rest of your life. You see, even though you will not know how to use your powers, there is always a chance you will discover how to use them yourself, or encounter a rogue magician willing to teach you – though that is highly unlikely. By law, the Guild must make sure you cannot use magic, even if you had all the help you needed.'

A chill had grown within Sonea as he spoke. Looking down at the table, she considered what Rothen had told her. Had he deliberately phrased the truth so that it sounded less frightening? Probably. Her suspicions grew stronger as she realised that Rothen had only *voiced* the revelation that she would be freed. She had not seen it in his mind and known it to be true . . .

She looked up at the red-robed magician. How could she trust anything *he* said? She could not think what he had to gain from lying, however, since she would discover the truth once she had learned Control.

'Why are you telling me this?'

He gave her a lopsided smile. 'Like I said, I'm on your side. You need to know the truth and . . . I can offer you an alternative.'

She straightened. 'What alternative?'

He pursed his lips. 'It will not be easy. Has Rothen explained about guardianship yet?'

She shook her head.

He rolled his eyes. 'He hasn't told you anything! Listen.' He leaned forward and placed his elbows on his knees.

'Guardianship allows magicians to control the training of novices. Rothen has claimed guardianship of you since the Purge. When I heard this, I decided to place a counter-claim. This forces the Guild to hold a Hearing – a meeting – where it will be decided which of us will be your guardian. You will help me win my claim, then—'

'Why would they hold a Hearing when I'm not going to join the Guild?' Sonea injected.

He raised his hands in a placating gesture. 'Hear me out, Sonea.' Taking a deep breath, he continued. 'If you refuse to join the Guild, your powers will be blocked and you'll be sent back to the slums. If you agree to stay, however, and I win your guardianship, I can help you.'

Sonea frowned. 'How?'

He smiled. 'You'll simply vanish one day. You can go back to the slums if you want. I'll teach you how to make your magic undetectable – and your powers will not be blocked. They will hunt for you at first, but if you are smart, they won't find you this time.'

She stared at him in disbelief. 'But you'd be breaking the Guild's laws.'

He nodded slowly. 'I know.' Different emotions shifted over his face. He rose and walked to the window. 'I don't like to see people forced to be what they don't want to be,' he told her. 'Look.' Turning, he crossed the room and held out his hand to her. The skin of his palm was callused and scarred.

'Swordplay. I am a Warrior, as you so astutely noted. It's the closest I can get to what I once wanted to be. When I was a boy, I dreamed of being a swordsman. I practised for hours each day. I dreamed of learning under the greatest teachers.'

He sighed and shook his head. 'Then my magical potential was discovered. It wasn't much, but my parents wanted to have a magician in the family. I would bring their House great prestige, they said.

'So I was made to join the Guild. I was too young to refuse, too full of doubts to know that magic wasn't my real calling. My powers aren't strong and, though I have learned to use them well, I don't enjoy them. I have kept up my fighting skills, though most other magicians regard honest, face-to-face battle with disdain. That is as close as I can get to the life I dreamed of.'

He looked up at her, his eyes bright. 'I won't let Rothen do the same to you. If you do not want to join the Guild, then I will help you escape. But you must trust me. Guild politics and laws are convoluted and confusing.' He moved back to his chair, but did not sit down. 'Do you want me to help you?'

Sonea looked down at the table. His story, and it's passionate delivery, had impressed her, but parts of it made her uneasy. Was keeping her magic worth becoming a fugitive again?

Then she considered what Cery would say. Why should the higher classes have a monopoly on magic? If the Guild would not accept anyone from the lower classes, then why shouldn't those classes have their own magicians?

'Yes.' She looked up and met his eyes. 'But I need to think about it. I don't know you. I want to check this guardianship thing before I agree to anything.'

He nodded. 'I understand. Think on it, but do not take too long. Rothen has managed to convince Administrator Lorlen that he must keep everyone away from you – to keep the truth from you, no doubt – until you have learned

Control. I risk much by defying that decision. I will try to visit again soon, but you must have an answer for me. I may not have a third opportunity.'

'I will.'

Looking at the door, he sighed. 'I had better go. It would do you no good if he found me here with you.'

Moving to the door, he opened it a crack and peered out. Pausing only to give her one last, grim smile, he slipped out. The door clicked shut behind him.

Alone again, Sonea sat and stared at the table, the magician's words running circles in her mind. She could not see any reason for Fergun to lie to her, but she would check every claim he had made: the blocking of powers, guardianship, and his story of broken dreams. By questioning Rothen carefully, she might trick him into confirming much of what Fergun had said.

But not tonight. She was too unnerved by the visit to be able to put on a calm face if Rothen returned. Rising, she entered her bedroom and closed the door.

CHAPTER 23

ROTHEN'S FRIEND

'There were no classes today.'

Rothen looked up from the book he was reading. Sonea was leaning on the window sill, a small circle of mist forming on the glass from her breath.

'No,' he replied. 'It's a Freeday. We don't have classes on the last day of the week.'

'What do you do, then?'

He shrugged. 'That depends on the magician. Some visit the races, or pursue other sports and interests. Some visit their families.'

'What about novices?'

'The same, although the older novices usually spend the day studying.'

'And they still have to clear the paths.'

Her eyes were following the progress of something beneath the window. Guessing what it was, Rothen chuckled. 'Clearing the paths is one of many duties they're given during their first year of study. After that, they do chores only as punishment.'

She looked at him, her eyebrows rising. 'Punishment?'

'For childish pranks or being disrespectful to their elders,' he explained. 'They're a bit old for smacking.'

The corner of her mouth twitched, and she looked back out of the window. 'So that's why he looks so grumpy.'

Noting that her fingers were drumming softly on the frame of the window screen, Rothen sighed. For two days she had been learning rapidly, grasping the Control exercises faster than any novice he had taught before. Today, however, her concentration had failed several times. Though she kept it well hidden, showing that her mental discipline had improved, it had been clear that something was on her mind.

At first he had blamed it on himself. He had not told her of Dannyl's visit, believing that the prospect of meeting a stranger would distract her from her lessons. She had sensed that he was keeping something from her, and had become suspicious.

Realising his error, he told her of the visit.

'I was wondering when I'd meet more of you,' she had said.

'If you don't want visitors tonight, I can tell him to come another time,' he had offered.

She had shaken her head. 'No, I'd like to meet your friend.'

Surprised and pleased by her reaction, he had tried to resume the lessons. She still had trouble keeping her attention on the exercises and he had sensed her frustration and impatience growing. Each time they had taken a break, she had returned to the window to stare outside.

He looked at her again and thought about how long she had been locked in his rooms. It was easy to forget that his living quarters were a prison to her. She must be tired of her surroundings, and was probably bored.

Which made it a good time to introduce her to Dannyl, he decided. The tall magician intimidated those who didn't know him, but his friendly manner usually put them quickly at ease. He hoped she would grow accustomed to Dannyl's company before Lorlen visited.

After that? Watching her drumming fingers, he smiled. He would take her out and show her the Guild.

A knock interrupted his thoughts. Rising, he opened the main door. Dannyl stood outside, looking a little tense.

'You're early,' Rothen noted.

Dannyl's eyes brightened. 'Should I come back later?'

Rothen shook his head. 'No, come in.'

Looking back, Rothen watched Sonea's face as Dannyl stepped into the room. She gave the tall magician an assessing look.

'Dannyl, this is Sonea,' he said.

'Honoured to meet you,' Dannyl said, inclining his head.

Sonea nodded. 'And I you.' Her eyes narrowed slightly, and a smile crept over her face. 'I think we've met before.' She looked down. 'How is your leg?'

Dannyl blinked, then his mouth twitched into a half smile. 'Better, thank you.'

Covering his mouth, Rothen tried unsuccessfully to choke back a laugh. Pretending to cough, he waved toward the chairs. 'Sit down. I'll prepare some sumi.'

Sonea left the window and took a seat opposite Dannyl. The pair regarded each other warily. Moving to a side table, Rothen placed the utensils for making sumi onto a tray.

'How are your lessons going?' Dannyl asked.

'Good, I think. What about you?'

'Me?'

'You're teaching Rothen's class, aren't you?'

'Oh. Yes. It's . . . challenging. I haven't taught anyone before, so I almost feel as if I've got more to learn than the novices.'

'What do you normally do?'

'Experiments. Small projects, mostly. Sometimes I assist with larger work.'

Rothen carried the tray to the table and sat down. 'Tell her about the thought imprinter,' he suggested.

'Oh, that's just a hobby.' Dannyl waved a hand dismissively. 'Nobody's interested in it.'

'What is it?' Sonea asked.

'A way to transfer images from the mind onto paper.'

Sonea's eyes brightened with interest. 'Can you do that?'

Dannyl accepted a cup of sumi from Rothen. 'No, not yet. Lots of magicians have tried over the centuries, but nobody's been able to find a substance that can hold a picture for long.' He paused to sip the hot drink. 'I've made up a special paper out of the leaves of anivope vines which can hold the image for a few days, but the edges blur and the colours start to lose their intensity after about two hours. Ideally, the picture would be permanent.'

'What would you use them for?'

Dannyl shrugged. 'Identification, for a start. It would have been handy to be able to do this when we were looking for you, for example. Rothen was the only one of us who had seen you. If he'd been able to make pictures of you, we could have carried them with us to show people.'

Sonea nodded slowly. 'What do the pictures look like when they've lost colours?'

'Faded. Blurry. But you can still see what they were, in some cases.'

'Can . . . can I see one?'

Dannyl smiled. 'Of course. I'll bring some around.'

Sonea's eyes sparkled with curiosity. If Dannyl set up his experiment here, Rothen mused, she could see it for herself. Looking around, he pictured transferring the clutter of vials and presses from Dannyl's guestroom to his—

'I'm sure Dannyl won't mind if we visit his rooms for a demonstration,' he said.

Dannyl's eyes went round. 'Now?'

Rothen opened his mouth to reassure his friend, then hesitated. Sonea was watching eagerly. He considered them both.

Dannyl obviously did not intimidate her at all. Of the two of them, she seemed the least bothered by the other's presence. Dannyl's rooms were on the lower floor of the Magician's Quarters, so they would not be going far.

'I don't see why not,' he replied.

—*Are you sure that's wise?* Dannyl sent.

Sonea's eyes flickered toward him. Ignoring the question, Rothen regarded Sonea carefully. 'Would you like that?'

'Yes,' she replied, turning to look at Dannyl. 'If you don't mind.'

'Not at all.' Dannyl glanced at Rothen. 'It's just . . . my rooms are a bit untidy.'

'A bit?' Rothen lifted his cup to finish the last of his sumi.

'Don't you have a servant?' Sonea asked.

'Yes,' Dannyl replied. 'But I have warned him not to touch any of my experiments.'

Rothen smiled. 'Why don't you go on ahead and make sure we have somewhere to sit.'

Sighing, Dannyl rose. 'Very well.'

Following his friend to the door, Rothen slipped outside. At once, Dannyl spun about to stare at him.

'Are you mad? What if someone sees you both?' Dannyl whispered. 'If you're seen taking her outside your room, Fergun will say you have no reason to keep him from her.'

'Then I'll let him visit.' Rothen shrugged. 'The only reason I wanted her isolated was to stop him visiting at a time when any unfamiliar magician would have frightened her. But if she is this calm and confident around you, I don't think she'll be worried by Fergun.'

'Thanks,' Dannyl replied dryly.

'Because you look more intimidating than him,' Rothen explained.

'Do I?'

'And he is much more charming,' Rothen added, smiling. He waved toward the stairs. 'Go on. Get downstairs. When you're ready – and the corridor is clear – let me know. Just don't take too long cleaning up, or we'll *both* think you had to hide something.'

As his friend hurried away, Rothen returned to his room. Sonea was standing before her chair, looking a little flushed. She sat down again as he cleared the table.

'He doesn't sound like he wants visitors,' she said doubtfully.

'He does,' Rothen assured her. 'He just doesn't like surprises.'

Picking up the tray, he carried it to the side table, then took a sheaf of paper out of a drawer and wrote a quick note to Tania, letting the servant know where they were. As he finished, he heard Dannyl call his name.

—There's a bit of space here now. Come down.

Sonea rose and looked at Rothen expectantly. Smiling, he moved to the door and opened it. Her eyes flickered about as she stepped outside, taking in the wide corridor and its numerous doors.

'How many magicians live here?' she asked as they started toward the stairs.

'Over eighty,' he told her, 'and their families.'

'So there are people other than magicians here?'

'Yes, but only the spouses and children of magicians. No other relatives are allowed.'

'Why not?'

He chuckled. 'If we had every relative of every magician living here, we would have to move the entire Inner Circle into the Grounds.'

'Of course,' she said dryly. 'What happens when the children grow up?'

'If they have magical potential, they usually join the Guild. If they don't, they must leave.'

'Where do they go?'

'To live with relations in the city.'

'In the Inner Circle.'

'Yes.'

She considered this, then looked up at him. 'Do any magicians live in the city?'

'A few. It's discouraged.'

'Why?'

He gave her a crooked smile. 'We're supposed to keep an eye on each other, remember, to make sure none of us get too deeply involved in politics, or plot against the King. It's harder to do that if too many of us live outside the Guild.'

'So why are some allowed to?'

They had reached the end of the corridor. Rothen started down the spiral staircase, Sonea following.

'Many reasons, all unique to the individual. Old age, illness.'

'Are there any magicians who decided not to join the Guild – who learned Control but not how to use magic?'

He shook his head. 'No. The young men and women who join us haven't had their powers released yet. After that they learn Control. Remember, you are unique in that your power developed on its own.'

She frowned. 'Has anyone left the Guild before?'

'No.'

She considered this, her expression intent. From below came Dannyl's voice, and another. Rothen slowed, giving Sonea plenty of time to become aware of the other magician.

Then she shied to one side as a magician floated up the stairwell, his feet resting on nothing but air. Recognising the magician, Rothen smiled.

'Good evening, Lord Garrel.'

'Good evening,' the magician replied, raising his eyebrows as he noticed Sonea.

Sonea stared at the magician, her eyes wide. As Garrel's feet reached the level of the higher floor, the magician stepped onto the solid surface of the corridor. He glanced down at Sonea once, his gaze bright with interest, then strode away.

'Levitation,' Rothen told Sonea. 'Impressive isn't it? It takes more than a little skill. About half of us can do it.'

'Can you?' she asked.

'I used to all the time,' Rothen told her. 'But I'm out of practise now. Dannyl can.'

'Ah, but I'm not the show-off that Garrel is.'

Looking down, Rothen saw Dannyl waiting at the bottom of the stairs.

'I prefer to use my legs,' Rothen told Sonea. 'My former guardian always said that physical exercise is as necessary as mental exercise. Neglect the body and—'

'—and you neglect the mind,' Dannyl finished with a groan. 'His guardian was a wise and upright man,' he told Sonea as she reached his side. 'Lord Margen even disapproved of wine.'

'Which must be why *you* never liked him much,' Rothen observed, smiling.

'Guardian?' Sonea echoed.

'A tradition here,' he explained. 'Lord Margen chose to guide my training when I was a novice, as I chose to guide Dannyl's.'

She fell into step beside him as he started toward Dannyl's rooms. 'How did you guide him?'

Rothen shrugged. 'Many ways. Mostly, I filled in the gaps in his knowledge. Some were there because of the neglect of a few teachers, others were due to his own laziness or lack of enthusiasm.' Sonea glanced at Dannyl, who was smiling and nodding in agreement.

'By helping me with my work, Dannyl also learned more through experience than he would in classes. The idea of guardianship is to help a novice excel.'

'Do all novices have guardians?'

Rothen shook his head. 'No. It is not common. Not all magicians want or have time to take responsibility for a novice's training. Only those novices which show considerable promise have guardians.'

Her eyebrows rose. 'So why . . .' She frowned, then shook her head.

Reaching his door, Dannyl touched it lightly. It swung inward and a faint smell of chemicals wafted into the corridor.

'Welcome,' he said, ushering them inside.

Though the guestroom was the same size as Rothen's, half of it was taken up with benches. Contraptions covered the surfaces and boxes were stacked beneath. Dannyl's work was neatly laid out and organised, however.

Sonea looked around the room, obviously amused. Though Rothen had seen Dannyl's rooms many times, he always found it strange encountering an Alchemy experiment set up in living quarters. Space in the University was limited, so those few magicians who wanted to pursue interests like Dannyl's often used their own rooms.

Rothen sighed. 'It's easy to see why Ezrille despairs of finding you a wife, Dannyl.'

As always, his friend grimaced. 'I'm too young to have a wife.'

'Nonsense,' Rothen replied. 'You just don't have the space for one.'

Dannyl smiled and beckoned to Sonea. She drew closer to the benches and listened as he explained his experiments. He brought out a few faded pictures and she examined them closely.

'It can be done,' he finished. 'The only challenge is to stop the image fading away.'

'Couldn't you get a painter to copy it before it does?' she suggested.

'I could.' Dannyl frowned. 'That would circumvent the problem, I suppose. He would have to be a good painter. Fast, too.'

Handing the samples back, she moved to a framed map on the wall nearby.

'You don't have paintings,' she said, glancing around the room. 'They're all maps.'

'Yes,' Dannyl replied. 'I collect old maps and plans.'

She approached another. 'This is the Guild.'

Rothen moved to her side. The plan was clearly labelled, in the neat writing of the Guild's most famous architect, Lord Coren.

'We are here.' Dannyl pointed. 'In the Magicians' Quarters.' His finger slid across to a similar rectangle. 'That is the Novices' Quarters. All novices who come to learn in the Guild are housed there, even if they have homes in the city.'

'Why?'

'So we can make their lives a misery,' Dannyl replied. Sonea gave him a very direct look, then snorted softly.

'The novices are removed from their family's influence when they come here.' Rothen told her. 'We have to wean them off the little intrigues the Houses are always indulging in.'

'We get plenty of new novices who have never needed to get out of bed before midday,' Dannyl added. 'It comes as quite a shock to them when they learn how early they have to rise for class. We'd have no hope of getting them to lessons on time if they lived at home.'

He pointed at the circular building on the plan. 'This is the Healers' Quarters. Some of the Healers live there, but most rooms are reserved for treatment and classes.' His finger moved to a smaller circle within the garden. 'This structure is the Arena. It is used as a practice area for the Warriors. There is a shield around it, supported by the masts, which absorbs and contains the magic of those within and protects everything outside. We all add our power to the shield from time to time to keep it strong.'

Sonea stared at the plan, watching as Dannyl's finger

moved to the curved building next to the Magicians' Quarters.

'This is the Baths. It is built where a stream once ran down the hill from a spring up in the forest. We have piped the water into the building where it can be drawn into tubs and heated. Next to it is the Seven Arches, which contains rooms for entertaining.'

'What are the Residences,' Sonea asked, drawing his attention to a label and an arrow that pointed off the page.

'Several little houses where our oldest magicians live,' Dannyl explained. 'Here, you can see them on this older map.'

They crossed the room to a yellowing map of the city. Dannyl pointed to a row of tiny squares. 'There, beside the old cemetery.'

'There are only a few buildings in the Guild on this map,' Sonea noted.

Dannyl smiled. 'This map is over three hundred years old. I don't know how much of Kyralian history you know. Have you heard of the Sachakan War?'

Sonea nodded.

'After the Sachakan War, there wasn't much left of Imardin. When the city was rebuilt, the greater Houses took the opportunity to set out a new city plan.

'You can see how it was built in concentric circles.' He pointed to the centre. 'First, a wall was erected around the remains of the old King's Palace, then another around the city. The Outer Wall was constructed a few decades later. The old city was named the Inner Circle, and the new area was divided into the four Quarters.'

His finger circled the Guild. 'The entire Eastern Quarter was given to the magicians in gratitude for driving out the Sachakan invaders. The decision wasn't made carelessly,' he added. 'The Palace and Inner Circle drew water from the spring in those days and building the Guild around the supply reduced the chance of anyone poisoning it – as had been done during the war.'

He pointed to the small rectangle in the Grounds. 'The first structure made was the Guildhall,' Dannyl continued. 'It was built with the local hard grey stone. It housed both magicians and their apprentices and provided space for teaching and debate. According to the history books, a spirit of unity had taken hold of our predecessors. Through the sharing of knowledge, new ways to use and shape magic were discovered. It did not take long before the Guild had become the largest and most powerful school of magicians in the known world.'

He smiled. 'And it kept growing. When Lonmar, Elyne, Vin, Lan and Kyralia formed the Alliance, part of the agreement was that magicians from all lands would be taught here. Suddenly, the Guildhall wasn't big enough, so they had to construct several new buildings.'

Sonea frowned. 'What happens to magicians from other lands when they finish learning?'

'Usually they return to their homeland,' Rothen told her. 'Sometimes they stay here.'

'Then how do you keep an eye on them?'

'We have ambassadors in each land who keep track of the activities of foreign magicians,' Dannyl told her. 'Just as we vow to serve the King and protect Kyralia, they swear service to their own ruler.'

Her eyes moved to a map of the region hanging nearby. 'It doesn't seem smart to teach magicians of other lands. What if they invade Kyralia?'

Rothen smiled. 'If we didn't allow them to join the Guild, they would start their own, as they did in the past. Whether we teach them or not won't prevent an invasion, but by doing so, we control what they are taught. We do not teach our own people differently, so they know they are not being treated unfairly.'

'They wouldn't dare attack us, anyway,' Dannyl added. 'Kyralians have strong magical bloodlines. We produce more magicians than any of the other races, and stronger ones.'

'Vindo and Lans are the weakest,' Rothen told her. 'Which is why they are not common here. We get more Lonmar and Elyne novices, but their powers are rarely impressive.'

'The Sachakans used to be powerful magicians.' Dannyl looked up at the map. 'But the war ended that.'

'Leaving us the most powerful nation in the region,' Rothen finished.

Her eyes narrowed. 'So why doesn't the King invade the other lands?'

'The Alliance was made to prevent it,' Rothen told her. 'As you so astutely reminded me the first time we spoke, King Palen refused to sign it at first. The Guild suggested that it might not remain uninvolved in politics if he did not.'

Her mouth curled into a faint smile. 'What stops the other lands fighting each other?'

Rothen sighed. 'A great deal of diplomacy – which does not always work. There have been several minor confrontations since the Alliance. It is always an awkward situation for the Guild. Disputes usually revolve around borders and—'

Hearing a timid knock, he stopped. He looked at Dannyl and knew from his friend's expression that they were thinking the same thing. Had Fergun heard that Sonea was out of his rooms already?

'Are you expecting anyone?'

Dannyl shook his head and moved to the door. As it opened Rothen heard Tania's voice and sighed with relief.

'I brought your meal down,' the servant said as she entered the room. Two other servants followed, carrying trays. Setting their burdens down on the only empty table, they bowed and left.

As the aroma of food filled the room, Dannyl made an appreciative noise. 'I didn't realise so much time had passed,' he said.

Rothen regarded Sonea. 'Hungry?'

She nodded, her eyes sliding to the food.

He smiled. 'Then I think that's enough history for now. Let's eat.'

CHAPTER 24

UNANSWERED QUESTIONS

Reaching the end of the University corridor, Dannyl halted as the door to the Administrator's office opened. A blue-clad figure stepped out and started toward the Entrance Hall.

'Administrator,' Dannyl called.

Lorlen stopped and turned around. Seeing Dannyl approaching, he smiled. 'Good morning, Lord Dannyl.'

'I was just coming to see you. Do you have a moment?'

'Of course, but only a moment.'

'Thank you.' Dannyl rubbed his hands together slowly. 'I received a message from the Thief last night. He asked if we knew of the whereabouts of a man who was Sonea's companion while she was hiding from us. I thought it might be that young man who tried to rescue her.'

Lorlen nodded. 'The High Lord received a similar inquiry.'

Dannyl blinked in surprise. 'The Thief contacted him directly?'

'Yes. Akkarin has assured Gorin that he will let him know if he finds the man.'

'I will send the same reply, then.'

Lorlen's eyes narrowed slightly. 'Is this the first time the Thieves have contacted you since you captured Sonea?'

'Yes.' Dannyl smiled ruefully. 'I had assumed I would

never hear from them again. Their message came as quite a surprise.'

Lorlen's brows rose. 'It came as quite a surprise to all of us that you had been talking to them at all.'

Dannyl felt his face grow warmer. 'Not all. The High Lord knew, though I have no idea how.'

Lorlen smiled. 'Now *that* does not surprise me. Akkarin might not appear to show any interest, but don't think he isn't paying attention. He knows more about people, both here and in the City, than anyone else.'

'But you must know more than he when it comes to the Guild.'

Lorlen shook his head. 'Oh, he knows more than I ever do.' He paused. 'I am meeting him now. Do you have anything you wish me to ask him?'

'No,' Dannyl replied hastily. 'I should be going, myself. Thank you for your time, Administrator.'

Lorlen inclined his head, turned and strode away. Starting back down the corridor, Dannyl soon found himself passing through a crowd of novices and magicians. With the first classes of the day about to start, the building was filled with activity.

He considered the Thief's message again. There had been an undertone of accusation in the letter, as if Gorin suspected that the Guild was responsible for the man's disappearance. Dannyl did not believe that the Thief would blame the Guild for his problems as easily as the average dwell did – or that he would contact the High Lord if he didn't have good reason to.

So Gorin must believe that the Guild was capable of finding the man for them. Dannyl chuckled as the irony of the situation occurred to him. The Thieves had helped the Guild find Sonea, now they wanted the same kind of favour in return. He wondered if they would offer as large a reward.

But why did Gorin think the Guild knew where the man was? Dannyl blinked as the answer came to him.

Sonea.

If Gorin thought that Sonea knew where her friend was, why hadn't he contacted her directly? Did he believe she would not tell them. The Thieves *had* sold her to the Guild, after all.

And her companion might have good reasons for disappearing, too.

Dannyl rubbed his brow. He could ask Sonea if she knew what was going on, but if she didn't know that her friend was missing the news might upset her. She might suspect the Guild of causing her friend's disappearance. It could ruin all that Rothen had achieved.

A familiar face appeared among the novices before him. Dannyl felt a small twinge of dread, but Fergun did not look up. Instead, the Warrior hurried past and turned into a side passage.

Surprised, Dannyl stopped. What could have absorbed Fergun so completely that he had not even noticed his old foe? Moving back down the corridor, Dannyl peered down the side passage and caught a glimpse of red robes before the Warrior turned another corner.

Fergun had been carrying something. Dannyl hovered at the passage entrance, tempted to follow. As a novice, he would have seized any opportunity to discover any of Fergun's little secrets.

But he wasn't a novice any more, and Fergun had won that war long ago. Shrugging, he started back down the corridor toward Rothen's classroom. Lessons were due to start in less than five minutes, and he had no time for spying.

After a week of darkness, Cery's senses had sharpened. His ears could pick up the shuffle of insectile feet, and his fingers could feel the slight roughness where rust nibbled at the metal skewer he had pulled from the hem of his coat.

As he pressed his thumb against the sharp point, he felt his anger simmering. His captor had returned twice more with food and water. Each time, Cery had attempted to find out why he had been imprisoned.

All his efforts to draw Fergun into conversation had failed. He had cajoled, demanded, even begged for an explanation, but the magician had ignored every word. *It wasn't right*, Cery fumed. Villains were supposed to reveal their plans, either by mistake or during a bout of gloating.

The faintest rapping reached Cery's ears. He lifted his head, then leapt to his feet as the sound grew into footsteps. Gripping the skewer, he crouched behind the door and waited.

The steps stopped outside the door. He heard the latch click, and tensed as the door began to slide inward. Light spilled into the room, illuminating the empty plate he had left just before the door. The magician took a step toward it, then paused and turned toward the coat and trousers lying half hidden under a blanket in the corner.

Leaping forward, Cery stabbed the skewer at Fergun's back, aiming for the man's heart.

The skewer struck something hard and slipped through his fingers. As the magician spun around, something slammed into Cery's chest, throwing him backwards. He heard a crack as he hit the wall, then pain ripped through his arm. Crumpling to the floor, he cradled his arm, gasping.

From behind came a long, exaggerated sigh.

'That was stupid. Look what you made me do.'

Fergun stood over him, arms crossed. Gritting his teeth, Cery glared up at the magician.

'This is no way to thank me after I went to all the trouble of bringing you blankets.' Fergun shook his head, then dropped into a crouch.

Trying to shrink away only brought another wave of pain. Cery smothered a cry as Fergun grasped the wrist of his injured arm. He tried to pull away, but the movement brought another stab of pain.

'Broken,' the magician muttered. His eyes seemed to have fixed on something far beyond the dusty floor. The pain suddenly dulled, then a warmth spread slowly through Cery's arm.

Realising he was being Healed, Cery forced himself to remain still. He stared up at Fergun, noting the sharp jaw and thin lips. The man's blond hair, usually combed back, now fell over his brow.

Cery knew he would remember this face for the rest of his life. *One day I'll have my revenge*, he thought. *And if you have done anything to Sonea, expect your death to be slow and painful.*

The magician blinked and released Cery's arm. He stood up, then grimaced and passed a hand over his brow.

'It is not wholly healed. I can't waste all my powers on you. Treat it gently, or the bone will come apart again.' His eyes narrowed. 'If you try something like that again,

I will have to bind you – to stop you harming *yourself*, you understand.'

He looked down. The plate he had been carrying lay broken, food scattered across the floor. The bottle lay nearby, water slowly leaking from a crack near the cork.

'I wouldn't waste that if I were you,' Fergun said. Bending, he picked up Cery's skewer, turned and strode out of the room.

As the door closed, Cery lay on his back and groaned. Had he really expected to be able to murder a magician with a skewer? He carefully prodded his arm with his fingertips. A mild tenderness was all that remained.

In the darkness the smell of fresh bread was strong and brought a growl from his stomach. Thinking of the spilled food, he sighed. His only indication of the time passing was hunger, and he had estimated that the magician's visits came every two days or more. If he didn't eat, he would grow weak. Even worse was the thought of the crawling things the food would attract from the corner he used for other bodily functions.

Pushing himself onto his knees, he crawled forward, hands searching the dusty floor.

Sonea caught her breath as the blue-robed magician stepped into the room. Tall, slim, with his dark hair tied at the nape of his neck, he could have been the assassin she had seen under the High Lord's house. Then the man turned to face her and she saw that his features were not as harsh as those of the man she remembered.

'This is Administrator Lorlen,' Rothen told her.

She nodded at the magician. 'Honoured to meet you.'

'I am honoured to meet you, Sonea,' the man replied.

'Please, sit down,' Rothen said, waving toward the chairs.

As they settled into chairs, Tania served the bitter drink the magicians seemed to prefer. Accepting a glass of water, Sonea watched the Administrator sip from his cup. He smiled appreciatively, but as he looked at her his expression became sober.

'Rothen was concerned that you would be frightened if I was to approach you when you first came here,' he told her. 'So you must forgive me for not coming sooner. As Administrator of the Guild, I wish to offer a formal apology for the trouble and distress we have caused you. Do you now understand why we had to find you?'

Sonea felt her cheeks warm. 'Yes.'

'That is a great relief to me,' he told her, smiling. 'I have some questions, and if you have any, please don't hesitate to ask. Are your Control lessons going well?'

Sonea glanced at Rothen and received a nod of encouragement.

'I think I'm improving,' she replied. 'The tests are getting easier.'

The Administrator considered this, nodding slowly. 'It's a bit like learning to walk,' he said. 'You have to think about it at first, but once you have done it for a while, you don't need to think about it at all.'

'Except that you don't walk in your sleep,' she added.

'Not usually.' The Administrator laughed, then his gaze became keen. 'Rothen has told me you don't wish to stay with us. Is that true?'

Sonea nodded.

'May I ask why not?'

'I want to go home,' she told him.

He leaned forward. 'We will not stop you seeing your family and friends. You could visit them on Freedays.'

She shook her head. 'I know, but I don't want to stay here.'

Nodding, he relaxed against the back of his chair. 'We will regret losing someone of such potential,' he told her. 'Are you sure you want to give up your powers.'

Remembering Fergun's words, her heart skipped. '*Give up my powers?*' she repeated slowly, glancing at Rothen. 'That is not how Rothen described it.'

The Administrator's eyebrows rose. 'What has he told you?'

'That I won't be able to use them because I won't know how.'

'Do you believe you could teach yourself?'

She paused. 'Could I?'

'No.' The Administrator smiled. 'What Rothen has told you is true,' he said. 'But knowing how the success of your lessons depended on maintaining trust between you, he has left it to me to explain the laws regarding the release of magicians from the Guild.'

As she realised he was about to confirm whether Fergun had spoken the truth, Sonea's heartbeat quickened.

'The law states that every man and woman whose powers are active must either join the Guild or have his or her powers blocked,' he told her. 'Blocking can't be done until full Control is established but once in place, it effectively prevents a magician from using magic in any way.'

In the silence that followed the two magicians watched her closely. She looked away, avoiding their eyes.

So Rothen *had* been keeping something from her.

Yet she understood why he had. The knowledge that magicians were going to meddle with her mind would not have made it easy for her to trust him.

Fergun had been right, though . . .

'Do you have any questions, Sonea?' Lorlen asked.

She hesitated, remembering something else that Fergun had said. 'This blocking isn't . . . uncomfortable?'

He shook his head. 'You won't feel anything. There is a sensation of resistance if you try to perform magic, but it is not painful. Since you are not used to using magic, I doubt you'll ever notice the block at all.'

Sonea nodded slowly. The Administrator regarded her silently, then smiled. 'I'm not going to try and talk you into staying,' he said. 'I only wish you to know there is a place here for you if you want it. Do you have any other questions?'

Sonea shook her head. 'No. Thank you, Administrator.'

He stood, his robes rustling. 'I must return to my duties now. I will visit you again, Sonea. Perhaps we can have a longer talk.'

She nodded and watched Rothen usher the Administrator from the room. As the door closed, Rothen turned to regard her.

'What do you think of Lorlen, then?'

She considered. 'He seems nice, but he's very formal.'

Rothen chuckled. 'Yes, he can be.'

He moved into his bedroom, then returned wearing a cloak. Surprised, Sonea watched him stride toward her. Another cloak was draped over his arm.

'Stand up,' he said. 'I want to see if this will fit you.'

Rising, she stood still as he draped the cloak over her shoulders. It fell almost to the floor.

'A bit long. I'll have it shortened. For now, you'll have to take care not to trip.'

'This is for me?'

'Yes. To replace your old one.' He smiled. 'You'll need it. It's quite cold outside.'

She looked at him sharply. 'Outside?'

'Yes,' he replied. 'I thought we'd take a walk. Would you like that?'

Nodding, she looked away, not wanting him to see her face. The thought of getting out had filled her with an intense longing. She had been inside his rooms for less than three weeks but she felt as if months had passed.

'We're meeting Dannyl downstairs,' he told her, moving toward the door.

'Now?'

He nodded and beckoned. Taking a deep breath, she approached the door.

Unlike the previous time, the corridor was not empty. A pair of magicians stood several paces to the right, and a woman in ordinary dress walked to the left, flanked by two small children. All stared at Sonea in surprise and curiosity.

Rothen nodded to the watchers and started toward the stairs. Following, Sonea resisted the temptation to glance behind. No floating magicians appeared in the centre of the staircase as they descended. Instead, a familiar tall magician waited at the bottom.

'Good evening, Sonea,' Dannyl said, smiling.

'Good evening,' she replied.

Turning, Dannyl gestured grandly at a pair of large doors at the end of the lower floor corridor. They slowly swung open, letting in a gust of cold air.

Beyond them was the courtyard she remembered seeing when she had explored the Guild with Cery. It had been night then. Now a murky twilight was growing, making everything seem muted and unreal.

Following Rothen through the doors, Sonea felt the bite of cold air. Though it set her shivering, she welcomed it. *Outside* . . .

Warmth slid over her skin, and she sensed a vibration in the air around her. Surprised, she cast about, but could see nothing to mark the change. Rothen was watching her.

'A simple trick,' he told her. 'It's a magical shield that holds in warmth. You can walk in and out of it. Give it a try.'

She took a few steps back towards the doors and felt the cold on her face. Her breath began to mist in the air. Reaching out, she felt her hand pass into warmth again.

Rothen smiled encouragingly and beckoned. Shrugging, she moved back to his side.

The back of the University towered to her left. Looking around, she identified most of the buildings she had seen on Dannyl's plan. Her eye was drawn to an odd structure on the other side of the courtyard.

'What is that?'

Rothen followed her gaze. 'That is the Dome,' he told her. 'Centuries ago, before we made the Arena, most training for Warriors was held in there. Unfortunately, the only people who could see what was going on were those inside, so teachers had to be strong enough to protect themselves from any stray magic that might be loosed by their pupils. We don't use it any more.'

Sonea stared at the structure. 'It looks like a big ball has been sunk into the ground.'

'It has.'

'How do you get in?'

'Through an underground passage. There's a door like a giant round plug which can only be opened inwards. The walls are three paces thick.'

The doors to the Novices' Quarters opened. Three boys hurried outside, wrapped in cloaks. They moved around the courtyard, tapping the lampposts standing around the edge of the paving. At their touch, the lamps began glowing.

Once all the lamps in the courtyard were alight, the three boys separated and ran in different directions. One headed down the front of the Novices' Quarters, the other disappeared into the gardens on the other side of the University, while the third dashed between the Baths and the Magicians' Quarters, where a long path curved up into the forest.

Dannyl looked at Rothen questioningly. While the two magicians teased each other like old friends, Sonea had noticed that Dannyl always deferred to his former guardian.

'Where to?'

Rothen nodded toward the forest. 'This way.'

Sonea stayed beside Rothen as the magician crossed the pavement and started along the path. The novice, having finished lighting the lamps, hurried back toward the Novices' Quarters.

As she passed the back of the Magicians' Quarters, a movement in one of the windows caught her eye. Looking up, she saw a fair-haired magician watching and felt a shock as she recognised him. He quickly withdrew into the darkness. Frowning, she turned her attention back to the path. She had no idea when Fergun would visit again, but when he did, he would want to know if she was going to accept his offer. She needed to come to a decision soon.

Until her talk with Lorlen, she hadn't discovered whether all of the claims Fergun had made were true. She had been waiting for opportunities to steer her conversations with Rothen to vows and guardians, or Fergun himself, but few had come. Could she ask him directly without raising his suspicions?

While Rothen had told her what a guardian did, he hadn't mentioned that he intended to be hers. She would not be surprised if he had decided that she did not need to know unless she chose to stay.

Once she had learned Control, she had two choices: return to the slums with her powers blocked, or help Fergun win her guardianship so that she could return with her powers intact.

As they reached the forest, Sonea looked into the maze of trunks. Fergun's plan made her uneasy. It involved a great deal of deception and risk. She would have to pretend that she wanted to stay, possibly lie to ensure Fergun won her guardianship, make a vow she intended to break, then break that vow – and the King's law – by leaving the Guild.

Had she become so fond of Rothen that the idea of lying to him bothered her? *He is a magician*, she reminded herself. *His loyalties are with the Guild and the King*. While she believed that he did not want to lock her away, for instance, he would if ordered to.

Or was it the idea of breaking a vow that worried her? Harrin and his friends cheated and stole all the time, but they regarded the breaking of a vow as an unforgivable offence. To keep their standing with others, they did all they could to avoid making one.

Of course, if a vow could not be avoided, awkward situations could be evaded if it was phrased sloppily . . .

'You're very quiet tonight,' Rothen said suddenly. 'No questions?'

Sonea looked up at Rothen and found him regarding her fondly. Seeing his smile, she decided it was time to risk asking a few unprompted questions.

'I was wondering about the vow magicians make.'

To her relief, his brows didn't lower with suspicion, but rose with surprise. 'There are two, actually. The Novices' Vow and the Magicians' Vow. One is made when novices enter the Guild, the other made at graduation.'

'What do they swear?'

'Four things.' Rothen held up the fingers of his left hand. 'The novices vow to never deliberately harm another man or woman unless in defence of the Allied Lands.' He tapped the first finger, then the others as he continued. 'To obey the rules of the Guild, to obey the laws of the King and orders of any magician unless those orders involve breaking a law, and to never use magic unless instructed by a magician.'

Sonea frowned. 'Why can't novices use magic unless a magician tells them to?'

Rothen chuckled. 'Plenty of novices have harmed themselves while experimenting without guidance. Magicians still need to take care, however. All teachers know that if they tell a novice to "go practise", without specifying exactly *what* they should practise, the novice will interpret the order as "go practise anything you wish". I can remember using that reasoning to justify spending a day fishing.'

Dannyl snorted. 'That's nothing.'

As the younger magician began telling her of his own exploits as a novice, Sonea considered the Novices' Vow. It contained nothing she would not have expected. She did not know what all the rules of the Guild were. Perhaps it was time to ask Rothen about them. The last two parts appeared to have been added purely to keep novices in line.

By leaving the Guild with her powers unblocked, she would be breaking the second part of the vow. Strangely, she had felt no reluctance to break a law unless it meant breaking a vow.

When Dannyl finished his anecdote, Rothen continued his explanation. 'The first two parts of the Magicians' Vow are the same,' he told her. 'But the third part changes to be a pledge to serve the ruler of one's own land, and the fourth becomes a promise to never use evil forms of magic.'

Sonea nodded. By letting her escape, Fergun would be breaking a law *and* the Magicians' Vow.

'What is the punishment if a magician breaks the Vow?'

Rothen shrugged. 'That depends how it was broken, which land the magician lives in, and the judgement of their ruler.'

'What happens if they are Kyralian?'

'The worst penalty is death, which is reserved for murderers. Otherwise, the strongest punishment is exile.'

'You . . . block the magician's powers and send them away.'

'Yes. None of the Allied Lands will accept them. It was part of the agreement.'

She nodded. She couldn't ask him what Fergun would face if the Guild discovered he had arranged for her to leave with her powers intact. A question like that was sure to make Rothen suspicious.

If she agreed to Fergun's plan, she would have to hide well, or face similar punishment. The Guild would not offer her another chance to join them. She would have no choice but to rely on a Thief to hide her again – though she was sure Faren would do so eagerly if her powers were unblocked and controllable.

What would they ask her to do in return? She grimaced as she considered the prospect of spending the rest of her life hiding and doing the bidding of a Thief. All she really wanted was to be with her family.

Looking up at the snow covering the ground on either side of the path, she felt a pang of worry as she thought of her aunt and uncle shivering in some tiny room somewhere. This would be a hard time for them. They would have few customers. With Jonna's baby growing and Ranel's bad leg stiffening in the cold, how were they getting deliveries done? She should return to help them, not perform magic for a Thief.

But if she returned with magic, she was sure Faren would make sure her aunt and uncle lived well, and she would be able to Heal . . .

Yet if she co-operated with Rothen, she could be back with her aunt and uncle in a few weeks. Fergun's plans might take months . . .

It was so hard to decide.

Frustrated, she wished, as she had so many times before, that she had never discovered her powers. They had ruined her life. They had nearly killed her. They had forced her to feel grateful to the hated magicians for saving her life. She just wanted to be rid of them.

Rothen slowed. Looking up, Sonea realised that the path came to an end at a wide, paved road ahead. As they reached it, several small, neat houses came in sight.

'These are the Residences,' Rothen told her.

The blackened skeletons of a few houses lay between some of the buildings. Rothen offered no explanation. He continued on to where the road ended in a large circle for turning a carriage. Walking over to a fallen tree trunk beside the road, he sat down.

As Dannyl folded his long legs and joined the older magician, Sonea looked around at the forest. Through the trees she saw a row of dark shapes in the snow, too regular to be natural.

'What are they?'

Rothen followed her gaze.

'That's the old cemetery. Shall we have a look?'

Dannyl turned abruptly to stare at the older magician. 'Now?'

'We've already come this far,' Rothen said, rising. 'It won't hurt to go a little further.'

'Couldn't it wait until morning?' Dannyl cast an anxious look at the distant shapes.

Rothen raised his hand and a tiny speck of light suddenly sprang into existence just above his palm. It expanded rapidly into a round globe of light, then floated up to hover above their heads.

'I guess not.' Dannyl sighed.

Snow crunched under their boots as they started toward the cemetery. Sonea's shadow stretched to one side, then was joined by another as a second sphere of light flared into existence over Dannyl's head.

'Afraid of the dark, Dannyl?' Rothen said over his shoulder.

The tall magician did not reply. Chuckling, Rothen stepped over a fallen log and entered the clearing. Several rows of stones stretched into the gloom.

Drawing closer, Rothen sent his light forward to hover just above one of the stones. The snow melted quickly, revealing markings on the surface. As the light rose higher again, he indicated Sonea should move closer.

A decorative design had been carved around the edge of the slab, and she could see marks at the centre which might once have been words.

'Can you read it?' Rothen asked.

Sonea ran her hand over the engravings.

'Lord Gamor,' she read, 'and a year . . .' She frowned. 'No, I must be wrong.'

'I believe it says twenty-five of Urdon.'

'This is seven centuries old?'

'It certainly is. All of these graves are at least five centuries old. They're quite a mystery.'

Sonea looked up at the rows of stones. 'Why are they a mystery?'

'No magicians have been buried here since then, and none are buried outside of the Guild either.'

'Where are they buried?'

'They aren't.'

Sonea turned to regard him. A faint noise whispered among the trees nearby and Dannyl turned abruptly, his eyes wide. She felt the hairs on the back of her neck begin to rise.

'Why not?' she asked.

Rothen moved forward and looked down at the grave. 'A magician four centuries ago described his magic as a constant companion. It can be a helpful friend, he said, or a deadly adversary.' He looked back at Sonea, his eyes hidden under the shadows of his brows.

'Think of everything you have learned about magic and control. Your powers developed naturally, but for most of us, we need to have our abilities triggered by another magician. Once that is done, we are bound by the demands of our powers for the rest of our lives. We have to learn to control them, and we have to maintain that control. If we don't, our magic will eventually destroy us.' He paused. 'For all of us, at the moment of our death, our grasp over our power ends and the remaining magic within us is released. We are, literally, consumed by it.'

Sonea looked down at the grave. Despite Rothen's shield of warmth, she felt cold to the bone.

She had thought that she would be rid of magic once she had learned Control, but now she knew that she would never be free of it. No matter what she did, it would always be there. One day, in some house in the slums, she would just flare out of existence . . .

'If we die a natural death, this is rarely a problem,' Rothen added. 'The strength of our power usually fades in our last years. If our death is unnatural . . . There is a old saying: it takes a fool, a martyr, or a genius to murder a magician.'

Looking at Dannyl, she suddenly understood his discomfort. It was not the presence of the dead that disturbed him, but the reminder of what was going to happen to him when he died. But he had chosen this life, she reminded herself. She hadn't.

Neither had Fergun. Forced to become a magician by his parents, he faced this end too. She wondered how many magicians entered the Guild reluctantly. Surprised by her newfound sympathy, she looked down at the headstone.

'So why are these graves here?'

Rothen shrugged. 'We have no idea. They shouldn't be. Many of our historians believe that these magicians drained all their power once they knew they were dying, then made sure they died at the point of exhaustion by stabbing themselves or taking poison. We know they chose other magicians to be attendants at their death. Perhaps making sure they died at the right moment was the attendant's task. Even a little remaining power can be enough to destroy a body, so the timing would have been important, especially as the magicians of that time were extraordinarily powerful.'

'We don't know if that's true,' Dannyl added. 'The stories of their powers may have been exaggerated. Heroes tend to gain improbable strength when their tale is told over and over again.'

'We have books written during their lifetimes,' Rothen reminded him. 'Even diaries of the magicians themselves. Why would they exaggerate their own abilities?'

'Why indeed?' Dannyl replied dryly.

Turning away, Rothen led them back, over the snow they had trampled on their approach.

'I believe that those first magicians *were* more powerful,' Rothen said. 'And we have been growing weaker ever since.'

Dannyl shook his head, then looked down at Sonea. 'What do you think?'

She blinked at him with surprise. 'I don't know. Perhaps they had some way of making themselves stronger.'

Dannyl shook his head. 'There are no ways of increasing

a magician's strength. What he is born with, he's stuck with.'

They reached the road and continued on. Night had descended completely and lights glowed in the windows of the houses along the road. As they passed a burned ruin, Sonea shivered. Had it been destroyed when the occupant passed away?

The magicians remained silent as they continued down the road. Reaching the beginning of the path, Rothen sent his floating light ahead to illuminate the way. In the lull in conversation, the chirping of insects in the forest seemed louder.

As the Magicians' Quarters came into sight, Sonea thought of all the magicians who lived there, each keeping their power under control even as they slept. Perhaps those early city planners had another reason for giving the magicians an entire quarter of the city to themselves.

'That's all the exercise I need for tonight, I think,' Rothen said suddenly. 'And it's just about time for the evening meal. Will you join us, Dannyl?'

'Of course,' the tall magician replied. 'I would love to.'

CHAPTER 25

A CHANGE OF PLANS

The sun hovered above the distant towers of the Palace like an enormous magician's globe light, sending long stripes of orange light into the gardens.

As they walked along the path, Sonea was quiet. Brooding. Rothen knew she had guessed the intention behind the excursions he had been taking her on, and was mentally hardening herself until no sight could tempt her to stay in the Guild.

He smiled. Though she might be determined to dismiss everything she saw, Rothen intended to show her as much as he could of the Guild. She needed to see what she was rejecting.

Surprised by her continuing determination to leave, Rothen had found himself pondering his own life. Like all children of the Houses, he had been tested for magical ability at about the age of ten. He remembered how excited his parents had been when potential had been found. They told him he was lucky and special. From that day, he had looked forward to joining the Guild.

Becoming a magician had never been a possibility for Sonea. She had been taught to see them as an enemy to be blamed and hated. In the face of her upbringing, it was easy to see why she considered joining the Guild a betrayal of the people she had grown up with.

But it didn't have to be. If he could convince her that she could eventually use her powers to help her people, she might decide to stay.

Reaching the end of the University, Rothen turned right. As they passed the gardens on the other side of the building, the gong rang, marking the end of classes. Knowing this was usually followed by novices rushing from the University to their quarters, Rothen had chosen a longer, but quieter, route to the Healers' Quarters.

He was looking forward to this excursion. Healing was the noblest of the magicians' skills, and the only magic which Sonea appeared to value. Knowing that the Warrior arts were unlikely to impress her, he had taken her to see them first. However, she had been more unsettled by the demonstration than he expected. Despite the teacher's explanation of the rules and protections used, she had flinched away from the combatants as soon as they began their mock battle.

Though Dannyl's mind-printing experiment had demonstrated one use of Alchemy, it was, in reality, only a hobby. If he was going to impress her, he needed to show her something that was more useful to the city. He hadn't yet decided what it should be.

As they neared the circular Healer's Quarters, Rothen glanced at Sonea again. Though her expression was guarded, her eyes were bright with interest. He stopped before the entrance.

'This is the second Healers' Quarters to be built,' he told Sonea. 'The first was quite luxurious. Unfortunately, our predecessors experienced problems with a few wealthy patients who assumed they could buy permanent residency. When the University and the other Guild buildings were constructed, the old Healers' Quarters was demolished and this replaced it.'

Though the exterior was attractive, the Healers' building was not as impressive as the University. Moving through the open doors, Rothen led Sonea into a small, undecorated entrance hall. A fresh, medicinal smell permeated the air.

Two Healers, a middle-aged man and a younger woman, looked up as Rothen and Sonea entered. The man regarded Sonea dubiously and turned away, but the young woman smiled and came forward to greet them.

'Greetings, Lord Rothen,' she said.

'Greetings, Lady Indria,' he replied. 'This is Sonea.'

Sonea nodded. 'Honoured to meet you.'

Indria inclined her head. 'A pleasure to meet you, too, Sonea.'

'Indria will be giving us a tour of the Healers' Quarters,' Rothen explained.

The Healer smiled at Sonea. 'I hope you find my tour interesting.' She looked at Rothen. 'Shall we begin?'

Rothen nodded.

'This way, then.'

Leading them to a pair of doors, Indria willed them open and ushered Rothen and Sonea into a wide, curved corridor. They passed several open doors, and Sonea took the opportunity to glance into the rooms beyond.

'The lower floor of the building is dedicated to treating and housing patients,' Indria told them. 'We can't expect sick people to climb up and down stairs, can we?' She smiled at Sonea, who managed a bemused shrug in reply.

'The upper floor has rooms for lessons and for the Healers who live here. Most of us live in this building rather than in the Magicians' Quarters. It allows us to respond quickly to an emergency.' She gestured to her left. 'The patients' rooms are those which have nice views of the gardens or the forest.' She waved to the right. 'The interior rooms are our Treatment Rooms. Come, I'll show you one.'

Following the Healer through one of the open doors, Rothen watched as Sonea examined the room. It was small, containing only a bed, a cupboard and several wooden chairs.

'We do minor healing and simple treatments here,' Indria told Sonea. She opened the cupboard to reveal several rows of bottles and boxes. 'Any medicines we can prepare quickly or mix beforehand are kept in easy reach. We have other rooms upstairs where more complicated preparations are made.'

Leaving the room again, Indria led them to a passage entrance next to the Treatment Room. She pointed to a door at its end. 'At the centre of the building are Healing Rooms,' she said. 'I'll just check this one's empty.'

Hurrying down the passage, she peered through a glass panel on the door. Turning to look back at them, she nodded.

'It's free,' she told them. 'Come in.'

Moving down the passage, Rothen smiled as Indria held the door open for him. The room they stepped into was larger than the first they had seen. A narrow bed stood in the centre and the walls were lined with cupboards.

'This is where we perform major Healing and surgery,' Indria told them. 'No-one is allowed in here during treatment except Healers – and the patient, of course.'

Sonea's eyes roved around the room. She moved to a gap in the far wall. Indria followed.

'The medicine preparation rooms are right above us,' the Healer explained, pointing up into the alcove. Sonea leaned forward and peered up to the room above. 'We have Healers that specialise in making medicines. They lower freshly made mixtures down these chutes as we need them.'

Her curiosity satisfied, Sonea moved back to Rothen's side. Indria moved to a cupboard. She opened it and took out one of the bottles.

'We have the greatest store of knowledge on medicine in the world here in the Guild,' she said with unconcealed pride. 'We don't just cure people with our Healing power. If we did, we wouldn't be able to keep up with the demand for our services.' She shrugged. 'Not that we do anyway. There just aren't enough Healers.'

Opening a drawer, she pulled out a small piece of white material. Turning to Sonea, she paused, then looked up at Rothen questioningly. Realising what she was going to do, he shook his head. Indria bit her lip, looked at Sonea, then down at the objects in her hands.

'Ah, perhaps we'll skip this part of the tour.'

Sonea eyed the bottle, her eyes afire with curiosity. 'What part?'

Indria turned the bottle so Sonea could see the label. 'It's an anaesthetic cream,' she explained. 'I usually spread a little over a visitor's palms to demonstrate the potency of our medicine.'

Sonea frowned. 'Anaesthetic?'

'It makes your skin go numb so you can't feel anything. The effect wears off after an hour.'

Sonea's eyebrows rose, then she shrugged and held out her hand. 'I'll try it.'

Catching his breath, Rothen stared at Sonea in surprise.

This was remarkable. Where had her distrust of magicians gone? Pleased, he watched as Indria unscrewed the bottle and poured a little of the paste onto the square of material.

Indria frowned at Sonea anxiously. 'You won't feel anything straightaway. After a minute you'll feel as if your skin is really thick. Do you still want to try it?'

Sonea nodded. Smiling, Indria gently wiped the paste over Sonea's palm.

'Now be very careful not to get any on your eyes. It won't make you blind but, believe me, having numb eyelids is a *very* peculiar sensation.'

Sonea smiled and examined her hand. Returning the bottle to its shelf, Indria dropped the cloth into a bucket inside one of the cupboards, then rubbed her hands together.

'Now let's go upstairs and have a look at the classrooms.'

She led them out of the room and back to the main corridor. They passed several Healers and a few novices as they walked around the building. Some regarded Sonea with curiosity. Others, to Rothen's dismay, frowned with disapproval.

'Indria!'

The Healer turned, her green robes flaring out at the abrupt movement. 'Darlen?'

'In here.'

The voice came from one of the nearby Treatment rooms. Indria strode to the doorway.

'Yes?'

'Give me a hand, will you?'

Indria turned and grinned at Rothen. 'I'll ask if the patient minds having an audience,' she said quietly.

She stepped into the room and Rothen heard several voices talking quietly. Sonea glanced at Rothen, her expression unreadable, then looked away.

Indria appeared in the doorway and beckoned. 'Come in.'

Rothen nodded. 'Give me a moment.'

As the Healer retreated, Rothen looked at Sonea closely. 'I don't know what you'll see in there, but I don't think Indria would invite us in if it was anything ghastly. If the sight of blood bothers you, however, we probably shouldn't enter.'

Sonea looked amused. 'I'll be fine.'

Shrugging, Rothen gestured to the door. Going through, she saw that the room was set up the same as the one they had previously entered. On the bed lay a boy of about eight years. His face was white and his eyes were red from crying. The voice that called for assistance belonged to a young man in green robes, Lord Darlen, who was gently unwrapping a blood-soaked bandage from around the boy's hand. A young couple sat on wooden chairs, watching anxiously.

'Stand over here, please,' Indria instructed, her voice suddenly stern. Rothen backed into a corner, and Sonea followed him. Darlen glanced at them, before turning his attention back to the boy

'Does it hurt any more?'

The boy shook his head.

Rothen looked at the couple. Despite signs they had dressed hastily, their clothes were opulent. The man wore a fashionable long coat with gemstone buttons and the woman wore a simple black cloak with a fur trimmed hood.

Beside him, Sonea made a small sound. Rothen looked

back to the bed and saw that the last of the bandages had been removed from the boy's hand. Two deep cuts crossed his palm and blood was dripping from the wounds.

Darlen pulled the boy's sleeve up and grasped his arm tightly. The flow of blood stopped. He looked up at the parents.

'How did this happen?'

The man flushed and his eyes slid to the floor. 'He was playing with my sword. I forbade it, but he . . .' The man shook his head, his expression grim.

'Hmm,' Darlen turned the hand over a little. 'He should heal well, though he'll have scars to treasure for the rest of his life.'

The woman made a small choking noise, then burst into tears. Her husband put an arm about her shoulders and looked at the Healer expectantly.

Darlen turned to Indria. She nodded and went to the shelves. From a drawer she produced more pieces of white material, a bowl and a large bottle of water. Moving to the bed, she gently bathed the hand. When it was clean, the Healer carefully placed his palm over the boy's and closed his eyes.

A stillness followed. Though the mother made the occasional sniff, all sound seemed to be muted. The boy began to fidget, but Indria leaned forward and lay a hand on his shoulder.

'Stay still. Don't break his concentration.'

'But it itches,' he protested.

'It won't for long.'

Catching a movement beside him, Rothen looked down to see that Sonea was rubbing her palm. Darlen drew in a deep breath and opened his eyes. He looked down at the hand and ran his fingers across it. Instead of deep wounds, fine red lines now crossed the boy's palm. Darlen smiled at the boy.

'Your hand is healed now. I want you to bandage it every day. Don't use it for at least two weeks. You don't want to spoil all the work I just did, do you?'

The boy shook his head. He lifted his hand and traced the scars with a finger. Darlen patted his shoulder.

'After two weeks, exercise it gently.' He looked up at the parents. 'There should be no permanent damage. Eventually he'll be able to do everything he could before, including wielding his father's sword.' He leant down and poked the boy's chest gently. 'But not until he's grown up.'

The boy grinned. Darlen helped him off the bed, smiling as the boy ran to his parents and was enveloped in their arms.

The father looked up at Darlen, his eyes glistening, and opened his mouth to speak. The Healer lifted a hand to stop him, then turned to look at Indria.

She gestured for Rothen and Sonea to follow her. They quickly slipped out of the room. As they began to stroll down the corridor, Rothen could hear the father expressing his thanks.

'Looks easy, doesn't it?' Indria grimaced. 'It's actually very hard.'

'Healing is the most difficult of all the disciplines,' Rothen explained. 'It requires a finer control and many years of practise.'

'Which is why it doesn't appeal to some of the youngsters,' Indria sniffed. 'They're too lazy.'

'I have many novices who are far from lazy,' Rothen told her archly.

Indria grinned. 'But you are such a wonderful teacher, Rothen. How could they not be the most dedicated pupils in the University?'

Rothen laughed. 'I should come to the Healers more often. You're so gratifying.'

'Hmm,' she said. 'We don't usually see you unless it's to grumble about indigestion or the burns you get from your silly experiments.'

'Don't say that,' Rothen put a finger to his lips. 'I'm taking Sonea on a tour of the Alchemy rooms next.'

Indria gave Sonea a sympathetic look. 'Good luck. Try not to fall asleep.'

Rothen straightened and pointed to the stairs. 'Get on with the tour, you insolent girl,' he commanded. 'Only a year since graduation, and already you think you can give cheek to your elders.'

'Yes, my lord.' Grinning, she gave a mocking bow then started down the corridor.

Sliding aside one of Rothen's windows screens, Sonea looked through the glass at the swirling snow. She rubbed her palm absently. Though feeling had returned hours ago, the memory of numbness was still strong.

She had expected Rothen to show her the Healers at work, and that she would have to resist the desire to be able to do it herself. Despite her determination to remain unaffected, seeing a child healed before her eyes had stirred up unwanted feelings. Though she had known she had the ability to do such things, only at that moment had she understood what she could be capable of.

Which had been Rothen's intention, of course. Sighing, she tapped on the edge of the window screen. As she had expected, he was trying to tempt her into staying by showing her all the wonderful things she could do with her magic.

But surely he hadn't expected her to be impressed by the previous day's Warrior demonstration. Watching novices throw magic at each other was not going to tempt her to stay. Perhaps he had only intended to show her that the fights were harmless. Guided by strict rules, they were more like games than real battles.

When she considered that, it was no longer difficult to see why they had reacted as they had when she had 'attacked' them in the North Square. They were too used to 'inner shields' and tallying 'hits'. It must have come as quite a shock to see what magic did to an undefended person.

She sighed again. A tour of the Alchemy rooms would probably come next. Against her will, she felt a twinge of curiosity. Of all the disciplines, Alchemy was the one she understood least.

She frowned at a knock on the main door. Tania had bid them goodnight hours ago and Rothen had not been gone long. Her heart skipped as a name raced through her mind.

Fergun.

He would want an answer, and she hadn't decided yet. She reluctantly crossed the room, hoping the visitor was someone else.

'Who is it?'

'Fergun. Let me in, Sonea.'

Taking a deep breath, she grasped the handle. At once, the door swung inward. The red-robed magician slipped gracefully into the room and closed the door behind him.

'How can you open it?' she asked, frowning at the handle. 'I thought it was locked.'

Fergun smiled. 'It was, but it will open when the door handle is turned by someone inside at the same time as someone outside.'

'Is it meant to?'

Fergun nodded. 'It's a precaution. Rothen might not be around to open the door in an emergency. Someone else can if, for instance, you started a fire.'

She grimaced. 'Hopefully *that* will never be a problem again.' She gestured to the chairs. 'Have a seat, Fergun.'

He glided to the chairs and sat down. As she took the seat opposite, he leaned forward eagerly.

'So, are your Control lessons going well?'

'Yes . . . I think.'

'Hmm, tell me what you did today.'

She smiled ruefully. 'I had to lift a box off the floor. That wasn't easy.'

Fergun drew in a sharp breath, his eyes widening, and Sonea felt her heart skip in response. 'What he is teaching you is not a Control exercise. He is showing you how to use your magic. If he is doing that, you must already have Control.'

Sonea felt a thrill of excitement and hope. 'He said he was *testing* my Control.'

Fergun shook his head gravely. 'All magic is a test of Control. He wouldn't be teaching you to lift objects unless your control was sufficiently established. You're ready, Sonea.'

Leaning back in her chair, Sonea felt a smile pulling at the corners of her mouth. *At last!* she thought. *I can go home!*

An unexpected twinge of regret followed the thought. Once gone, she might never see Rothen again . . .

'So, are you satisfied that what I told you is true – that Rothen has kept information from you?'

She looked at Fergun and nodded. 'Most of it. Administrator Lorlen explained the blocking of power to me.'

Fergun looked surprised. 'Lorlen himself. Good.'

'He told me it would not be unpleasant, and that I'd never notice it after.'

'If it works properly. The Guild hasn't needed to do it for many, many years.' He grimaced. 'The last time they did, they messed it up a little – but you should not worry about that. Accept my help and you won't have to take the risk.' He smiled. 'Are we going to work together?'

She hesitated. Doubts ran through her mind.

Seeing her expression, he asked: 'Have you decided to stay, then?'

'No.'

'Then are you still undecided?'

'I'm not sure about your plan,' she admitted. 'Parts of it, anyway.'

'Which parts?'

She drew in a deep breath. 'If I become a novice, I'll have to make a vow that I know I'm going to break.'

He frowned. 'And?'

'I'm not . . . happy about doing that.'

His eyes narrowed slightly. 'You're worried about breaking a vow?' He shook his head. 'I am willing to break the King's law for you, Sonea. Though I'm sure we can make it look as if you escaped on your own, there's a chance my part in it will be discovered. I am willing to take that risk for your sake.' He leaned forward. 'You must decide whether the King has the right to take your power from you. If he doesn't, then what value is there in the vow?'

Sonea nodded slowly. He was right. Faren would agree, and so would Cery. The Houses had kept magic to themselves for too long – and then used it against the poor during the Purge. The dwells would not look down on her for breaking the Novices' Vow. It was their opinion that mattered, not the King's or the magicians'.

If she returned to the slums with her powers unfettered and taught herself magic, she could teach others too. She could start her own secret Guild.

It would mean relying on Faren to hide her from the Guild again. It would mean she could not return to her family. It would mean she might eventually use her powers to help and heal people – which might make the risks worth taking.

She looked at the magician sitting opposite her. Would Fergun be so keen to let her go if he knew what she was thinking? She frowned. If she became his novice, he might need to enter her mind to teach her. He might discover her plans and, not liking the consequences of helping her, change his mind.

Much of his proposal forced her to rely on him. She did not know him, had not seen into his mind.

If only she could leave – escape – without his help.

She felt a sudden thrill. Perhaps she could. She had achieved Control. Rothen didn't know that she knew. He would have to admit it eventually, and once he did, he would be wary of her attempting to escape. But not now. Now was the perfect time to try.

What if she did not get the opportunity, or failed?

Then she would accept Fergun's offer. For now, however, she had to delay him.

Looking at Fergun, she sighed and shook her head. 'I don't know. Even if your plan does work, I'll still have the Guild hunting for me.'

'They won't be able to find you,' he assured her. 'I will teach you how to hide your powers. They'll find no clue to your location, and eventually give up. You're not the only one who got tired of the hunt last time, Sonea. They won't search forever.'

'There are some things you don't know,' she told him. 'If I return to the slums with magic, the Thieves will want me to work for them. I don't want to be their tool.'

He smiled. 'You'll have magic, Sonea. They can't make you do anything you don't want to.'

She looked away and shook her head. 'I have family, Fergun. The Thieves might not be able to hurt me, but they can hurt others. I . . .' She rubbed her face, then looked at him apologetically. 'I need more time to think.'

His smile vanished. 'How long?'

She shrugged. 'A few weeks, maybe?'

'I don't have that long,' he told her, his expression darkening. '*You* don't have that long.'

Sonea frowned. 'Why not?'

Rising abruptly, he took something from within his robe and dropped it onto the table before her.

She sucked in a breath as she recognised the dagger. So many times, she had watched the blade being carefully and lovingly sharpened. She could remember the day, many years before, when the rough picture of a familiar rodent had been etched into the blade.

'You recognise it, I see.'

Fergun stood over her now, his eyes glittering.

'I have the owner of this knife locked in a dark little room that nobody here knows of.' His lips stretched into a nasty smile. 'Just as well they don't, since they might get a bit worried if they saw how big some of these rodents can grow.' Dropping into a crouch, he placed his hands on the arms of her chair. Sonea shrank back, appalled by his malicious stare.

'Do what I tell you, and I will release your friend. Give me any trouble, and I will leave him there forever.' His eyes narrowed. 'Do you understand me?'

Stunned, unable to speak, Sonea could only nod.

'Listen carefully,' he said. 'I'm going to tell you what you need to do. First, you're going to tell Rothen that you've decided to stay. When you do he'll announce that you've achieved Control, so he can get you into the Guild before you change your mind again. There'll be a Meet in a week, and a Hearing to decide who will be your guardian will be held afterwards.

'At this Hearing you're going to tell everyone that, during the Purge, I saw you before Rothen did. You'll tell them I looked at you after the stone flashed through the barrier and before it struck.

'When you tell them this, the Higher Magicians will have no choice but to grant me your guardianship. You'll enter the Guild, but I assure you, it won't be for long. Once you have performed a little task for me, you'll be sent back where you belong. You'll get what you want, and so will I. You have nothing to lose from helping me, but . . .' he picked up the dagger and ran a finger along the blade, 'you'll lose that little friend of yours if you don't.'

He held her gaze as he slipped the dagger back into his

robes. 'Don't allow Rothen to find out about this. Nobody knows where the little ceryni is but me, and if I can't bring him food he's going to get very, very hungry.'

Rising, he glided to the door and opened it a crack. Looking back at her, he sneered. Sonea's heart lurched as she suddenly remembered where she had seen him before. He was the magician she had knocked out during the Purge.

'I expect to hear Rothen proclaiming his success tomorrow. I'll see you after.' He slipped through the door and pulled it closed behind him.

Sonea listened to his faint footsteps hurrying away, then pressed her hands over her eyes. *Magicians.* She hissed a curse. *I will never, ever trust them again.*

Then she thought of Rothen, and her anger faded. Even though he had deceived her into believing she hadn't achieved Control yet, she was sure Rothen's intentions were good. He had probably been delaying things to give her time to decide if she really wanted to leave. If that were true, he had done nothing that she would not have done herself, had she been in his place – and she was certain that he would help her if she asked.

But she couldn't ask him. A smothering helplessness rushed over her. If she didn't do what Fergun told her, Cery would die.

Curling up in the chair, she wrapped her arms about herself. *Oh Cery*, she thought. *Where are you? Didn't I tell you to make sure you didn't get caught?*

She sighed. Why was Fergun doing this? She thought of the first time she had seen his sneer, and shivered.

Revenge. Simple, petty revenge for the humiliation of being knocked unconscious by a rebellious dwell. It must infuriate him that, instead of punishment, she was being invited into the Guild. But why bother when she didn't want to stay?

She considered his words. '*Once you have performed a little task for me, you'll be sent back where you belong.*' To have joined the Guild, then be sent away . . . He *was* going to make sure she was punished for striking him.

He was going to make sure she would never be able to change her mind and return to the Guild.

CHAPTER 26

THE DECEPTION BEGINS

In the air between the two palms – one large and aged, the other slim and callused – two specks of coloured light danced like tiny insects. The lights spun around each other, dipped and circled in a complex game. The blue light suddenly darted toward the yellow. The yellow turned into a ring of light and, as the blue spark shot through it, Rothen laughed.

'Enough!' he exclaimed.

The shadows around them ceased dancing as the two specks blinked out. Looking around at the dim room, Rothen was surprised to see how late it was. Flexing his will, he created a globe of light and sent the screens sliding over the windows.

'You're learning fast,' he told her. 'Your Control over your power is growing.'

'I mastered Control days ago,' she replied. 'You didn't tell me.'

Surprised, Rothen turned to regard her. She met his gaze steadily. There had been no hint of doubt in her voice. Somehow she had worked it out for herself.

Leaning back in his chair, he considered the situation. If he denied it, she would only grow more resentful when she learned the truth. It would be better to explain his reasons for delaying.

Which meant he had run out of time. He had no reason to keep her here any longer. In a day or two she would be gone. He could ask Lorlen to delay the blocking but he knew, as he considered her now, that he would not be able to change her mind in a few short days.

He nodded. 'A few sessions ago I thought you'd reached a point where I'd normally consider a novice's Control was adequate. I felt, for you, that it was particularly important to test your Control over your power, since we won't be around to help you if something goes amiss.'

Instead of relief, he saw only apprehension in her gaze. 'Not that I think anything will go amiss,' he assured her. 'Your control is—'

'I'm going to stay,' she told him.

He stared at her, momentarily too surprised to speak. 'You're *staying*?' he exclaimed. 'You changed your mind?'

She nodded.

He leapt to his feet. 'That's *wonderful*!'

Sonea stared up at him with wide eyes. He wanted to pull her to her feet and give her a hug, but he knew he would only frighten her. Instead, he strode to the cabinet at the back of the room.

'We must celebrate!' he told her. Taking out a bottle of pachi wine and some glasses, he brought them back to the chairs. She watched, still and silent, as he pulled the stopper out of the bottle and poured some of the yellow liqueur into the glasses.

Sonea's hand shook as she accepted a glass. Rothen sobered, realising that she must be feeling overwhelmed – and a little scared, too.

'What changed your mind?' he asked as he sat down.

She bit her lip gently, then looked away. 'I want to save someone's life.'

'Ah!' He smiled. 'So it was the Healers that impressed you most.'

'Yes.' She admitted. Taking a sip, her face lit with delight. 'Pachi wine!'

'You've had it before?'

She smiled. 'A Thief gave me a bottle once.'

'You've never told me much about the Thieves. I didn't want to ask in case you thought I was trying to get information from you.'

'I never found out much about them,' she replied, shrugging. 'I spent most of my time alone.'

'I assumed they wanted you to perform magic in exchange for their help?'

She nodded. 'But I never really gave the Thief what he wanted.' A crease appeared between her brows. 'I wonder . . . will he think I've broken our agreement by staying here?'

'He didn't succeed in helping you,' Rothen pointed out. 'How can he expect you to fulfil your side of the exchange?'

'He spent a lot of effort and used a lot of favours to hide me.'

Rothen shook his head. 'Don't worry. The Thieves won't bother you. They told us where to find you.'

Sonea's eyes widened. 'They *betrayed* me?' she whispered.

He frowned, disturbed by the anger in her eyes. 'I'm afraid so. I don't think they wanted to, but it was clear that your powers were growing dangerous.'

She looked down at her glass and brooded in silence for some time.

'What happens now?' she asked suddenly.

Rothen hesitated as he realised he would have to explain the guardianship claims to her. The thought of being placed in the care of a magician that she did not know or trust might be enough to change her mind again, but he had to warn her of the possibility.

'There are several matters that must be resolved before you are sworn in as a novice,' he told her. 'You need to have good reading and writing skills, and be taught basic calculations. You'll also need to understand the rules and customs of the Guild. Before then, your guardianship must be decided.'

'Guardianship?' She leaned back in her chair. 'You said only very gifted novices have guardians.'

Rothen nodded. 'From the beginning, I knew that you would need the support of a guardian. As the only novice not from the Houses, you may find things a little difficult at times. Having a magician prepared to be your guardian might help to counter that, so I placed a claim on you.

'But I am not the only magician who wants the honour. There is another, a younger magician named Fergun. When two magicians claim a novice's guardianship, the Guild must hold a Hearing to decide which claim will be granted. The Guild rules say that, if more than one magician wishes to claim a novice's guardianship, the one who first recognised the novice's magical potential is granted the honour, so it is usually a simple decision.' He grimaced. 'But not this time.

'We didn't discover your magic by the usual tests. Some magicians believe that I, being the first to see you, recognised your powers first. Others say that Fergun, being the one your rock struck, was the first since he experienced the effects of your powers.' Rothen chuckled. 'Apparently, the Guild has been arguing about it for months.'

He paused to take another sip of wine. 'The Hearing will be held after the next Meet, which will occur in a week's time. Afterwards, you will continue your lessons with either me, or Fergun.'

Sonea frowned. 'So the novice doesn't get to choose their guardian?'

He shook his head. 'No.'

'Then I better meet this Fergun,' she said slowly. 'Find out what he's like.'

Rothen regarded her closely, surprised at her calm acceptance of the situation. He should be pleased, he told himself, but he could not help feeling a little disappointed. It would have been more gratifying if she had protested at the idea of being removed from his guidance and company.

'I can arrange for you to meet him, if you wish,' he replied. 'He will want to meet you. So may others. Before then, I should teach you some of the rules and customs of the Guild.'

She looked up, her eyes brightening with interest. Relieved to see her curiosity return, Rothen smiled.

'For a start, there is the custom of bowing.'

Her expression changed to dismay. Rothen chuckled sympathetically.

'Yes. Bowing. All non-magicians – apart from royalty, of course – are expected to bow to magicians.'

Sonea grimaced. 'Why?'

'A gesture of respect.' Rothen shrugged. 'Silly as it may seem, some of us get quite offended if we are not bowed to.'

Her eyes narrowed. 'Do you?'

'Not usually,' he told her. 'But there are times when neglecting to bow is obviously intended to be rude.'

She considered him warily. 'Do you expect me to bow to you from now on?'

'Yes and no. I don't expect it in private, but you should bow when we are outside these rooms, even if just to accustom yourself to the habit. You should also use the honorific. Magicians are referred to as Lord or Lady, except in the cases of the Directors, Administrators and the High Lord, for whom you must use their title.'

Rothen smiled at Sonea's expression. 'I didn't think you'd like it. You may have grown up in the lowest class in society, but you have the pride of a king.' He leaned forward. 'One day everyone will be bowing to *you*, Sonea. That will be even harder for you to accept.'

She frowned, then picked up her glass and drained it.

'Now,' Rothen continued, 'there are the rules of the Guild to cover as well. Here.' He reached forward and poured her another glass of wine. 'Let's see if these are any easier to stomach.'

Rothen left just after dinner, no doubt to spread the news. As Tania began to clear the table, Sonea moved to a window. She paused to look at the screen covering it, and realised for the first time that the complex pattern printed on it was actually made up of tiny Guild symbols.

Her aunt had owned an old, mould-spotted pair of screens. They had been the wrong shape for the window of their room in the stayhouse, but her aunt had leaned them up against the glass anyway. When the sun shone through the paper, it had been easy to ignore their flaws.

Instead of the usual pang of homesickness at the memory, she felt a vague longing. Looking around at the luxurious furnishings, the books and the polished furniture, she sighed.

She would miss the comforts and the food, but she was resigned to that. Leaving Rothen would not be so easy, however. She liked his company – his conversations, their lessons, and talking mind to mind.

I was going to leave anyway, she reminded herself for the hundredth time. *I just hadn't thought about how much I'd gained here.*

Knowing that she would be forced from the Guild had made her realise what she was losing. Pretending that she wanted to stay was going to be far too easy.

Just as well Fergun doesn't know, she mused. *It would make his revenge so much sweeter.*

Fergun was risking much to pay her back for humiliating him. He must be very angry – or very sure he could get away with it. Either way, he was prepared to put a lot of effort into having her barred from the Guild.

'Lady?'

Turning, Sonea found Tania standing behind her. The servant smiled.

'I just wanted to tell you that I'm glad you've decided to stay,' she said. 'It would be a poor shame if you didn't.'

Sonea felt her cheeks grow hot. 'Thank you, Tania.'

The woman folded her hands together. 'You look like you're all full of doubts. You're doing the right thing. The Guild never take in poorer folk. It'll do them good to see you doing everything they can, and just as well as they.'

A sliver of cold ran down Sonea's back. This wasn't just about revenge!

The Guild didn't *have* to invite her to join them. They could have blocked her power and sent her back to the slums. Yet they hadn't. For the first time in centuries, the magicians had considered teaching someone from outside the Houses.

Fergun's words echoed in her mind. '*Once you have performed a little task for me, you'll be sent back where you belong.*' Back where she *belonged*?

She had heard the contempt in his voice, but hadn't understood the significance. Fergun didn't just want to make sure *she* didn't enter the Guild. He wanted to make sure no dwell was ever given the chance again. Whatever 'task' Fergun had planned for her would prove that dwells were untrustworthy. The Guild would never consider inviting another dwell into their ranks.

She gripped the window sill, her heart beating fast with anger. *They are opening their doors to me, a dwell, but I'm going to walk out as if that means nothing!*

A familiar feeling of helplessness crawled over her. She couldn't stay. Cery's life depended on her leaving.

'Lady?'

Sonea blinked at Tania. The servant laid a hand lightly on her arm.

'You will do well,' Tania assured her. 'Rothen says you're very strong, and you learn quickly.'

'He does?'

'Oh, yes.' Tania turned and picked up her basket, laden with dishes. 'Well, I'll see you in the morning. Don't go worrying. Everything will be fine.'

Sonea smiled. 'Thanks, Tania.'

The servant grinned. 'Goodnight.'

'Goodnight.'

The servant slipped out of the door, leaving Sonea alone. Sighing, she stared out of the window. Outside it was snowing again, white flakes dancing in the night.

Where are you Cery?

Thinking of the dagger Fergun had shown her, she frowned. It was possible that he had found it; that he did not have Cery locked away . . .

Leaving the window, she dropped into a chair. There was so much to think about: Cery, Fergun, the Hearing, guardianship. Despite Tania's assurances, she was not going to get much sleep during the next few weeks.

Every Threeday, Dannyl joined Yaldin and his wife for the evening meal. Ezrille had started the routine years before when, concerned that Dannyl had not found himself a wife, she began to worry that he would grow lonely if he had to end every day by himself.

As he relinquished his empty plate to Yaldin's servant, Dannyl gave a little sigh of contentment. Though he doubted he would ever sink into the melancholy Ezrille feared, it was certainly better eating in company than by himself.

'I have heard rumours about you, Dannyl,' Yaldin said.

Dannyl frowned, his contentment evaporating. Surely Fergun wasn't at it again. 'Oh, what rumours?'

'That the Administrator is so impressed with your negotiations with the Thieves that he is considering you for an ambassadorial role.'

Dannyl straightened and stared at the old magician. 'He is?'

Yaldin nodded. 'What do you think? Does travelling appeal?'

'I . . .' Dannyl shook his head. 'I've never considered it. Me? An ambassador?'

'Yes.' Yaldin chuckled. 'You're not as young and foolish as you once were.'

'Thanks,' Dannyl replied dryly.

'This could be good for you,' Ezrille said. She smiled and pointed a finger at him. 'You might even bring back a wife.'

Dannyl gave her a withering look. 'Don't start that again, Ezrille.'

She shrugged. 'Well, since there's obviously no woman in Kyralia who is good enough for—'

'Ezrille,' Dannyl said sternly. 'The last young lady I met stabbed me. You know I'm cursed when it comes to women.'

'That's ridiculous. You were trying to catch her, not romance her. How is Sonea going, anyway?'

'Rothen says she's progressing well with her lessons, though she's still determined to leave. She's become quite chatty with Tania.'

'I suppose she'll feel more comfortable with servants than with us,' Yaldin mused. 'They're not as high above her status as we are.'

Dannyl winced. Once he wouldn't have questioned the remark – he would have agreed with it – but now that he had conversed with Sonea, it seemed unfair, even insulting. 'Rothen would not like to hear you say that.'

'No,' Yaldin agreed. 'But he is unique in his opinions. The rest of the Guild feel that class and status are very important.'

'What are they saying now?'

Yaldin shrugged. 'It's got beyond friendly wagers over

the guardianship claim now. A lot of people are questioning the wisdom of having someone with her dubious background in the Guild at all.'

'Again? What are their reasons this time?'

'Will she honour the vow?' Yaldin said. 'Will she be a bad influence on other novices?' He leaned forward. 'You've met her. What do you think?'

Shrugging, Dannyl wiped the sugar from his fingers onto a napkin. 'I'm the last person you should ask. She stabbed me, remember?'

'You're not ever going to let us forget it,' Ezrille remarked. 'Come now, you must have noticed more than that.'

'Her speech is rough, though not as bad as I expected. She has none of the manners we're used to. No bowing or "my Lord".'

'Rothen will teach her that when she's ready,' Ezrille said.

Yaldin snorted softly. 'He better make sure she knows before the Hearing.'

'You're both still forgetting that she doesn't want to stay. Why would he bother to teach her etiquette?'

'Perhaps it would be easier all round if she did leave.'

Ezrille gave her husband a reproachful look. 'Yaldin,' she scolded. 'Would you send the girl back to poverty after showing her all the wealth here? That would be cruel.'

The old man shrugged. 'Of course not, but she wants to go and it'll be easier if she does. No Hearing for a start, and the whole issue about taking in people from outside the Houses will be forgotten.'

'They're wasting their breath arguing about it,' Dannyl

said. 'We all know that the King wants her here, under our control.'

'Then he won't be too happy if she sticks to her intention to leave.'

'No,' Dannyl agreed. 'But he can't make her take the vow if she doesn't want to.'

Yaldin frowned, then glanced at the door as someone knocked on it. He waved a hand lazily, and the door swung open.

Rothen stepped inside, beaming. 'She's staying!'

'Well that settles that,' Ezrille said.

Yaldin nodded. 'Not everything, Ezrille. We still have the Hearing to worry about.'

'The Hearing?' Rothen waved a hand dismissively. 'Leave that to another time. For now, I only want to celebrate.'

CHAPTER 27

SOMEWHERE UNDER THE UNIVERSITY

Curling up in a chair, Sonea yawned and considered the day so far.

In the morning, Administrator Lorlen had visited to ask her about her decision, and to explain, over again, about guardianship and the Hearing. She had felt a pang of guilt as he expressed genuine pleasure that she was staying – a feeling she grew familiar with as the day continued.

Other visitors had come: Dannyl, then the stern and intimidating Head of Healers, and an old couple who were friends of Rothen's. Each time someone had knocked at the door she had tensed, expecting Fergun, but the Warrior had not appeared.

Guessing that he would not visit until she was alone, she was almost relieved when Rothen left after dinner, saying he would be absent until late and that she should not wait up for him.

'I'll stay and chat with you, if you like,' Tania offered.

Sonea smiled in gratitude. 'Thank you, Tania, but I think I'd like to be alone tonight.'

The servant nodded. 'I understand.' She turned back to the table, then paused as a knock came from the door. 'Shall I answer that, Lady?'

Sonea nodded. Taking a deep breath, she watched as the servant opened the door a crack.

'Is the Lady Sonea present?'

Hearing the voice, Sonea felt her stomach sink with dread.

'Yes, Lord Fergun,' Tania replied. She glanced anxiously at Sonea. 'I will ask if she wishes to see you.'

'Let him in, Tania.' Though her heart had begun to race, Sonea managed to speak calmly.

As the servant stepped away from the door, the red-robed magician moved into the room. Inclining his head to Sonea, he placed a hand on his chest.

'I am Fergun. I believe Lord Rothen has told you about me?'

His eyes shifted to Tania then back again. Sonea nodded.

'Yes,' she said. 'He has. Will you sit down?'

'Thank you,' he said, bending gracefully into a chair.

—Send the woman away.

Swallowing, Sonea looked up at Tania. 'Is there anything more you need to do, Tania?'

The servant glanced at the table, then shook her head. 'No, Lady. I will return later for the dishes.' She bowed, then slipped out of the room.

As the door closed behind her, Fergun's friendly expression vanished. 'I was only told this morning that Rothen has announced you ready. It took you some time to tell him.'

'I had to wait for the right moment,' she replied. 'Or it would have seemed strange.'

Fergun stared at her, then waved a hand dismissively. 'It is done. Now, just to make sure you understand my instructions, I want you to repeat them to me.'

He nodded as she recited what he had told her to do.

'Good. Do you have any questions?'

'Yes,' she told him. 'How do I know if you really have Cery? All I've seen is a dagger.'

He smiled. 'You'll just have to trust me.'

'Trust *you*?' She snorted loudly and forced herself to stare into his eyes. 'I want to see him. If I don't, I might have to ask Administrator Lorlen if blackmail is a crime in the Guild.'

His lip curled into a sneer. 'You're in no position to make such threats.'

'Aren't I?' Rising, she strolled to the high table and poured herself a glass of water. Her hands shook and she was glad she had her back to him. 'I know all about this kind of blackmail. I've lived with the Thieves, remember? You need to make it clear that you can carry out your threat. All I've seen is a dagger. Why should I believe you have its owner?'

She turned to meet his gaze and was gratified to see his stare falter. He clenched his fists, then slowly nodded.

'Very well,' he said, rising. 'I will take you to him.'

She felt a thrill of triumph, but it quickly faded. He wouldn't have agreed if he didn't have Cery locked away. She also knew that, when someone's life was being traded for something, the hardest part was stopping the kidnapper from killing their captive as soon they had what they wanted.

Moving to the door, Fergun opened it and waited for her to step through. As she entered the corridor, two magicians stopped and stared at her in alarm, then relaxed as Fergun joined her.

'Has Rothen told you about the buildings of the Guild?' Fergun asked brightly as they started toward the stairs.

'Yes,' she replied.

'They were constructed about four hundred years ago,' he said, ignoring her. 'The Guild had grown too large . . .'

The end of the week at last! Dannyl thought jubilantly as he stepped out of the classroom. The possibility that Sonea would be joining the Guild hadn't occurred to several of the novices. They had been discussing it all day, and he had been forced to keep two back as punishment when they had become too much of a distraction for the others.

Sighing, he placed books, paper and writing box under his arm, and started down the University corridor. As he reached the staircase he froze, unable to believe what he saw in the hall below him.

Fergun and Sonea had just stepped into the University. The Warrior looked around the hall, then checked the stairs opposite Dannyl. Taking a step backwards out of sight, Dannyl listened as the pairs' footsteps moved under him, fading as they started down the ground floor corridor.

Keeping his steps as quiet as possible, Dannyl descended the stairs. He moved across the hall to the lower corridor entrance and peered around the corner. Fergun and Sonea were several paces away, walking quickly. As he watched, they turned into a side passage.

Heart beating faster now, Dannyl made his way down the corridor. He slowed as he reached the side passage, realising it was the same one that he had observed Fergun hurrying down a few days ago. He risked a quick glance.

The passage was empty. Starting down it, he listened carefully. The faintest sound of Fergun's voice drew him to a door that led to the inner passages of the University. Slipping through, Dannyl followed the voice along a few more passages until, abruptly, it ceased.

The silence sent his skin prickling. Had Fergun realised he was being followed? Was he waiting for his pursuer to catch up?

Reaching a bend in the corridor, Dannyl mouthed a curse. Without Fergun's voice, he had no idea if he was about to stumble upon the magician. Taking a cautious look around the corner, he sighed in relief. It was empty.

He started forward, then slowed as he found himself facing a dead end. It wasn't technically a dead end, as none existed in the University. One of the doors would lead to a side passage that would meet the main corridor. Yet if Fergun had gone that way, Dannyl would have heard a door close. Fergun hadn't been trying to be quiet.

But he might have if he had detected someone following him.

Taking the handle of the door leading to the side passage, Dannyl turned it. The hinge creaked dramatically as the door opened, as if it wanted to reassure Dannyl that he would have heard Fergun opening it. Moving through, Dannyl found the side passage empty.

Exploring further, he saw that the main corridor was also empty. Puzzled, Dannyl retraced his steps and tried other doors, but found no sign of Sonea or Fergun.

Shaking his head, he made his way back out of the University, his head buzzing with questions. Why had Fergun taken Sonea out of Rothen's rooms? Why had he led her into the deserted inner passages of the University. How could they have disappeared?

—Rothen?

—Dannyl.

—Where are you?

—In the Night Room.

Dannyl scowled. So Fergun had waited until Rothen was absent before approaching Sonea. Typical.

—*Stay there. I'm coming to meet you.*

Pulling the blanket closer around his shoulders, Cery listened to the chattering of his teeth. The temperature of the room had dropped slowly over several days and was now cold enough to freeze the moisture on the walls. Somewhere above, winter was tightening its grip on the city.

The magician now brought a candle with each meal, but it only lasted a few hours. When darkness came again, Cery slept or paced the room to keep his blood warm, counting the steps so that he did not bump into the walls. He hugged the water bottle to his chest to prevent it freezing.

A soft sound caught his attention and he stopped, sure that he had heard footsteps behind his own. Only silence followed. Sighing, he returned to his pacing.

In his mind, he had rehearsed countless conversations with his captor. After his unsuccessful attempt at killing the magician, Cery had spent many hours considering his situation. Breaking out of the cell was impossible, and he was no threat at all to his captor. His fate was entirely in the magician's hands.

Though it brought a sour taste to his mouth, he knew his only chance of escape lay in gaining the magician's good will. It seemed an impossible task – the magician was not inclined to talk and obviously regarded Cery with disdain. *For Sonea's sake*, Cery thought, *I have to try*.

Sonea. Cery shook his head and sighed. It was possible she had been forced to tell him that she needed the Guild to teach her to control her powers, but he doubted it. She hadn't been tense or frightened, only resigned. He had seen how her powers had reacted to her emotions, how dangerous they had become. It was not hard to believe that her magic would have eventually killed her.

Which meant that taking Sonea to the Thieves had been the worst decision he could have made. By putting her in a situation where she was forced to use magic every day, her powers had been encouraged to grow, perhaps speeding her toward losing control of them much sooner.

She would have reached that point eventually, no matter what he had done. Sooner or later, the Guild would have found her – or she would have died.

Grimacing in the dark, Cery thought of the letter the magicians had sent, claiming they did not intend to harm Sonea and offering her a place among them. Sonea hadn't believed them. Neither had Faren.

But Cery had an old acquaintance among the Guild servants. The man might have been able to confirm the truth, but Cery hadn't asked.

I didn't want to know. I wanted us to be together. Sonea and I, working for the Thieves . . . or just together . . .

She was not one for the Thieves – or for him. She had magic. Whether she liked it or not, she belonged with magicians.

He felt a twinge of jealousy then, but he pushed it away. In the dark he had begun to question his hate for the Guild. He could not help thinking that, if the magicians had gone to so much trouble to save her – and many of the slum dwellers – from her powers, they could not be as indifferent as the dwells thought.

And what better future could he imagine for Sonea?

She could have wealth, knowledge and power. How could he deny her that?

He couldn't. He had no claim on her. The knowledge brought an ache like bruising after a blow to the chest. Though his heart had leapt the moment she had appeared in his life again, she had never expressed anything more than the fondness of friendship.

Hearing a faint noise, he stilled. In the distance, he could hear the faint but growing slap of shoes against stone. As the footsteps drew closer, he moved back to allow room for the magician to enter. From the quick pace, it sounded as if Fergun was in a hurry.

The footsteps did not slow as they reached the door, but continued past.

Cery took a step forward. Was it his captor, merely walking past on the way to another destination? *Or was it someone else?*

He rushed to the door and raised a fist to hammer on it, then froze, seized by doubts. If he was right, and Fergun was using him to blackmail Sonea, would he endanger Sonea by escaping and ruining Fergun's plans?

If Fergun had told Sonea too much, he might kill her to hide his crime. Cery had heard many stories of kidnapping and blackmail gone wrong, and he shivered as he remembered the unpleasant endings of some of those tales.

The footsteps had faded beyond hearing now. Cery rested his head against the door and cursed. It was too late. The stranger was gone.

Sighing, he resolved to keep trying to befriend Fergun, even if only to learn the magician's plans. Once more, conversations ran through Cery's mind. When footsteps reached his ears again, he almost believed he had imagined them.

But as they grew louder he knew they were real. His heart began to race as he realised he was hearing two sets of footsteps. The owners stopped outside the door, and Cery heard Fergun's voice, muffled by the door.

'Stop. We're here.'

The lock clicked, and the door swung open. A globe of light hung over Fergun's head, dazzling Cery's eyes. Despite the brightness, Cery recognised the silhouette of the other visitor. His heart leapt.

'*Sonea!*'

'Cery?'

Sonea reached up to her face and pulled a blindfold away. She blinked at him, then smiled and stepped into the cell.

'Are you all right? You're not sick or hurt?' Her eyes roved over him, looking for signs of injury.

He shook his head. 'No. You?'

'I'm well.' She glanced at Fergun, who was watching them with interest. 'Fergun hasn't hurt you?'

Cery managed a wry smile. 'Only when I asked for it.'

Her brows rose. Turning, she regarded Fergun with narrowed eyes.

'Give me some time to talk to him alone.'

Fergun hesitated, then shrugged. 'Very well. A few minutes, no more.'

He gestured and the door swung shut, leaving them in complete darkness.

Cery sighed. 'Well, we're trapped together.'

'He won't leave me here. He needs me.'

'What for?'

'It's complicated. He wants me to agree to join the Guild so he can have me break a law and get kicked out. I think it's his way of getting revenge for me knocking him out in the Purge – but I'm guessing it's also about convincing the Guild that they shouldn't take in dwells. It doesn't matter. If I do what he says, he'll let you go. Do you think he will?'

Cery shook his head, though he knew she couldn't see him. 'I don't know. He hasn't been nasty. Thieves would've been worse.' He hesitated. 'I don't think he knows what he's doing. Tell someone.'

'No,' she replied. 'If I tell someone, Fergun will refuse to reveal where you are. You'll starve.'

'Someone else must know about these passages.'

'They might take days to find you, Cery. We walked a long way to get here. You could even be outside the Guild.'

'It didn't seem far to m—'

'It doesn't *matter*, Cery. I wasn't going to stay, so there's no sense in risking your life.'

'You weren't going to join the Guild?'

'No.'

His heartbeat quickened. 'Why not?'

'Lots of reasons. Everyone hates magicians, for a start. I'd feel like I was betraying the people I know if I joined them.'

He smiled. It was so like her to see it like that. He took a deep breath. 'Sonea, you *should* stay. You need to learn how to use your magic.'

'But everyone will hate me.'

'No they won't. Truth is, they'd love to be a magician if they had half a chance. If you turn the magicians down, everyone will think you're mad, or stupid. They'd understand if you stayed. They wouldn't want you to give it all up.' He swallowed hard, and forced himself to lie. 'I don't want you to give it all up.'

She hesitated. 'You wouldn't hate me?'

'No.'

'*I* would.'

'The people who know you wouldn't think it was wrong,' Cery told her.

'But . . . I'd still *feel* like I'd changed sides.'

Cery sighed. 'Don't be *stupid*, Sonea. If you were a magician, you could help people. You might be able to do something about stopping the Purge. People would *listen* to you.'

'But . . . I belong with Jonna and Ranel. They need me.'

'No they don't. They're doing fine. Think how proud they'd be. Their own niece in the Guild.'

Sonea stamped her foot. 'It doesn't matter, Cery. I *can't* stay. Fergun said he'll kill you. I'm not going to abandon a friend just so I can do a few magic tricks.'

A friend. Cery's shoulders drooped. Closing his eyes, he let out a long sigh. 'Sonea. Do you remember the night we spied on the Guild?'

'Of course.' He could hear the smile in her voice.

'I told you that I knew someone, a servant in the Guild. I could have gone back to that man, and asked him to find out what the Guild planned for you, but I didn't. Do you know why?'

'No.' She sounded puzzled now.

'I didn't want to find out that the Guild really wanted to help you. You'd just come back and I didn't want you going away. I didn't want to lose you again.'

She said nothing. Her silence told him nothing. He swallowed, his mouth dry.

'I've had lots of time to think here,' he told her. 'I've . . . well, I've told myself to face up to it. There's nothing between us 'cept friendship, so its unfair . . .'

A soft gasp escaped her. 'Oh, Cery,' she breathed. 'You never said anything!'

He felt his face burning, and was grateful for the dark. Holding his breath, he waited for her to speak, hoping she would say something to show she felt the same, or, perhaps, that she would touch him . . .

The silence stretched on until he could stand it no longer. 'Well, it doesn't matter,' he told her. 'What matters is that you don't belong in the slums. Not since you found your magic. Now you might not fit in real well here, either, but you have got to give it a go.'

'No,' she told him firmly. 'I've got to get you out of here. I don't know how long Fergun intends to use you to blackmail me, but he can't keep you down here forever. I'm going to make him bring me messages from you so I know you're alive. If he doesn't, I'll stop co-operating. Remember the story about Hurin the carpenter?'

'Of course.'

'We'll do what he did. I don't know how long it will take before he frees you but I—'

She stopped as the door clicked open. The magician's light fell upon her face and Cery felt his heart twist.

'You've been in here long enough,' Fergun snapped.

Sonea turned back to Cery, gave him a quick hug, and stepped away. He swallowed. Somehow the brief encounter hurt more than her earlier silence.

'Stay warm,' she told him. Backing away, she stepped

past Fergun into the passage. As the door closed, Cery hurried forward and pressed his ear to the wood.

'Do what I tell you and you'll see him again,' Fergun said. 'Otherwise . . .'

'I know, I know,' Sonea replied. 'But just you remember what Thieves do to those who break their promises.'

You tell him, Cery thought, smiling grimly.

It was clear from the moment Dannyl entered the Night Room, that he was worried about something. Extracting himself from a circle of questioning magicians, Rothen walked across the room to greet his friend.

'What's wrong?'

'I can't tell you here,' Dannyl said, his eyes flickering about.

'Outside then?' Rothen suggested.

They walked out into falling snow. White flakes fluttered all around them, hissing as they met Rothen's shield. Dannyl moved to the fountain and stopped.

'Guess who I saw in the University just now.'

'Who?'

'Fergun and Sonea.'

'Sonea?' Rothen felt a twinge of anxiety, but pushed it away. 'He has the right to talk to her now, Dannyl.'

'Talk to her, yes, but take her from your rooms?'

Rothen shrugged. 'There is no rule against it.'

'Aren't you concerned?'

'Yes, but it will do no good to protest, Dannyl. It's better that Fergun is seen to overstep his welcome, than I protest at his every move. I doubt she would have gone with him if she didn't want to.'

Dannyl frowned. 'Don't you want to know where he took her?'

'Where?'

A look of vexation crossed Dannyl's face. 'I'm not sure, exactly. I followed them into the University. Fergun took her into the inner passages. After that I lost them. They just disappeared.'

'They vanished before your eyes?'

'No. I could hear Fergun talking, then everything was silent. Too silent. I should have heard footsteps, or a door closing. Something.'

Once again, Rothen pushed away a feeling of unease. 'Hmm, I *would* like to know where he took her. What could he possibly have to show her in the University? I'll ask her tomorrow.'

'And if she doesn't tell you?'

Rothen stared at the snow-covered ground, considering. The inner passages of the University led to small, private rooms. Most would be empty, or locked. There was nothing else there . . . except . . .

'I don't suppose he's shown her the underground passages,' he murmured.

'Of course!' Dannyl's eyes brightened, and Rothen instantly regretted his words. 'That's it!'

'It's highly unlikely, Dannyl. Nobody knows where the entrances are except—'

Dannyl wasn't listening. 'It makes sense now! Why didn't I think of them?!' He pressed his hands to the side of his head.

'Well, I would suggest strongly that you keep out of them. There are good reasons for the ban against using them. They're old and unsafe.'

Dannyl's eyebrows rose. 'So what about the rumours that a certain member of the Guild uses them on a regular basis?'

Rothen crossed his arms. 'He can do as he pleases, and I'm sure he's capable of surviving if a passage collapsed. I'm also sure he wouldn't approve of you snooping around. What will you say if he discovers you in there?'

The light in Dannyl's eyes faltered as he considered that. 'I'd have to time it carefully. Make sure I knew he was elsewhere.'

'Don't even consider it,' Rothen warned. 'You'll get lost.'

Dannyl snorted. 'It can't be any worse than the slums, can it?'

'You're *not* going, Dannyl!'

But Rothen knew that, once Dannyl's curiosity was roused, nothing would deter his friend but the threat of expulsion. The Guild wasn't going to cast him out for breaking a minor rule. 'Think carefully, Dannyl. You don't want to ruin your chance to become an ambassador, do you?'

Dannyl shrugged. 'If I can get away with negotiating with the Thieves, I doubt a little snooping around under the University will earn me much disapproval.'

Defeated, Rothen turned and started back toward the Night Room. 'That may be so, but sometimes it matters whose disapproval you earn.'

CHAPTER 28

THE HEARING BEGINS

'Don't worry, Sonea,' Tania whispered as they reached the front of the University. 'You'll be fine. The magicians are just a gaggle of old men who'd rather be sipping wine in their rooms than sitting in a draughty old hall. It will all be over before you know it's started.'

Sonea couldn't help smiling at Tania's description of the Guild. Taking a deep breath, she followed Tania up the stairs of the grand building. As they passed through the huge open doors, she caught her breath.

They had entered a room full of staircases. Each was made of melted and fused stone and glass, and looked too frail to support a man's weight. The stairs spiralled up and down and around each other like an elaborate piece of jewellery.

'The other side of the University isn't like this!' she exclaimed.

Tania shook her head. 'The back entrance is for novices and magicians. This is the way that visitors come, so it has to be impressive.'

The servant continued through the room and started down a short corridor. Sonea could see the bottom half of another pair of enormous doors ahead. As they reached the end of the corridor, Sonea stopped and stared around in awe.

They stood at the threshold of an enormous room. White walls stretched up to a ceiling of glass panels that shone brightly in the gold light of the afternoon sun. At the level of the third floor, a web of balconies crisscrossed the room – so delicate that they seemed to float in the air.

Before her stood a building. A building *within* a building. The rough grey walls made a dramatic contrast to the airy white of the Hall. A row of slim windows were spaced, like soldiers, along it's length.

'This is the Great Hall,' Tania said, indicating the room. 'That,' she pointed to the building, 'is the Guildhall. It's over seven centuries old.'

'That's the *Guildhall*?' Sonea shook her head in disbelief. 'I thought they replaced it.'

'No.' Tania smiled. 'It was well made and has historical value, so it would have been a shame to tear it down. They took the inside walls out and made it into a hall.'

Impressed, Sonea followed the servant around the building. Several more openings led out of the Great Hall. Tania pointed to a pair of doors in the side of the Guildhall. 'That's where you'll go in. They're having their Meet now. The Hearing will start when it's finished.'

Sonea's stomach began to flutter again. A hundred magicians sat inside, waiting to decide her fate. And she was about to stand before them all . . . and deceive them.

She felt a sickening wave of apprehension. What if, despite her co-operation, Fergun did not win the claim? Would he still let Cery go?

Cery . . .

She shook her head as she remembered his halting admission in the dark cell. 'I didn't want to find out that the Guild really wanted to help you. You'd just come back and I didn't want you going away. I didn't want to lose you again.'

He loved her. Surprise had left her speechless at first, but when she thought back to the times she had noticed him watching her, how he would sometimes grow hesitant when talking to her, and how Faren had occasionally behaved as if Cery was more than just a faithful friend, it all made sense.

Did she feel the same way? She had asked herself the question countless times since their meeting, but she could not answer with certainty. She didn't feel like she was in love, but perhaps the fear that gripped her when she considered the danger he was in meant she was. Or would she feel that concern for anyone she loved, whether as a friend or more than a friend?

If she loved him, wouldn't her heart have leapt with joy at his admission? Wouldn't she feel gratified that he had tried to rescue her, rather than guilty that his regard for her had led to his capture?

Surely, if she did loved him, she wouldn't have to ask herself these questions.

Pushing the thought aside, she drew in a deep breath and let it out slowly.

Tania patted her shoulder. 'Hopefully it won't be long, but you never know . . .'

A firm click echoed through the Hall, then the doors Tania had pointed to swung open. A magician stepped out of the building, then another. As more appeared, Sonea began to wonder why so many were leaving. Had the Hearing been cancelled?

'Where are they going?'

'Only the ones who are interested in watching the Hearing will stay,' Tania told her.

While some of the magicians left the Great Hall, others gathered into small groups. A few looked at her, their eyes bright with curiosity. Unsettled, Sonea avoided their gaze.

—Sonea?

She started, then looked toward the Guildhall.

—Rothen?

—It was a short Meet – over quickly. You'll be called in soon.

Looking toward the Guildhall doors, Sonea saw a dark figure emerge. Her heart skipped as she recognised him.

The assassin!

She stared at him, sure that this was the man she had seen the night she had spied on the Guild. He wore the same grim, brooding expression she remembered. His black robes snapped around him as he strode across the room.

A few magicians turned and nodded to him, offering the same wary respect she had seen Faren give an assassin of the Thieves. He inclined his head in reply but did not stop. Though she knew she would draw his attention if she kept staring, she could not take her eyes from him. His gaze flickered to hers, lingered a moment, then shifted away.

She jumped as a hand touched her shoulder.

'There's Lord Osen.' Tania was pointing toward the Guildhall doors. 'The Administrator's assistant.'

A young magician stood there, watching her. As she met his eyes, he beckoned.

'Go on,' Tania whispered, patting Sonea on the shoulder again. 'You'll be fine.'

Sonea took a deep breath and forced herself to walk across the Hall to the door. When she reached the young magician, he inclined his head politely.

'Greetings, Sonea,' he said. 'Welcome to the Guildhall.'

'Thank you, Lord Osen.' She quickly sketched an awkward bow. Smiling, he gestured for her to follow him into the Guildhall.

The scent of wood and polish filled her senses as she stepped inside. The hall seemed larger than it had appeared on the outside, the walls rising up to a dark ceiling high above. Several magic globe lights hovered under the rafters, filling the room with a golden glow.

Rows of tiered wooden seats extended down the length of the building on each side. Sonea felt her mouth go dry as she saw the robed men and women watching her. Swallowing, she looked away.

Osen stopped and indicated that she should stay where she was, then climbed a steep arrangement of tiered seats to her right. These, she knew, were for the Higher Magicians. Rothen had drawn a diagram of the seating arrangement so she could memorise the magicians' names and titles.

Looking up, she saw that the topmost row was empty. Rothen had assured her that the King rarely attended Guild ceremonies. His chair at the centre was larger than all others, and the royal incal had been stitched onto the cushioned back.

A single chair stood below it. Sonea felt a vague disappointment as she saw that it was empty. She had hoped to catch a glimpse of the High Lord.

Administrator Lorlen sat at the centre of the middle row. The seats on either side of him were empty. He was talking to Osen and a long-faced man in the seat below him who wore a black sash over his red robes. This, Sonea recalled, was Lord Balkan, the Head of Warriors.

To Balkan's left sat the stern Lady Vinara, the Head of Healers, who had visited Rothen after he had announced that Sonea would be staying. To his right was an old man with an angular face and a large nose – Lord Sarrin, the Head of Alchemists. Both were watching Lorlen intently.

In the lowest row of seats were the Principles – the magicians who controlled and organised lessons in the University. Only two seats were occupied. Sonea frowned as she struggled to remember why, then looked up at Lord Balkan. The Warrior held both positions, she recalled.

Osen straightened and descended to the floor again. The higher magicians turned to regard the hall. Rising, Administrator Lorlen lifted his chin and surveyed the magicians in the hall.

'The Hearing to decide the guardian of Sonea will now begin,' he intoned. 'Would Lord Rothen and Lord Fergun, as claimants to that role, please approach the front.'

Hearing the scrape of booted feet, Sonea looked up at the rows of magicians. A familiar figure was making his way down to the floor. As Rothen stopped a few steps from Osen, he looked at her and smiled.

She felt an unexpected pang of fondness and started to smile in return, but then she remembered what she was about to do and she looked down at the floor. He was going to be so disappointed in her . . .

Another set of footsteps filled the hall. Looking up, she saw that Fergun had stopped a few paces from Rothen. He, too, smiled at her. She quelled a shudder and looked at the Administrator instead.

'Both Lord Rothen and Lord Fergun have claimed guardianship of Sonea,' Lorlen told the audience. 'Both believe they were the first magician to recognise her potential. We must now decide which claim shall be honoured. I leave the proceedings of this Hearing to my assistant, Lord Osen.'

The young man who had led her into the room stepped forward. Taking a deep breath, Sonea stared at the floor and tried to steel herself for what she must do.

'Lord Rothen.'

Rothen turned to face Lord Osen.

'Will you please tell us of the events that led you to recognise Sonea as a potential magician.'

Nodding, Rothen cleared his throat. 'On the day I recognised Sonea's powers – the day of the Purge – I was paired with Lord Fergun. We had arrived at the North Square and were assisting in the barrier shield. As always, a group of youths started throwing stones.

'I was facing Lord Fergun at the time. The shield was about three paces from us, on my left. At the edge of my vision I saw a flash of light in the vicinity of the shield, and simultaneously felt the shield waver. I glimpsed a stone flying though the air just before it struck Lord Fergun on the temple, knocking him unconscious.'

Rothen paused, glancing at Fergun. 'I caught Lord Fergun as he fell. When he was safely lying on the ground I searched for the one who had thrown the stone. That is when I saw Sonea.'

Osen took a step towards Rothen. 'So this was the first time that you saw Sonea?'

'Yes.'

Osen crossed his arms. 'At any point in time did you see Sonea performing magic?'

Rothen hesitated. 'No, I did not,' he admitted reluctantly. A low murmur began among the magicians seated to his right, but it quickly died away as Lord Osen glanced in that direction.

'How did you know it was she who threw the stone that broke through the shield?'

'I judged the direction from which the stone had come, and guessed that it had to be one of two youths,' Rothen explained. 'The closest – a boy – was not even paying attention. Sonea, however, was staring at her hands in surprise. As I watched she looked up at me, and I knew from her expression that she had thrown the stone.'

'And you believe that Lord Fergun could not have seen Sonea before then?'

'No, Lord Fergun could not have seen Sonea at all that day,' Rothen said dryly, 'due to the unfortunate nature of his injury.'

A few chuckles and coughs echoed in the hall. Lord Osen nodded, then moved away. He stopped in front of Fergun.

'Lord Fergun,' he said, 'will you please tell us of the events of that day as you saw them.'

Fergun inclined his head graciously. 'I was assisting with the barrier in the North Square as Rothen has described. A group of youths came forward and began throwing stones at us. I noted that there were about ten of them. One was a young girl,' Fergun glanced at Sonea. 'I thought she was behaving strangely, so when I turned away I continued to observe her in the corner of my eye. When she threw her stone I thought nothing of it, naturally, until I beheld a flash of light I realised she must have done something to break the barrier.' Fergun smiled. 'This surprised me so much that, instead of deflecting the stone, my first reaction was to glance at her to confirm that it was, indeed, her.'

'So you realised that Sonea had used magic *after* the stone broke through the shield, and *before* it struck you.'

'Yes,' Fergun answered.

The hall echoed with voices as this was discussed. Gritting his teeth, Rothen resisted the urge to stare at Fergun. The Warrior's story was a lie. Fergun had never glanced toward Sonea. Rothen stole a quick look at her. She stood quietly in the shadows, her shoulders slumped. He hoped she understood how important her account would be in confirming his story.

'Lord Fergun.'

The room fell silent at this new voice. Rothen looked up at Lady Vinara. The Healer was regarding Fergun with her famous, unblinking stare.

'If you were looking at Sonea, how is it that the stone struck your *right* temple? That would indicate to me that you were looking at Rothen at the time.'

Fergun nodded. 'It all happened very quickly, Lady,' he said. 'I saw the flash and *glanced* at Sonea. It was only a fleeting look – and I recall wanting to ask if my companion had seen what this girl had done.'

'You did not even attempt to dodge?' Lord Balkan asked, his tone disbelieving.

Fergun smiled ruefully. 'I am not accustomed to having stones thrown at me. I believe surprise overrode the instinct to duck.'

Lord Balkan looked at the magicians beside him and received slight shrugs. Watching them closely, Osen nodded as no more questions came. He turned to regard Rothen.

'Lord Rothen, did you see Fergun glance at Sonea between the time the stone broke through the barrier and when it struck him?'

'No,' Rothen replied, struggling to keep anger from his voice. 'He was talking to me. The stone cut him off in the middle of a sentence.'

Osen's brows rose. He glanced at the Higher Magicians, then looked up at the audience.

'Does anyone have an account that contradicts or adds to what we have heard?'

Silence answered him. Nodding slowly, Osen turned to regard Sonea.

'I call on Sonea as witness to this event.'

Moving from the shadows at the side of the hall, Sonea walked forward to stand a few paces from Fergun. She glanced up at the Higher Magicians, then bowed quickly.

Rothen felt a pang of sympathy for her. A few weeks before, she had been terrified of him and now she faced a hall of magicians, all watching her intently.

Osen gave her a quick smile of encouragement. 'Sonea,' he said. 'Please tell us your version of the events we are discussing.'

She swallowed and set her gaze on the floor. 'I was with the other youths. They were throwing stones. I didn't usually do that – I usually stayed with my aunt.' She glanced up and blushed, then continued on in a rush. 'I guess I got dragged into things. I didn't start throwing stones straightaway. I watched the others and the magicians. I remember I was . . . I was angry, so when I did go to throw a stone I pushed all that anger at the stone. Later I realised I had done something, but at the time everything was so . . . confusing.' She stopped and seemed to collect herself.

'When I threw the stone it went through the barrier. Lord Fergun looked at me, then the stone hit him and Ro – Lord Rothen caught him. The rest of the magicians were looking everywhere, then I saw Lord Rothen looking at me. After that, I ran.'

A cold rush of disbelief struck Rothen. He stared at Sonea, but her eyes remained fixed on the floor. Glancing at Fergun, he saw that a sly smile curled the man's lips. As the Warrior realised he was being watched, the smile vanished.

Helpless, Rothen could only clench his fists as the rest of the Guild voiced their approval.

The half-seen vision of the Guildhall wavered as anger, disbelief and hurt flowed over Dannyl's mind. He stopped, alarmed.

—What's wrong, Rothen?

—She lied! She supported Fergun's lie!

—Careful, Dannyl cautioned. *You'll be heard.*

—I don't care. I know *he's lying!*

—Perhaps that's how she saw it.

—No. Fergun never looked at her. I was talking to him, remember?

Dannyl sighed and shook his head. Rothen had finally seen Fergun's true character. He should have been happy, but how could he be? Fergun had won again.

Or had he?

—Have you found anything yet?

—No, but I'm still looking.

—We need more time. With Sonea supporting Fergun, they'll probably make a decision in the next few minutes.

—Delay them.

—How?

Dannyl drummed his fingers on a wall.

—*Ask to talk to her.*

Rothen's presence vanished as his attention returned to the Hearing. Grimacing, Dannyl regarded the walls around him. Every magician knew that there were entrances to the underground passages inside the University. He had guessed that those entrances must be well hidden or novices would be flouting the rule all the time.

As he had expected, a simple search of the passages had revealed nothing. Though he was sure that he would eventually find something if he kept examining the walls closely, there wasn't time for that.

He needed another clue. Footprints, perhaps. The underground passages were probably dusty. Fergun must have left some evidence. Eyes on the floor, Dannyl started along the corridor again.

Turning a corner, he collided with a short, plump figure. The woman gave a little yelp of surprise, then stepped back, a hand pressed to her heart.

'Forgive me, my Lord!' She bowed, the water in the bucket she carried sloshing. 'You were walking so quietly, I didn't hear you coming!'

He looked at the bucket, then smothered a groan. Evidence of Fergun's passing would be regularly cleaned away by the servants. The woman moved past him and continued down the corridor. Watching her, it occurred to him that she probably knew more about the inner passages of the University than any magician.

'Wait!' Dannyl called.

She stopped. 'Yes, my Lord?'

Dannyl walked toward her. 'Do you always clean this part of the University?'

She nodded.

'Have you needed to clean up any unusual messes? Muddy footprints, for example?'

The servant's lips thinned. 'Someone dropped food on the floor. The novices aren't supposed to bring food in here.'

'Food, eh? Where was it dropped?'

The servant gave him an odd look, then led him to a painting further down the corridor.

'It was on the painting, too,' she said, pointing. 'Like they'd been handling it.'

'I see.' Dannyl narrowed his eyes at the painting. It was of a view of a beach, with tiny spiral shells carved into the frame. 'Thank you,' he said. 'You may go.'

Shrugging, she bowed quickly and hurried away. Dannyl examined the painting carefully, then lifted it off the wall. Behind it was the usual wooden panelling of the inner passages. Running his hand over it, he extended his senses beyond and drew in a breath as he detected metal shapes. Following their contours, he found a section of the panel that gave beneath his probing fingers.

A soft sliding noise followed, and a section of the wall moved aside. Darkness and cold air confronted him. Flushed with triumph and excitement, he replaced the painting, created a globe light and stepped through.

A steep stairway descended to his left. Finding a lever on the inside of the door, Dannyl pressed it and the door closed. He smiled to himself and started down the stairs.

The passage was narrow and he had to stoop to avoid brushing his head on the ceiling. A few faren webs clung to the corners. As he reached the first side passage, he reached into a pocket and drew out a jar of coloured paste.

Unstoppering it, he wiped a little of the contents onto the wall beside him.

The paste would slowly change from white to a clear, hard coating over the next few hours, giving him a marker that would soon be unnoticeable. Even if he was exploring in a few hours, he could still find his way out by looking for the clear coating.

He looked down and laughed aloud.

Footprints stood out clearly in a thick layer of dust. Dropping into a crouch, Dannyl identified the familiar imprint of a magician's boots. From the number of tracks, it was clear that someone had scuffed this passage many times.

Rising, he followed the footprints for several hundred paces. Reaching another side passage, he was dismayed to find the prints led down both the main passage, and the new one. He dropped to his haunches again and examined them closely. There were only four sets of prints in the side passage, two of magician's boots, two of smaller shoes. The prints in the main passage were fresher, and numerous.

A faint sound touched his ears then – a very human-sounding sigh. Dannyl froze, a chill slowly running up his spine. The dark beyond the reach of his globe light seemed thick and full of unpleasant possibilities, and he suddenly felt sure that something was watching him.

Ridiculous, he told himself. *There's nothing there.*

Taking a deep breath, he stood and forced himself to look only at the tracks. Moving forward, he followed them for another hundred paces, finding more side passages with older tracks.

Again, he felt a nagging certainty that he was being followed. Behind his footsteps there was the echo of softer treads. The faintest breeze brought a smell of rot and something alive, but filthy . . .

He turned a corner and his imaginings fled. Ahead, about twenty paces away, the footprints ended at a door. He took a step forward, then went rigid with terror as a figure moved out of the side passage beside him.

'Lord Dannyl. Might I inquire as to your reasons for being here?'

Staring at the man, Dannyl's mind seemed to divide into two. While one part babbled excuses, the other watched helplessly as the first made an utter fool of itself.

And at the edge of his mind a familiar presence was projecting both sympathy and smug satisfaction.

—I told you not to go down there, Rothen sent.

In the lightless silence, the sound of his stomach grumbling was loud. Cery rubbed his belly and continued to pace.

He was certain now that more than a day had passed since his last meal, which meant that a week had gone by since he had seen Sonea. Leaning against the door, he cursed Fergun with every unsavoury ailment he could think of. Between the words he heard the sound of footsteps and froze.

His stomach growled fiercely in anticipation. The footsteps were slower, taunting him. They drew closer, then stopped. The faint sound of voices reached him. Two voices. Both male.

He drew in a quick breath and pressed his ear to the door.

'. . . tunnels are extensive. It is easy to become disorientated. Magicians have been lost for days and returned starved. I suggest you retrace your steps.' The voice was stern and unfamiliar.

Another voice replied. Cery caught only a few words, but he understood enough to know that the other magician was apologising. The voice was also unfamiliar, but he could easily imagine Fergun's voice becoming faint and high if he was babbling so.

The stern magician clearly did not approve of Fergun's presence in the passages. He was unlikely to approve of Fergun keeping prisoners down here either. All Cery had to do was call out, or hammer on the door, and Fergun's trap would be unsprung.

He raised his fist, then paused as the voices stopped. Hasty footsteps led away, then another set approached. Biting his lip, Cery backed away from the door. Which magician was it? Fergun or the stern stranger?

The lock clicked. Cery shied back against the far wall. As the door opened light filled the room and he closed his eyes against the glare.

'Who are you?' boomed an unfamiliar voice. 'What are you doing down here?'

Opening his eyes, Cery's relief changed to astonishment as he recognised the man standing in the doorway.

CHAPTER 29

TO DWELL AMONG MAGICIANS

'She said he was doing it so that no-one will ever think dwells could be magicians,' Cery finished.

The magician narrowed his eyes. 'That does sound like Fergun.' As the dark gaze shifted to Cery again, a small frown creased the magician's brow. 'The Hearing is taking place now. I can reveal Fergun's crimes, but only if I have proof that he is the man you speak of.'

Cery sighed and looked around the room. 'I've got nothing 'cept the things he gave me, but he has my knife and tools. If you found them, would that be enough?'

The man shook his head slowly. 'No. What I need is in your memories. Will you allow me to read your mind?'

Cery stared at the magician. *Read* his *mind?*

He had secrets. Things his father had told him. Things Faren had told him. Things even Faren would have been surprised to know. What if the magician saw them?

But if I don't let him read my mind, I can't save Sonea.

He couldn't let a few musty secrets keep him from saving her – and the magician might not see them, anyway. Swallowing his fear, Cery looked up at the magician.

'Sure. Do it.'

The magician regarded Cery soberly. 'It will not harm or hurt. Close your eyes.'

Taking a deep breath, Cery obeyed. He felt fingers touch

his temples. At once, he became aware of another mind. It seemed to drift in behind his own, then a voice spoke from . . . somewhere.

—Think of the day your friend was captured.

A memory flashed before his eyes. The other mind seemed to catch and steady it. Cery found himself in a snow-filled alley. It was like a vision, clear and yet lacking fine detail. He saw Sonea running away from him, and felt an echo of the fear and despair he had felt as he had hammered against the invisible barrier that had separated them. Turning, he saw a man wearing a cloak, standing behind him.

—This is the man who captured you?

—Yes.

—Show me how.

Once again a memory flashed through his mind, was caught and replayed. He stood outside the Magicians' building, looking up at Sonea. Fergun appeared. Chased him. Caught him. The blue-robed magician and his companion appeared, took Cery to Sonea. His memory sped on. He was leaving Sonea and walking through the Magicians' building. Fergun was suggesting they go through the University. They entered the building and travelled down passages.

Then Fergun opened the secret door and forced him through. The blindfold touched his face again, and he heard his own steps as he walked down the underground passage. He faced the cell again, walked inside, heard the door close . . .

—When did you see him next?

Memories of the magician's visits followed. Cery saw himself searched and robbed of his possessions, then relived his failed attack and was healed. He saw Sonea enter the room and heard their conversation over again.

After that, the other mind brushed over his, then seemed to fade away. Cery felt the magician's fingers lift from his temples. He opened his eyes.

The magician was nodding. 'That is more than enough,' he said. 'Come with me. We must hurry if we wish to attend the Hearing.'

He turned on his heel and strode out of the room. Following, Cery felt relief rush over him as he stepped out of the cell. He looked back once, then hurried after his rescuer.

The man strode quickly down the passage, forcing Cery into a jog to keep up. The passage met another, then several more. None looked familiar.

They reached a short flight of stairs. The magician climbed these then bent to stare at the wall. Seeing a small dot of light around the magician's eye, Cery guessed that there was a spy hole.

'Thanks for helping me,' he offered. 'There's probably nothing a petty thief could offer in return, but if you need anything just ask.'

The magician straightened and turned to regard him soberly.

'Do you know who I am?'

Cery felt his face warm. 'Of course. There's nothing the likes of you would ever need from me. Seemed right to offer, though.'

The ghost of a smile touched the magician's lips. 'Do you truly mean what you said?'

Suddenly uneasy, Cery shifted from foot to foot. 'Of course,' he said reluctantly.

The man's smile became a little more pronounced. 'I'm not going to force you to make a bargain with me. No matter what you say, Fergun's actions must be revealed and punished. Your friend will be free to go, if that is what she wants.' He paused, his eyes narrowing slightly. 'But I might contact you some time in the future. I will not ask for anything beyond your abilities, or that will compromise your place with the Thieves. It will be up to you to decide if what I ask is acceptable.' He lifted an eyebrow. 'Is that reasonable?'

Cery looked down. What the man was proposing was more than reasonable. He found himself nodding. 'It is.'

The magician extended his hand. Taking it, Cery felt a strong grip. He looked into the man's eyes, and was pleased to see that the dark stare was steady.

'Agreed,' Cery said.

'Agreed,' the magician repeated. He then turned back to the wall. After checking the spy hole again, he grasped a lever and pulled. A panel slid sideways. The magician stepped through, his light following.

Cery hurried after and found himself in a large room. A desk stood at one end, with chairs arranged before it.

'Where am I?'

'In the University,' the man replied, sliding the panel back into place. 'Follow me.'

The magician strode across the room and opened a door. Following the man through, Cery found himself in a wide corridor. Two green-robed magicians stopped to stare at him, then looked up at his guide. They blinked in surprise, then inclined their heads respectfully.

Ignoring them, the magician strode to the end of the corridor, Cery following close behind. As they passed through a doorway, Cery looked up and gasped. They had entered a room filled with fantastic spiralling staircases. To one side the doors of the University stood wide open, revealing snow-covered ground and a view of the Inner City. Cery turned full circle, then realised that the magician was already several paces down the corridor.

'Harrin's never going to believe me,' he muttered as he hurried after him.

'That's not what happened,' Rothen told her.

Sonea looked away. 'I know what I saw,' she answered. 'Do you want me to lie?' The words left a bitter taste in her mouth. She swallowed and tried to look puzzled by his question.

Rothen stared at her, then shook his head. 'No, I would not. If it was discovered that you had lied today, many would question if you should be allowed to join the Guild.'

'That's why I had to do it.'

Rothen sighed. 'Then that is truly how you remember it?'

'I said that, didn't I?' Sonea sent him a pleading look. 'Don't make it any harder than it already is, Rothen.'

His expression softened. 'All right. Perhaps I missed something that day. It is a shame, but it can't be helped.' He shook his head. 'I will miss our lessons, Sonea. If there's . . .'

'Lord Rothen.'

They turned to see Osen walking toward them. Rothen sighed, then walked back to his place. As Fergun started toward her, she smothered a groan.

When Rothen had asked for time to speak with her, Fergun had promptly asked for the same. What did he plan to say? All she wanted now was for the Hearing to be finished and over with.

Fergun gave her a sickly smile as he reached her side. 'Everything going as planned?' he asked.

'Yes,' she nodded.

'Good,' he crooned. 'Very good. Your story was convincing, if a little badly spoken. Still, it had a charming honesty.'

'I'm glad you liked it,' she said dryly.

He looked up at the Higher Magicians. 'I doubt if they will want to discuss this any longer. They will make their decision soon. After that, I will arrange a room for you in the Novices' Quarter. You should *smile*, Sonea. We want people to believe you are filled with delight at the prospect of being my novice.'

Sighing, she forced the corners of her mouth upward into what she hoped the distant magicians would take as a smile.

'I've had enough of this,' she said between her teeth. 'Let's go back and get it over with.'

His brows rose. 'Oh, no. I want my full ten minutes.'

Pressing her lips together, Sonea resolved to avoid saying another word. When he spoke to her again she ignored him. Seeing the flicker of annoyance in his eyes, she found it much easier to smile.

'Lord Fergun?'

She turned to see Lord Osen beckoning. Letting out a sigh of relief, she followed Fergun back to the front of the hall. The room still hummed with voices. Osen lifted his hands.

'Quiet, please.'

Faces turned back to the front and the hall settled into an expectant silence.

In the corner of her eye, Sonea could see Rothen staring at her. She felt another pang of guilt.

'From the accounts given today, we can clearly see that Lord Fergun was the first to recognise Sonea's abilities,' Lord Osen. 'Does anybody contest this conclusion?'

'I do.'

The voice was deep and strangely familiar, and it echoed from somewhere behind her. Scraping and the rustle of robes filled the hall as all shifted in their seats. Sonea turned around and saw that one of the huge doors was standing slightly open. Two figures were striding down the aisle toward her.

As she recognised the shorter one she gave a cry of joy. 'Cery!'

She took a step forward, then froze as she saw Cery's companion. Whispered questions drifted to her ears from either side. As the black-robed magician neared, he gave her an appraising look. Disturbed by his gaze, Sonea turned her attention to Cery.

Though pale and dirty, Cery was grinning happily. 'He found me and let me out,' he told her. 'Everything's going to be fine.'

Sonea looked questioningly at the black-robed magician. His lips curled into a half smile, but he said nothing. Moving past her, he gave Osen a nod then started up the stairs between the Higher Magicians. No-one protested as he settled into the seat above the Administrator.

'For what reason do you contend this conclusion, High Lord?' Osen asked.

The room seemed to tilt beneath her. She stared at the black-robed magician. This man was no assassin. He was the Guild's leader.

'Evidence of deception,' the High Lord replied. 'The girl has been forced to lie.'

Sonea heard a strangled sound to her right. Turning, she saw that Fergun's face was white. She felt a flare of triumph and anger and, forgetting the black-robed magician, jabbed her finger at Fergun.

'He made me lie!' she accused. 'He said he would kill Cery if I didn't do what he said.'

From all around came gasps and hisses of surprise. Sonea felt Cery grip her arm tightly. She turned to look at Rothen, and as he met her eyes she knew he understood everything.

'An accusation has been made,' Lady Vinara observed.

The hall quietened. Rothen opened his mouth to speak, then frowned and shook his head.

'Sonea. Do you know the law regarding accusations?' Lord Osen asked.

Sonea drew in a sharp breath as she remembered. 'Yes,' she replied, her voice shaking. 'A truth read?'

Osen nodded, then turned to face the Higher Magicians. 'Who will perform the truth read?'

Silence followed. The Higher Magicians exchanged glances, then looked up at Lorlen. The Administrator nodded and rose from his chair.

'I will perform the truth read.'

As he descended to the floor, Cery pulled on her arm. 'What's he going to do?' he whispered.

'He's going to read my mind,' she told him.

'Oh,' he said, relaxing. 'That's all.'

Amused, she turned to regard him. 'It's not as easy as you'd think, Cery.'

He shrugged. 'It seemed easy enough.'

'Sonea.'

She looked up to see that Lorlen had reached her side.

'See Rothen over there, Cery?' She pointed to Rothen. 'He's a good man. Go stand beside him.'

Cery nodded, then squeezed her arm and moved away. As he reached Rothen's side, she turned to face Lorlen. The Administrator's expression was sober.

'You have experienced a sharing of minds while learning Control,' he said. 'This will be a little different. I will be wanting to see your memories. It will take a great deal of your concentration to separate what you want to show me from anything else that you think of. To help you, I will prompt you with questions. Are you ready?'

She nodded.

'Close your eyes.'

Obeying, she felt his hands touch the sides of her head.

—Show me the room that is your mind.

Drawing up the wooden walls and doors, she sent Lorlen an image of the room. She sensed a fleeting amusement.

—Such a humble abode. Now, open the doors.

Turning to face the double doors, she willed them open. Instead of houses and a street, darkness stretched beyond. A blue-robed figure stood within it.

—Hello, Sonea.

The image of Lorlen smiled. He strode across the darkness and stopped at the doors. Extending a hand, he nodded to her.

—Bring me in.

She reached out and took his hand. At her touch, the room seemed to slide under his feet.

—Don't be afraid or concerned, he told her. *I will look at your memories, then I will be gone.* He moved over to a wall. *Show me Fergun.*

Focusing on the wall, she created a painting. Within it she placed an image of Fergun's face.

—Good. Now show me what he did to make you lie for him.

It took no force of her will to animate the image of Fergun. The painting swelled to fill the wall and changed to show Rothen's guest room. Fergun strode toward them and placed Cery's knife on the table in front of her.

I have the owner of this knife locked in a dark little room that nobody here knows of . . .

The scene blurred and then Fergun was crouching in front of them, larger than reality.

Do what I tell you, and I will release your friend. Give me any trouble, and I will leave him there forever . . . When you tell them this, the Higher Magicians will have no choice but to grant me your guardianship. You'll enter the Guild, but I assure you, it won't be for long. Once you have performed a little task for me, you'll be sent back where you belong.

You'll get what you want and so will I. You have nothing to lose from helping me, but . . . he picked up the dagger and ran a finger along the blade, *you'll lose that little friend of yours if you don't.*

She felt a wave of anger from the presence at her side. Distracted, she glanced at Lorlen, and the painting faded into the wall. Turning back, she willed it to appear again.

Drawing on her memory, she filled the painting with an image of Cery, dirty and thin, and the room he had been imprisoned in. Fergun stood to one side, looking smug. The smell of stale food and human waste flowed from the painting into the room.

At this scene the Lorlen image shook his head. He turned to face her.

—This is outrageous! It is fortunate, indeed, that the High Lord found your friend today.

At the mention of the black-robed magician, Sonea sensed the painting change. As she turned toward it, Lorlen followed her gaze and drew in a sharp breath.

—What is this?

Within the frame stood the High Lord, dressed in blood-soaked beggar's clothes. Lorlen turned to stare at her.

—When did you see this?

—Many weeks ago.

—How? Where?

Sonea hesitated. If she let him see the memory, he would know that she had trespassed and spied upon the Guild. He had not entered her mind to see that, and she was sure he could not complain if she pushed him out.

But a part of her wanted him to see. There could be no harm now in letting the magicians discover her intrusion, and she craved an answer to the mystery of the black-robed magician.

—Very well. It began like this . . .

The painting changed to show Cery leading her through the Guild. She felt Lorlen's surprise, then a growing amusement as the image jumped from scene to scene. She was spying through windows one moment, running through the forest the next, and looking at the books Cery had stolen. She sensed amusement from Lorlen.

—Who would have guessed that was where Jerrik's stolen books went? But what of Akkarin?

Sonea hesitated, reluctant to uncover that memory.

—Please, Sonea. He is our leader and my friend. I must know. Was he hurt?

Drawing up the memory of a forest, Sonea projected it

into the painting. Once again she moved through the trees to the grey house. The servant appeared, and she dropped down between the bushes and the wall. The tinkle that had attracted her to the grille rang in her imaginary room.

The High Lord stood in the painting again, this time wearing a black cloak. The servant arrived and she sensed recognition from Lorlen.

—*Takan.*

It is done, the High Lord said, then removed his cloak to reveal the bloodstained clothes. He looked down at himself in disgust. *Did you bring my robes?*

At the servant's mumbled answer, the High Lord pulled off the beggar's shirt. Beneath it was the leather belt strapped to his waist and the dagger pouch. He scrubbed himself down, then moved out of sight and returned wearing black robes.

Reaching for the pouch, he removed the glittering dagger and began to wipe it on a towel. At this she sensed surprise and puzzlement from Lorlen. The High Lord looked up at the servant.

The fight has weakened me, he said. *I need your strength.*

Dropping to one knee, the servant offered his arm. The High Lord ran the blade over the man's skin, then placed a hand over the wound. Sonea felt an echo of the strange fluttering within her head.

—*No!*

A wave of horror swept over her. Startled by the force of Lorlen's emotions, Sonea's concentration snapped. The painting went black, then disappeared completely.

—*It can't be! Not Akkarin!*

—*What is it? I don't understand. What did he do?*

Lorlen seemed to gather his emotions to himself. His

image slowly faded to nothing and she realised he had left her mind.

—*Do not move or open your eyes. I must think this over before I face him again.*

He was silent for several heartbeats, then his presence returned.

—*What you have seen is forbidden,* he told her. *It is what we call black magic. By using it, a magician can take strength from any living creature, human or animal. For Akkarin to be using it is . . . is terrible beyond belief. He is powerful – more powerful than any of us . . . Ah! This must be the reason for his extraordinary strength! If that is so, then he must have been practising these vile arts before he returned from abroad . . .*

Lorlen paused as he considered this.

—*He has broken his vow. He should be stripped of his rank and expelled. If he has used these powers to kill, the penalty is death . . . but . . .*

Sonea sensed anguish from the magician. Another long silence followed.

—*Lorlen?*

He seemed to collect himself again.

—*Ah, I am sorry, Sonea. He has been my friend since we were both novices. So many years . . . and I had to find* this!

When he spoke again there was a cold determination behind his sending.

—*We must remove him, but not now. He is too powerful. If we confront him and he fights us, he could easily win – and each killing he made would make him stronger. With his secret revealed and no reason to hide his crime, he could kill indiscriminately. The entire city would be in danger.*

Shocked by what he was describing, Sonea shivered.

—*Do not fear, Sonea*, Lorlen soothed. *I will not allow that to happen. We can't confront him until we know we can defeat him. Until then, we must not let anybody know about this. We must prepare in secret. That means you must never speak of this to anybody. Do you understand?*

—Yes. But . . . must you let him remain the Guild's leader?

—Unfortunately, yes. When I know we are strong enough, I will gather all the magicians together. I will have to move quickly, without warning. Until then, only you and I can know of this.

—I understand.

—I know you want to return to the slums, Sonea, and I would not be surprised if this discovery has increased your determination to leave, but I must ask you to stay. We will need all the help we can get when the time comes. Also, I fear that, though I do not like to think it, you may be an attractive victim for him. He knows you have strong powers. You would be a potent source of magic. With your powers blocked, and living out of the sight of those who would recognise the death brought by black magic, you would be the perfect victim. Please, for your sake and ours, stay here with us.

—You want me to live here, right under his nose?

—Yes. You will be safer here.

—If you couldn't find me without the Thieves' help, how would he?

—Akkarin has finer senses than the rest of us. He was first to know when you started using your powers. I fear he would find you easily.

She sensed that he truly feared for her safety. How could she argue with the Administrator of the Guild? If he believed she would be in danger, then she probably was.

She had no choice. She had to stay. To her surprise, she felt no anger or disappointment, only relief. Cery had told her that she should not consider herself a traitor by becoming a magician. She would learn to use her magic, master the skills of Healing, and, perhaps, one day, she would take what she knew and help the people she had left.

And it would be satisfying to thwart those magicians who, like Fergun, believed that dwells should not join the Guild.

—*Yes*, she sent. *I will stay.*

—*Thank you, Sonea. Then there is one other we must trust with our secret. As your guardian, Rothen may have reason to go into your mind again, particularly when the time comes to teach you Healing. He may see what you have shown me today. You must tell Rothen about Akkarin, and of all that I have said to you today. I know he can be trusted to remain silent.*

—*I will.*

—*Good. Now I am going to release you and confirm Fergun's crime. Try not to show any fear of Akkarin. If it helps, don't look at him at all – and keep your thoughts buried deep.*

Feeling his hands lift from her temples, she opened her eyes. Lorlen regarded her solemnly, his eyes bright, then his expression smoothed and he turned to face the Higher Magicians.

'She speaks the truth,' he said.

A shocked silence followed Lorlen's words, then the room began to buzz with exclamations and questions. Lorlen lifted a hand and the room fell silent again.

'Lord Fergun imprisoned this young man,' Lorlen gestured toward Cery, 'after he had told me he was going to escort him to the gates. He locked him in a room underneath the Guild, then told Sonea that he would kill her friend if she did not lie at this Hearing to confirm his story. Having won his claim, he intended to force her to break one of our rules, so that she would be publicly expelled.'

'*Why?*' Lady Vinara hissed.

'From what Sonea understands,' Lorlen answered. 'To dissuade us from offering a place in the Guild to other commoners.'

'She wanted to leave anyway.'

All eyes turned toward Fergun. He stared defiantly at the Higher Magicians.

'I'll admit I got a little carried away,' he said, 'but I only wanted to save the Guild from itself. You would have us welcome thieves and beggars into the Guild, without asking whether we, or the Houses, or even the King we serve, wishes it. It may seem a small thing to let a beggar girl into the Guild, but what will it lead to?' His voice rose. 'Will we let more of them in? Will we become a Guild of Thieves?'

A murmur followed and, looking at the magicians on either side, Sonea saw several heads shaking.

Fergun looked at her and smiled. 'She wanted to have her powers blocked so that she could return home. Ask Lord Rothen. He will not deny it. Ask Administrator Lorlen. I asked her to do nothing that she did not already want.'

Sonea clenched her fists. 'Nothing I did not already want?' she spat. 'I did *not* want to make the Novice's Vow and then break it. I did *not* want to lie. You *imprisoned* my friend. You threatened to *kill* him. You are . . .' she stopped, suddenly aware that all eyes were watching her. Taking a deep breath, she faced the Higher Magicians. 'When I first came here it took a long time before I saw that you were not . . .' she paused, not liking the image she saw of herself, standing in the Guildhall calling the magicians names. Instead she turned to point at Fergun. 'But *he* is everything I had been taught to believe all magicians are.'

Silence followed her words. Lorlen regarded her solemnly, then slowly nodded. He turned to face Fergun.

'You have committed numerous crimes, Lord Fergun,' he said. 'Some of them of the most serious nature. I need not ask you to explain yourself; you have done so quite well enough already. A Hearing to discuss your actions and decide your punishment will be held in three days. In the meantime, I suggest that you co-operate with our investigations.'

He strode past Osen and climbed the stairs between the Higher Magicians. The High Lord watched him, a half smile curling his lips. Sonea shivered as she imagined the conflicting emotions that Lorlen must feel under that gaze.

'The issue we have gathered to discuss is now irrelevant,' Lorlen announced. 'I hereby grant guardianship of Sonea to Lord Rothen, and declare this Hearing ended.'

The hall filled with voices and the thunder of booted feet as the magicians rose from their seats. Sonea closed her eyes and sighed. *It's over!*

Then she remembered Akkarin. *No, it isn't*, she reminded herself. *But, for now, that is not for me to worry about.*

'You should have told me, Sonea.'

Opening her eyes, she found Rothen standing in front of her, Cery at his side. She looked down.

'I'm sorry.'

To her surprise Rothen gave her a quick hug. 'Don't apologise,' he told her. 'You had a friend to protect.' He turned to regard Cery. 'I apologise on behalf of the Guild for your treatment.'

Cery smiled and waved a hand dismissively. 'Get me my stuff back, and I'll forget about it.'

Rothen frowned. 'What are you missing?'

'Two daggers, a few knives, and my tools.'

'Tools?' Rothen echoed.

'Picks.'

Rothen lifted an eyebrow at Sonea. 'He's not joking, is he?'

She shook her head.

'I'll see what I can do.' Rothen sighed, then looked over Sonea's shoulder. 'Ah! Here's a man more familiar with the ways of Thieves – Lord Dannyl.'

Feeling a pat on her shoulder, Sonea turned to find the tall magician grinning down at her.

'Well done!' he told her. 'You have done me, and the rest of the Guild, a great service.'

Rothen smiled crookedly. 'Feeling particularly cheerful, Dannyl?'

Dannyl gave his friend a haughty look. 'Who was right about Fergun, then?'

Sighing, Rothen nodded. 'You were.'

'*Now* do you understand why I dislike him so much?' Seeing Cery, Dannyl's expression became thoughtful. 'I think the Thieves are looking for you. They sent me a message asking if I knew where a companion of Sonea's had disappeared to. They sounded quite concerned.'

Cery looked up at the tall magician appraisingly. 'Who sent the message?'

'A man named Gorin.'

Sonea frowned. 'So Gorin was the one who told the Guild where to find me, not Faren.'

Cery turned to stare at her. 'They *betrayed* you?'

She shrugged. 'They had no choice. It was a good thing they did, actually.'

'That's not the point.' A gleam had entered Cery's eyes. Guessing what he was thinking, Sonea smiled.

I do love him, she thought suddenly. *But right now it's a friend's love.* Perhaps, if they had time together, without all the distractions they'd had for the last months, it would grow into something more. But that wasn't going to happen. Not now that she was joining the Guild and he was returning, most likely, to the Thieves. Knowing this, she felt a small pang of regret, but pushed it away.

Glancing around the hall, she was surprised to see that it was nearly empty. Fergun still stood nearby, among a group of magicians. As she looked toward him he caught her eye and sneered.

'Look at them,' he said. 'One consorts with beggars, the other with Thieves.' His companions laughed.

'Shouldn't he be locked up or something?' she mused aloud.

Rothen, Dannyl and Cery turned to regard the magician.

'No,' Rothen replied. 'He'll be watched, but he knows that there's a chance he won't be expelled if he appears repentant. Most likely he'll be given a duty to perform that nobody wants, probably one that will involve working in some remote place for several years.'

Fergun scowled, then turned on his heel and strode toward the door, his companions following. Dannyl's smile widened, but Rothen shook his head sadly. Cery shrugged and turned to regard her.

'What about you?' he asked.

'Sonea is free to go,' Rothen replied. 'She'll have to stay

another day or two, however. By law she must have her powers blocked before she returns to the slums.'

Cery looked at her, his brows knitting. 'Blocked? They're going to block your magic?'

Sonea shook her head. 'No.'

Rothen frowned, then looked at her closely. 'No?'

'Of course not. It would make it a bit difficult to teach me, wouldn't it?'

He blinked. 'You're really staying?'

'Yes.' She smiled. 'I'm staying.'

EPILOGUE

In the air above the table floated a speck of light. It slowly expanded until it was a globe about the size of a child's head, then rose up to hover near the ceiling.

'That's it,' Rothen told her. 'You've made a globe light.'

Sonea smiled. 'Now I really do feel like a magician.'

Rothen looked at her face and felt his heart warm. It was hard to resist the temptation to keep teaching her magic when it obviously gave her so much pleasure.

'At the speed you're learning, you'll be weeks ahead of the other novices when you start lessons in the University,' he told her. 'At least in magic. But . . .' Reaching to a pile of books beside his chair, he started to sort through them. 'Your calculation skills are far behind,' he said firmly. 'It's time we got stuck into some real work.'

Sonea looked down at the books and sighed. 'I wish I'd known what tortures you were going to put me through before I decided to stay.'

Chuckling, Rothen slid a book across the table. He paused, then narrowed his eyes at her.

'You haven't answered my question yet.'

'What question?'

'When did you decide to stay?'

The hand reaching for the book froze. Sonea looked up at him. The smile she gave him did not extend to her eyes.

'When it occurred to me that I should,' she said.

'Now, Sonea.' Rothen shook a finger at her. 'Don't get evasive on me again.'

She leaned back in her chair. 'I decided at the Hearing,' she told him. 'Fergun made me realise what I was giving up, but that wasn't what changed my mind. Cery told me he'd think I was stupid if went home and that helped, too.'

Rothen laughed. 'I like your friend. I don't approve of him, but I like him.'

She nodded, then pursed her lips.

'Rothen, is there any chance at all that someone might be able to hear us?' she asked. 'Servants? Other magicians?'

He shook his head. 'No.'

She leaned forward. 'Are you *absolutely* sure?'

'Yes,' he said.

'There's . . .' she paused, then slipped out of her chair and knelt down beside him, her voice dropping to a murmur. 'There's something Lorlen said I had to tell you.'

LORD DANNYL'S GUIDE TO SLUM SLANG

blood money – payment for assassination
boot – refuse/refusal (don't boot us)
capper – man who frequents brothels
clicked – occurred
client – person who has an obligation or agreement with a Thief
counter – whore
done – murdered
dull – persuade to keep silent
dunghead – fool
dwells – term used to describe slum dwellers
eye – keep watch
fired – angry (got fired about it)
fish – propose/ask/look for (also someone fleeing the Guard)
gauntlet – guard who is bribeable or in the control of a Thief
goldmine – man who prefers boys
good go – a reasonable try
got – caught
grandmother – pimp
gutter – dealer in stolen goods
hai – a call for attention or expression of surprise or inquiry
heavies – important people
kin – a Thief's closest and most trusted
knife – assassin/hired killer
messenger – thug who delivers or carries out a threat
mind – hide (minds his business/I'll mind that for you)
mug – mouth (as in vessel for bol)
out for – looking for
pick – recognise/understand
punt – smuggler
right-sided –

trustworthy/heart in the right place
rope – freedom
rub – trouble (got into some rub over it)
shine – attraction (got a shine for him)
show – introduce
space – allowances/permission
squimp – someone who double-crosses the Thieves
style – manner of performing business
tag – recognise (also means a spy, usually undercover)
thief – leader of a criminal group
watcher – posted to observe something or someone
wild – difficult
visitor – burglar

GLOSSARY

ANIMALS

aga moths – pests that eat clothing
anyi – sea mammals with short spines
ceryni – small rodent
enka – horned domestic animal, bred for meat
eyoma – sea leeches
faren – general term for arachnids
gorin – large domestic animal used for food and to haul boats and wagons
harrel – small domestic animal bred for meat
limek – wild predatory dog
mullook – wild nocturnal bird
rassook – domestic bird used for meat and feathers
ravi – rodent, larger than ceryni
reber – domestic animal, bred for wool and meat
sapfly – woodland insect
sevli – poisonous lizard
squimp – squirrel-like creature that steals food
zill – small, intelligent mammal sometimes kept as a pet

PLANTS/FOOD

anivope vines – plant sensitive to mental projection
bol – (also means 'river scum') strong liquor made from tugors
brasi – green leafy vegetable with small buds
chebol sauce – rich meat sauce made from bol
crots – large, purple beans
curem – smooth, nutty spice
curren – course grain with robust flavour
dall – long fruit with tart orange, seedy flesh
gan-gan – flowering bush from Lan
iker – stimulating drug, reputed to have aphrodisiac properties
jerras – long yellow beans
kreppa – foul-smelling medicinal herb
marin – red citrus fruit
monyo – bulb

myk – mind-affecting drug
nalar – pungent root
pachi – crisp, sweet fruit
papea – pepper-like spice
piorres – small, bell-shaped fruit
raka/suka – stimulating drink made from roasted beans, originally from Sachaka
sumi – bitter drink
telk – seed from which an oil is extracted
tenn – grain that can be cooked as is, broken into small pieces, or ground to make a flour
tugor – parsnip-like root
vare – berries from which most wine is produced

CLOTHING AND WEAPONRY
incal – square symbol, not unlike a family shield, sewn onto sleeve or cuff
kebin – iron bar with hook for catching attacker's knife, carried by guards
longcoat – ankle-length coat

PUBLIC HOUSES
bathhouse – establishment selling bathing facilities and other grooming services
bolhouse – establishment selling bol and short term accommodation
brewhouse – bol manufacturer
stayhouse – rented building, a family to a room

PEOPLES OF THE ALLIED LANDS
Elyne – closest to Kyralia in position and culture, enjoys a milder climate
Kyralia – home of the Guild
Lan – a mountainous land peopled by warrior tribes
Lonmar – a desert land home to the strict Mahga religion
Vin – an island nation known for their seamanship

OTHER TERMS
cap – coins threaded on a stick to the value of the next highest denomination
dawnfeast – breakfast
midbreak – lunch
simba mats – mats woven from reeds